Upper King Street

Valerie Perry

ISBN: 1460904079
ISBN-13: 9781460904077
LCCN: 2011902066

This book is a work of fiction. Names, characters, places and incidents are products of the author's imagination. Any resemblance to actual events, locales or individuals living or dead is entirely coincidental.

To My Parents

Rosemarie S. Perry
James "Russell" Perry d.1985

To My Aunt and Uncle

Brigitte S. Oberer
Wilhelm F. Oberer

Acknowledgements

I would like to thank the individuals who made this book a reality. Thank you to my father who always said that dreams do come true and that the sky is the limit when you believe that something will happen. Thank you to my uncle, for telling me one day "stop going to workshops and just self-publish." Thank you to twin sisters my mother and my aunt for sheparding me; for all the stories you have told, the many trips to Europe and the support.

A special thank you to Lese Corrigan who graciously provided original cover art for this novel. Many thanks to my circle who listened to me and offered advice as I read this novel aloud weekly if not daily. My sister, Adrienne Barton, Gail Widner, Katherine Carey, and Anne Marie Crevar who also printed and bound a copy for me; making it a dream come true. Thank you too for twin girls Ava and Anya who give me such joy.

I am grateful for my friends who supported me. Thank you Joan and Chad Mc Donald for all the suggestions while we idled on your front porch, thanks to Karl Clark, John Skelton and my Tuesday Night Burger Boys for sustaining me with support, food and excellent company. A special thanks to my aunt Irma Morbitzer and my uncle Hanns Sohm for trips to Paris and Prague. Thank you to Judy Middleton, Carroll Ann Bowers, Betty Guerard, and Leigh Handal who always asked each day at work. Thank you to Julie Wing, Greer Farrell, Les Schwartz, Joe Gartrell and everyone else that cheered me on including the many museum house interpreters and master gardeners at the Aiken-Rhett House, the Nathaniel Russell House and my friends at Historic Charleston Foundation.

Thank you to April Goyer who helped me focus on my priorities and make them realities. Much gratitude to Jonathan Poston who has taught me all things Charleston over the years. To Kevin Eberle and his great legal mind, his wit and the correct definition and usage of the word "Flaneur". Thank you to Christopher DiMattia who told me to stop talking about writing and to just do it.

Thanks to the team at CreateSpace that held my hand through the production. There are so many people who offered assistance. Thank you for your support, your insight, your suggestions and your belief in me and my first book. As this one begins its printed journey the next book is being written and the third already is rambling around in my head.

Chapter 1

I'm not ambitious to get rich. If I can...own a piece of land and some...dogs, give my family...[and friends] some tomfooleries—everybody ought to have a few tomfooleries—I'm content with my lot. I love this Low Country of ours and couldn't breathe away from it.

Great Mischief, Josephine Pinckney

April 2007

Lucy found herself off on a sunny spring day and started out on her bike. She didn't care where she went. It was just enough to drink in her environs and let the architecture take her over. Early into the ride, she stopped at the uptown Baptist Church with its surrounding yard, filled with antebellum tombstones bearing the names of the Charleston elite. The fluted columns and swags of the monuments welcomed her to the land of the past, a place where she was familiar and happy. The churchyard bore no relationship with its current occupants, as its dead were members of an Anglican church associated with a church downtown. No matter, the names came off her lips as she touched this and that and connected the lineage of the dead and imagined their lives so long ago. After ten minutes of scurrying around, she jumped on her bike again, anticipating her next new/old find. This was her passion, her love, her destiny—discovering the many layers of her town.

She managed to avoid the potholes on Rutledge that could be considered traffic-calming devices, and are a hazard of a city built on landfill. Her eyes filled with the beauty of old walls, varying architecture, from pre- and post-revolutionary, Federal, Greek Revival, Italianate, and the prevailing vernacular single houses. She stopped at St. Michael's Episcopal Church, locked her bike, and wandered into its graceful interior. Its English Baroque architecture resembled St. Martin-in-the-Fields in London, and Lucy loved it. For its meringue. The interior of the church was cool in temperature, and she brushed her hand on the pew where George Washington and later Robert E. Lee had worshipped. She opened the box and sat in that very pew, closing her eyes to pray for her mother, who had died many years ago. After a few minutes of polite silence, she gazed around her and took in the Tiffany stained glass of St. Michael the Avenger and the many tributes to the dead. She glanced at her watch, sighed, and launched herself from the church.

The light at the Four Corners of Law, at the corner of Meeting and Broad Streets, was red, and it gave her an opportunity to gaze up at the steeple. She smiled to herself remembering when she had climbed to the steeple, once illegally after Hurricane Hugo and once legally when an acquaintance who rang bells for the church invited her to help the group ring on the Saturday before Easter just a year ago. Both experiences were magical. The first with the thrill of being somewhere where she wasn't to be at midnight in the hot July night with the stars murky under the haze of humidity, the other before noon, and she remembered being a bit breathless after counting the ninety-seven steps from the bottom to the top and then the sheer joy of pulling the rope on the smallest bell.

In her great excitement, she hadn't listened to the instructions properly, and before she knew it, her feet were in the air by three feet and only a little tinkling sound came from her bell. The other ringers, very serious types, nicely barked orders in an attempt to help her ring the bell correctly. She listened, embarrassed and flushed, and before she knew it, she heard it: the prettiest sound to her ears, the soft clanging of the smallest bell, and she was creating that noise as the clapper continued to sway side to side. She cycled through the intersection thinking that the bells had crossed the Atlantic Ocean many times. They were world travelers by now. First they had come to Charleston from a foundry in Whitechapel in London, England. During the American Revolution, they were taken as war prizes by the British and went from whence they came. They came home again following that successful war won by the colonials. During the Civil War, they had been sent overland to Columbia, the capital city, for safekeeping. However, Columbia had been burned and the bells damaged, so they traveled after the war back to England for recasting. They lived in relative harmony back in their perch above Broad Street until the winds of Hurricane Hugo hit in 1989, when they were damaged again. They were again sent back to London to the same foundry, recast, and now they lay in their bell tower, reposed and ringing in the day at noon or heralding the hours what seemed like every day of the week and for weddings and services.

Lucy cycled past Hibernian Hall, the Greek Revival Irish bastion of social activities. Behind her to her right, on cobblestoned Chalmers Street, lay the Fireproof Building that housed the South Carolina Historical Society. Its classical beauty was designed by Robert Mills, America's first architect and a Southern son, and completed in 1826. She was happy, smiling. She didn't think of the dishes left in the sink or the coffeemaker left on, as she was in such a rush to be in the moment in her city, the crown jewel of all of America. Today, was hers, and it was filled with remembering why she lived there and nowhere else. The Low Country inspired her from its built environment to its marsh grasses and green water. In fact, she was the queen of her universe, and all was well and beautiful.

As she sailed by the market, she thought about long-ago postcards that showed the Charleston Eagles, buzzards that littered the streets and denuded the market of its offal. She smiled, shook her head, and pedaled on. She passed down Anson Street marveling at Goldsmith's Row, intact simple frame buildings from the late nineteenth century, and pondered the gentrification that had occurred during the rehabilitation of Ansonborough in the twentieth century. Today was not about dark things. It was about goodness and light and embracing the goddess within. Badness always attracts twice the vibration of good. Today was Lucy's day. She finally came home two hours later and visualized her house—her house—that she and the bank owned. Her mood was untempered with the endorphins kicking in, and she said like a mantra: *I'm home. This is my beautiful house. Humble, no mansion, but how would I heat another?*

She turned off the coffeepot, patted her Bouvier des Flandres, Toulouse, donned an apron, and left the back door open. Refreshed from her ride, she would now tackle the small back garden. She needed to weed, start seeds, and deadhead. It was April, and the nasturtiums were popping up, holding their sunny round leaves to the sun. She always planted them on Valentine's Day, as she had been told by her grandmother so many years ago. Their orange, yellow, and red blossoms filled the pots and beds heralding spring's arrival. The blossoms would be plucked several times a week and added for spice and color to her salad at dinner. The borage was getting taller and missed most of its leaves, as Toulouse nibbled this delicacy. Each year she would drive thirty minutes to John's Island with one of her best friends to the Garden of Eden that was Pete's Plants, a local nursery. After strolling the nursery, which always played Vivaldi, Mozart, or Haydn, she would happen across healthy camellias, native azaleas, and acanthus, and then finally she would limit her purchase to the borage. For several years now, she had purchased the borage exclusively for her dog, as she had read somewhere that borage and comfrey soothed nervous temperaments. Toulouse loved the plants, and it certainly seemed to calm him.

Her back garden was small and lovingly planted. She had spent her hard-earned money on shrubs from local nurseries, where the roots were not bound and the plants cared for. She had wasted money early on at the big chain stores, where plants dried out and then were given an abundance of water. Usually they did not survive. The initial investment was a little higher, but the quality of plants was well worth it. Her gaze swept back and forth admiring her landscape and the borrowed landscape of her neighbors. In the shade, fatsia cohabited with Aspidistra, or cast-iron plant, as it is commonly called. The camellias included Pink Perfection, Betty Sheffield Blush, and Alba. A few azaleas peppered the beds with names like George Tabor, Pride of Summerville, and Pride of Mobile. In dappled shade she grew a profusion of ferns that broke up the color. Rosemary was easy to root, and those herbs were planted strategically for their texture as well as for use in the kitchen and bath. Hydrangeas bloomed in summer, waving their lace caps in lavender and fuchsia, and the oakleaf and white snowball enjoyed part shade. In partial to mostly sun, she had planted nightshade plants, brugmansia and datura, for their dramatic color and shape. Columbine loved the dappled light, and pansies and impatiens added more color. The honeysuckle and confederate jasmine covered the fence and mixed with the autumn-blooming clematis. In May the passion vine, with its unusual purple flower and triangular stamen, would herald the warmth of summer. This backdrop of beauty gave her a sense of satisfaction, but her grass did not. Although she had purchased grass time and time again, it looked ratty against the verdant backdrop.

She dropped to her knees and began clipping and weeding. Her windows were open, allowing the music from NPR to soothe her as she worked. Joshua Bell was on the violin, stretching the bow back and forth on his 1713 Stradivarius, reminding her that she needed to reserve *The Red Violin* from the library. Lulled into the trance of the music and her task, she almost missed the sound of the gate opening to her side yard. Her gaze took a moment to adjust, and she was faced with a good-looking man whom she had seen around town but didn't know. She became a little worried that Toulouse would herd him. Well, actually he usually nipped males in the rear. A Bouvier thing, that's all.

He was medium in height, and his body had seen many hours of exercise. His dark hair was slightly shaggy, and his eyes were dark silver-blue.

"Hi, I'm Samuel O'Hara, and I read the ad on Craigslist, left you a message, and then drove around the neighborhood and saw the For Rent sign. I'm wondering about the apartment."

Young, probably would be late with the rent, she thought. She looked at his shoes, noticing boots, and thought about clodhopping above her.

"Well," she said, "It's above my house. Those stairs there lead to it. It's about six hundred square feet, hardwood floors—well, actually pine floors—claw-foot tub, but not a stand-up shower. It's cute, but men usually don't prefer it."

"Why's that?" he questioned

"Well, this is tight space, and mostly it's that it doesn't have a stand-up shower. Also there are challenges that I've had with male tenants. I've had problems with noise, and they never close the gate properly, and then Toulouse gets out and goes on a walkabout and a swim-about in the water and the pluff mud. I'll be more than happy to show it to you, but I will need three references from previous landlords."

"Okay, may I just look at it to see if it will work?"

What was it about him that unnerved her? Was it that he seemed so self-possessed and sure that she would rent it to him, or was it the thought of those boots thunking off late at night and she would wake up to that noise? It was always easier to rent to girls. Her favorite tenants were schoolteachers or reference librarians, women who understood her frugality and who read and were quiet, people who were respectful of her space below. She bragged to friends about her customer service ethic at work, but here she was sighing, getting up slowly, and asking the potential tenant to give her a moment. She grabbed the keys off the ring and walked up the metal steps to the aerie above her brick ersatz Tudor cottage and ushered him in.

"There it is. Take a look about. The walls are beaverboard. That fabric was used until nineteen fifty, when wallboard was invented, and the material is fragile, but I love it. Because of the peak roof, a stand-up shower is out of the question. Keep in mind you need to place a window treatment on that small window because the neighbors can see in. We're very close, building-wise, up here."

"One small closet?"

"Yes, but you have the attic for storage, so summer clothes can go in storage bins there in the winter and vice versa. Sorry, that's what I tell my female tenants. Men don't usually question the closet. Maybe you're a clotheshorse?" She giggled then and looked at his boots again.

"Ah, no, I'm no clothes...What did you say? Horse? I just have some extra gear. So it's five hundred and fifty a month?"

"It includes water."

"I'll think about it."

"Okay. Don't forget those references."

Good, she had put him off with her unfriendliness. He wouldn't be coming back. No boys, however cute. She went back to gardening, finished weeding, and then cut a bouquet of fresh flowers for her dining room table. As she arranged the flowers, the phone rang. Her assistant in the gallery was talking so fast she couldn't understand a word she said.

"Gabriella, slow down. Get off the chandelier. Now tell me what's going on. Yes, okay. Yes, it sold yesterday. Yes, yes, okay, give me the number. Sure, thanks. Yes, indeedy, Yankees are difficult, but they buy our art. Yes, I'll take care of it."

She no sooner hung up when the phone rang again. Her friend Diana invited her for dinner. She returned the necessary work call and continued her day. After walking Toulouse in Hampton Park, she traipsed over with a bottle of wine and made herself at home at Diana and Weston's patio table. She looked around her in amazement at their paradise. Diana's garden was picturesque. A sculptor by training, she had an uncanny eye for color and texture, and her art was everywhere. Weston, a talented architect, had designed their garden house, a beautiful folly that was useful and where Diana refrigerated bulbs and stored seeds, paint, stone, and her garden accoutrements. Guests could also stay the night in the loft.

Diana came out and embraced her friend. "How's it going? I haven't seen you in two weeks and you're only a block away. What's up?"

Lucy sighed. "Do you know I don't think this place can be prettier? Just when I think my beds are journeying for yard of the month, I come here. It's just glorious. I've been busy. My tenant above me moved out, so I've been showing the 'love nest,' and then today we had a disgruntled customer at the gallery. I just bought several Prentiss Taylor prints from a lady on Limehouse Street, and this man—rude, rude, rude—was trying to talk me down on the price on one of them. I refused, and he stormed off. So he must have Googled the prints, as he came back today and wanted to buy it. Meanwhile, yesterday that really wealthy couple on Charlotte Street came in and fell in love with them and made the purchase of all three. Anyway, Mr. New Jersey gave Gabriella a hard time, and I had to call him and talk him down. So Monday he's going to come in and look at the other prints. No biggie, but jeez, why are people so rude?"

"Well, it's not just Northerners, and you know that. When I was at the store just the other day, I ran into Weston's friend that owns the bike shop. He looked straight at me and walked by even though I said hello."

"Well that's 'cause he's still pissed after we got him when we had drinks at Rue. Remember?"

"Oh yeah, I forgot about that. Oh well. That was too perfect. What was it I said? Oh yes, the quote from *Pride and Prejudice*, something about gentlemanly-like manners."

"Jeez, Diana, it was hysterical. On another topic, I was accepted to the program in England. Isn't that fantastic?" In sotto voce she mentioned, "And you know, I showed the place to this really cute guy today."

"Really? How cute, and were you nice to him?"

"Cute and not exactly..."

She had rented to two men in the past who hurled their shoes off late at night. One had played Ravi Shankar loudly at 3:00 a.m., and when she called to remind him that it was a school night, he told her to f- off. She had to evict each of them when they ignored her phone calls that rent had been due. The calls were made each week and ignored. She finally cycled to the magistrate's office and filed the necessary paperwork, posted the sign on the door, and mailed the certified letter. Renting to boys was just an awful idea. The last one had tried to insert himself into her life, even trying to sleep with her, which was not acceptable. In Lucy's mind, this was a conflict, as theirs was a business arrangement, and it just would not do.

"What is wrong with you? You haven't had a date since last year with R—I mean the not-boyfriend, and you're headed for forty. Come on, girl, what are you thinking? You won't try the Internet. You won't try speed dating. How do you think you will meet someone?"

"Diana, I did try the Internet once, remember, a few years ago? Remember that guy, Henry? I was supposed to meet him at the restaurant at the old rice mill, and thank goodness we had just added him on to Violet's birthday celebration and I didn't meet him one-on-one. I had told him that I would be in a black dress, and I described myself without going into detail. He had sent me his picture, so I knew what he looked liked. That afternoon I spilled coffee with half-and-half all over my dress, and I had to go home to change, and then I wasn't wearing black at all. I decided to wear that pretty white linen dress that looks like it's from the fifties. At the eleventh hour, John from the city called.

Remember, he was that quiet IT guy that I saw for a while and later said he couldn't continue to see me because my life was too crazy? But of course, when he was bored, he always called and wanted to do something, and he did have fun, and of course he was never right for me, but back to that night.

"So there we were, all eight of us sitting on the banks of the Ashley River, when I saw a man that looked like Henry, but certainly could not be Henry, as he was about sixty, and Henry said he was forty-five. He was wearing khaki Bermuda shorts, a white button-down shirt, and a school tie, the ones with heraldry and the like, and he had on kneesocks and bucks. He was surveying the room with one hand on his hip, and then I noticed he was carrying a European walking stick with all kinds of painted metal decorations. He would swing the stick up and down and side to side. I was awestruck that this was the man with whom I had such nice chats with on e-mail and on the phone, and here in front of me was this absolute weirdo who looked as if he should be walking about the mountains, hills, and dales of Switzerland, so I ducked under the table to hide from him and stayed there for a little while. I'll never forget John's face as he peered at me, his head upside down, and he said, 'Lucy, what are you doing down there?' and I told him briefly the story and told him to look up, and he said, 'Oh no, that just will never do.' No one paid me any attention, and I think it was that the martinis were so good, and after about five minutes, John peered under the table again and said the coast was clear."

"Oh, Lucy!" Diana was laughing. "I had completely forgotten about that, but that's not how it ended, is it?"

"Oh no. We all went home, and there were fourteen messages on my answering machine, all from Henry. He said he was coming over to settle this one way or another. I was scared, and for the first time since I owned my little house, I was glad that the protector guards were on my windows and doors, as at that time I had not found someone to take them off. I knew he was hammered, so I set my alarm for seven that Saturday, knowing I'd wake him up. He deserved it after all that impolite behavior, and so I called him and said, 'Henry what were you thinking, sending me a photo that was at least twenty years old? You lied about your age, and you probably made up your entire profile.' He was hungover, and I was strident and caught him off guard, and he said, 'Everybody lies on the Internet. In fact, everyone lies, period.' Well, I let him have it then. I was peevish and, to tell the truth, a little sleep-deprived and anxious, but now the sun was bright, and I wasn't afraid anymore, and I felt strong and told him if he ever contacted me again,

I would let Toulouse attack him and carry off what didn't get a rise with the help of Viagra. When I think back on it, it is hilarious and a little frightening. No, I don't want to go back to the Internet. I think some people find the love of their life there, but it's not for me."

"Are we discussing Lucy's love life again?" Weston queried.

The two looked at him together and replied in unison, "Maybe."

Diana raised a winged eyebrow, and Lucy knew she would give him the scoop later that night. Soon it was time for dinner, and the three friends watched the sunset glow from peach to pink to deep red, before twilight claimed the night.

Chapter 2

Travel and change of place impart new vigor to the mind.

Seneca

Samuel O'Hara couldn't get the song "*Travelin' Man*" by Widespread Panic out of his head as he stepped into the Rutledge Avenue bar near the ballpark with the best burgers in town. He propped himself on the barstool and looked at his friend Paul. "I'll take a Bud Light."

"Here you go, man. Did you look at the rental? I've heard it's nice."

Sam ran his fingers through his dark hair.. "Sure, it's clean, freshly painted, and small. There's not enough room to swing a cat in it, though, but otherwise it's perfect, and I might add your friend is a bitch."

"Lucy? She's a sweetheart. When Phoebe had little Trey, she brought over food constantly, even babysat so Phoebe could do the books for this place and get some rest. Did I ever tell you how she found us our house? That girl is great."

"No, she's not. She's rude, and she's a snob, and her dog, some furry beast, bit me. She's high maintenance, like every other Southern girl, and then I asked her about storage, and she pointed to the small closet and asked me if I needed more space, implying that I was gay or something. It's time for me to buy another house. That's the only way to figure this out."

"Well, if you're going to stay in Charleston, you're only going to meet Southern girls. Shit, why would you buy another house? Just put your stuff in storage."

"Yeah, whatever, give me another Bud Light."

A woman in her midtwenties walked by him and smiled appreciatively, taking in his high cheekbones, strong chin, dark blue eyes, and straight nose. He was not quite six feet in height, and his body was lean and well muscled.

"If I buy the house, my stuff will be stashed. Storage places are always getting ripped off. Besides, I know a couple of guys that are looking for a rental, and I trust them."

Samuel was from Salem, Massachusetts. He had visited Charleston with his parents while in high school. They owned a house on Kiawah Island, and his summers had been filled with sand, sun, golf, and long hours in the surf. He fell in love with the local food, the heat, and the beautiful landscape. Each year his parents would pack up the Volvo station wagon and drive two days from Salem. Both parents were professors at Boston University, and the summers offered them time to relax and prepare for the fall semester. For Samuel it was the dramatic difference between the coastlines of his home and Charleston that held him captive. His favorite memories included the drive through John's Island with its rural roads shielded by a canopy of live oak trees. The island was a haven of beauty with its blue-green water, salt marshes, palmettos, and scrub myrtles. The summer meant John's Island fruits and vegetables, strawberries in June and watermelon and tomatoes in July. His mother loved visiting the local farms and purchasing this organic cornucopia for all of their meals.

He grew up in an educated household where he and his sister, Elizabeth, were expected to study hard and also to live life. His mother was a true Francophile and specialized in French history, specifically the Napoleonic period. His father taught African-American studies, and the history of the Civil Rights Movement was his passion. By the time Sam graduated from high school, he had decided to attend the College of Charleston, partly because of the beautiful campus and the reputation of the school, but also to stake his independence from his family. His father had purchased a single house on the Eastside, on America Street near Mary Street, as it was a better investment to buy a property than pay rent for his son. He expected Sam to manage the mortgage by having roommates. He felt that this way his son would understand at an early age the responsibility and commitment of home ownership. He had ensured that his children were responsible with money, as he had opened checking accounts for them at the age of fifteen. Sam had always had three roommates while in school, and he managed to pay the note each month and made three hundred dollars on top of it.

By the time he had graduated from C of C, he was able to purchase the house from his parents. His father was so impressed with his hard work and business acumen, that he sold him the property for the purchase price of four years before. During the school year, he'd worked part-time more from boredom than for the need of money. His grandmother had died his senior year in high school and left him and Elizabeth a small but generous inheritance. During the summers he had worked in construction for a preservation contractor. He learned vital skills for restoring windows and doors, as well as carpentry, painting, and repairing brownstone.

He earned a double major in historic preservation and business, knowing that his business background would serve him well. After sending off countless resumes and working countless internships, he realized that the field of preservation was hard to break into, and without a master's degree, there was little hope of working for the organizations like Historic Charleston Foundation, The Preservation Society of Charleston, Drayton Hall, Middleton Place, or the National Park Service. He also discovered that employers and local businesses didn't need to pay salaries that a person could live on in the twenty-first century. Like him, everyone seemed to want to live in Charleston. For the past eight years, since finishing school, he had purchased, restored, or rehabilitated houses on the Eastside and then sold them. He bought his second house by taking out a home equity loan on his first house. It was a nine-hundred-square-foot freedman's cottage that was a wreck. Once getting it clean from the forty years of decrepitude and filth, he uncovered vernacular woodwork and rustic faux-finished surfaces under the modern paint. He restored the house beautifully and did the work by himself. He learned the Board of Architectural Review process when he added the addition on the back. He purchased a third property soon after, another freedman's cottage that had been gutted by fire. The interior was badly damaged, and if it had had any interesting details, they had been lost forever. He sold that house to a young couple. He was a firefighter, and she taught at the magnet school on Calhoun Street.

He'd cleared twenty-five thousand dollars after the sale, not much for all that sweat equity, but he was building his street and the community. He learned rapidly that the preservation groups needed to be his allies, and after purchasing a house, he invited them to see the property, photograph it if they wanted, and shared his vision. Yes, he would rebuild the windows, no problem. Yes, he would save the hardware, but some was missing. Could they help him? It was not an easy situation, and there was a great deal of criticism for add-ons, but he learned to research the properties and find a footprint of an original outbuilding, thereby convincing them to support his applications. He did not mind the suggestions of replacing six-over-six windows rather than two-over-two if enough six-over-six survived.

He chose the Eastside as his project zone because he lived there and the houses were smaller and less expensive than other areas of the historic district. The BAR seemed to be somewhat supportive of any rehabilitation of the Eastside, as it still had not boomed in the past fifteen years like Cannonborough, Elliottborough, the Westside, Hampton Park Terrace, Wagener Terrace, and North Central. The Eastside had problems with drugs and vacant and boarded-up houses in a state of demolition by neglect. His neighbors loved him or hated him. The drug dealers would get in his face and say, *"Fuck you. I'm gonna kill ya, man."* His neighbor across the street, Mrs. Manigault, baked him pies and cakes each Saturday and waved to him each day. On Sunday morning he watched as her family and friends picked her up for church. She sang beautifully in the choir of Emmanuel AME church at the age of seventy-eight. When she needed something from the Harris Teeter, or the PIG, he happily shopped for her and refused her cash when he returned. He simply asked her to tell him stories of her life. She spoke at length of the Civil Rights Movement, about being an LPN, and the unfortunate salary discrepancies between whites and blacks.

He reveled in her stories and learned to bake at her side. She taught him how to make a mean coconut cake and a Lane's cake that contained so much butter, sugar, and fruit that it should be served with a Lipitor. He learned how to make casseroles. Growing up in New England, he'd thought casseroles were a Midwestern thing, but Mrs. Manigault corrected him and told him it was an African thing, a Southern thing. She asked him to call her Mrs. Annie, and she wanted to torque his cooking up and teach him to fry chicken. She told him to buy lots of baking soda. He didn't know what that was about, but he bought all the ingredients, and when he started his first grease fire, he understood.

"Maybe I should grill out and avoid frying altogether," he'd said as soon as the fire was out.

"No, honey, you got to get your rhythm. That's why I saved your house." She had laughed.

Sometimes her dialect was so strong that he missed the nuances. He respected her and liked her on so many levels. She was exquisitely beautiful, wore gloves and a hat to church, and was the kindest soul he had ever met—and she was smart. She had a street savvy that amazed him.

As time progressed, he realized what jobs were worth the price. On occasion he still purchased a neighbor's house for more money than it was worth and created beauty while clearing a marginal profit. He used a few of his friends for the jobs and was able to make a decent living.

His mantra was to travel for at least one month a year. He had visited Central and South America, England and Ireland, Germany, Hungary, and the Czech Republic, as well as France, Italy, Spain, and Portugal. His parents had always traveled, and his wanderlust stemmed from an innate curiosity that they had fostered at an early age.

This year had been very successful, as he had finished three houses. With the sale of the last one, he had decided that it was now time to take a break, take off for several months. He'd be able to handle his business over the Internet and with his cell phone. His roommate and sometime partner would manage the old house on America Street. The two new roommates were set to move in, but he needed to get his electronics stored safely, his computer, high-definition TV, and the expensive stereo he had spent so much money on. He couldn't help it that day. Usually he didn't spend much money on things, but he had sold one of the houses and the owner of the store on the corner of King and Spring Streets had talked him into spending five thousand dollars on equipment that rocked out. When he listened to the sounds of Tool, STP, or The Killers, he turned the volume up marginally, and it amazed him by the quality of sound. He didn't know the new roommates that well, and that was why the apartment would have been perfect.

Paul had told him that Lucy was a nester. She rarely left home, and that would have been the perfect place to store his stuff. But not now, he thought. Three references, forget it. What a bitch. It was supposed to be so easy. His next trip would take him to the Orient, where he would dive into China, Vietnam, Cambodia, Thailand, and Japan, and he planned to be gone for six months. The rent from his tenants would pay the note, pay for the small apartment, and make him a small monthly profit. The kicker had been when she kept looking at his boots. He knew that look. His mother had drilled him as a young boy to quietly take off his shoes and not drop them like a moron. She may be nice to Paul, but he had absolutely no use for her. Besides, she had too many freckles, and people of Scots-Irish birth didn't age well. He preferred dark-haired, blue-eyed girls like Jessica anyway, not strawberry blondes with eyes the color of a swamp.

Sam paid his tab and added 25 percent gratuity. "Good night, Paul, I'll talk to you later."

"So what are you going to do about your stuff?"

"Maybe I'll buy a place in West Ashley, keep a room and rent it out. I know of a couple of friends who are looking for a place."

"That's complicated, isn't it? I mean, why don't you leave your stuff at the house? And that better happen soon, right?"

"June first."

"Wow, man, how do you figure it out?"

"Well, no wife and no kids, right? Just me, not even a ferret to look after. Good night."

He drove around Avondale the next day and looked at the houses available for sale. He found a ranchburger with three bedrooms, made an offer with cash on the table. He called his contacts and booked the surveyor, termite inspector, and home inspector. The house would close in two weeks, and his life would be on track. He called his friends who needed a place to live and showed them the property. They would lease it for six months, and from there they would decide to buy it from him or find something else.

They were a strong couple. One of the guys worked construction with him and looked like the built gay character of the movie *The Full Monty*. The crew had named him "Sheffield." He was out of the closet and had a better relationship with his partner than many of Sam's married straight friends besides Paul and Phoebe. Sheff's partner, Drew, was a sharp young tax lawyer who supported Yellow Dog Democrats and was invited to every rich Republican house in town. They, like so many gay couples, wanted to move to the burbs close to town to enjoy a sense of autonomy. The owner of the ranchburger, a widow of eighty who had kept up the house, was relieved that she could now go to an active retirement community, near her children living in Mt. Pleasant. Drew and Sheff would keep the place up, probably make improvements, and his electronics were secure. In a little over one month, he would be in a different country, learning the culture and viewing sites he'd never seen. E-mail and text messaging would keep him in the loop.

Chapter 3

"We pass by another of his houses which is newer built and very good gardens, called Barmstone...the house is all built with Brick and so good Bricke that at 100 years standing no one brick is faulty...the front looks very uniform...with Compass windows ... and the door enters in the side of [a] tower which was the old fashion in building and is like my brother Say's house at Broughton; out of the entry you come into a lofty good Hall... the parlour and drawinge-room are well proportion'd roomes and the wainscoate is all well-carv'd in the moldings of the doores and chimneys are finely carv'd with staggs and all sorts of beasts woods and some leaves and flowers; and birds and angels, etc."

The Journeys of Celia Fiennes, Celia Fiennes

July 2007

"I can't believe I'm at Petworth and that we've just enjoyed the tour of the house, the private galleries, and the lectures, and now we're in the midst of the fantastic grandeur of Capability Brown. I think I will just die, right now, it's so exquisite." Lucy sighed.

Lucy's classmate rolled his eyes. "Dear girl, have you never traveled?"

Taken aback, Lucy became hurt and gave her friend the stink eye. "Yes, thank you, I have traveled. My first junket to Europe was when I was ten. Just not like this. Petworth is the quintessential country house that links the South Carolina Low Country to England. The masters that crafted the woodwork in our environs were copying this astonishing beauty. Grinling Gibbons's work was recreated in a more rusticated way on the banks of the Ashley River by 1738. That's so early. The resemblance between the halls is amazing, although Drayton Hall is on a much smaller scale. There they were, though, those sons and daughters of the British gentry carving their niche in the wilderness of the New World. The mantels at Drayton Hall are straight from the designs of Inigo Jones's and William Kent's books. It's just so fantastic to see this. But then I wouldn't expect you to understand my excitement because this is what you do and you've cataloged almost all of the English houses for the National Trust. You are a little jaded, you know."

"Sorry, you just seem too exuberant about everything. Truly, it's odd to me the way that you have these astonishing rules and then you seem to be so emotional and passionate about buildings. Not that I don't understand the passion, but jeez, you're a little extreme," Nigel said.

"Hah. I'm not the only emotional one. I heard that after you left the pub last night, you were sort of enveloped in silk. Am I right?" She giggled.

"Damn, that was a textile experiment gone completely wrong. I was teasing her, and she thought I was flirting with her. I'm happily married. There was nothing emotional about it."

"All right, really, you are my best friend in this program, so can we be nice-nice?"

"What is 'nice-nice,' another phrase of Lucyspeak?"

"Yes, it is. It's a word that means be nice and polite. So nice-nice, please? By the way, that painting by Washington Allston—wasn't it beautiful?"

"Yes, it was, Lucy, and another link to your Carolina coast, I presume."

Her days in England were a fantasy of twenty-seven houses in twenty-one days. One day they enjoyed lunch at the teahouse on the grounds of Broughton Castle, known for its intricate ceilings and chimneypieces. She saw Chatsworth, associated with Elizabeth Shrewsbury, one of the most important women of the Elizabethan period and the place that Jane Austen had based Darcy's house, Pemberley, in *Pride and Prejudice*. She witnessed the woodwork at Belton House attributed to Edmund Carpenter and Grinling Gibbons. There she thought of the relationship of Edith Wharton and her brilliant friend and architect Ogden Codman, Jr., and how this house had served as the vision for The Mount in the Berkshires in Massachusetts. Places she had only seen in books. Each house had many stories, and many had connections to America and the South. Her colleagues were some of the finest curators, directors, and museum professionals in the field. Their knowledge was monumental. The scholars' ages ranged from twenty-five to sixty, and all offered valuable knowledge and experience. Lucy was one of a handful who were not on scholarships, and the other two both were savvy art dealers from New York.

Her two best friends were men, Nigel and Rupert. Nigel was married and lived in Sussex, where he cataloged properties. She had recently heard endless hilarious stories of his wife and child while riding the bus back to the campus. Rupert grew up in Cheyenne, Wyoming, and was one of the sharpest curators of art she had ever met. He worked at the Museum of Fine Arts in Boston. She was older by five years than both of them. Age did not matter here, as it was all about the exchange and broadening of knowledge. They entered the houses with great decorum, and when they were allowed to wander, each ran in a different direction to find the paintings painted by those gods of art that included Lely, Van Dyck, Kneller, Benjamin West, Angelica Kauffman alongside those painted by Caneletto, Turner, Romney, and Reynolds to name a few. They would reunite moments later and review their visual inventory. At Kedleston they were amazed by Robert Adam's use of fantasy. They marveled at the merpeople furniture made by Linnell and were awestruck at the fishing pavilion.

Chatsworth, with its extraordinary Baroque architecture, seemed the most exquisite of the houses with its art collection, deer park, acres and acres of gardens, fountains, maze, and sheep and chickens. After leaving Chatsworth, they piled in the back of the bus and discussed all they had seen and realized that they never stopped talking. Their camaraderie was such that they shared everything about their lives in those weeks. Lucy enjoyed the mornings and would rise early at 6:00 a.m. and stroll the grounds where they were staying. Each week they moved to another university, where they stayed in the dormitories. She wrote copious notes in her journal about each day's outing and thanked her lucky stars that Diana and Weston had loaned her their digital camera. At first she had been an idiot with the memory stick, but one of her colleagues who was a techie sorted her out to her complete satisfaction. She studied each person and learned all of their names within three days. By doing so she created a relationship with them and was able to seamlessly fit in with almost everyone except the expert who knew everything about ceramics, especially Chinese export ware. Lydia had dated Nigel in the nineties, before he had secured his amazing wife.

Lydia still felt a hold on him and despised that he spoke so closely with the brash girl from the American South. Lydia didn't like how Lucy seemed too close to Nigel, too intimate. He had never laughed with her as he laughed with Lucy, that woman who always had too many lipsticks in her handbag and was always handing out tissues, plasters, and the like. Lucy, in Lydia's mind, was altogether too forward, and she insinuated herself into everyone's business. The others never minded, though, and Lydia thought they were just a bunch of gits, the lot of them.

Day after day they toured houses, attended lectures, and were given the gift of art and history, architecture and decorative arts. At Belton House, Lucy was spellbound during the lecture on Chinese and Japanese porcelain. She delighted in the bedchamber with its Asian paper with applied birds and was thrown over by the painted decoration and the weavings of the tapestry by John Vanderbank, the Chief Arras Worker of the Great Wardrobe, said to have been commissioned in 1691. At Belton it had poured buckets, and Nigel had entrusted Lucy to his notebook. No sooner than he was out of reach did Lydia reached for it and demand that she hand it over.

"Give me the book, Lucy."

"No. Nigel handed it to me, and he's my friend." She knew her voice sounded high and strident.

"Oh, he's your friend, is he? Is there something in the book that the two of you are hiding?"

"No, of course not. What would we have to hide?" Lucy felt like a ferret. Why had everybody left and here was Lydia reaching out and grabbing the book? Lucy didn't know what was written in Nigel's notebook, all she knew was that Lydia now had it. She felt terrible. It began to rain so hard that the Baroque architecture was obscured, and they ran for the bus.

Nigel boarded the bus and began to sit next to Lucy. She looked terrible as if she had done very wrong.

"Lydia has your notebook. I'm sorry."

He looked at her, and his eyes darkened in annoyance while she looked down at her hands clutching her own journal and bag. He strode down the aisle and requested his notebook.

Lydia patted the seat next to her, and he sat. "Why do you like that stupid woman? She's not even pretty. Barely attractive in an Irish kind of way," she said.

"Give me my journal, Lydia, thank you. As usual, you are in a peevish mood. Why does Lucy exasperate you so? She's quite fun, you know. Very amusing in her storytelling. She has quite a lovely and fun life at home, so many good friends, and everything with her is an adventure."

"She's annoying and insipid and not very bright, that's what I think, and it's damn annoying that these Americans seem that they can just pluck Jane Austen out of everywhere. Yes, Austen is a fine novelist, but not Dickens, not Dryden, Shakespeare, nor Chaucer. And it's always

Pride and Prejudice, not *Mansfield Park*, not *Sense and Sensibility*, nor *Emma*. Don't you take notice? It's as if she watched the movie over and over—I doubt she even read the book."

"I think you're jealous, Lydia, and there's nothing going on if that's why you wanted the journal. My Sophie would love her. She is much like Soph's American sister-in-law, and they are the best of friends. I might add she has an excellent manner at picking out the artists, and she was quoting Celia Fiennes earlier."

"Not so keen on ceramics, though. Er, and how is Sophie? Has she lost the weight from the baby?"

"You are too much. Sophie and Robin are very well, and she is the love of my life. By the way, Lucy doesn't claim to be an expert on ceramics, like someone I know. Enough. I'm resting now."

By the end of third week, Lucy and her colleagues were finished, cooked, fried, and done. Those staying in London gathered and hashed and rehashed the time and after a dinner of fish and chips at the Duke of Wellington pub, not far from the Tate Modern museum. They broke up and said endless farewells, promising each other to visit, room together at conferences, and maybe start a stateside program. Lucy clung to Nigel and cried and said they must come visit, please? She hugged Rupert and made him promise to stay in touch, promise please?

After she left, both Nigel and Rupert eyed one another. Rupert started first. "Good luck, we'll e-mail, right? I'll keep up with her. I think she fell in love with you, you know. I hope she's going to be okay."

Nigel laughed. "Oh, Rupe, she fell in love with the program. Our Lucy loves men, and her heart is still mending from that idiot that hurt her, the not-boyfriend, remember? We just needed to love her, listen to her, and remind her that all men aren't that bad."

"But they are, aren't they? Look what happened to me on the trip."

"I never read him right. I think he's still on the fence. Sorry."

"It's okay. All right, so I'll see you. If you come to America, I'll show you Boston."

"We'll keep in touch."

"Cheers."

"Cheers."

Lucy packed her bags thinking about all she had learned, her new friends, everything. She glanced about the room, took a shower, and finished packing. She double-checked the bathroom that she shared with three others and found her razor and puff. Tomorrow she was home, home to her cottage, and all would be well.

Lucy's flight touched down in Charleston at five before seven. It was the end of July, and she knew that it was hot and humid, ninety-eight degrees, and as hot and damp as the inside of one's mouth. As she deplaned, she was hit with the smell of pluff mud and heat before walking into the cool air-conditioning of the airport. She went to baggage claim and snatched her black suitcase, easily identifying it with the winged griffon emblazoned on the small label of the Attingham Summer School. She was prepared to take a shuttle into town when, to her amazement, a familiar SUV pulled alongside her.

Her friends Benjamin and Sebastian hollered out, "Need a lift, baby?"

She smiled broadly at her two friends and said, "Absolutely."

On the way home, they told her that they had been at Weston and Diana's, and now, as they spoke, a group was gathering to welcome her home. Home, Lucy thought, home to her wonderful friends, her cottage, and tomorrow she would pick up her furry boy, Toulouse.

She regaled them with her stories of the trip, and they filled her in about all that had happened while she was away. Violet was dating a friend of Sebastian's, a math teacher. Diana had found a spot on Spring Street for a floral shop, Rachel had passed her real estate exam, and there was something more that they couldn't tell her. By eleven she was home in her house with all of the things she loved. It seemed so odd to be home, to be tucked in the sheets, with no bus to board the following day. She closed her eyes, and sleep crept over her, taking her to Morpheus's side.

The next day, her friends Ella and Ryan came to visit. She was still groggy from her flight when they called at the kitchen door. She offered them coffee. As she looked at them, she noticed an exuberance that she didn't quite remember from before she left. Ella had lived above her several years ago before she purchased her own house. While living there she had met Ryan. Ella was one of three tenants who had lived in the "love nest" and had not moved out to move in with her boyfriend or become engaged.

Here was Ella now, holding out her right hand, showing a marquise-cut emerald with diamond baguettes on either side. At her astonishment, Ryan and Ella burst into laughter.

Ella said, "We couldn't come last night, and we asked the gang not to tell you. Obviously they didn't."

Ryan held his fiancée's hand and looked at Lucy. "I proposed the week after you left, so when you called to check in, we kept quiet because we wanted to tell you face-to-face."

"It wasn't the love nest, though, was it? I'm just wondering about it, you know, if the spell is broken?" Lucy naively questioned.

They looked at each other, Ella a petite, trim forty-five-year-old looked at her twenty-six-year-old handsome, loyal man and said, "No, the spell isn't broken. It just took a while to figure it out."

"Wow. This is fantastic! I just wish I had champagne. Well, Ella, it's not that I'm smart and gorgeous like you, but this does give me hope."

Ryan winked at her. "Baby, we brought champagne and provisions. Now get rid of some of those rules, Lucy, and you'll find the right guy."

Ryan popped the cork of the bottle of Saint-Hilaire champagne, and they toasted to the couple's bliss and their imminent nuptials. Ella removed eggs, bacon, and toast from her enviro grocery bag and soon whipped up what Lucy would remember as a happy feast.

Chapter 4

Oh!
THE PLACES YOU'LL GO!
You'll be on your way up!
You'll be seeing great sights!
You'll join the high fliers
who soar to high heights.

Oh, The Places You'll Go!, Dr. Seuss

It was the end of July. Samuel had visited China, where he spent two weeks in Beijing and two in the countryside. He had visited the glories of the Forbidden City, had walked the Great Wall, where he hiked up and tobogganed down. He had sipped tea in teahouses, wandered the streets, listened to traditional Chinese music, seen acrobatic shows and amusement parks. After Beijing, the country was quiet. The unusual beauty of the landscape was breathtaking. He followed his *Lonely Planet* guides and viewed temples and shrines tucked away like jewels waiting for discovery.

The first two weeks of his trip had been spent in Thailand. Although Bangkok wasn't his scene, he spent four days there before taking the train twelve hours to the north to drink in the city of Chiang Mai. At Chiang Mai he met Americans visiting from Chicago. They spent two days touring the city. At first he enjoyed their company, but at the end of the three-day adventure of hiking, elephant rides, and white-water rafting, he was ready to abandon them in search of more adventure. It had been nice to share things they had in common. However, five days with strangers had tested his nerves. He searched the islands to the south, where he snorkeled and dove in azure blue, water where he was stunned by rocks jutting out of the sea at Koh Tao, which translated to "Turtle Island." While he snorkeled, he was amazed that he could see up to seventy-five feet and was awed by the iridescent and vibrant colors of the fish as they swam by.

Now he was off to Cambodia to see the World Heritage Site Angkor Wat, considered one the most spectacular wonders of the world. He planned on spending four or five days there. He e-mailed friends, bringing out his notes and hitting the highlights of his stay. Sheff and Drew wrote to say that they were enjoying the house and couldn't believe how comfortable it was. They were even looking at buying the place from him. They were still thinking, though. He scrolled down and read the part about the kitchen needing a rehab and that they had purchased old brick to lay a patio. He laughed out loud as he read on that they had fertilized the old gardenia bushes and they had not disappointed. Sam knew they were nesting, probably even landscaping. They noted that they had repainted all but his room and that the place had a fresh look. He imagined that they had taken down the widow's window treatments and hung tailored drapes or plantation shutters. It had been the best idea on his part. They never disappointed. They noted that his stuff was safe and not to worry. They had their own electronics that were quite superior, as Drew required the very best technology could offer. Sam sighed in relief.

The next e-mail was from his roommate Whit. The roommates were fine, if not a little rowdy, and it was best that Sam had moved the electronics. They had forgotten to mention that they played in a pseudo eighties punk band called Devo Lives. He told Mrs. Annie that he would make sure they didn't practice after nine. He also told the punks that they had to find a different place to rehearse.

Sam sighed again. The third e-mail came from Paul and was lengthy, updating him on the scene of the bar, how he was planning to expand it. Should he buy a place downtown with outdoor seating? What did Sam think of the new menu that was sent as an attachment? Phoebe, his wife, and little Trey were growing. She was pregnant again. All good news.

His parents and sister, Elizabeth, had written him chatty missives, and his mother encouraged him not miss the sites of Angkor Wat. As he read, he said, *Yeah, yeah, I'm there now.* He replied to the e-mails, and before shutting the computer down, he realized another had just arrived—Mrs. Annie, God love her. She told him politely about the roommates after she had asked how he was. Her niece was staying with her and had brought her computer. Wasn't the Internet a blessing? Serena had talked her into cable, and now she was going to give her her older laptop, as she needed a new one. She didn't have anyone's e-mail but his, as it was on the card he had given her. How was the Far East, she asked, and please put me on your what's-it-called list.

She then said, *I have to tell you about a house. Mr. Smith down the street died.* Sam skipped over the list of ailments, maladies, and hospital stays. *Sorry, buddy, but you were ninety-seven. We can't live forever; just go ahead and give up the ghost.*

The family wanted to sell the house, but it was a wreck. *Yes, it is,* thought Sam. Would he be willing to buy it for sixty-thousand? Sam's throat worked very hard. The land was worth more than that. He didn't want to rip them off, but if he were to rehab the place right, it would cost a small fortune, and dirt in Charleston wasn't cheap. Sam e-mailed Mrs. Annie: Yes, he would buy the house. Yes, she would be included in his blanketed e-mails. He was proud of her new technology skills. Would she please have the family e-mail him? No need for Realtors, he would pay for the inspection, termite letter, and handle the attorney fees. Make it easy on the family in their time of grief.

Sam knew that Mrs. Annie had cooked for Mr. Smith. She had read to him, and he, Sam, had made those grocery runs. The children, in their sixties, were successful and lived "off." They sent Mr. Smith nice ties and cuff links, knowing he liked to dress well. They rarely visited, as they thought his house was a pit. Sam sighed again. It always happens to the old. They do right by their kids, give, and when they need help, everyone is too selfish and they jump ship.

Sam e-mailed his attorney, his inspectors, and the mortgage loan officer. He would e-mail the family's contact info at the end of the week. He e-mailed Sheff about mothballing the property as soon as he wrote him next. All was going better than planned. Another property secured while he was thousands of miles away. His attorney was a good friend and loved to be in the loop of Sam's effort of rehabbing properties. He was active in all of the preservation efforts in town and tried to get Sam to speak at public meetings.

Sam had finally laid down the law. He had said, *"Look, Brooks, I'll do my part on the Eastside, okay?"*

Eventually Brooks backed off. Brooks would handle everything in his prompt legal manner. While Samuel was exploring the ancient city of Angkor Wat in Cambodia, Brooks would be *ching-chinging* his hourly fees.

Chapter 5

This city is the oldest I have yet seen in America...The appearance of the city is highly picturesque...in one street you seem to be in an old English town and in another in some continental city of France or Italy. This variety is extremely pleasing to the eye.

Fanny Kemble, nineteenth-century English actress

December 2007

It was Sunday, and Lucy was going to her grandmother's house. She went for three o'clock dinner every week and then met her friends at Paul's bar around seven. This particular Sunday, her Grandmere would entertain several of Lucy's cousins. Her independent, right-winged cousins now lived in big, modern houses in Mt. P, either in the new urbanism neighborhood where everything was brand new or those where the houses were a minimum of three thousand square feet. The houses boasted business offices, master suites, closets bigger than her largest bedroom, and even massage rooms off of the exercise rooms. They sent their children to Ashley Hall School, a fabulous property said to be designed by William Jay and where girls were educated to the nth degree, and to Porter-Gaud, another illustrious private school.

Lucy parked her vintage turquoise Karmann Ghia on the block. Today would be stressful, but Grandmere loved her, so all was right with her universe. She lovingly gazed at the house before entering. It was a large mid-nineteenth-century Greek Revival house with exterior masked piazzas. Its Carolina gray brick was muted, and the brownstone sills fashioned with Greek keys and marble window pediments set off its beauty. The pointing needed to be done, but that would be left to a different generation of Barwicks, Camerons, Bennetts and the lot. Grandmere had not done work since she had added central heat and air and upgraded the kitchen after Hurricane Hugo's fierce winds swept the city in 1989. Before that, she and her husband had made necessary repairs in the 1960s to keep the grandeur of the house intact. Lucy couldn't worry about that, though. She remembered as a child the spring parties when the house and her grandparents were larger than life. She remembered one particular party when they hosted a famous architect from England, and he commented on the heat and the size of the bugs. Immediately it seemed that a huge palmetto bug swarmed and landed in his fresh gin and tonic, only to quietly sit on top.

Her grandfather had hesitated only for a second and plucked the drunk insect out of his guest's cocktail and said, *"Imagine what your forebears thought of India!"* To this day, Lucy imagined the horrified Londoner repeating the story.

She walked up the stairs and turned the knob, allowing herself into the house. They would all be in the double parlors. She sidestepped everyone and walked down the hall quietly. Her grandmother's cook stood by the gas range and sputtered quietly to herself.

"Hey Stella," Lucy said quietly. "Who are we dealing with today?"

Stella turned toward Lucy and said, "Hey, sugar, give me a hug."

Lucy loved Stella. She had always been so good to her after her mother died and after her father had had to leave. Stella was filled with wisdom, was kind and generous of heart, and knew the Cameron and Barwick family's many secrets. When Lucy had told Stella she was looking for a house ten years ago, Stella told her about her uptown neighborhood, how diverse it was. Yes, there were still issues with drugs, but the neighborhood was strong. Trust her, Lucy would like it. It was all mixed up with black folk, white folk, and all classes. Stella and her husband, Mack, had bought their house in 1970, as it was close to his job at the navy yard and close to her work on Legare Street. One of Stella's friends had died, and Stella had found the Realtor handling the house, and Lucy had signed the deposit check that day. Stella promised her she would never regret it.

That first night, Lucy had cried in the dark house, not understanding that the electricity didn't work. She cried even harder when she realized no church bells would wake her in the morning. As she was in the consequences of a full meltdown, there had been a knock at her door. There stood Stella and Mack with a casserole in hand.

Mack had looked at Lucy and said, *"What're you doing in the dark, girl?"* He and Stella had no trace of the Gullah dialect of their upbringing, as in their days at school it had been eradicated completely.

Lucy, still crying had said, *"The inspector told me I would have to replace the wiring. I guess it must be that bad."*

Mack had looked at her and said, *"Where's the breaker box?"*

She'd lifted a finger, pointing into the hall. Mac asked for a flashlight. Lucy handed him her only vestige of light. Within seconds the house was blazingly lit in every room.

She had looked at Mack and said, *"My hero."*

"No, not your hero, Lucy, just remember that when they switch over the power, you usually turn the breakers off."

"Oh."

Mack and Stella were two of Lucy's favorite people. True to her word, Stella had included Lucy in neighborhood functions and had forced her to join the neighborhood association, where they tirelessly went to meetings and the mayor's office, held bake sales, and planted trees.

"Well, there aren't any diverse people here today. Two sets of your cousins, the lot of them, and a nice young lawyer, your age, one of their friends. Your uncle and aunt couldn't make it, as he has a big case in Columbia tomorrow."

Lucy nodded. Her uncle Gardiner took his clients seriously, and like many lawyers of his generation, giving up Sunday dinner was something you did.

"You should be all right. Those cousins of yours mostly just annoy you," Stella said.

"Absolutely. And since they think I prefer your company, which I do, more than theirs, it will be fine to scoot back here before dessert is served."

Lucy entered the parlor.

Her cousin Russell was pouring a glass of wine for his wife when he noticed her. "Lucy, honey, where have you been? It's two thirty. We expected you earlier." His lawyer voice was honed and polished.

He had been a prompt child and now was a stickler for timeliness. She felt sorry, as always, for his staff. "Hi, Russ, I was in the kitchen." She smoothed her gray wool skirt and adjusted the Hermès scarf that had been her mother's.

He was tall and broad-shouldered, dark-haired from his Huguenot lineage, and quite attractive but uptight. He and his wife, Stephanie, had met at USC while both were in law school. Stephanie was pretty, tall, slim, and had not aged. Between her personal trainer, Botox or Restalyne, and her therapist, they had taken a beautiful, smart woman and turned her into someone with an air of celebrity. She had a greedy side to her, though, and not enough positive thinking or proper meditation would eradicate this from her system. Stephanie wore a stunning polka-dot dress in black and celadon. It was cut along the lines of a 1960s vintage dress made famous by the likes of Audrey Hepburn. She smiled her BriteSmile, showing over white teeth at Lucy and said, "We've brought a friend for you to meet."

The way she said it reminded Lucy of that scary Jodie Foster movie with Anthony Hopkins. What was it? Oh yeah, *Silence of the Lambs.* What was that line? *"I had an old friend for lunch."* Ick. She really couldn't stay that long.

Her Grandmere had seen her now. Lillian Barwick was still beautiful although her eighty-sixth birthday was right around the corner. "Lucy, have you been here long?"

She looked around her. The French chandeliers that members of the Barwicks had purchased on a grand tour in France 150 years ago scintillated. She mused at the ceiling medallions with their Greek key design bound by rosettes in guilloche and finished with acanthus leaves. The house was elegantly furnished in a way that spoke old Charleston with portraits by Theus, Savage, Sully, and Osgood placed against the muted jasper green painted walls. The furniture was a mix of late eighteenth century Charleston-made chests-on-chests, tea tables, and Pembroke tables. The mahogany gleamed under Stella's careful eye. The sofa was early Empire and one of Lucy's favorites with its heavily carved winged paw feet and its turned rail. The fabrics on the seat furniture were a hodgepodge of blues, greens, reds, and faint yellows. The draperies tied them all together, as did the worn yet beautiful Aubusson carpet.

"Well, er, Grandmere, Russ and Steph here were holding me captive. I narrowly missed the lamentations of soccer games and music lessons. However, if you can stand the abject torment of any of my boredom, I'll discuss it with you, but otherwise I am all ears to hear about your week, which I'm sure has been quite exciting, as it always is."

Lillian Barwick laughed. "Let me introduce you, dear, to this fabulous friend of Russell's. This is Drew Simmons, and quite a remarkable man. In fact, I absolutely want you to sit on either side of me. Drew, my granddaughter Lucy Cameron, she shares many of your interests. And I believe she thinks I have a life of adventure, which I do not. Russell, Stephanie, Blake, and Molly? It's time for dinner."

At six, Lucy left the table, saying she must help Stella. There was just too much work for one person. She had enjoyed dinner very much, and Drew was a fantastic dinner partner.

He had slipped her his card and told her to call him. Very nice indeed, she would enjoy introducing him to her friends. She almost skipped to the kitchen to help Stella. On arriving, she noticed that Stella was wiping counters and that, besides the dessert plates, all was cleaned and straightened. They washed and dried the nineteenth-century blue-and-gold Barwick Derbyshire plates, and Lucy noted that today had been pleasant. She asked Stella if Christmas would work with her sister and father coming? After all, Grandmere would be visiting Aunt Aurora in Prague, so there didn't need to be a family brouhaha.

"Maybe, honey. Don't put all your eggs in one basket."

As she left the house, she strolled to the Karmann Ghia. She thought about her Grandmere, and love surged for her. Her cousins were *so* uptight, but she had been given the gift of Drew's conversation.

She felt him before she saw him. It was the not-tenant of the boots cycling down the street. She hadn't seen him for a while. Huh.

Lucy waved and said, "Hello."

He looked at her briefly, said, "Hi," and picked up speed.

Odd, she thought. *Oh well.*

It was now time to meet her friends at Moe's Crosstown Tavern. Sebastian and Ben were there, holding down the fort in what they called the "bat cave," a corner table and booth. Lucy shut out the dark December sky with purple clouds squirreling away. She entered the tavern and hugged her friends.

"How was dinner?" they questioned in unison.

"It was actually great. I met this nice attorney, and my cousins behaved. No politics. It was quite civil and nice."

"So this attorney, our type or your type?" asked Benjamin.

"Definitely your type, but my family believes he's my type."

Sebastian yawned. "What's his name?"

"Drew Simmons, Simon, something like that."

Ben looked at her, eyes dancing. "That's rich, sweetheart. It's Simon, Andrew Simon. He's from Virginia and has the same-first-name-could-be-last-name thing. He and his partner Sheff are regulars here on burger night."

Lucy giggled. "That's hilarious. God, what a joke on good ole Russ and Steph. I bet they've already asked him for political contributions. Oops, he's not a Log Cabin Republican, is he?"

Sebastian leaned his dark, handsome face to her and growled, "Yellow Dog Democrat, they both are Yellow Dogs."

The three friends ordered drinks, and the men ordered food. Lucy was happiest with her friends, as they were never pretentious, always entertaining, and smarter than she.

"Great, just unbelievable." Sam spied the Karmann Ghia as he pulled up to the bar on his bike.

For six months he had had the most amazing time of his life. He had arrived at his parents' house, where he had enjoyed Thanksgiving with his tight-knit group of family and friends. After a week and a half in Salem, he had flown to Charleston, where he was staying with Sheff and Drew until December thirty-first, when the Devo Lives boys would vacate his house.

He hoped he wouldn't run into her. He'd hang with Paul and have his beer at the bar before he cycled home. He shook his head. Why did he find her so annoying? She wasn't anything to him, nothing at all. Just another snooty Charleston girl.

Walking in, he caught sight of Benjamin and Sebastian. "Hey guys, what's happening?"

"Not much," Ben replied. "How was your trip? I can't believe it's been almost six months. Was it amazing?"

Sam regaled them with stories of beautiful scenery, pagodas, temples, beaches, exotic food, and a culture so different to his own. He told them that he had met a beautiful girl who was quite direct about initializing a liaison and was, unbeknownst to him, a Thai ladyboy. That it had thrown him for a loop. They both knew he would never step out on Jessica, and there was never a danger of him getting involved, but still, that was something. Out of the corner of his eye, he saw Lucy scoot along the banquette. He stared at her. She actually looked nice, even pretty, when she didn't have dirt smudged on her nose.

She extended her hand and said, "We were never properly introduced. I'm Lucy Cameron."

He shook her hand. "Samuel O'Hara, but I go by Sam."

Ben invited him to join them, and he agreed. He wasn't sure why exactly, but he did.

Sam's humor was infectious as he continued to ramble on with tales from his journeys. Lucy listened to his voice, enjoying his Massachusetts dialect. She liked how he said "won't" and "out." She was impressed that he had gone so far for so long, and by himself. When he told them about Angkor Wat, she felt for the first time in her life that she would like to go to the Far East—until he told them about the live land mines. At Phnom Penh, he was faced with the history of the brutality and the violence of the Khmer Rouge and the killing fields. By nine thirty, Lucy was ready for home. She said her good nights and "Nice to see you again" to Sam. She pulled her car into the drive. It was time to take Toulouse around the block and call it a night. Tomorrow was a workday, after all.

Chapter 6

A kiss can be a comma, a question mark or an exclamation point. That's basic spelling that every woman ought to know.

Theatre Arts, Mistinguett (Jeanne Bourgeois)

The next day Lucy opened the shop in the French Quarter. The street was quaint with colonial houses and churches. The French Quarter was home to the Dock Street Theatre, one of the first theaters in America, where Farquhar's *The Recruiting Officer* was performed in 1736, while the Gothic edifice of the French Huguenot Church added interest and beauty across the street. St. Philip's Episcopal Church lay at a bend with its large portico stretching over the sidewalk. There were two cemeteries for St. Philip's, one on the church side and one opposite. Legend had it that the church side was for Charlestonians initially, while the stranger's side was for those from off. There were former signers of the Declaration of Independence and US Constitution on the church side, while John C. Calhoun's tomb lay on the opposite side of the street.

Lucy tended to walk down the street and take her lunch some days in the cemeteries. She looked for Barwicks, Smiths, and other family members. Grandmere's family rested in both St. Philip's and the French Hugeunot Church, but like so many Huguenot families, most of Grandmere's ancestors had aligned themselves with the English roughly seventy years after arriving to this coastal wilderness in 1680. Today she would walk to Waterfront Park. Few visitors were in town, and she could enjoy the blue sky and the warm December day.

It was the first week of December. She needed wreaths for the shop and her house. As it was slow, she left a note on the door that she would return by eleven thirty. She locked the shop and walked to Broad Street, headed for the Four Corners of Law and the basket weavers of African descent who sold wreaths this time of year. She visited her favorite weaver, a lady in her eighties named Beatrice who lived in Mt. Pleasant. Beatrice offered her two wreaths made of greenery and popcorn berries.

Lucy sat on the coping of the Judicial Center and wrote her check. They spoke of this and that, and Beatrice told her that the lights on Broad Street that hung in the palmettos had been finished that day. They talked of how others rushed Christmas and that it just wasn't right to put up decorations before Thanksgiving. Beatrice mentioned that, now that her husband had passed, she was scaling back, nothing on the roof this year. Not the Santa and sleigh, she had given it to neighbors. Lucy told her that she placed white lights around the arch of her doorway and a star in the window. That was enough for her.

Back in the shop Lucy, looked at her new acquisitions. She had purchased four original Alice R.H. Smith prints from Grandmere's friend who was moving to the exclusive facility for the aging on James Island. Lucy smiled when she looked at them. Was it really last week when Sadie offered her the art at such a low price? She remembered how she quickly increased the amount and wrote the check.

Sadie had gazed at the amount and then asked her, *"Would you like to see the Hirsch sculptures?"*

"Oh, yes, absolutely, but I probably can't afford them." She had seen the Hirsches and rubbed her hands with glee. *"They are just lovely. He had such talent."*

"He was a friend of the family, you know. Which one do you like the best?"

"Oh, I think that one, the danseuse. She's radiant, isn't she?"

"Good choice. It is my favorite, and now she is yours."

"Oh, Sadie, I couldn't possibly. It's too dear."

"Just be a good girl and say thank you. Those children of mine, they have enough, and their children, well, they never see me. I doubt they would appreciate it, and they will never miss it."

"Thank you. I will treasure it."

"I know you will." She had touched Lucy with a liver-spotted hand. Long fingers bent with arthritis cupped her cheek.

"So, we meet next week. Let's see what I can offer you for purchase then."

"Yes, ma'am, and Sadie, this is the best Christmas gift a girl could ever have. Thank you!"

Lucy tried not to sell Charleston Renaissance art out of the Low Country, or "off," as the locals said. She would offer it to the local institutions first, selling it for less than its worth. Her second choice was to sell to local collectors. After receiving a BA in art history at the University of South Carolina, she had taken a position at a local gallery where she learned everything about the Charleston Renaissance. Her mentor was older and realized her enthusiasm and eye.

He thought nothing of closing the shop if he felt that they should both travel across America to find prints and paintings that needed to come home. Often people did not realize the value in what they had and were more than happy to part with the objects. In one case he had received a tip about an upcoming garage sale in Los Angeles. It was said that the deceased had descended from a wealthy planter family who had lived on the Pee Dee River. She had borne no issue and had not kept in touch with her few siblings and cousins in South Carolina, many of whom had predeceased her. She had chosen California in hopes of being successful on the silver screen and had played bit parts in movies and TV and was able to enjoy a comfortable living. Her death at ninety-five made few headlines. Huger Sinclair's contact was quite positive that she had never parted with anything in her life.

Lucy organized their trip, and by 6:30 a.m. on a Saturday morning in the early 1990s, with precious little sleep, they were stalking the house, waiting for the sale to begin. Amongst the recliners and sofas, bedpans, and hospital bed were stacks of prints, some in their original frames, some loose. They were priced from a dollar to fifteen dollars. The sellers had acquired the house after the owner's death and wanted to clear out the detritus. Lucy and Huger Sinclair were quietly going through them when he told her to look around for anything else. While he haggled with an overtired woman, she gazed around her and saw a small bronze sculpture marked fifty dollars. She knew it had been crafted by Anna Huntington of Brookgreen Garden fame. She had continued her search high and low and found two Chinese export plates for ten dollars each. She would not pull a Huger, no haggling for these objects.

There had been nothing else of significance. She wasn't interested in the vintage clothes, shoes, and mink stoles, but then her eyes darted to an exquisite black cloche with its original box settled amidst 1940s compacts and cigarettes cases made of sterling silver and brass inscribed with the initials of the dead. It was marked seventy-five dollars, a little high. She placed it on her head after checking for moth holes and decided that she would bargain for this one thing.

As she checked out, she spoke to the owner of the house. She was exhausted. The closing was hell, there was no family, and the lady's friends wouldn't clear the things out. Well, in truth, how could they? They were all as ancient as she had been. The place was a wreck. The last owner had chain-smoked, and everything was brown; wasn't it a wonder that she lived until ninety-five? They just wanted to get rid of this stuff. They hadn't even touched the attic. At the mention of the attic, Lucy came alive. She introduced herself and handed her card to the lady and said, "I would be extremely interested in what's in the attic. Would you call me please? I would love to help you sort through it."

"Thanks, I'll do it."

"Do you have a card, or I can write down your name? "

"I can't leave the desk, but yes, let me give you my name."

"I'm Phyllis Richardson." She then gave Lucy her phone number, and Lucy had promised to keep in touch.

Lucy no longer cared to bargain for the hat. This was all meant to be.

"Listen, Lucy, is it? Just give me a hundred for everything, okay?"

"Thank you, that's so very nice."

"To tell you the truth, you've been the first nice person today, so thank you."

"You're welcome, and I'll keep in touch."

She had to remember Mr. Sinclair's quote to her over the years. *"It's all fair, Lucy, in love and war."* She hadn't quite understood what that meant until that day. They had returned to their hotel, where they looked at the works. Most were prints and drawings that were valued from two hundred fifty to a thousand dollars, but they had struck gold when they unwrapped what seemed like ancient wrapping from the 1940s. There lay two museum-quality exquisite pastels on silk executed by Elizabeth O'Neill Verner. Those would garner a small fortune. The drawings were myriad. Here a stack of works by Alfred Hutty, there originals from the book *A Woman Rice Planter* by Alice R.H. Smith. Almost all of the artists of the Charleston Renaissance were represented in this body of work, stored in boxes and never unwrapped so they remained in pristine condition.

Huger Sinclair had looked over his glasses at her and said, "This was a very worthy trip indeed, Lucy. We found many important treasures. And what did you find besides what seems to be a stunning vintage cloche?"

Lucy had unwrapped the two Chinese export plates, one famille rose and one grisaille, both late eighteenth century. She then offered the bronze sculpture to him. "That was unbelievable. These plates were only ten dollars each, and they are so lovely, no chips or hairline cracks, and the sculpture was fifty dollars."

"Well the plates are definitely yours, but what do you want to do with this?" He took the small sculpture of Diana, the goddess of the hunt, in his hands. She was beautifully crafted.

Lucy raised her eyes and drew in her breath. "We did come here for inventory, so I suppose we should sell her, but..." She hesitated. How could she tell him she wanted this so desperately for her own?

"No, she shouldn't be sold. I think she found you, and you found her. She's yours, Lucy. I can tell you how I remember those early days finding such a treasure. It belongs to you."

Lucy had hugged him to her and thanked him. "It's a Huntington, isn't it? Mr. Sinclair, I can never be in your league, what with your eye, but I'm learning, you know. I'm having fun with it all, and I couldn't thank you enough for taking me under your wing."

"No, my dear, in a few years you will surpass me, trust me about that. My good eye stemmed from what I grew up with and, of course, my education. We are much alike in that manner. To answer your question, I do believe it's a Huntington. It has all the grace and beauty, but also it possesses power and strength. It's marvelous, and why wouldn't I take you under my wing, as you are the child of the woman I loved so dearly and who extended me much kindness when Charleston society shunned my lifestyle. Now let's go have an early dinner so I can pack for the flight tomorrow. I can say I'm not sorry to go, to leave this place of sprawl and excess concrete. Truly, it wears upon the eye."

He went back to Charleston, and she flew to San Francisco, where she spent a few days' time with her father and her sister. She'd boarded her flight from LAX to San Francisco. She was quiet, thinking about the bronze in her carry-on adding a little weight, and she smiled. She said hello to the flight attendant before taking her seat in coach. The flight didn't take long, and in roughly two hours, she was with her father, who lived in the Castro District. Her sister was busy in class at Berkeley, working on her master's degree, and didn't arrive until the next day.

As Lucy placed the wreath on the front door, she thought about the fortunate trip to L.A. so long ago and how it had led to her business success. She remembered all that Huger Sinclair had taught her. Once she was home, he had asked her to dispense of formality and to call him Huger. As the years went by, they became good friends. In 2000 he had had a scare with cancer and decided to sell her the business at a low price. He had had enough, and he wanted to see her flourish. Almost immediately after Lucy purchased the business, Phyllis Richardson in Los Angeles was moving, and she called Lucy about the items in the attic. After sorting the good from the bad, she had been able to sell the objects, netting enough income to purchase the tiny eighteenth-century building in which the gallery was housed.

The business transaction suited both Lucy and Huger. She would run the business, and his legacy would be carried on, although now it bore the moniker of Cameron Fine Art and Prints. He kept his house in Ansonborough and had a summer house in Cashiers, North Carolina. Between traveling, entertaining, and gardening, he told her his life was full. He didn't miss the gallery, but still offered her tips regarding art that he came across, and they enjoyed hunting for treasures together on the rare occasion and mostly closer to home.

Huger had been right; her eye was good, and it was just getting better. The largest gift he ever gave her was the gift of confidence. He would ask her why she knew that a work was good, and he would force her to articulate the strokes, the application, composition, and more. Sometimes she would rail at him. What about Abe Schwartz's work? It was appealing, had a vernacular bent. *"Ahh,"* he would say, *"but will you still have it in twenty years? One never knows with outsider art, does one?"* Lucy couldn't answer that question and still pondered it. She had grown up around Charleston Renaissance art at Grandmere's house, where each piece was treasured.

The artists had lived such rich lives, and their work chronicled Charleston in the late nineteenth century and early decades of the twentieth century. While the Northeast, Midwest, and West Coast cities embraced the Industrial Revolution following the Civil War, Charleston had still been recovering from the fire of 1861, the effects of the Civil War, the earthquake of 1886, and the hurricane of 1911. The artists painted and wrote about their past, a past that was tied to incredible riches from the planters and merchants, and to the harsh living conditions borne to enslaved African-Americans and the working poor. DuBose Heyward's book *Porgy* focused on Charleston's African-American community and the story of real-life Sammy Smalls. The story, laden with the rich culture of the Gullah people, became America's first opera composed by George and Ira Gershwin. Dorothy Heyward, DuBose's wife, was talented as well. She had met George Gershwin while aspiring to her own artistic pursuits, and she and her husband wrote the libretto.

The women of the Charleston Renaissance were of mythic proportions to Lucy. Josephine Pinckney's novels were Book of the Month Club realities, Beatrice Ravenel was the first female editor of the *Harvard Review*, Alice R.H. Smith's work with her father, *The Dwelling Houses of Charleston*, published in 1917, spurred the preservation movement. Her legendry artwork was based on Low-Country scenes, and she was inspired by Asian art. She was a prolific watercolorist and sketcher who captured the essence of the Low Country of the past and the present.

Her subjects were rice fields, plantations that survived and those that had been eradicated by time.

Elizabeth O'Neill Verner wrote and painted. She sketched a Charleston of the past, skillfully painting and drawing the vegetable- and fruit-sellers balancing their goods in baskets on their heads in the African fashion of porterage. She captured the essence of the city in a fugue state not quite in severe decay, but certainly with a rich patina and without economic momentum. Meanwhile, John Bennett, from Ohio, moved to Charleston and chronicled its history and stories, both white and black. His children's book *Master Skylark* had been received with critical acclaim. He and the rest were active in various civic pursuits, including the Poetry Society of South Carolina, which welcomed Gertrude Stein in 1934, where her lecture on nouns was not well received.

Lucy loved her job. She enjoyed her work and spent time in the months of December, January, and February researching the Charleston Renaissance and any artist, sculptor, or writer that inhabited their sphere. She sighed, now realizing that it was 4:00 p.m. The day had passed quickly, and she remarked to herself that she should make a list of things that she needed to do before the weekend. The phone rang, interrupting her thoughts.

"Happy Holidays, Cameron Fine Art, may I help you?" she inquired.

"Lucy, honey, it's me," her father stated.

"Hi, Dad, how are you? You're still coming for Christmas, aren't you? I haven't heard from you since Thanksgiving." Lucy knew she had sounded a little harsh, but she loved Christmas and wanted to see him.

"Well, actually, that's why I'm calling. Rut just found out that there is a great house at Tahoe that's available. We wanted to know if you would like to visit us."

Lucy fumed. Her father knew how she wanted him to see her place, what she had done with the garden. She would have to find someone to mind the shop. Besides, it was their turn to come. She had flown to California last year.

Stilling her frustration, Lucy said, "So, what do you propose?"

Her father took on the quick and concise CEO voice. "We'll send you the ticket, and you can come on the twentieth and leave on the twenty-seventh. That will give us time to enjoy each other, go skiing, and celebrate. Your sister thinks it's a great idea as she's pretty wiped out working on her dissertation and all. Think about it. It makes far more sense for one of us to fly than the four of us."

"Does the fourth mean that Maeve's Republican Raymond is coming too? I thought she kicked him to the curb again."

"They're fine, but I do believe I have two of the most high-strung, indignant daughters in this country. Just relax and think about it, honey. We'll have great fun, and you love the snow. Think about it, and let me know this weekend. But listen, I have to go. I have a meeting. I love you."

Lucy sat down, hurt at her father, his partner, and her sister. They never liked to come home to Charleston. It was too staid for them, too formal. Her father felt that Charleston was too conservative and he couldn't be himself. Likewise, Maeve, her only other sibling, liked everything on the West Coast and felt that Charleston on the whole was too confining. Lucy knew she would cave. She missed them, her father, his partner, and Maeve. They were smart, funny, and quick. Their lives were always new and exciting. The only glitch was Raymond, an attorney who turned every conversation into a political minefield.

Lucy looked at her list and added: *call Kennel for T.* That night she worked on her holiday cards, separating out those for Christmas and those for Hanukkah. She had found a vintage card from the 1940s with a shaggy dog wishing Happy Christmas. She had had them reprinted and now was hand-coloring the body charcoal and silver. She changed pencils for the large bow tied around the neck. She colored fifteen red bows, fifteen green bows, and fifteen royal blue bows. She added gold and silver to the mix, and by 9:30 p.m. she had almost completed her task. As she happily listened to Bing Crosby singing "I'll Be Home for Christmas," the phone interrupted her task at hand.

"Hi, Lucy, how are you? It's Drew."

"Hi, Drew, I'm great, just working on holiday cards. What's up with you?"

"Well, Sheff and I are having an impromptu gathering at our house on Saturday, and we wanted to know if you would like to come?"

"This Saturday, then, the sixth? That's St. Nicholas Day, right? Well, all right. What's the address, and what's the dress? I see...okay, casual. Can I bring anything? Sure, I'll bring a bottle of wine. Are Sebastian and Ben going? Great, I'll catch a ride with them. Thanks, Drew, it will be great to see you. What? Yes. Yes, I'd love to meet your friend who just got back. It'll be a pleasure."

No sooner had she clicked the phone off when it rang again. She glanced at the caller ID and knew she had to speak to Maeve.

"Hi, sis, how are you, and how's the dissertation?"

"It's going, Lucy. I'm learning so much more about Jean Rhys than I ever thought. In fact, she may just be the end of me, but it's coming.

Let's hope it's done this time next year. How are you, and how is the gallery?"

"It's all wonderful, lots of new inventory and people have been shopping"

That's great. Listen, I know you think Dad and I are sideswiping you with Christmas. It's just I'm really doing well and have good momentum, and Charleston always makes me think of Mom and brings me down. Can you please understand?"

"Ok, but I am a bit disappointed" Lucy added peevishly.

"Dad feels really bad, but Tahoe will be great, and it always gives me good energy."Maeve added.

"I understand, Maeve, but is recalcitrant Raymond going to be there the entire time? I don't think I can stand his politics, and well, you know how he feels about me. He's just so stiff. I don't quite get it, you know, your relationship."

"Lucy, I love him. I know it's crazy, but for the most part, he's great. I'll remind him to be nice to my sister. No comments about being a Dem in a red state and all that. He is a smart, wonderful man and is quite generous, and the sex is fantastic."

"Don't you think part of that is that he gets you so emotionally worked up? I don't know. Yes, I'll call Dad tomorrow and tell him I'm coming. Have you spoken to Grandmere?"

"No, not yet, I'll call her before she leaves for Prague."

"Don't forget to edit yourself, Maeve. She always clues in to ulterior motives."

"Too true, dear sister. Okay, so that's settled. I need a run before seriously getting down to my writing. Is your tree up?"

"Yes it is and it's a great big fat fraser fir."

"Great, Mom's ornaments from Europe on? ...And is that Bing in the background?

"Of course, to both"

Look, sis, I love you, okay?"

"Love you too. Bye."

Lucy poured a glass of wine. She was now enjoying Handel's *Messiah* as she stared at the tree covered in glass ornaments that her parents had purchased long ago when her father was in the army. They were her treasures, and each year she unpacked them with gentleness and reverence. She would miss the late-night Christmas service at St. Philip's, but family was most important, after all.

Drew and Sheff were pulling out all the stops. Sam felt that he was caught in a maelstrom of catering as they whipped together dips, ham biscuits fresh from the oven, cheeses, and more. He had offered assistance and was relegated to do what he knew. He packed ice chests with Heineken, Bud Light, Miller Light, and Sam Adams. He chilled bottles of Pinot Grigio, Chardonnay, and Riesling. He uncorked two bottles of Cab, two Pinot Noir, and two Merlot.

The house had been amazingly transformed. They had painted the walls in a palette of chocolate brown in the living room and Tuscan yellow in the dining room. The kitchen wallpaper of roses had been tossed in the trash, and its burnished walls of yellow-orange continued the feel of Italy. They had taken up the linoleum on the kitchen floor, and the Formica on the counters, and had relaid twelve-by-twelve tiles on all the surfaces. The house was a dream in the burbs. With their collection of mission and contemporary furniture, modern art and prints, Sam felt the house had been done in a masculine manner, without it screaming: *Too many electronics and not enough taste!* The tree was placed in a corner of the living room, topped with a Santa hat, and laden with a mishmash of ornaments and alight with large colored lights.

"So, Sheff, Drew, who's all coming tonight?" he queried.

"Our friends and your friends. About sixty. Drew's doing oysters outside, and then we'll have the rest of the food in the dining room. We think we have a present for you."

He grinned at his friends. They were always trying to fix him up. "Oh yeah, what's that? Please not a fishwife, and there's Jess still, you know."

"While you and Jess are on hiatus, just meet some people, and no, she's no fishwife," said Sheff. "Drew thinks this babe is perfect for you. She has her own business and is very independent. She loves kids, and she's, most importantly, smart, well traveled, and loves to learn. She's cute too."

"Well, what does she look like? I mean, is she tall, short, a bombshell, or a Jennifer Aniston type, you know? Come on."

"You'll meet her in an hour or so. It'll be fine."

She couldn't figure out what to wear. Her clothes lay in a heap in the guest room on the bird's-eye maple Victorian bed, its high headboard decorated with carved shells and flowers. It was all a disaster, and it seemed as though the clothes were welling into a sea of fabric discord, sweeping off the bed and onto the floor. She stood in her panties and bra, a matching set of azure blue bedecked with velvet and lace of a lighter shade and looked in the mirror. Garrison Keillor rambled in the background, on NPR, that in Lake Wobegon, all the women were strong and the children above average.

She laughed, and then she placed the cloche on her head and said, "Well, this is right—so what else will do?"

She ended up wearing a pewter silk Anne Klein cowl-neck blouse with a short black skirt. She added tights and Donald Pliner boots. Her outfit was eclectic and fun. She dodged into the bathroom and added Clinique lipstick in her favorite shade, Raspberry Rush, then waited for the boys to pick her up. She draped the cape on her shoulders and turned down the carols for Toulouse. The five-minute drive over the bridge to Sheff and Drew's was a fun time. She told them about Christmas and her disappointment. They told her to just have fun.

The house was packed. Lucy suggested to her friends that they go around back, which they did. The yard seemed to be illuminated with a million tiny white lights that sparkled amongst the camellias and mature trees. Drew was hefting oysters with a shovel on a temporary table of plywood and sawhorses. His handsome face, with its square jaw and chocolate-colored eyes, was alive with merriment. He welcomed them, and Lucy had to stand on her tiptoes to kiss him on the cheek. He gave her a bear hug, his strong arms circling her waist.

She touched his thick hair that was graying prematurely and said, "Hello, handsome man, Merry Christmas."

He smiled at her, showing strong, even white teeth, and a dimple appeared on the right corner of his mouth. "Hey Lucy, darling, you look perfect and hot. Where did you get that amazing vintage hat?"

"Oh, it's a long story. I'll tell you sometime. Is there anything I can do to help?"

"No, not at all, just dig in."

The ultimate hosts had provided gloves and knives for their guests. Lucy, Sebastian, and Ben dug into the melee, jostling friends and newcomers alike. Lucy heard a familiar laugh and turned to see Rachel heading in their direction.

"Hey Rache, take my place," she said. "I'm completely surfeit with our briny delights."

"Thanks, Lucy, how have you been?"

"Good, what about you? How's the new career? You never did tell me why you left the law firm, you know."

"Well, it's slow, but good. I've three active listings, and I sold two houses within the last three months. I stashed some money while I was at the firm, so I haven't been worrying about cash flow. What I didn't tell you last summer is that the firm fired the brilliant attorney I worked for and the new managing partner was just awful. All I can compare it to is *Harry Potter*. He was like Delores Umbridge, and he took all the light out of my Hogwarts. Suffice it to say, that when his name lit up on the phone, I felt sick, as if I were seeing the mark of the Dark Lord in the sky. I know it's silly of me to use the *Harry Potter* quotes. It just makes me feel better if I liken it to fiction. So now I'm on my own, no longer working my fingers to the bone as a paralegal. I've been planting and painting. I never had the time to do those things before. It's really quite wonderful."

"That's great, Rachel. Isn't it crazy how one person can ruin things for everyone? I knew that there had been a shake-up over there, but I didn't think it would affect you. I'm sorry that all happened."

Rachel had just turned fifty. She was tall, lean, and well muscled. She shook her short auburn hair. Her hazel eyes flashed sometimes green and then shot with copper in her pretty, narrow face with full red-rouged lips and a strong, straight nose.

"In the end, for me, it was for the best. Sometimes bad things happen to mix things up. I think this was a contrast that I needed so I could really achieve what I wanted."

The friends continued to talk until they heard Diana and Weston arrive. Always silly and cheerful, their conversation turned to Diana's possible acquisition of an acre in North Charleston where she could erect a greenhouse and cultivate flowers for her shop. She knew it would be a jump, and yes, she would have to hire extra staff, but why not take the leap? She was a perfectionist, and she felt that the flowers she had been ordering were not quite up to her standards. Yes, she would still have to order peonies and other flowers, but, a greenhouse, just think about it, even better to find someplace that already had a well.

Rachel offered to assist with the acquisition, and Lucy offered to help her friend seed up and plant when the deal was done. Diana told Rachel how they had all missed her, that it was months since she had been hanging with their regular pack. She understood that Rachel needed some time, but truly didn't they all miss her, she queried Lucy. Yes, Lucy said, and maybe they just needed to schedule time to get together. They didn't have to wait for an emergency beer night or anything.

Sam was stuck in the dining room. He was trapped between the dowager who was Sheff's grandmother, a proper lady who continued to ask him questions and remarked about the beauty of the Northeast, and a charming man in his late sixties. Every time he tried to disengage himself, his access was blocked yet again by a small mob that had gathered at the table. The man had introduced himself as Huger and said that he had owned a gallery for years, but was now happily enjoying retirement. Sam nodded as he listened about acquisitions of Charleston art. He had known that Charleston had had an artistic boom in the twenties, but he hadn't realized all the significant artists who had visited during this period, like Edward Hopper and Childe Hassam. He eventually shook hands with both of his conversationalists and slipped between the crowd to the kitchen.

"Where have you been, Sam?" Sheff queried as he thoughtfully stroked his trim beard. Sheff was tall, with a perfectly fit body that visited the gym on a regular basis. His auburn hair was sticking up, and his light blue eyes flashed.

"I was trapped. What can I do to help? How about if I check the beverage station, since that was my task earlier?"

"Great," Sheff said good-naturedly, nimbly carrying two platters while sailing to the dining room.

No sooner had he stepped outside, case of beer in hand, than Drew called him over. "Sam, I want you to meet a friend of mine. Lucy Cameron, meet Samuel O'Hara, world traveler."

He said hello and sized her up. So this was the girl his friends wanted him to meet. Two more who thought she hung the moon. She looked nice in her short skirt and boots. The hat was a little much, though, and who wears a cape these days? Something quirky there. They talked about the house and all that Drew and Sheff had done to it. They planned to buy it from him now. Wasn't it funny how things worked out? She asked him about his family and growing up in Salem. He noted that she giggled a lot and that she was constantly waving to someone walking by.

He was handsome, she thought. Nice teeth, nice eyes. Lucy quietly drank in his attractiveness. She could tell that he worked out regularly, that his arms were strong, and she wondered about the presence of six-pack abs. She told him that she would be traveling to California and then to Lake Tahoe for the holidays to spend time with her family. He told her about a house that he was trying to acquire and that he was staying in the city. Besides, he liked the peace and quiet of Charleston during this time. She noted that, historically, Charleston was quiet at the holidays and that in the 1830s, the English actress Fanny Kemble mentioned that Charleston's elite hastened away to the plantations on the Ashley and the Cooper Rivers or to the French Santee.

He liked the way she spoke with intensity, the way she formed her words and nodded her head.

As he bent over to retrieve another beer, she noticed how his pants fit and thought that he looked better in a pair of khakis than anyone she knew. Funny, she hadn't looked at a man like this in a long time. Ben and Sebastian came to claim her. They were ready to go and wanted to check out a bar on the way home. Lucy said she'd catch a ride back with Diana and Weston, only to be told that they had just gone.

Sam offered her a ride. He was going by a party downtown and could drop her. They said their good-byes, and he asked her for directions to her house. They kept up a steady conversation in the car until he pulled into her driveway. He walked her to the door. Taking her keys out of her hand, he unlocked the door for her.

"Well, good night then. It was really nice of you to give me a ride."

He leaned into her and briefly kissed her mouth, startling them both. "Merry Christmas, Lucy."

After walking inside, she touched her mouth with her right hand, unsure if the kiss had happened or if it was some fabrication in her mind. She thought that he was smart and funny, and he seemed very nice. Toulouse, her furry boy, greeted her and licked her face. Hugging him to her, she closed her eyes and thought, *This is a very merry Christmas indeed.*

Chapter 7

Were kisses all the joys in bed,
One woman would another wed

Sonnets to Sundry Notes of Music, IV, William Shakespeare

New Year's Day came quicker than she thought. It seemed that the trip to California had come and gone too quickly. Her dad and his partner, Rutherford, Rut for short, were excellent hosts, and even Raymond had behaved himself. Maeve had surprised her one evening after they watched *Doctor Zhivago*. They were both crying, talking about Lara, her fate, and the beauty of the movie. Lucy commented on the melancholic sound of the balalaika and the soundtrack as a whole. Maeve had asked her then if she wondered if their mother had committed suicide. Why would she have been following the truck so closely, if she hadn't meant to end it? Lucy wouldn't hear it. Their mother had probably been distracted. It had been raining hard, as it does in summer in the Low Country. She was driving in a near monsoon and didn't know how close she was. Besides, why would their mother want to do that? She had everything to live for. Maeve spoke about their father, his coming out when they were teens. Had their mother known? And what about his need to leave Charleston and its stifling traditions? She spoke about her own fears and dislike of a town thousands of miles away and was sorry that she felt that way; she just did. The two sisters cried until there were no tears left and agreed to always be honest and true with each other. They were too old to keep any secrets.

Lucy couldn't think about those things, dark things that she hadn't thought about for a long time. She needed to lighten her mood and dress for dinner. Today was the dinner party at Huger's. She would see old friends and probably meet someone new. Huger always had something up his sleeve, and his dinner parties were legendary. She took her time dressing. She had found a skirt and top on sale the day before in a shop on upper King Street and would wear it today. She would rescue the jet beads that had been her great-grandmother's from the bottom of her jewelry case and add the silver-and-black marcasite earrings. The day was warm, so no coat was needed, just a pashmina in case the evening became cool.

Huger's house in Ansonborough was a brick Greek Revival single house built one room wide and several rooms deep around 1840. The houses were a vernacular architectural form angled just right to catch the cool breezes in the heat of the summer from Charleston's harbor on the porches, called piazzas. Lucy noticed that the light-colored gray painted piazza was neatly swept and the planters were filled with purple violas, lavender pansies, and rocket-sized snaps. Calendulas proudly held up their full yellow heads to the attention of the sun. She rapped the brass lion-head knocker and marveled at Huger's taste as she always did. The terra-cotta planters and soft Charleston green painted wicker furniture offered an elegant but comfortable setting.

The house was crowded with twenty-five guests. The dining room table sat twenty, and then ten more would sit at a table set up in the parlor. The tables were set with white damask cloths, Haviland china, and Waterford crystal. Knife rests were positioned at each place setting with overlarge Victorian napkins folded into bishop's hats.

The art on the wall was representative of old Charleston style, here a Sully, there a Morse. One wall featured artists relating to the Charleston Renaissance: Hutty, Smith, Verner, Taylor, they were all there. The grouping also included a print by Prentiss Taylor, the prominent WPA artist who illustrated Langston Hughes's books. Lucy looked about her, eyeing the early nineteenth century painting of Shakespeare's Macbeth by John Blake White. Each wall held treasures. Hudson River artists' works, an original Angelica Kauffman, the list went on and on. Miniatures reposed comfortably on the mantelpiece with a seventeenth-century famille rose Chinese export garniture set. Rich Oriental carpets covered the original pine floors, while his furnishings featured Charleston-made tea tables, settees, and a secretary bookcase all made of mahogany with cypress wood serving as the secondary wood due to the high humidity and harsh heat. Venture cargo furniture graced the room too, a Duncan Phyfe 1820s sofa and a rare Townsend and Goddard side table from Newport, one of 144 pieces that was said to have been sent to Charleston from 1765–1768.

Huger's parties were always catered by a new and up-and-coming chef. He tried not to use the same person twice, as he wanted to give some fresh talent an opportunity. Only once had there been disaster.

More often than not, these young men and women rose to the occasion and became prominent fixtures in Charleston's dining institutions.

Huger hugged Lucy to him. He was tall and well built, and she felt small in his embrace when he kissed her cheek. "How's my girl?"

His handsome face broke into a smile, and she was reminded that he resembled the actor Christopher Plummer. The laugh lines around his eyes and his mouth deepened as he looked at her with genuine affection. He was dressed in a smart double-breasted suit with an Hermès cravat tucked into a heavily starched white shirt. His blue eyes twinkled while his graying blond hair waved in a fashionable cut.

"Good. All is well, and you?" She touched his facial hair. "I like the Vandyke. It really is charming with the soul patch. You look rather dashing, you know?" She handed him the slim volume that was tucked in her right hand. "I wanted to return this to you. I'm sorry it's taken so long, but I felt that Celia Fiennes just prolonged the trip to England for me. Thank you so much for recommending the book and for writing my letter of recommendation. It was a fabulous experience. I still return to my guide books and process all that I saw."

"All is well with me, Lucy. You didn't have to return the book. I knew it was safe in your keeping. And I knew you would enjoy the summer school, just as I did when I went so many years ago. It changes your life in a very special way."

"Yes, it does. I seem to look at everything differently now. Everything is so much more intense, and I understand so much better our ancestors and their mad inclinations for collecting and travel. Huger, I found my own copy of Celia's journeys online. It should be arriving any day. So, I'll continue to enjoy my excited and descriptive seventeenth-century traveler. I especially enjoyed her thoughts on Chatsworth and Belton House. By the way, I was doing some research on Southerners and the grand tour at the historical society, and I came across one of the Aiken travel journals. My new dead friend Joseph also describes in detail life along the River Derwent, the deerpark, and the glory of Chatsworth. It seems he was quite taken by it, as I was over a hundred fifty years later. I also wanted to ask if you would be willing to write another letter. I plan to apply for the summer course in Newport this year. I think it's time for another adventure, and I'm not familiar with the Northeast at all. Certainly, I know its history from books and pictures, but I would like to know more. By the way, who's our mystery guest? You always have one or two."

"Ah, well, I have invited a very talented chanteuse who has been performing spirituals and jazz all over town, and a young Yankee who loves his Red Sox."

"Hmm. They're all like that, aren't they? A little nutty about sports, the Red Sox and the Patriots, the Giants and Yankees. And do I know the Yankee?"

"I'm not sure. He's very nice and smart. You'll like him. I met him at Drew and Sheff's party, and he was a wonderful conversationalist. He's your dinner partner, and he happens to be straight. Lucy, I would be delighted to place pen to paper and submit another missive for your inclusion to the summer school. The more that you learn, the better your business will become, and you will love the Newport cottages. I would suggest that you spend a few days around Boston, though. You should visit Salem, too, and the Peabody Essex Museum, and visit the Jeremiah Lee House in Marblehead. There is just so much to see and do."

"That's all thrilling advice. If I am accepted, my friend Rupert, that I met last summer, has offered to squire me about. He's a curator at the Museum of Fine Arts in Boston, so I should be in good hands."

Lucy glided through the rooms with a glass of Pinot Gris in hand as she thought, *That is dear*. Huger, never using his computer in an important letter, but rather writing by hand, listing her attributes and virtues as to why she should be selected as a candidate for the course. He was known in the art world, as he had distinguished himself serving on various national boards over the years and actively helping institutions acquire works of art.

Dinner would be served at three thirty, starting with she-crab soup, followed by fresh greens, with the main course being a nouvelle version of Hoppin' John, venison, and collards. The Low-Country standard meat was ham, but Huger felt it was too pedestrian and that a person couldn't eat enough venison.

Huger announced dinner. As Lucy enjoyed the lively chatter and main course, she could not feel a bit disappointed that the chair next to her remained empty. As the plates were cleared for dessert, a knock came at the front door. The bartender let in a disheveled Samuel O'Hara. He walked up to Huger and apologized for his lateness, with great aplomb Huger noted he had arrived in time for dessert.

Lucy smiled at Sam as he took his seat. "Hi again."

"Hi to you. Look at you. That's a pretty getup." His eyes gazed down the length of her dressed in a black cut-velvet skirt and velvet top. "Looks like the jewelry is vintage."

"Yes, it is. It's from my great-grandmother. So what happened to you? You're looking a little out of sorts."

"I had a minor plumbing disaster at one of my rentals. I think I've fixed it, though. My tenant flushed a T-shirt down the toilet."

"Oh my gosh, are you kidding? Were they smoking crack or what?"

"No, I don't know. Tenants do the craziest things. She said she was cleaning the toilet, and her hand slipped on the handle, and *whoosh*. Anyway, it's fixed. This is amazing. What is this stuff?"

Lucy couldn't imagine who in the world possibly used an old T-shirt to clean a toilet when a scrub brush could handle the job. She stifled the criticism and smiled sweetly at him, tilting her head toward him. "Food of the gods, charlotte russe: ladyfingers with whipped cream, egg whites, and plenty of sugar and sherry or wine. But today's version hints of cognac, maybe even Courvoisier. Yes, I think that's definitely it. I was telling Huger that last year I was to make the charlotte russe for a dinner party, when one of my friends came over. He had been cocktailing at a party and decided to traipse uptown to surprise me and go with me. While there, he decided to add Courvoisier to it while I changed clothes before we went out. I didn't realize until we served it up later that it had been added. Amazingly, it made it better, so I think Huger decided to alter the recipe just a wee bit."

"Wow, so how was your Christmas? Did you have a good time with your family?"

"I did. My dad and his partner are so fun. I told you my dad was gay, right?"

"Yeah, I figured that out, but it's no big, right? I mean, we are who we are. Just take Drew and Sheff. They are the best guys and a wonderful couple. In fact, they are so rock solid, even more so than many of my straight friends."

"I know, they are very dear. I've just gotten to know them in December, and I really like them. It's just with my dad, sometimes people say, 'Did your mom know?' Well, it was different back then. My mom died when I was a kid, and there's this one old bat who we call the Un-Cassandra that always hints that, well, never mind. People can just be mean sometimes."

"Excuse me, but what's an Un-Cassandra?"

"You know, Cassandra from mythology, the Trojan War and all that, always seeing into the future or omniscient or something, but no one really believes her."

"Okay, got it, so the Un-Cassandra is what you call this woman who thinks she knows it all."

"Exactly." Lucy beamed.

Sam looked at her face. She was pretty. He liked the way that little lines winged around her eyes when she smiled. She was probably a little older than he was, maybe a couple of years. That didn't matter. She was fun and pleasant, and maybe, just maybe, he'd take her to dinner and learn more about her.

Guests became restless, and before the first could leave, the beautiful dark-skinned, sloe-eyed chanteuse named Enid stood up and said, "Huger, I think it's time for a few songs, and since the holidays aren't officially over until Twelfth Night, we should do carols as well." Her beautiful voice led them into jazzy versions of Christmas carols, spirituals, "Auld Lange Syne," and "Summertime."

Guests sang loudly and off-key before dissolving into laughter. Lucy introduced herself to Enid saying that she thought she looked familiar, Enid asked her where she lived, and they both laughed when they realized they lived two blocks from one another, but had never previously met. They promised to stay in touch and share seeds in February, as they were both fond of gardening. As promised, the day was the perfect beginning of the new year.

Chapter 8

Some wondrous pageant; and you scarce would start,
If from a beech's heart,
A blue-eyed Dryad stepping forth should say,
Behold Me! I am May!

"Spring", Henry Timrod

May 2008

Lucy never heard from Sam. He never called in the new year, and she wondered what had happened. The dinner had been so lovely, and he was so charming. She had thought that he would call her, but the phone never rang with his voice on the other end.

She was planning her trip to Newport, as she would leave within the week. She would enjoy another summer school where she would pack her days with history, architecture, and art. This would be a new learning experience, since she was unfamiliar with the Northeast. She would learn about the decorative arts of the Gilded Age, and she hoped to glean knowledge about the connections between Newport and Charleston. She would leave the first of June, missing all of Spoleto Festival USA except the first weekend. She planned to attend the opening night of Wagner's *The Flying Dutchman* with Grandmere. She enjoyed most operas—those by Verdi, Puccini, Mozart, and the like—but Wagner's operas were mythic displays of lights, costumes, and music. Grandmere said you either appreciated his works or you did not. The show's costumes were supposed to be outrageous; the performers were world-class. The tickets had sold out early, and Lucy knew the Gaillard Auditorium on Calhoun Street would be packed tonight.

Lucy cycled to work noting that she would put up the sign in the window that she was closing early. That way she would have time to take Toulouse to the park and get ready for the opera. It was warm today, and soon she would have to turn on the AC in her house. She would deal with that when she came home from Newport, she thought. Today she had to concentrate on being timely. Grandmere did not appreciate tardiness. She said she was too old to climb over strangers' feet in a concert venue. She was navigating with a cane now and still was not sure if it offered her any benefit. At three thirty, Lucy locked the door and jumped on her bike, tucking her hair inside her helmet.

Out of the corner of her eye, she saw a familiar dark head. She closed her eyes and ignored him. She pedaled down State Street, cutting through the market. She heard her name called and cycled faster, down Anson Street, past the old mattress factory that had been converted to a residence. She didn't take time to enjoy the bougainvillea that grew in abundance on the corner of Anson and George Streets, nor the plumbago that covered the iron railing. She ignored the beauty of Ansonborough, with its stuccoed facades and Greek Revival brick edifices. She was sure that she lost him when she came to the stop sign at Calhoun Street. Traffic was not participating with her. It seemed that there were hundreds of cars crowding the street. She heard him before she saw him. His Trek's brakes squealed as he stopped next to her.

"Hi, Lucy. How're you doing?"

She looked at his handsome visage. "I'm fine, Sam. All is well. I haven't seen you in a while." Her tone was slightly accusatory.

"Look it. I've been busy. I meant to call you, but it just seemed that all these projects got in the way, and my uncle was ill, so I took April off and went to help him out with his business."

"I'm sorry to hear that. Is he better then? What does he do?"

"Yes, he is better. Thanks for asking. He's my dad's brother and is a decorative painter, also named Samuel O'Hara, and my godfather. He needed some help with his accounting and all, and I had the time to help him. He's a really wonderful man. Just salt of the earth, you know, no nonsense and as generous as the day is long. He's also the last generation of decorative painters in our family."

"No kids?" she queried.

"No, he always had this string of lady friends, but, it's like he got hurt a long time ago and always kept everyone at arm's length. I think that was easier for him."

"Hmm. I guess I know how that works. I'm glad he's got you, though." She grinned at him slightly.

"Yeah, you know, family is extremely important in my neck of the woods. Down here you all throw out the love word so frequently. 'Oh, he's my cuz, and I love him,' but then that same cuz causes a scene, and he doesn't have the support. I guess it's a regional thing. Anyway, you'll like this considering you research things to death. I just found out that my ancestor Samuel O'Hara did work in Charleston. I found the info at the South Carolina Historical Society. I was researching his work in Mass, when he disappears and takes out an ad that he's removing himself—yup it says that—to Charleston. His ads then show up in the Charleston paper. He turns up in Mass later on, though, after eighteen twenty. While I was with my uncle, he said that he thought that one of the Samuel O'Haras in our family had lived here. It was a matter of going through family papers and the Bible in order for us to find the dates. My great-aunt Margaret loved to research things, too, so it helped that she had sorted family letters and documents. I come from a long line of pack rats; they don't throw anything out."

"That's fabulous. He probably left here when we went into a recession. You know, our Gilded Age, when we're referred to as 'Little London' is from around seventeen fifty or so until eighteen twenty, not forgetting the disastrous economic condition during the Revolution. After that, the rich still had plenty of money, of course. They rebuilt, but they just did not have the gazillions they had before; now some did, and they traveled abroad and afar, but now it was a bit changed, and that would have affected the craftsmen. They would have followed the money, and even though there were gigs in the South, New York, Boston, and Philadelphia would have been better markets. Plus there would have been a closer radius of environs. There's the whole Industrial Revolution to consider as well. I hope you'll consider sharing those documents with the staff at the historical society. They are always so very helpful," she said.

He smiled at her, showing those even white teeth, and said that he had told the archivist that he would make copies the next time he was home. Lucy smiled back at him, thinking about how handsome and smart he was.

A horn blew behind them. The SUV driver, most likely a harried soccer mom, inched into their space while chatting on a cell phone. They both pulled onto the sidewalk. She had lost a little weight and was now still fit, but almost thin, Sam thought. Her heart-shaped face looked younger, and her eyes were edgier than he remembered.

"Listen, can I give you a call sometime? I'd like to get together. Maybe we could go to a movie or something."

Lucy looked at him and thought, *What is it about men and movies?* A movie was a terrible date. You just sat there like bumps on a log. You couldn't talk, and then they always wanted to see something like *Lara Croft: Tomb Raider*, so at the end of the movie, they can't help but compare your absolute plainness with the hot sex-o-matic Angelina Jolie. Just a terrible idea.

Instead she said, "That would be nice. I'm going away, though, for a week and a half to your world of the Northeast to study the Gilded Age."

He gave her his card. "Well, then the ball's in your court. Why don't you give me a call when you return?"

"Great, thanks. See you 'round."

Lucy picked up Grandmere. She was early. There would be no problems with navigating their seats. Grandmere looked beautiful in a lavender silk dress, her hair freshly coiffed. Lucy's simple chocolate linen dress hung on her. She had tried earlier to cinch it with a belt, but that made it hang awkwardly in places. She ended up dragging out the ironing board and the Rowenta and smoothing the creases that the belt had made. She focused on jewelry, adding earrings, a pendant, and bracelet of amber that Aunt Aurora had sent her from Prague for her birthday a few years ago.

"Lucy, you can't lose another ounce. Your clothes are all extremely large on your frame, and you're looking like one of those cocaine model waifs." Grandmere shook her head at Lucy.

Lucy giggled slightly thinking how funny that her Grandmere read trash tabloids. "I know, I know. I'm eating. I think I'm just getting more exercise, that's all, but I do find it interesting that you keep up with that sort of thing. Tonight should be wonderful, though. The costumes are supposed to be brilliant."

"Yes, I'm sure it will be quite divine. I do enjoy Wagner. You seem preoccupied, dear. Have you seen that young man, again? Because he is no good, no good at all."

She couldn't possibly be talking about Sam, Lucy thought, and then she remembered the time she had introduced Grandmere to the not-boyfriend. They had had an argument, and he was angry and she petulant.

"No, Grandmere, I am not seeing him. It's been over for a while now."

The opera was all that Lucy expected and more. Grandmere commented how Spoleto was just the most magical festival. She had only been disappointed once. "Remember?" she said to Lucy, "It was that odd occurrence called a poetry slam that you took me to, and there were those extremely rude, salacious, and filthy pieces that some of those people read."

"Grandmere, at the time you said you didn't like it, but you did say that art came in all form and fashion."

Grandmere smiled and harrumphed at her favorite granddaughter. After the opera, they enjoyed sitting outside of a tapas restaurant and ordered glasses of champagne with a floating raspberry while nibbling on shrimp and goat cheese canapés.

"So are you ready for Newport, Lucy? It is a lovely town. I think you will really enjoy it."

"I am, and I want to thank you so much for helping with the tuition. It means an awful lot to me."

"Absolutely, what am I to do with my money? It's always important to support my girls and their education."

Grandmere's subsidies had supported both Maeve and Lucy in their various ventures of travel and study. Grandmere had been the same with her other grandchildren and her own children. There had been three: Celeste, Lucy's mother; Gardiner, the son who had studied law, a tradition that his sons continued; and her favorite, her youngest and most talented, Aurora, the girl who had always shown such spunk and independence.

Lost in thought, Lillian Vander Horst Carpentier Barwick thought of Aurora as a small child, how she would say, *"Roar, my Rora. Roar for me."* The name was an old one, one that was in the Barwick family Bible, and it had suited the small but strong-lunged infant. The girl had always been a little minx with mischievous eyes and had had an incredible knack in mimicking sounds. Those days were long past, but her Aurora continued to speak loudly through her art. Of all her grandchildren, Lucy was most like Aurora, although she had a quieter bent. Where Aurora needed international lights, Lucy, much like her mother, was comforted by home. She smiled thinking Rora would be home this week visiting while her Czech husband Georg would premier his symphony during Spoleto.

Lucy interrupted her grandmother's musings.

"Grandmere, are you all right? I was worried for a moment. You were so quiet."

"I'm sorry, Lucy, just an old woman musing."

"Never that. You seemed to be lost in your own reverie, though."

"I was just thinking how nice it will be to have Rora and Georg here. They are just so pleasant and lovely. I enjoy their company so. He's so cosmopolitan and has such old-world manners, and as you know, she is always up to something. I'm sure she will kidnap me one day, and we will be off to Beaufort or to Georgetown so she can be inspired by the marsh, creeks, ruins, and the sea."

"You enjoyed visiting them in Prague, didn't you?"

"Oh, yes, child, and they ferried me everywhere. They have such a lovely life together. I just wish you could find someone that suits you as well."

"Well, there's hope, right? Aunt Aurora didn't meet him until nineteen ninety-one, after the Velvet Revolution, and she was forty-five by then, right, and I'm not quite forty yet."

"Yes, but she always maintains that he came at the right time. She was already established with her art, and they have their shared interests and their individual interests. In the end it's all about respect, my dear, respecting each other's past and present."

Lucy dropped her grandmother off at the mansion on Legare Street. She opened the car door and helped her up the steep steps to the house and then up the steeper steps to her bedchamber. Grandmere never called it a bedroom, but a chamber, as her mother and her mother's mother had. Lucy volunteered to help Lillian into her night things, and Lillian remarked that she was old, but not decrepit, but that it would be a pleasure if Lucy could lock up the house.

Lucy checked all the doors of the main house, and they were locked. The back houses, the kitchen and carriage houses, were occupied by some of the ballet crew for Spoleto, and Lucy hoped they would not impose a loud revelry upon Grandmere's sleep. One year Grandmere told her about a French circus troupe that had stayed and how they had woken her at three in the morning. She had called out for them to hush the nonsense, and before she knew it, they had climbed like monkeys onto the second-story piazza and entertained her with so much champagne and acrobatics that the next day she was ruined by a night of raucous entertainment. Lucy remembered that that was a time after Papa died, her grandfather, and that Grandmere needed all the fun she could have, as she missed him with terrible abandon.

On her way home, Lucy thought about Grandmere's words. Respect was supposed to be so simple, but it wasn't. People had issues with control, and when one person tried to control the other, then respect was tossed out of the window, discarded like the day's trash. Aurora and Georg liked and respected each other before they began their relationship, and if one loved the other more, Lucy never knew. Unlike her last relationship.

Lucy did not want to be honest with herself and think about the not-boyfriend and why it ended badly. She began obsessing and opened her memory to the last month they had spent together and thought hard on the arguments and the issues. He didn't like her friends. He didn't like that she rode her bike to work. It was too dangerous to cross the Crosstown. He didn't like Toulous because he looked like a sloth, and it didn't matter how often she bathed him. He, the not-boyfriend, thought that Toulouse smelled like a primate—that was his term. *In fact,* she thought, *why did he even see me? He didn't like me. I was too independent, too odd.*

He needed someone like Jessica, his old girlfriend, someone who watched TV and baked cookies and brownies from the box and carted them to the office on a weekly basis. Lucy always thought those kinds of people were a little odd. Why do you have to cook for your coworkers? Shouldn't they like you for who you are? And truly, Lucy did love the occasional brownie, but why did people suck up like that? In fact, in England she had looked like a veritable suck-up; her carry-on was packed with tissues and Band-Aids and the like because Violet was worried that she would need them. Certainly, at home she was always getting scratched by a rose bush or bumping into things while moving things about, but when she traveled, she channeled Lillian, Aurora, and her mother's grace and never had a small disaster.

Back to the not-boyfriend, he was looking for someone who was his type of normal, whatever that was.

She changed her clothes, looking at her body in the mirror, remembering his touch and missing it and trying to block all of the memories rushing through her mind. She remembered what Diana had said to her last year when it was finally over in April.

"He's definitely the not-boyfriend, Lucy. He's boring and totally beige—there is no color whatsoever in his life. He's just not for you!"

Diana didn't like that the not-boyfriend wouldn't spend time with Lucy's friends. She felt that Lucy was losing her independence and becoming wishy-washy. She noted that her wacky, fun friend always complained and that she never read anymore, just seemed to be glued to court TV or mini-dramas. Funny, if asked what he thought of himself he would have said he was a flaneur, a man about town. He'd drop words like that. At first she thought it was amusing that he learned a new word each week. Later she would think that he was behaving in a pretentious manner.

Lucy remembered that they sat too much. He was always tired from work and didn't want to go for a walk or ride bikes. They ate bad food, too much mac and cheese and fried everything, from shrimp to chicken. She felt sick when she couldn't fit in her size-eight skirts and pants and had succumbed to dressing in loose dresses that she referred to as her muumuu wardrobe. In the end it was all meant to be. He had gone back to his past girlfriend, Jessica, a no-nonsense, tall, solid-sized girl comfortable in clothes from Talbots, Lands' End, or L.L. Bean, the one he intended to marry now. Like him, she was an engineer, and they had all that surveying in common. Lucy sighed and thought at least she had her figure back, even if the sixes were hanging on her. She fished the Sonata out of the cabinet. She would pop just one, and in thirty minutes Morpheus would claim her and ease her mind. No more thoughts of empty relationships that had ended in a train wreck.

Chapter 9

"It is within the possibility that Newport may become an educational center. Fashion may go elsewhere, the rich people may tire of their great houses, which could be turned into schools and colleges.

Maud Howe Elliott

"Hi, Lucy, I'm calling everyone to remind them to come to my annual Carolina Day party. It's next Saturday at my house. It starts at five and will probably wrap up around nine. No, you don't need to bring anything, just yourself. I'm not sure, the usual crowd, you know, friends, neighbors, that sort of thing. All right, I'll see you then."

Lucy loved Brooks's Carolina Day parties. They were filled with good food, and she always met someone new, an aspiring writer, historian, or an eclectic artist. One year she had met a neurosurgeon who was interested in Buddhism. His friends were eclectic and a good mix. She wanted to tell her childhood friend all about her trip to Newport and the links she had found to Charleston. He would be very impressed with the information and would then research the topics further. Grandmere always said that Brooks and Lucy should write a book on Charleston. They were both passionate about the history, culture, and historic preservation movement, and Grandmere thought they could create a good story. Maybe they should think about that again. Lucy arrived with a bottle of wine in hand. The party was in full swing, with children running about the back lawn. Although the temperature was in the nineties, Brooks did not have the AC on in his house. He refused to turn it on until the Fourth of July, and she remembered one year he had gone as long as July fifteenth .

The house had been built in 1917, a traditional craftsman four square that had been converted into apartments by the 1960s. Brooks had returned the house to its former glory and had performed most of the work on his own. No stranger to hard work, Brooks was an absolute snob regarding architecture and paid attention to even the most minute detail. His house was situated under a massive live oak that provided shade on one-third of Parkwood Street.

Sam saw her as she entered the side yard. She was wearing a colorful skirt and a pink T-shirt and wore a ridiculously large straw hat. He shook his head wondering where she kept her myriad chapeaus. He sidled up to her, gazing sideways to see under the brim.

"Hello, Ms. Cameron, how are you doing on this brilliant hot day?"

"Oh, hi, Sam, how are you? You just pop up everywhere, don't you?"

"Well, I could say the same thing about you. How do you know Brooks?"

"Ah, we've known each other all of our lives. We've sort of been in each other's pockets forever."

"Good friends, then. He's a great guy. I met him at a Board of Zoning Appeals meeting a couple of years ago. We've been friends ever since, and he's a great attorney."

"Yes, he is that. He's a brainiac and can get any real estate deal hammered out."

"So, let me get you a drink, and tell me how you liked Newport."

Lucy sipped the wine and jumped into her subject. She was charmed by Newport. The city was exquisite, so similar to Charleston but very different. Her classes were wonderful. She learned so much. In fact, did he know that one of the rooms at The Breakers was finished with platinum leaf? Everything was just amazing. She had spent a few days after in Boston and had spent a day in his hometown of Salem. It was a lovely town with beautiful houses, large and small, and she enjoyed how it was situated on the water. The witch stuff was a little maddening, and she couldn't imagine how many crazies came out at Halloween. All in all she was quite impressed with the Northeast as a whole, and she loved that it was so liberal. She felt quite at home there. Of course she had been to the Peabody Essex Museum, as well as two of the house museums that had impressed her. How did he like the Chinese House? She noted that her friends had driven her to Marblehead; unfortunately the Jeremiah Lee House had been closed, but the bookshop in town was impressive, and she had purchased a first edition of Consuelo Vanderbilt's *The Glitter and the Gold* there. Can you believe it for only a dollar more than the new paperback reprint?

She blabbed on how Marblehead was so colorful and that the people were so hospitable. She described the flight home and how her rollerboard was too heavy to lift because of the books she had purchased. She dissolved into laughter as she rattled on that the male flight attendant with a great deal of swish made her march to the back and unload the heavy objects before she could trundle down the passageway and heave the luggage above her in the overhead bin. She giggled and continued on about how the balding, heavy passenger from Columbus, Ohio, with the spot of grease on his tie had commented about women and shopping. She related that she had shot the man the stink eye and the stick mouth and queried the stranger if his wife was fond of first editions. He'd looked at her crosswise and said, *"No, she prefers shopping for clothes at the mall."* She giggled then and said wasn't that a stitch? Her exuberance made Sam smile.

He asked her if she wanted to go cycling the next morning. She quickly acquiesced and said it would be a pleasure. They continued to talk about his projects and the house he was now rehabilitating. He explained to her how he kept the costs down by doing the majority of the work on his own. And that he liked to feel the spirit of each house as it took shape. She asked after his uncle, and he told her he was a bit better, but that he felt he needed to be there for him. She smiled with sincerity when she told him that he was a good nephew, a gem. Sam left the party at nine and drove to Paul's house.

Phoebe opened the door and whispered, "I just got the little one down, and I'm exhausted. You two keep it down, or someone will be dealing with more than a baby whining."

Paul handed his friend a beer, and they sat on the front stoop of the brick bungalow that Paul and Phoebe had purchased a few years ago.

"So how was the party?"

"It was great. I won't stay long; Phoebe seems beat. I saw Lucy. She was under this pretty stupid-looking hat. I had to look underneath it to even see her. Is she a little crazy, do you think? I asked her to go on a bike ride tomorrow. That should be safe. Lucy Cameron, she is something."

"Finally, brother, finally. To answer your question, Phoebs and I are both beat. The little girl just doesn't sleep. Trey, on the other hand, was a dream at this age. So, I can't believe it has taken you this long to ask our Lucy out. She is a little crazy, but in the best possible way. She's really funny. Have you noticed that? She has this way of making fun of everything."

"Yeah, I know. She cracks herself up and everything. Even a two-hour plane ride is some kind of adventure with her. I'm just...I don't know. I'm still missing Jess. You know, we still e-mail, but since she's been working in Birmingham, it just made sense to see others. I just haven't been able to do it yet. I haven't seen her in six weeks, and I just miss her."

"When does she finish her residency? It's been longer than most, right? Is she going to try to come back here?"

"End of August she wraps it up, unless she extends her stay, which she says they would like her to do. The plan was for her to work at the Medical University if she can get a position. Her residency has been longer than most, as she wanted additional training. The last thing she told me was that she was sending out her CV. So we'll see. Lucy might just be fun to hang with, someone to spend time and do things that are light."

"Yeah, but don't hurt her. She was crazy about the last guy, and I don't know why. They'd come in the bar for burgers, and he was always rude. Never a thank-you and I never felt that he liked her. He didn't like her friends, that's for sure. When she was with him, she was always down, you know, and that's not what's supposed to happen if you are in love."

"Do I know this guy?"

"Probably, he's one the group of engineers that worked on the new bridge that comes in regularly. He's a big guy, about six-six. He plays pool a lot and flirts with all the chicks. His name's Randolph and gets really pissed if you call him Randy. He's pretty much a useless bastard, and I'm glad he dumped her. She deserves better."

"Still, no one likes to be dumped. I'll let you know how the 'date' goes."

"All right, man, I better check on Phoebe and the kids. See you later."

Sam was looking forward to their ride. He'd get to know her better. It would be interesting to discover her favorite sites in town. They were to meet at eight thirty at Marion Square and would go from there.

His phone rang, and he saw Jess's number pop up on the screen. "Hey angel, how are you?"

"I'm wiped—just totally wiped. I was on call yesterday and worked a fourteen-hour shift today. I hope I can survive all of this. The hours are just grueling, but I'm learning so much, and I really like being a doc. How are you, and how are the houses going?"

"It's great. Everything's going as planned. I've got the matrix down, you know, and I'm really pleased with the work of the subs. Knock on wood, I've been lucky this go-round. But look, angel, let me come over there and take care of you. My schedule is flexible. I'm turning into a pretty decent cook with the help of Mrs. Annie. Think about it, and let me know."

"Thanks, Sam, but I'm okay. Just bitching a little because I'm tired. We said we'd see other people, and if I land in Charleston, we'll see how it goes, right? Look, I better go. I need to get some shut-eye because things will start early tomorrow."

"I miss you, Jess and I love you. I want us to be together like we used to be, *you* know that."

"I know, Sam. Please, let me sort things through. I need more time, okay? Good night."

"Good night, Jess."

He hung up, disappointed. She had rushed him off the phone. He loved her, and he could feel that something was just not right. They had met his sophomore year in college. He had gone to his roommate's house in Kingstree for Easter, and she was home from the University of Georgia, where she studied premed. She had been accepted to medical school at the Medical University of South Carolina and had always wanted to specialize in pediatrics. From the first day they met, they seemed as if they were made for one another. She ran marathons and was smart and beautiful with long black hair and blue eyes. But Jess's best feature was a calm demeanor. Something had changed, though, six months ago, after she had extended her residency in Birmingham. She had called him one night and told him quietly that she thought they needed to see other people. They had started this all when they were so young, and she wanted to make sure that they were absolutely right for each other. The only way she could do that was to meet other men and date them.

The last three years of driving back and forth had been wearing on her. He acquiesced. He knew she was the one for him, and he could wait. He was good at waiting. The house-acquiring process had taught him well. He could wait as long as it took. But why shouldn't he enjoy a woman's company while she made up her mind?

Chapter 10

"With my kiss, my soul beside it
Came to my lips and there I kept it,-

'Kissing Helena', Percy Bysshe Shelley

He saw Lucy by the fountain. Her hair was shoved underneath a baseball cap bearing the image of The Breakers, the Newport mansion built by Cornelius Vanderbilt II. She was looking at the old Grant's building, shaking her head.

"Hi, Lucy, guess you don't approve of the design of the rooftop terrace?"

"I hate this building, just hate it! It was better when it didn't have this thing that looks like a large spider on steroids sitting on top. Yuck! Don't you think it's hideous? Come on!"

"Well, it's going to go away eventually, right? I thought a developer is planning to build condos there. It will have to go through BAR, so it should be okay."

"Really? Okay, do you really think so? The price of dirt is so expensive that they cheap out on the materials. Look at half the new stuff going up around town—-cheap, cheap, cheap—and the height, scale, and mass issues are all out of proportion. And I'll tell you something else. If one board goofs it up, they make room for every other board to goof it up. Look at Planning Commission. If they change the zoning or allow three-X zoning in areas, they are allowing a behemoth to go up. There's just no way it can't be goofed up, like the proposed hotel on this very square. It will put the old Citadel in permanent shade, you just watch."

"Wow. Don't hold back now. I mean, feel free to express yourself," he said with a laugh in his voice. "Some of my architect friends don't feel the hotel's out of scale. But let's go. Where do you want to go first?" Sam was laughing to himself. He had never seen this side of Lucy. This ride might just be very interesting.

"Well, actually, I had planned two loops that I wanted to run by you. I thought we could head west and turn on Rutledge, take Rutledge to the Battery, then take Meeting to Tradd, Tradd to Church, Church through the market to Ansonborough and then Mazyck-Wraggborough, or we could head east and do the reverse, ending with Radcliffeborough. Depending on the time, I suppose we could go down Limehouse and Legare. What's your pleasure?"

"Hmm, I think I will let Miss Lucy Cameron show me her Charleston. You choose."

"Okay, let's go west. It's quiet this morning, so we can go down Rutledge Avenue and cruise by Colonial Lake."

As it was early, the streets were quiet, and Lucy and Sam had the town to themselves. She stopped at the corner of Montagu Street and Rutledge Avenue and listed the history of the houses in quick succession: "Mid-nineteenth century built by an Edisto Planter for his third wife. That one with the Tower of the Winds portico has its original oculus window that works like a skylight. Just beautiful. They don't survive in Charleston because of hurricanes. That one is my favorite. It has an exquisite Federal interior. It just sold. Let's hope the new owners are sensitive."

She rattled dates, architectural styles, and builders in such quick succession that he was having a hard time keeping up. Lucy was something, smart and knowledgeable. He told her that, although he had studied Charleston's architectural heritage, she pointed out buildings, iron fences, and gates and curious turrets he had never noticed. Charleston was like that, she said. Every day you could find something old that was new to the eye. He noticed her long legs and slender figure and thought again that she was pretty in a very unique, Lucy kind of way. Shading her eyes, she turned left onto Broad Street and pointed to a Victorian house where a friend of hers had lived. She stopped and began laughing as she told him that her friend had come home one day and found that the entire plaster ceiling in her bedroom had fallen. But the funniest part of the story was not the falling plaster, but rather the plumbing. The entire plumbing had been made up of black garden hoses and duct tape. Sam mentioned that the owner must not have watched the contractor. Lucy laughed. Nope, it was an older woman, and she knew the garden hose and duct tape would outlive her, and it did by a couple of years. They turned south of Broad, down Legare Street, and he stopped her in front of Grandmere's house.

"Who lives there? I saw you there once."

"My grandmother and unless you want to be interviewed I suggest we move on."

He pointed to a house on Limehouse Street with its prominent Greek Revival door looming over the street and mentioned that Brooks had pressed him into service to be a docent for the preservation society one year for the fall tours. He had been so impressed with the private collection and remarked that it was amazing how the family had inherited so many treasures. She added that many of the new people now used these houses as second and sometimes third residences, and they weren't interested in having Charleston furniture or paintings by Sully, Osgood, or Morse. They tended to furnish their retreats used during Spoleto or the winter months with comfortable, cushy furniture and had decorator art or giclées hanging on the walls. At one point she stopped her bike at the corner at Tradd and Logan Streets and began ranting of the importance of interior easements. She gave him an example of a house on Church Street, where the simple yet beautiful Georgian candle-wicked cornice had been replaced by a large one that was out of scale with the house. He thought she would foam at the mouth when she went on about the need for people to respect a house just as people should respect one another.

"You know," Lucy said, "it's like this. The garbage collector doesn't have but an eighth-grade education, but he picks your trash up every week. He picks up your baby's diapers, your dog's poo, and the lettuce that has become foul in the fridge. Respect him for doing his job for being an integral part of the community. Because if all of us were doctors and lawyers, we'd be all the same, and really, we'd be awfully boring. Housing stock is the same. If it's all mixed up, it works. If it's not, well, then you're anywhere and not someplace special. Are you following me?"

"I am. I'm with you completely. I told you yesterday that I live on the Eastside, right? People are always disrespecting the Eastside because they see it as a place filled with drug dealers. But it's a neighborhood, and it's good. A lot of the older folks just do what they can, just trying to maintain it all on a fixed income, and the flippers just want to fuck it all up and make a profit using cheap materials. I'm just happy that the BAR goes up to Line Street. I feel as if they have my back. Just think what would happen if it didn't exist."

"I know; things like that make me crazy. My friend Violet tells me all the time that I love buildings more than people, and maybe she's right. It's just that, even though the preservation groups are excellent at what they do, homeowners who have money and have never owned an historic property just don't get it, and they do really bad stuff. So, like our friend Brooks, I'm a house advocate. You know, Sam, what makes me the saddest is the fate of a freedman's cottage. Most people just ruin them or want to take them down, and in my neck of the woods, they are everywhere. Some of the interiors have all this great vernacular architecture and distinctive paint colors."

"I know. Didn't Brooks tell you about my freedman's cottage rehab? The wallboard was failing, and when I took it off, the plaster was in really good shape. It was painted from the chair rail to the baseboards to resemble mahogany. It survived on three of the walls. My uncle came to visit me, and he reproduced the fourth wall, and the room looks incredible. Of course, I followed his instructions and painted marine varnish over the grain painting in order to encapsulate it. To tell you the truth, most of my tenants want to paint over it, and I tell them no way. Listen, Lucy, this has been great, but it's almost noon, and I have plans at two, so maybe we can head back?"

All she heard was, *We're done*. Maybe she should rethink a movie as a first date. "Sure, I'm sorry. I just tend to get lost around architecture, that's all."

She looked at him and then heard the pealing of the bells, first St. Philip's, then St. Michael's, and before long, the entire peninsula rang with the sweet cacophony.

"That's one of the reasons I love this place. Why don't we cycle to my house, and I can show it to you?" Sam said.

"Sure, that would be nice."

He showed her the before-and-after photographs, and she complimented him on the sensitive rehabilitation of his property. After Lucy left, Sam stood on the second-floor piazza, looking at her disappearing figure. That girl was something, he thought. Kind of crazy and extremely passionate. He wondered what it would be like to be involved with her. Definitely a roller coaster ride.

Lucy and Sam continued to see each other all of July. By early August, she began to think he was gay. They had enjoyed concerts, dining out, cycling, and lazing on the beach at Sullivan's Island. They exchanged books on architecture and art, and he helped her paint her spare bedroom strawberry pot blue and complimented her on her color choice. He was nice and sensitive and smart, but he hadn't made a pass at her. He hadn't even kissed her on the cheek. She liked him a little too much and told Diana one evening over drinks.

"What I don't quite understand, Diana, is that he hasn't done anything to show his affection. I know there's the whole three-date rule that some people espouse, but we're now looking at six weeks and many outings. We seem to have fun together, but maybe he's just not interested in me sexually. I just don't get it. And these things are always so complicated. I can't say, 'Look, Samuel O'Hara, don't you ever think about intimacy with me?' and 'I really would like to jump you.' I can think that, but let's face it, it's not something that you can verbalize, or he'll think I'm pushy or suffer from Tourette's syndrome. I just don't know what to do. It's sort of a quandary. Maybe he's gay."

"Luce, honey, why don't you just enjoy the company and the attention? It seems like he's always doing something nice for you, helping you around the house. Didn't he just help you move furniture so you could take your carpets up and have them cleaned? That was nice. And doesn't he invite you for dinner? It seems that you see each other quite often."

"He does take me out, and he's a good cook, and we see each other two or three times a week and sometimes more. I don't know. It's just I've been a cover before, and I'm just not sure if this is the same thing. He's really nice, though, and it sure is fun to have someone that wants to do things besides sit on the sofa. Did I tell you that the not-boyfriend sent me an invitation to his wedding? Imagine the audacity."

"Well, ask Sam to go. Wear a pretty dress and hat, and let him squire you there. It will make you feel better, and you'll finally have the closure you need. Where are they getting married, and where's the reception?"

"I suppose she's Catholic; their wedding is at the cathedral. The reception is at Society Hall. What do I get them, AutoCAD?"

"Nice, I'm sure you'll find something suitable. There are several great shops on Upper King that have wedding-type gifts. Maybe we should go there and take a look around. And back to Sam, even if he is gay, isn't it wonderful to have someone decent in your life that makes you feel like a million bucks? All of your friends like him, and if you really think he's gay, ask Ben or Sebastian. They'll know for sure."

Sure enough, Lucy and Diana went shopping and found impersonal and decorative placemats and napkins that would serve as the perfect gift. The couple's online registry listed the wall colors of their new house, and the linens would work in the kitchen or the dining room. Lucy asked Diana if she thought this was all a bit presumptuous, and Diana said no, she thought it was quite helpful for all parties. It was always so ridiculous and a waste of time to have to exchange things. Truly, Lucy should be grateful for their organization.

The two friends preferred the locally owned stores, as they felt that they should support local entrepreneurship instead of the chains, and the sales associate couldn't have been nicer wrapping the gifts in ice blue tissue paper and wrapping the box in white paper and finishing it with an ice blue ribbon. Lucy was always amazed at how the staff could smooth the paper just right and make those perfect lines at the corners of the box before placing it in an oversized bag so it would not be dinged or dented. The bow was a work of art, and she said so to Diana.

Diana rolled her eyes at her friend and said, "Don't you wrap your works of art, Lucy?"

"Certainly, but rarely as a gift, and then it's different. You have to be careful with paintings so that the paint doesn't chip or crack, you know?"

"Of course I know that," said Diana, "but no bows?"

"Oh no," Lucy demurred, "just our signature adhesive sticker, clear and with the logo, all very simple, yet with distinction, I hope." Lucy raised both eyebrows and cocked her head to the right.

Diana sighed and said maybe she would come by and take a look, and since Lucy offered her so much guidance and advice, perhaps she could reciprocate? Lucy smiled at her dear friend and thanked her and asked her why she hadn't thought of that herself. Both women giggled as they left the store, passing the precious candles, stationary, and other gewgaws that were never a necessity of life, but made it all more genteel.

Lucy called Ben and Sebastian and invited them over for drinks and dinner. It was a hot, balmy evening with the temperature in the midnineties. Her garden was lit with Christmas lights, and Johnny and June Carter Cash were crooning about Jackson. While grilling the chicken shish kababs, she mused aloud.

"So, do y'all think Sam's gay?"

"I wish!" Benjamin said. "He's really good-looking, but most of all, he's a great guy. What made you think that?"

"Oh, I don't know. It's just we've been seeing each other for a while now, and nothing's happened, not even a kiss."

"Perhaps, he's old-fashioned, puritan stock and all that," Sebastian said darkly.

"Maybe."

"Look, Lucy, just enjoy it, okay? But if you do have sex, do you have what you need?"

"Oh, yes, Ben. Don't worry, I have an arsenal of protection thanks to the two of you and your Christmas gifts—so naughty—including that fun but silly pop-up book."

Ben looked her in the eye, his strawberry blond hair a shade darker than her own, and then glanced at Sebastian, whose wide grin stretched over his handsome face. "*The Kama Sutra* is a classic piece of literature and art, and even though you are trying to be all prissy, you know you like it, especially in pop-up form."

Sebastian and Ben had allayed her fears. They were probably right. She just needed to stop worrying about it. She was feeling and looking happy, and if it was meant to be it would happen.

ꕥ

That same day, Paul and Sam were laying the patio with salvaged brick behind Paul's house when Paul asked the question. "So, my friend, are you getting any action? It seems to me that you're spending a lot of quality time with Lucy. Just curious, that's all."

Sam looked hard at his good friend. The day was hot and humid, ninety-eight degrees and not a cloud in sight. "You know, that's none of your business. We're having fun. I'm getting to know her, and I like her, but I'm not ready to go there. Besides, there's Jess, and I just can't do that yet."

"Well, have you heard from Jess? Do you think she's having a good time?"

"She's good. I don't think she's seeing anyone. I don't want Lucy getting any ideas, and besides, you are the one that told me not to hurt her feelings, remember?"

"Got it. Well, you can always be friends with benefits."

"I don't do that or booty calls. You know me better than that. It's too confusing, and someone always falls for the other, and it gets messy. Her ex is getting married next weekend, and I'm going to the wedding with her to show support."

"Well, that should be interesting."

ꕥ

August's heat was unbearable. Lucy had popped on her bike only in the evenings. To catch a breeze, Sam and Lucy went to baseball games at the Joe. They sat high in the stands and cooled off with the warm breeze drifting off the Ashley River. He loved baseball, even if a minor league team was playing. She enjoyed tagging along and watching his enthusiasm as he cheered the home team on. She thanked him for agreeing to go the wedding and told him she had found a dress on sale and a new hat. He raised his eyebrows wondering what this one was like. Probably something large. Had she ever thought of adding a bird or two? She punched his arm and spoke of Victorian hats with peacock plumes and horrified him when she described the hats that were currently on exhibition at the museum.

"So this wedding, will I know some of the guests, do ya think?"

"Of course, you know this town. It's three degrees of separation rather than six. I'm sure all of his work colleagues will be there, as well as hers, and then probably some of his friends from kickball and the bar."

"I thought he just sat on the sofa. He actually plays kickball?"

"Yes, indeedy, but I think in the past it was so he could meet girls. That's how we met. My friend Edie had lost all this weight and signed up for the league and asked me to come watch. Anyway, after the game, we went out to Paul's bar for a beer, and I met him. He seemed nice and smart and had all of this confidence that I found attractive. The next thing I knew, we were seeing each other. Anyway, I don't even know why I'm telling you all of this, but I'm just glad that it's not me walking down the aisle to him."

He squeezed her hand. "Well, let's just enjoy the party, right?"

She called Ben when she got home. "He squeezed my hand, Ben, and I don't know how to explain it, but I think there just might be something there."

"Good for you, baby. Now just roll with it and listen on Saturday, just look your best, okay? Be happy. People always find happy people attractive. And Lucy, be a Girl Scout."

"I'm always a Girl Scout, Ben. Be prepared and all that. Good night."

Chapter 11

She walks in beauty, like the night
Of cloudless climes and starry skies;
And all that's best of dark and bright
Meet in her aspect and her eyes...

"She Walks in Beauty", George Gordon, Lord Byron

Lucy woke before six. Toulouse was sprawled on her bed, his shaggy head on a pillow near hers. She hugged his head and held him close. She felt alive, more so than she had in a long time, and she did have to credit Sam's excellent company. He just made her so happy. And today she didn't feel sad that Randolph was marrying Jessica. She felt good about that too. They had never been right together, always at sixes and sevens with another if she was honest. Sam would pick her up at five fifteen. By the time they would find parking, it would probably be between five thirty and five forty-five. She looked at the new hat on the hatstand and smiled. Today she would be feeling like Holly Golightly from *Breakfast at Tiffany's*. Her sleeveless dress was a new design based on a sixties pattern. Its pale pink linen lines were clean with black piping at the neck and hem. The hat was a black straw picture hat that reminded her of the scene with Andie McDowell in *Four Weddings and a Funeral.*

She had found the narrow pale-pink-and-black polka-dot grosgrain ribbon and hot glued it in place to the hat. She would add black patent strappy sandals that she'd found in the back room of the shoe store in South Windermere for $19.99. The heels were higher than what she usually wore, but they weren't quite the skyscrapers that the retail associate tried to convince her that she absolutely needed. She wondered if Sam would like her hairdo, as she had cajoled her hairdresser to take two inches off. It now swung in a short bob framing her face.

The temperature was roughly eighty-five degrees, as it was early, and she decided to catapult out of bed and take her furry boy for a walk.

The two walked to Hampton Park, enjoying the fountain and noticing the beautiful plantings in the beds and along the borders.

The city's horticulture team was legendry in their knowledge and talent with plant materials. Native species grew alongside with cultivars from distant Australia and New Zealand. The hydrangea allee still boasted blooming lace caps and mopheads, and Lucy smiled to herself and thanked God for allowing her to live by all of this beauty. After circling the park three times, Lucy walked Toulouse home. She made coffee and retrieved her list. Today was hers alone. She would invite Sam in for a glass of champagne tonight. Then she would see how it would go. She needed to run the vacuum and clean. It seemed that Toulouse had shedded another Bouvier. She would pick up champagne, Camembert, caviar, toast points, and fresh fruits and berries. God knows that they would bob and weave at the reception, hardly ingesting a thing. Her edible flowers were no longer in bloom, so instead she would garnish the plates with raspberries. Presentation was always important. She might even plan a nap so her eyes would be refreshed. She added to her list: *do nails and toes*. Yes.

Today would be perfect.

He was right on time. She gazed about the house, noticing that it looked very tidy and clean. It looked lovely, she had to admit. She wandered in the back. She shouldn't act like she was too eager. *Calm. Be calm*. She reminded herself not to be a maniac. Sam was wearing a blue linen suit with a white button-down with the top button unbuttoned. She noticed his smooth skin and the dark hair that ran on his upper chest. A blue, gray, and white striped silk tie lay around his neck. He nodded at her.

"Lucy, you look very nice. I like the hat. And the shoes."

All she could intone was, "Thanks."

"So, I think we're going to have a storm this evening. I was watching the news, and it looks like we're getting the aftermath of Charlie."

"Well, hopefully it won't rain until after the reception."

During the wedding he looked at her to see if she was okay, hoping that she was over this guy. He noticed that she smiled as they exchanged vows. There was nothing false in her expression. He knew more people than he thought he would. He was a little surprised that several of his friends were also friends with Randolph although the two of them had never met.

The reception was laden with heavy hors d'oeuvres expertly prepared and garnished. She was not surprised to see the chef replenishing items and was happy to know that another one of Huger's talented friends was forging ahead with his own business. Like other locals, they didn't use the plates, but bobbed and weaved at the food table sampling this and that, shrimp paste sandwiches, crab dip, ham biscuits, and strawberries drenched in what was probably Grand Marnier and then dipped in chocolate. At nine thirty they headed out the door only to hear the first clap of thunder.

When they pulled up to Lucy's house, they were caught in the maelstrom with drops saturating them in the moments it took to reach the door. The temperature had dropped, and she opened the windows, letting in the rich smell of the rain. She placed out the cheese and fruit and handed him the bottle of prosecco. They laughed about the weather, spoke about the guests, and were amazed at the champagne toast of the best man. She didn't know that Randolph's friend was that articulate. What did Sam think? They sat at the dining room table sipping champagne when she placed a raspberry in his glass and one in her own.

He realized he was a little tipsy and thought twice before filling their glasses. She stood up and looked out the window, noting that the storm was in full swing now. She stood in front of him when he placed his hand on her shoulder.

She turned into him, looking up into his eyes, thinking how handsome he was and how she was happy he was here in her little house. How they were safe from the storm as it rattled the windows in their sashes. She kissed Sam on the cheek and smiled at him. He held her face in his hands, telling her that he liked her new haircut and that she had looked prettier than the bride could ever be.

He twirled her around and held her with her back to his chest. He held her loose yet tight and conformed her to his form. As droplets of rain careened through the window and slightly dappled her toes, she closed her eyes thinking she was the luckiest girl alive. Roots Music Karamu played Bob Marley and other reggae music on the stereo, but she was oblivious as she heard her own symphony. Their bodies moved, swayed together in a vertical, comfortable dance that seemed very familiar. He turned her to him and held her face closely in between his hands.

"Lucy, is this what you want?"

She looked into those eyes, sometimes sapphire, sometimes dark pewter and said, "Please say you'll stay the night."

She led him to her bedroom. The walls were an umber rose hue called Ruby Begonia with off-white trim on the baseboards and crown molding. They opened the windows together, letting in the fresh air, laughing in anticipation as they batted at the dotted Swiss sheers that covered bamboo shades. He laid her in the garden that was her duvet cover, situating her amidst hydrangeas and cabbage roses on a muted blue linen background. The mahogany bed occupied the majority of the room, while two Empire chests were situated against opposite walls. He barely noticed the paintings on the walls, some abstract, some realistic; he did notice the graceful bronze dancer reposing on the delicate rosewood desk and thought it could be a sculpture of Lucy.

He slipped the zipper of her dress down and gently moved her dress from her shoulders, kissing her body as the fabric slid between them. He marveled at her body. She was strong and fit, yet her curves filled his hands. He kissed her legs, ending at her feet where he unstrapped her sandals. He continued plundering her body with sweet kisses and left no surface untouched, always to return to her mouth, which he kissed deeply. He smiled at her and enjoyed viewing her tiny, lacy pink underthings fixed with small satin bows at the straps below her shoulders and on the fabric by her hips. Lucy smiled at him, pulling him gently so that her mouth was on his. They teased each other until their breathing came long and hard. He wanted the heat of her body next to him so he could touch and taste her intimately. Their bodies worked together like call and response, and Sam didn't know if he had ever felt this way before.

Lucy had never known this passion, the way he held her and kissed her and finally took possession of her body, jolting her so she felt that her head was filling with constellations of stars and planets. Moments passed, and she realized that he was stroking her back, then her breasts and thighs.

"Sam," she said quietly. "Whatever just happened, that was amazing."

He laughed, holding her body so that it touched the length of him. "You are pretty wonderful, Lucy. All that passion."

They lay together listening to the rain pounding the windows and spoke quietly of nothing of consequence. She didn't remember falling asleep, but she woke to featherlight kisses in the middle of the night. He touched his mouth to her shoulder, her collarbone, her breasts, coaxing and teasing her body into a wakeful state of excitement. She kissed him back, rolling him underneath her and tasting his body with her tongue, enjoying the texture of his skin and his scent. Her hands and her mouth found intimate territory, and she teased him with her tongue, eliciting his pleasure with her skillful repertoire.

His hands never left her body, and he pulled her to him, needing to be deep inside her to feel the final crescendo. He took them both through a storm of emotion, leaving them breathless and sated. Lucy held his face in her hands and kissed his eyes, his nose, his lips, and chin. She snuggled against him, placing her head near his neck, under his chin, and gave a little giggle.

"Samuel O'Hara, thank you for a magical night."

He held her tight, rolling her over to her side, and kissed her softly.

Sam woke to the smell of coffee brewing and bacon frying. He was thirsty and a little woozy from the lack of sleep and too much alcohol. He heard Brahms on the stereo and was glad that Lucy wasn't rocking out this morning like she always did. The kitchen was clean, last's night's evidence of champagne tucked away in the refrigerator. She had laid the dining room table with colorful plates boasting flowers. He couldn't look at their overbright surfaces. The napkins were freshly starched, and he wondered when she had woken up. She was showered and dressed in a simple cotton azure sundress exposing the length of her long legs. Last night's lovemaking appeared nowhere in sight until his gaze rested on her swollen mouth and pink chin.

"Good morning." She beamed. "How do you like your eggs?"

"You're awfully cheerful. How long have you been up?" He leaned forward and kissed her.

She kissed him back and smiled. "A couple of hours. It's so cool out. Quite wonderful, in fact, so I took Toulouse to the river and back. Tide's high and everything looks so refreshed by the rain. Did you sleep well?"

"You are something. I don't think sleep was really on the agenda last night, do you? And I'd like my eggs sunny-side up, please."

"Consider it done, that's how I like mine." She poured him coffee, added cream, and handed him the mug.

"So, what do you have planned today?" she inquired.

"Paul and I are going sailing, that's the plan. You?"

"Not sure, maybe work in the yard for a while and go down to hang out with Diana and Weston this afternoon. You never know what they're doing. Diana has endless projects, and Weston, well, he's been doing all this research on green design. I can't wait to see the new project that he's working on: geothermal heat, solar panels, a vegetative roof terrace. He's LEED certified, you know. It should be pretty grand. I just love them. You know, they are just such an incredible couple. They are each so creative in their different ways and so terrific together. Plus, Sam, you know what I appreciate the most in both of them?"

"What's that?"

"Integrity, decency, no false pride. They are just extremely good."

After he left, Lucy angled herself in her bedroom doorway. She would not wash the linens today. She may not even make the bed. She wanted to hold him close to her, and seeing the room in a case of dishabille made her feel that last night wasn't just eight hours past, but that he was with her. She held the sheets close to her and was hit by a rush of his scent. No cologne, just Samuel's masculine scent, and it was very dear to her.

Sam met Paul at the marina. He was better now, hydrated and not so woozy. He knew that Lucy was passionate, and he had expected good sex, but what happened last night took his breath away. Yes, she wasn't twenty-one and inexperienced, but he had no idea of the scope of her sexual talent, and to admit it, yes, it had felt fantastic, but he was a little worried that the inner Lucy could be that sensual and that good. It wasn't as if he needed to help her along. It was as if she had taken him on the whole crash course of "Fear of Flying." It bothered him just a little. They left the Ashley River Marina and set sail in Charleston Harbor. The vintage boat angled beautifully in the water, its teak hull gleaming in the bright sun. It belonged to a friend of Paul's who lived mainly in Chicago and part-time in Charleston.

"You're quiet today."

"Yeah, just a little hungover. I went with Lucy to the wedding, and then we drank champagne at her house."

Paul studied his friend and noted his pensive mood and the furrowed line between his eyebrows. Something had happened, that was for sure.

"Yeah, how was the wedding? Phoebe and I hoped that you would have fun and that Lucy was all right. Do you want to talk about it?"

"It was fine, good food, music, and all. I knew a lot more people than I thought I would. I think Lucy had fun. She gets a little amped up, though, doesn't she?"

"Sure, but that's part of her charm. I really don't know anyone like her, you know?"

"Yeah, I know."

"I do not know how to describe it, Diana. It was if I was in a Maxfield Parrish painting; I can't really believe it happened."

"That's lovely, waterfalls, mountains, peaks, and valleys."

"Yes, exactly, but it was also as if he touched the very depths of my soul."

"Just enjoy it, Lucy. Don't rush things. Just enjoy it all."

Lucy started plucking Florida betony out of the flower bed marveling at the long white root system. She was quiet for a few moments, reliving the night before in her mind.

"I just wonder, maybe, if he's the one. We have so much fun together, and I laugh so hard when I'm with him. It's just amazing."

"Don't try so hard, and don't rush it. It's a dance, you know. You need to let him lead sometimes, and you need to take a step back. Don't scare him off with all of that intensity of yours. Now why don't you help me root these white hydrangeas?"

Lucy and Diana quietly worked together, no longer discussing Sam, but laughing about Diana's latest employee. She was a retired teacher and a friend of Weston's mother. The challenge was that she wasn't nice to the other employees. She was always bossing them around and insulting them about their body art. The customers loved her, though, but what was Diana to do, as some of her best young floral designers were threatening to quit?

Lucy looked up at her friend. "You know, I think I still have that customer service training on my jump drive, the one I helped Liz develop for her culinary students. We could switch out some of the slides, add the different flowers and arrangements, and you could go through it with her one-on-one."

"I don't even want to put that much energy in to it. Why can't she just go away? And what is it with you and PowerPoint? You're always up to a new slide show."

"Somehow that never happens. Bad people hang on and ruin the atmosphere for all the good staff members; that's why people get fired. To ease your conscience, I would talk to her, have a mini-intervention, and make her watch the customer service show. The worst thing that could happen is you do absolutely nothing, and the good people see it as a sign of poor leadership, and they bail. Then the evil educator wins, and you, my friend, will be in a pickle. No, I say nip it in the bud. Ha! Flowers, get it? It might seem of little consequence now, but wait a month or so, and it could be quite intolerable. This is your business, not anyone else's. Manage it as you always have others', with a firm yet conscientious hand. I love PowerPoint. It's so much fun to do, and now that I have all these images, I'm just happy to do it."

"Oh, Lucy, I guess you're right. I guess she's been bullying me, too, and I've questioned my ability. I see my arrangements as art, not just flowers in vases. And she questions the curly willow that is my signature."

"What, she questions the curly willow? Look, Diana, your name is representative of the goddess of the hunt. You are not a mealy-mouthed Mellie Wilkes. Well, actually, she wasn't so mealy-mouthed, but you know what I mean. You, like everyone else, hate confrontation, but you are so strong. What's with this woman?"

"I don't know. She's from Maine. I'm really beginning to think there's something to your theory about people from the Northeast."

"Aha. The truth is out. I'm always telling you the challenge is all that cold weather. Five months of the frozen tundra and anyone would become grumpy and incorrigible. Think about it. They also get the SAD syndrome from not a lot of light. Here the winter is short, and listening to the maudlin tunes of Sarah McLachlan is *charmant* at the holidays, but imagine if you are in the 'bleak midwinter' and then there's late winter, too. Crabbiness would become second nature, and then negativity is the result. Give her the training, document it, and then kick her to the curb. Easier said than done."

"I know, and then there's my mother-in-law's factor. How do I say to her, 'Your friend is a true bitch, and thanks a lot for dumping her on me'? Instead I would have to say, 'Izzie isn't working out. She's a little tough on the young, talented staff that I've cultivated, and I understand she's a new widow and all and that her children have not done right...' Do you see what I mean?"

"Yes, but here we go again. Just because Louise doesn't want Izzie to be part of her bridge group, why does that mean that you have to suffer? Truly, what is with mother-in-laws thinking that they can thrust their ill-wanted friends on their sons' wives? That's crazy. Also it's a control thing because you know that irascible Izzie is going back and reporting out everything about you in her own grumpus fashion, and what is Izzie short for anyway, Isabelle, Isabella, or Isadora? Why would you call yourself Izzie, or did someone else call her Izzie in a tizzy and it just stuck? All right, now I'm rethinking this—kick Izzie to the curb. 'Izzie, I found out about this great program that needs retired teachers, and it pays...' You get it?"

"Okay, but I haven't seen anything in the paper like that for a while. Have you?"

"No, but I'll call my friends at the community foundation. They know everything. You never need my help really. You are always so good and strong, but in this case, I'm there for you. You can count on it."

"Thanks, Lucy, and thank you for talking me through it. Weston has been under so much strain with his projects, especially the green ones, as they are just expensive on the front end. I just don't want him to think that I can't handle this."

"Jeez, Diana, you have my back every day. This is the least I can do, and I'll e-mail you the show. You should be able to open it. Just think it through and use your good judgment. It will all work out. It always does."

They finished potting up the last of the hydrangeas, and Lucy soon said her good-byes. On her way home, she thought how lucky she was that her one employee, Gabriella, was so good. Sometimes a little anxious, but that could apply to Lucy as well.

❦

Besides that brief cool weekend, the heat of August continued through the end of September, and although Lucy did not see Sam as much as she would have liked, they spent the weekends together and dined together once during the week.

She cooked him dishes, and they dined al fresco in her small backyard. They cycled and visited the Gibbes Museum of Art, the Charleston Museum, and other area sites. He showed off his culinary skills, preparing the local dishes that Annie had taught him. They shared books and magazines. He offered her his *Preservation* magazine, and she offered him her editions of *Art and Antiques*. The time they spent in her bedroom was magical to them both and they continued to surprise each other every time.

One evening Sam popped over to her house, and they shared the task of cooking together. He lit the grill and placed fresh chicken kebabs next to the counter. Lucy had prepared the salad and was marinating portabello mushrooms. Toulouse ambled back and forth between the grill and the kitchen. He and Sam had become friends, and Toulouse always sat beside him while they ate. The patio table was set with Lucy's sterling, a vibrant tablecloth, and white stoneware. As always, she used her great-grandmother's oversized damask napkins.

Sam marveled at her easy sense of style and could not help to ask, "So, Lucy, do you set aside one day a week to starch and iron napkins?"

"No, but I do like to iron. My Aunt Aurora gave me a Rowenta iron a few years ago, and boy howdy, it has changed my life. I like the way that starch smells as well, just so clean. My mom always starched linens. She would say that before you set the table, you must lay the foundation to have a table properly set. She always surprised us with different napkin folds too. She loved to entertain. How about your mom, any crazy linen thing?"

"No, we always had the table nicely set at the holidays, Christmas, Thanksgiving, and Easter, but she tends to entertain in a casual manner. We have this big farmhouse table in the kitchen, and it's the center of family activity and dining for the most part. She's more of a nouvelle cuisine type, and any dish from Provence. She's a bit of a Francophile."

"That's really wonderful, though, isn't it? That she has that passion for what she does and carries her interest in France in her everyday life too. Sam, did I tell you I'm going to Prague? No? My Aunt Aurora called the other day and asked if I wanted to visit. So I'm going at the end of next month to see her. Her husband is traveling to Poland, Latvia, and Lithuania at that time while various symphonies will be performing his new compositions. It should be wonderful. Maeve will be joining us as well, so it should be a wonderful girl party."

"Prague is one of my favorite European cities. It's just terribly crowded in the summer, and there's such a crush of tourists, but its fine in the autumn, and you will have the insider's view. You have been, though, right?"

"Yes, but it was short and a family gathering, so we only went to the main attractions, and I never saw the *Infant of Prague* and his trappings."

"Lucy, it should be a great trip, and after this hot summer, the cool weather will definitely be refreshing. I'll dig up my guidebooks and give them to you. If you can, you should see Tel□, a magnificent World Heritage Site, and the castle at Karlštejn as well. I also made notes on restaurants. There's the Good Soldier Schweik in the Malá Strana that serves incredible goulash. I'll get it to you this week."

They sat companionably and chatted and soon washed up. Sam said he had an early morning and he needed to leave. He pecked her on the mouth, tousled Toulouse's furry head, and left by the side door. Lucy smiled as she prepared for bed, thinking how easy Sam was, no false pride, no self-absorption, just a great guy. Her last thoughts before sleep claimed her was that she was so happy in his company.

Chapter 12

Take this kiss upon the brow!
And, in parting from you now,
Thus much let me avow –
You are not wrong who deem
That my days have been a dream;
Yet if hope has flown away
In a night, or in a day,
In a vision, or in none
Is it therefore the less gone?
All that we see or seem
Is but a dream within a dream

"A Dream within a Dream", Edgar Allan Poe

Sam called to say he had dropped off the guidebooks and that he would be busy the next two weeks. She shouldn't count on him—he would be working day and night on his properties, and he had had to let the plasterer go. The house on Hanover Street needed more work than he had earlier anticipated, but that's how it always was. He would call her soon, not to worry. He was just a little overwhelmed. Lucy told him that she understood; projects always loomed larger than one thought. She told him she would miss his company and wished him good luck. The second week turned into a third, and Lucy was anxious, since she hadn't seen him. She called him, and he had been short with her on the phone, and she couldn't help but wonder if there wasn't something else.

They had had such a good time, had been honest with each other. She had followed Diana's sage advice about not contacting him too much. Now she was getting ready to leave in a week for her trip, and she just wanted to be with him and hold him, even if it were for an hour and a half. She decided to whip up some brownies and stop by the next day after work. She wore her Lily knockoff skirt with a bright pink T-shirt and added flat pink silk sandals. She was pleased with her image and added sunglasses before she left the gallery, locking it up at 6:00 p.m.

She drove to the house, a large clapboard single house looming over the street. It was taller than its neighbors and had simple Greek Revival details. Brackets had been switched out at a later date, and Victorian bargeboards had been added, in her judgment around the 1870s, when the house was in her heyday. She noted all the exterior work that was needed and wondered what it was like on the interior. Sam was right. He was just busy, that's all. She stepped on the piazza, noticing that many of the balusters were missing and that the floor was sagging.

She remembered a conversation with Brooks about piazzas and how they come and go in Charleston because of the climate. *That's right,* she thought, *we do live in a petri dish.* She called his name.

"Up here, Lucy."

She looked about her, noticing the cracked plaster in the rooms off the stair, and then climbed the stairs, avoiding the missing treads and noticing the new rat traps he had placed in strategic places.

"Hi, Sam, I brought brownies."

He looked tired. His hair was sticking out at all ends, but it added to his handsomeness, she thought. Strong arms, abs, and a beautiful tush. What was she thinking? She leaned in and hugged him. He did not hug her back. She cocked her head and looked at him. Was something wrong?

"It's a great house, although it's a total wreck, but you've done this plenty before."

"Yes, but not on this scale. It's big."

He asked if he could come by later, around eight thirty. He would then be able to work some more, go home, and clean up.

She could only say, "Great," and that she wouldn't keep him.

Sam arrived a little before nine. He was pensive, and there was no evidence of his usual positive disposition. They sat at the dining room table, and he took her hands in his. He looked at her and said that he had enjoyed her company, that he did not remember when he had felt so free before. He had not laughed with anyone like he did with her. He had been getting behind on his projects, though, and their relationship wasn't reality-based; it was spontaneous and a fantasy, and real life meant that there was so much more. He should never have slept with her those many nights. His heart was otherwise engaged and had been since his junior year in college. She was a doctor and was moving back in early November, and it was just best that he and Lucy should part ways. He did not know if they could be friends because they had been too intimate. He was sorry, and he knew he was hurting her, but it would all be best in the end. For perhaps the second time in Lucy's life, she could not find words to speak.

She finally asked him when this all had come about, and he told her that Jessica had called him three weeks ago to tell him the news of her new position at the hospital. They spent more time talking. After a while Lucy stood up and quietly asked him to leave.

"Just go. I would not have thought you were capable of this. No discussion, just your decision. I didn't even count in your life's equation, did I?"

She was softly crying now. He touched her shoulder, squeezed it, and pulled her to him gently.

For three days she tried to center herself, tried not to remember his pewter-colored eyes and the scent and feel of his body. She couldn't and wouldn't think about what happened between them, after he had taken her in his arms and before he left her house. She finally sent out an e-mail to her girlfriends. She typed the message:

Emergency whine/wine night at Lucy's. Please be there. I need you.

The girls called each other and questioned what was going on. Diana was the first to arrive. She held a bottle of red in one hand and white in the other. Lucy's face was swollen, and Diana was sorry to see her friend hurting so much.

"Lucy, what happened?"

"I was Jessicaed again. Sam had a girlfriend all along. She was living in Alabama, and they were taking some time off, but she's coming back now, and, well, there it is."

"Oh, honey, I'm so sorry. I had no idea. Are Ben and Sebastian coming too?"

"No, they are all friends with him now. They do the boys' burger night once a week. I'm sure they'll find out soon enough."

Rachel was the next to arrive, followed by Ella, Katie, and Violet. The friends listened to Lucy, expressing sympathy and frustration.

"So he never let on that there was someone else, Lucy? He just said he was busy? And then what happened?" Ella inquired.

"Well, actually, he came over about three weeks ago and said he was going to be busy with the two houses he purchased in late summer. He dropped off guidebooks and then stopped calling. I called him and popped by three days ago with brownies. He then came over and delivered his dramatic monologue. He had it all figured out, you know."

Katie had not dated in three years and offered her own advice. "Well, you shouldn't have slept with him. You know better than that. Momma always said, 'Why buy the cow when you get the milk for free?'"

"Shush, Katie, this is no time for being negative. Lucy already feels bad enough, and it seems like she enjoyed the sex. We're not living in the sixties, you know," Rachel stridently chimed.

Ella, also wanting to know the full story, asked, "What do we know about this Jessica? Just that they dated in college and after and that she's a doctor. We don't know if Sam is falling back into that habit because maybe this relationship scared him and the other is comfortable. Lucy, you have a fantastic trip coming up, and I know that it feels like your heart is broken, but you never know what will happen, right?"

"You're right, Ella. Every relationship is different. Look, Lucy, you are a beautiful, smart woman, and if Sam is not for you, there are plenty of others out there. Life is sometimes like a game, we all know that, and sometimes, the person that you thought you loved the most wasn't worthy of all the love you have to give. Meanwhile, and I know this doesn't help, you had an amazing summer filled with beautiful memories. If he is the one, he'll come back," Diana added.

"Jeez," Violet sighed." This is just a little too *Jonathan Livingston Seagull* for me. If you love something, set it free and all that. I say Lucy deserves to have her cry, and we get him somehow. I could always ask my friend in the code office to watch his work and make it hard for him. Stop work orders, things like that. That'll fix his little red wagon."

"That won't get anyone anywhere. He was honest, he pleaded his case, it was probably even hard for him to do so, but at least he wasn't seeing you both at the same time. If she's been away for a while, she may have changed, or she might not be the girl he remembered at all. Machinations will do nothing, Violet, but make Lucy look petty and spiteful," Ella stated.

"I agree. Ella is right, and Lucy, you will see him; our town is so small. You must take the high road, and you know that. Otherwise you'll be viewed a bitch or a shrew, and you are neither. So let's talk about something else. I know you're hurting, but you've dwelled on this alone for three days before you called us together. We need to think of what you're taking on the trip. It's Thursday already, and you leave on Saturday. No, I say moping will not do. It doesn't suit you, my dear friend," Diana intoned.

"Thank you, all of you. I appreciate all your comments, but what I'm most concerned about is that he wasn't honest. Maybe he was that last night, but not before that. He lied by omission, and all those great times spent doing common fun things, the bike rides, dinners, seeing exhibits, and the sex—and Katie, the sex was worth all of my tears—he knew his heart belonged to another, and he couldn't or wouldn't tell me."

Ella patted her friend and filled her wineglass with Pinot Gris. "I hate to break it to you, but we all lie. We tell our coworkers who have gained ten pounds that they look great even though they should be in an eight and not a ten. We tell our mothers all is well when our hearts are breaking. We lie about everything, and I'm not talking about women. I'm talking about people. We lie in order to be polite. We lie in order to make things convenient for others and ourselves. We lie when we are confused, and we lie when we are just being plain bad. The deal is our world is too fast. Technology is everywhere. If we lived in the eighteenth or nineteenth century, we would have time to process. Time to make plans so that when we responded by mail, we would not be lying when we said we were otherwise engaged. Our problem is, because of all of this, we also want immediate gratification. I might add, as Americans, we are the absolute worst, as we have too much. Be hard on him if it makes you feel better right now, Lucy, but also take this time to look gently in your own heart."

Ella and Diana caught one another's eye. They had both been in Lucy's shoes. They never gave up, though. Love was there, somewhere, for Lucy. They both knew she just had to find it, whether it was in Sam's arms or another's.

Rachel commented that maybe emotionally Sam felt too close to Lucy and that the intimacy confused him. Sometimes people just get plain scared and then behave badly. Katie and Violet weren't so sure that Ella's words rang true. Diana finally gave them direction, and as they had on so many emergency nights at each other's domiciles, the girls cleaned up the glasses and food and departed. Diana asked Lucy if she needed anything. Yes, she would take her to the airport, and no, it was no problem, and she was happy to see her friend off.

Before Diana left, Lucy asked her about the problematic Izzie. They had not discussed her in a while. Yes, it was short for Isadora, and yes, she was gone. Diana had given her the information regarding the substitute teacher positions, so now she was the challenge of the Charleston County School System. The other coworkers had been so impressed with Izzie's complaints about Diana's ill treatment of her and the mandatory slide show that they had asked to see the customer service PowerPoint. They had all decided that they needed the training and it could be a useful tool in their work. It had all worked out. Izzie, to save face with Weston's mother, said that Diana had not challenged her properly and she was happy to work again in the classroom.

"Funny, isn't it? How it all sorts out."

"It is, my dear. It will for you, beloved friend of mine."

"I love you, Diana. You are little sister, and Ella, big sister. I just didn't realize how negative Katie and Violet can be sometimes, but they were probably just giving me their own version of support."

"Good night."

"Night, best to Weston and thanks for everything."

Chapter 13

I hold it true, whate're befall;
I feel it when I sorrow most;
'Tis better to have loved and lost
Than never to have loved at all....

"In Memoriam" Alfred, Lord Tennyson

Maeve and Aunt Aurora met Lucy at the airport. She was so happy to see them that tears welled in her eyes. Of course she had told them both over the phone about the breakup. Aurora was undaunted and reminded Lucy that she could talk about Sam, but this was their girls' trip, and it was about seeing sites and having fun. For the next ten days, they would do just that.

Each day took them on outings and journeys. On All Saints' Day, they traveled to Tel□, the World Heritage Site Sam had mentioned, and wandered the town. The Baroque architecture lifted Lucy's spirits. After touring churches and walking about, Lucy commented about the number of people carrying flowers and candles who seemed to be wandering in the same direction on foot and in old trucks and mule carts. Aurora remarked that they were honoring the dead and placing flowers on tombstones. Lucy and Maeve were touched at the thought and imagined that, in their own country, people rarely honored this tradition. One day they toured the Hrad□any, marveling at the St. Vitus Cathedral, the castle, and gardens. Another day took them to the Jewish Ghetto, where they visited all of the synagogues, including the Old New Synagogue with its mounding tombstones dating from the thirteenth century. Maeve and Lucy were grateful for the cool mornings where they could don heavy sweaters, and they thrived on the thick, strong coffee.

Each evening they cooked together in Aurora and Georg's chic condo in the Malá Strana, enjoying each other's company, although Lucy seemed preoccupied much of the time. They crossed the Vltava

River via the Charles Bridge and climbed the towers to view the panorama of the Golden City. Maeve had brought a book with her regarding Kafka's life and demanded that they visited all sites associated with one of her favorite authors. They embraced Kafka's environs and reflected on his books and short stories.

"Maeve," Aurora said one evening after Lucy went to bed, "she's not shaking the sadness, and I think the two of you need something else." She absently touched Georg's grand piano. "Although you are both so dear and great fun, I think you need to extend your stay in Europe elsewhere. Go to Rome and Florence. See something entirely new. I think Lucy needs you and your strength. She's pining here, and although she puts a bright smile on that face of hers, I can't help but feel this undercurrent of despair. I would like to offer you the plane tickets and cover the hotel. I know of a little hotel that is divine and near everything. It would be my treat to the two of you. And I don't think either of you have been there in a very long time. So tell me you can take some more time and do this. Our Lucy needs to be well and shake her pain before she goes home."

"Aunt Aurora, how can I thank you? Yes, I can take some more time, and all of the writers visited Rome, all of them. Yes, Lucy needs to snap out of it, and you've been far too kind to her. To tell you the truth, I was a little happy that she missed our big shopping day. I just couldn't help admiring all that we saw and was glad she and her mullygrubbing weren't with us. I know—I know by just looking at your face that you think I'm being mean-spirited, but I'm not. I'm just being forthright. Now if you hear on the radio that she's found with duct tape on her mouth, you will know that I reached the very end of my patience. Rome, I can't imagine, so much that I can understand better at this time of my life. We'll do ancient Rome, the Vatican City, and then all of its magnificent Baroqueness. Oh heavens, and Florence and maybe one day at Pompeii. This will be glorious. Let's just hope she doesn't become so maudlin that I push her under a bus."

Aurora shook her head. "Maeve, her confidence lies in tatters, and I think she has already been pushed under the bus. She's always been so supportive towards you, and now you must return all of her kindness, even if she is somewhat trying. Now, first things first, who do we need to call so we can make arrangements for her work and Toulouse before we start hatching this plan?"

"Well, I can e-mail the shop and ask them for the kennel info, as well as ask Gabriella to cover everything. I can do that now, and we should be in business by tomorrow night. Then we'll just have to order tickets." Maeve smiled and was quite pleased with herself.

"Exactly, Maeve, and I can e-mail the hotel tomorrow. It's quite old-fashioned, yet very clean, on the third floor of a Baroque building not far from the Villa Borghese."

The arrangements had all been made, including the airlines, by the following night. Aurora kept remarking how wonderful the Internet was and how she could never have planned this so effortlessly without it. While Lucy slept, the two consulted guidebooks, sitting in the elegant and smart living room adorned with Aurora's paintings and an eclectic mixture of modern and antique furnishings.

Maeve and Aurora told Lucy about the trip while at a crowded café the next day. She could not form an argument nor could she act poorly in public.

Inside Lucy felt that she had been manhandled and treated like a child. She whispered to Aurora, "I don't understand why we can't stay here another week. We've only been to a handful of churches and museums. Why do we need to go to Italy?"

Aurora arched her swan's neck and raised her perfectly groomed right eyebrow and felt sorry for Maeve. "Listen, Lucy, I know you are feeling very sad, but you have to move on. This is your life. You've been sad and miserable for nearly three weeks. You won't have time in Rome to think about Sam and his ungentlemanly-like manners, and you won't have time to stay hiding in bed. You will make another memory, not stretch this painful one out any further. Trust me. You need some excitement, a new adventure. Roman men are wonderful flirts, and you need that right now. Do not say a word that you can't afford it. I've shifted your flights, and you will leave from Rome back to Charleston; there was an insignificant charge to manage that, and I'm covering your hotel and flight there, and Gabriella is more than happy to have the extra hours. All you and Maeve are responsible for are food, admission tickets, and trains if you go to Pompeii and Florence. You have five days to get that heart in shape."

Lucy looked at her aunt and loved her, loved her for being pushy and complicated, generous and high-handed. "Okay, but what if Maeve pushes me over the edge of the Colosseum or down to the bottom of the Catacombs, something like that?"

Aurora laughed then and winked at her nieces. "Maeve has said the worst she will do is place duct tape on your mouth. I have booked separate rooms for you; that way you won't keep her up all the night wanting to rehash. So, girls, one last visit to the Church of the Lady Victorious?"

"Yes, please," they chimed together.

Lucy visited the *Infant of Prague* for the last time, rethinking the story of this seventeenth-century wax baby Jesus and wondering at how it survived through so much time. She prayed hard that God would give her strength and that he would help this hurt lessen. She knew she couldn't ruin this generous gift from Aunt Aurora, knew that she had to be good, as Maeve was jumping out of her skin with excitement. A single tear ran down her face. She thanked God for everything he had given her: life, her family, including Toulouse, her business and her little house, and yes, for that brief time with Sam. She knew that Maeve and Aurora had lit candles in honor of her mother, and she followed suit, thinking how her mom would have loved the adult Aurora, not just the wild bohemian artist, but the one who loved her nieces so purely and so well.

Chapter 14

I am in Rome! Oft as the morning ray visits these eyes
Waking at once I cry,
Whence this excess joy? What has befallen me?
And from within a thrilling voice replies,
Thou art in Rome!

"Italy, a Poem" Samuel Rogers

They landed in Rome at noon and took the train from the airport to the Termini. From there they had a five-minute walk to their hotel. The fall sky was brilliantly blue and gleamed on the sites along the way, here a fragment of an ancient wall, there a Baroque structure, and streets all finished in paving blocks. Maeve had planned everything with Aurora's detailed memory and guidebooks. Today was Baroque Rome. They didn't have much time, only five days, and they had to focus on the sites they wanted to see. So today they would tour the Villa Borghese, the Bernini fountains, the Triton and boat fountain, and the Trevi, the Spanish Steps, and the Keats-Shelley Memorial House.

They took off, map in hand. Maeve, the dark beauty, was sensibly dressed in comfortable black leather shoes, black pants, ruby turtleneck, and a vintage black-and-white silk scarf under a simple black coat. Lucy wore a gray wool skirt with an aqua cashmere sweater over a French-cuffed white blouse and a chic short leather jacket. Low-heeled black boots, a turquoise necklace, bracelet, and earrings finished her outfit.

She looked at her sister and said, "Maeve, honey, look, I'm going to promise not to be a pain. Okay?"

"Okay. First we're going in this direction to the Villa Borghese. I think we are in for a world of art. The guidebook says one room alone is dedicated to Carvaggio's works, and Bernini, of course. Look, Lucy, I think you're feeling better already. You look great, but I do think Grandmere is right. You just can't lose any more weight."

"I'm fine. I'm eating well, and I am feeling better, thank you. I think I'm inspired by your infectious attitude. Speaking of dearest Grandmere, isn't that scarf one of hers? I remember it from a picture."

"It is. She gave it to me the last time I was in Charleston. She wanted me to have something that reminded me that she is fun and not always so serious. I said to her, 'Are you sure you want to give me the one with polkie dots?' She laughed so hard, saying that for someone working on a PhD, I still had a lot of childishness. So here goes. Are you ready?"

They checked their handbags and cameras and began exploring the Baroque villa. Maeve marveled at the works of art, truly impressed with the decorative arts, the paintings, and the sculpture. It was too much to take in. They sighed in awe at the many sculptures and agreed that Bernini's *Apollo and Daphne* was exquisite. They wondered how he had carved her hands so beautifully, the way they turned to laurel leaves. Lucy marveled at his *David*, commenting to Maeve about his fierce and determined look.

She touched Maeve and said, "Goliath never had a chance."

They viewed Canova's *Venus*, remarking about Napoleon's sister Paolina who had married into the prestigious Borghese family, and Lucy added that Joseph Bonaparte had lived in America. After two hours the sisters had consumed so much art that they were famished for blue sky and fluffy clouds to cleanse their mental palate. They knew they had not experienced it all, but they were surfeit and complete, and the day had just begun. Maeve told Lucy that she needed to view the grounds to clear her head from all that beauty, although the grounds, with their plant materials, were another visual stimulant. They sat on a bench, and Lucy brought up the painted decoration.

"Maeve, it's just so beautiful, the painted walls, the ceilings and cornices, and the frescoes. Exquisite, just divine. I just don't know how we can do it all."

"We won't do it all, but we'll make a very large dent, and then we have to plan on another trip. Aunt Aurora knew what she was doing. She really did. I wonder how she knew that we would feel like this?"

"I'm not sure, but let's get to it."

They wandered about, enjoying the architecture. When a Baroque church beckoned, they got lost inside. They ended at the Keats-Shelley House and wandered about. Although Lucy enjoyed the Romantics, this was now Maeve's territory. A map on the wall sited the Spanish Steps. It marked where many of the authors had lived, the English and Americans mostly. They found Goethe's house and those of the

Brownings, Wordsworth's, and Coleridge's. They noted the others in quick succession, cramming their heads together and reading out loud.

"Look, there's James and Irving, Melville and Byron."

"You always loved Byron, Maeve. Remember on your twelfth birthday when you had a hissy fit when Mom and Dad said that the Castle of Chillon was too far away? And then you started quoting 'The Prisoner of Chillon' in the blue Volvo?"

"But they had planned it, Lucy. It was a big surprise. Remember the dungeon and the way that *LacLeman* had lapped at its walls. I'll never forget it. You know that vacation in Switzerland, in the lap of the Bernese Oberland, was just so fantastic. Three weeks in front of the majesty of the Eiger, Mönch, and Jungfrau, and to finish it all with Chillon. It was the year before, you know."

"That was the year you wrote your first volume of verse, and you glued dried flowers inside, gentians, alpine flowers and edelweiss. But Maeve, let's not bring the other up. Let's make a pact right now that we will not bring up troubling thoughts, or if we do, no longer than five minutes of discussion."

"You're right. This is our time. Demons can't haunt us here. Let's go upstairs to see where our man lived."

They wandered the spaces and saw where Keats had lived. They hovered over a first edition of Polidori's "The Vampyre" and read Mary Shelley's words at discovering Percy Shelley's drowning. They felt as intruders of the lives of those talented writers so young to have left this world. They were in awe of Keats's small spaces, and they noted his furniture, especially the Empire bed from the period and identical to the one where he hacked up the last vestiges of his life as he died from tuberculosis.

After leaving the museum, they stepped into a faintly drizzling world. Maeve noted it was as if Rome was crying in remembrance of such great talent. They asked a chicly dressed petite Asian girl who spoke beautiful Italian to take their picture in front of the steps. Maeve wanted to send it to one of her professors. After consuming a caffe latte, they strengthened their resolve and ran up the Spanish Steps, catching their breath and laughing before quietly entering the serenity of the Trinity of the Mount. From there they went to the Piazza Colonna, where they viewed the column erected to Marcus Aurelius after his successful defeats of the Germans in 180 AD. Lucy pointed to a small Baroque chapel with a cartouche of a *Madonna and Child*. Art was everywhere. Frescoes adorned walls, houses, and churches, making Lucy smile and forget the sadness that had clutched her heart.

The Trevi Fountain beckoned them, and they heard the rush of water before they saw its mammoth figures of Neptune and those who attended him attributed to Nicola Salvi, but also said to be based on designs by the hand of Bernini. The beauty and noise of the water inspired and calmed Lucy, and she felt some of her innate happiness returning. She smiled at Meave, and the sisters giggled together.

"Lucy, do you have any coins?"

"I do, but we're not throwing euros in the fountain. With lattes at four euros, we'll be broke before we're done. I don't think they would mind quarters, do you? Here, this is for you." She placed several coins in Maeve's hand. "Just one coin, two, or three? Let's see, one is for a return to Rome, two for love, and three for marriage."

"Oh no, Maeve, I don't think I'm up for two or three. I'm a little done in that arena this trip, but definitely one. I want to visit Rome again and again."

"Sounds good. Now we have to do it right and throw it over the shoulder. That's what all the books say. All right, one, two, three."

They heard the quiet splashes and knew that they had been successful. This would be the first of their many visits to the Eternal City as adults.

"Maeve, look," Lucy said as she wiggled her eyebrows.

In front of them, sitting on the fountain, were two heavy gladiator reenactors, one chatting noisily on a cell phone while the other sat in companionable silence, smoking a cigarette while sipping a Diet Coke. Lucy didn't know why she found this spectacle so amusing, but she did. She felt alive and happy. She was surrounded by a sea of people of all ages and from various and assorted countries and backgrounds.

The light was fading, and the sisters started their procession back to the hotel. They passed the Piazza Barberini, where they stopped in their tracks, admiring the Triton Fountain, so simple in its Baroque grandeur compared to the Trevi. Here, not a person surrounded the solitary figure except Lucy and Maeve. Roman inhabitants barely gazed at it as they quickly went on their way to cafés or home to surfeit themselves on a meal of pasta or veal.

Lucy could feel Maeve's silence and also a presence of melancholy that stole through her sister's essence. She wanted to say something but quickly halted any comment by pressing her fingers to her lips. Maeve was crying, crocodile tears streaming down her face, and she was whispering to herself. Lucy touched her arm, and Maeve smiled at her and began quoting.

"Getting and spending, we lay waste our powers:
Little we see in Nature that is ours;
We have given our hearts away, a sordid boon!
This sea bares her bosom to the moon;
The winds that will be howling at all hours,
And are up-gathered now like sleeping flowers;
For this, for everything, we are out of tune;
It moves us not. Great God! I'd rather be
A Pagan suckled in a creed outworn;
So might I standing on this pleasant lea,
Have glimpses that would make me less forlorn;
Have sight of Proteus rising from the sea;
Or hear old Triton blow his wreathed horn."

"Don't you see, Lucy? They were all amazed here, too, and Wordsworth's words, well, think about it. He's questioning life and all the trappings that are immaterial, and here this work of art by Bernini juxtaposes all of that with the solitary Triton. In the end, we all have to think about what is important in life, those core elements that make us tick, of being part of the universe and achieving, but not being tricked by trappings that are unimportant and unnecessary."

"*'The World is too much with us; Late and Soon,'* right, our lake brother, Wordsworth?" Lucy hugged her sister to her, telling her she loved her. She quietly thanked Aunt Aurora again for this trip, this beautiful gift. She thanked her lucky stars for a brilliant sister and for the parents who had made them both read so many classics at a young age.

Maeve stopped by Lucy's room later in the evening. "Let's plan tomorrow's trip. I just checked the schedule to Naples, and it will take roughly one hour to get there and then thirty minutes on the commuter train. If we leave on the eight thirty train, we should be able to spend the entire day there at Pompeii, or we could try to see Herculaneum too. What do you think?"

Maeve gazed at her sister and noticed the pale blue T-shirt that was too big for her frame. It had an angry dark-haired girl in pigtails throwing rocks. The logo read: Boys are stupid, throw rocks at them.

"Where on earth did you get that silly shirt?"

"I think tomorrow's trip sounds wonderful. I've been looking through the Pompeii book, and it seems that there is just so much to see and do." She looked down at the shirt. "Violet gave me this before I left, hoping that I would feel better if I wore it, and somehow I do. It's the silliness quotient; I can just think of someone throwing rocks at Sam and hurting him just a little."

They took the Eurostar to Naples the following day on their quest to Pompeii. The yellow commuter train rattled along the Amalfi Coast, and they shuttled through a paradise of tiled rooflines, buildings of muted blues, pinks, and yellows, and a tropical landscape. Several handsome Italian men smiled at them, and one looked intensely at Lucy and winked at her when he disembarked. They stepped off the train and were surrounded by friendly dogs of varying hues and sizes that seemed to be greeting them as they entered the ruins. They decided to tour the site without a guide, as they were both familiar with the map now, and they knew what they wanted to see. The panorama of ruins in front of them left them breathless, and everywhere they went, they could see Vesuvius in their line of vision.

They took turns reading from the guidebook about what they were touring, the Temple of Apollo, with its bronze statues, plaster casts of bodies, and amorphe. They followed the map as they went. Maeve had prepared a detailed list of all that she wanted to see. Lucy looked over her sister's shoulder and navigated them so they would miss nothing. They admired the depiction of a dog in the mosaic at the House of the Tragic Poet. They were bowled over by the frescoes and mosaics at the House of the Small Fountain and the House of the Large Fountain and the House of Apollo. They snapped digital pictures of it all, corresponding the numbers in Maeve's journal and marking the guidebook. They had walked for two hours when they sat on a stoop, quietly commenting on all they saw.

Maeve remarked at the timeless beauty of the frescoes and wondered exactly who had done all the work. Not one house was unadorned. They shook their heads, as they were amazed that all of this had been covered by ash for over fifteen hundred years. Lucy noted that the guidebook said the artisans probably consisted of masters and apprentices as well as slaves. Maeve asked how she knew that and added "smarty-pants" at the end. Lucy held the book to her sister and began quoting from page nine.

"I couldn't sleep last night, Maeve, so I read the book twice from cover to cover and oriented myself to the map. Finally I popped a

Sonata. I've been doing too much thinking, and although I am feeling better, I just can't quite fathom it all. And I have a confession. What made everything worse was that we were intimate 'one last time' that night because I wanted it, and he obliged me. After a significant while, I started crying because I was so unhinged that I would never kiss him again, never touch him, nor feel all those emotions that I have only ever felt with him. He tried to comfort me, and I couldn't control the crying, well, sobbing at that point—all right, to be truthful, wailing with huge tears—and I could feel my eyes swelling, and I just wailed harder. When I saw him out, I grabbed a nightie. I didn't even look to see which one, and it was...it was that sheer pink silk chemise. You bought the blue one and I the pink, remember? I just hope my neighbors were asleep. Imagine if they had seen me? And now I'm humiliated at my own weakness, that of my body and the absolute desperation of my soul. It would have been funny, if it had been in a book or in a movie like *Bridget Jones's Diary*, but it wasn't because it happened to me. My confidence is rattled, I feel unattractive, and I have to get back to my sassy self." She sighed.

Maeve had to look away. She felt sorry for Lucy and knew she was getting better, but she had to admit her sister did behave oddly sometimes. She sighed and replied, "Look, if that is the very worst that you did, it's not so very bad, is it? He surprised you with all that information, and you let your emotions completely run wild, but you didn't plead for him to stay, did you?"

"No, no pleading."

"Okay, let's banish Samuel O'Hara for the rest of this day. He will not steal this day from us. There is so much we still need to see, and I want to do it all. I think we should save Herculaneum for the next trip, and there will be another, as you know we are just scratching the surface. Most importantly, let's acknowledge your feelings, but we can't obsess, okay? You need to realize you are a beautiful woman and people love you. You're generous and kind and smart. I bet if someone were to ask Sam why he ended the relationship, he would say it had nothing to do with you, that it was all about him and where he is in his life. Most people are selfish, Lucy. Remember that."

"Hmm. I never thought about that. You are right, no more time spent on him. This is our girls' trip."

Lucy and Maeve soldiered on, adamant that they would see more than the six-hour tour conveyed. At the House of the Vettii, the girls giggled at the fresco of the warrior weighing his phallus. At the House of Octavius Quartio, the sisters marveled at the fountain that stretched nearly one block. The house's painted decoration was astounding and included the fated lovers Pyramus and Thisbe. Lucy looked at it closely, cricking her neck to the left and to the right, knitting her eyebrows as she stared at the fresco.

They boarded the train at five thirty. Sated and exhausted, they slipped into seats, chatting together of the wonders of Pompeii. They talked about the dogs that had followed them throughout the ruins, playfully jumping in their laps when they had stopped for water at the Forum, and how the security guard had thanked them for scratching the pooches behind the ears and on their backs. They interrupted each other as they had as children, finishing each other's sentences the way close siblings do. They caught the Eurostar at six thirty, and they sat in comfortable seats with a table between them.

Lucy fished the turquoise-colored Italian leather journal out of her bag. She smiled at her sister and thanked her for the new gift. It was just yesterday afternoon when Maeve had slipped into a stationery shop and purchased one for herself the color of deep cinnabar and one for Lucy. She had told Lucy as she handed it to her as they sipped a caffe latte in a cafe near the Spanish Steps that this would be the Rome journal. The battered, tear-stained one she had brought from home must be exiled immediately, as it carried too much sadness and the hashing and rehashing of the guy from Salem who had thrown Lucy under the bus when he kicked her to the curb.

The girls quietly journaled. By the time they reached the Termini train station, their stomachs were rumbling. They stopped at the *supermercato* and purchased fruit and yogurt and agreed to meet for dinner in thirty minutes' time. Their borrowed neighborhood boasted excellent restaurants within a four-block radius. This night they dined at Da Salvatore. Lucy ordered the ravioli, Maeve the veal scaloppine, and they shared a bottle of white wine. Their waiter, in his early twenties, was handsome and charming. They used their phrase book, and he happily answered them in both English and Italian. Maeve noticed the way he looked at her sister in appreciation. She had to admit it, Lucy was lovely, and her eyes were sparkling again, unlike the leaden look that they had had in Praha.

They walked, as they called it, "home," to their lodgings and Maeve said, "I've been thinking on your sleep shirt from the moment I saw it. As you know, Ray and I are doing well, but there are days that we all wish to throw rocks at them, men in general. This is what I've come up with—an edited version, of course. Men, stupid, mean, rocks. How's that?"

"That's great, and," Lucy giggled, "I think I want to add something to it. I know Pyramus and Thisbe are the tragic lovers. You know how the story goes. A lioness charges her, she loses her cloak, and it's ruined beyond repair. He finds the cloak and thinks she's dead, so he commits suicide, as he cannot go on, not one day, without her love. Today, as I looked at the fresco, I had a different thought. Let's say they live in the modern world where, as you reminded me, selfishness abounds. Would he really do that? I don't think so. So how's this? Men, straight, stupid, mean, rocks, gun, murder, suicide."

They laughed out loud. "See, Maeve, I figure our modern-day Thisbe doesn't look good in the detention center orange suit, and well, the boy just plain pissed her off. So she kills him and then says uh-oh and does herself in. Self-absorption can be manipulated best through mythology. Why else was the fresco of Narcissus directly across from it?"

"Oh, sister mine—you are getting better. Your sense of humor is back."

They had three days left. Tomorrow would be ancient Rome and the next day the Vatican City. The last day they would board the train and visit Florence.

Chapter
15

We have looked with much pleasure to this abode of the muses and our first impressions were altogether favourable. We went to the studio of (Hiram) Powers... We saw a duplicate of his Greek Slave it is the perfection of female loveliness...

1849 Travel Diary, Joseph Daniel Aiken

Lucy and Maeve stepped onto the Eurostar at 8:00 a.m. The train ride was uneventful, and the two girls quietly journaled. Lucy made notes about the catacombs that they had visited earlier, noting that over four hundred thousand remains had been placed over time in the hallowed place called San Callisto. Maeve journaled about the Colosseum and the many artifacts they had viewed at the Forum. While Maeve journaled on about the Arch of Constantine, Lucy was quickly jotting her thoughts down about St. Peters and its exquisite coloration, and then later the hues and shades of the exquisite tapestries and maps they had seen in the Vatican Museums. She couldn't help but smile to herself when she thought about the three times they had visited the Sistine Chapel, twice unexpectedly, as they became lost on the way to see the *Laocoön Group*, the masterpiece that Pliny the Elder had claimed to be the finest sculpture ever.

Lucy sighed and looked up from her leather-bound volume, where her penmanship had decidedly taken a downhill spiral, and rubbed her right hand with her left. She smiled at her sister and said, "I still can't believe last night. Truly this is the most magical place ever. I'm even thinking of selling everything, the lot of it, and moving here."

Maeve shook her head and smiled back. "You will never leave Charleston. That's not in your blood."

"But Aunt Aurora did, and maybe I will too!" she exclaimed as she shook her head, giggling.

"Last night was amazing, though. The singing. Just beautiful. Do you think they were the understudies?" Maeve questioned.

"No matter, really, is it after all, as it gave us both chill bumps for a fantastic hour. Only in Rome could we have been serenaded to the beauty of *La traviata* from nine until ten in the courtyard behind the hotel and outside of my bedroom. Even better was the flutter of the breeze lifting the curtains back and forth. What an exquisite gift."

"Magical, just magical. It would be wonderful if they performed again tonight. We will just wait and see," Maeve noted.

Lucy closed her eyes and thought of the exquisite memories of this trip that she would take home. Last night after dinner, she was feeling a wee bit maudlin, and then she had heard the woman's beautiful voice calling across the courtyard and the man's voice calling back. She laughed at him and began to sing, and he called back to her critically. Then she began again, a voice strong and melodious, and then he sang, and Lucy's world was made whole.

She had started crying for all of that beauty that unfolded several floors beneath her. She called Maeve and whispered for her to come over, and Maeve had said, *"What are you whispering about, and why do you have opera cranked on the TV? You don't even watch TV."*

"Just come over," Lucy had said.

She'd opened the door for Maeve, and the TV's dark screen faced her, but the music continued. Maeve had wrinkled her brow, and Lucy pointed out the window. The girls leaned out their heads, drinking in the voices, hearing the laughter as the performers stopped one another, corrected each other, and began again. It was an experience that neither Lucy nor Maeve would ever forget.

The train was slowing down, and the two glanced at each other in anticipation. Since they only had one day, they would do a blitzkrieg tour of the city. They had chosen to see the Palazzo Pitti and the Boboli Gardens over the Uffizi. They would tour the Academia with Michelangelo's *David*, and they would visit the Duomo, with its colorful façade of green, red, and white marble. A must-see included the Loggia dei Lanzi, where Lucy had to see Cellini's sculpture of Perseus holding the head of the slain Medusa. As this was their last day, they would try to fit in a little shopping at the end before leaving for Rome at seven.

They were awestruck at the sheer beauty of the Renaissance city. The architecture was exquisite, and everywhere they looked, they came upon sculptures, fountains, and handsome and stately buildings. Maeve remarked to Lucy that they were immersed in a city filled with art. They marveled at the baptistery near the Duomo and chatted merrily as they viewed the large gilded bronze doors that Michelangelo had named the Gates of Paradise. They were beside themselves beholding the beauty of the cathedral as they viewed colorful religious frescoes and stained glass. Maeve pointed a long finger to a painting they both knew from school of Dante and *The Divine Comedy*.

"Funny," Maeve said, "I knew that it was in Florence. I just didn't know it was in the Duomo."

They drank in the small and exclusive jewelers' shops as they crossed the Arno River at the Ponte Vecchio.

After two and a half hours at the Palazzo Pitti, Maeve looked at her watch and said, "Lucy it's one o'clock. We still have so much to see and do."

Lucy was surfeit for the moment, as she had seen three paintings by Artemisia Gentileschi, a room made of majolica, more Renaissance art than her mind could take in, and Dolci's masterpiece, the *Magdalene*, that had consumed so much time of that most gifted seventeenth-century Florentine painter's life. The Palazzo Pitti was all that she had expected and more.

Lucy looked at Maeve and she said, "Dolci's *Magdalene* has always been one of my favorites since college. It is absolutely perfect. I hoped I would see it. Thanks to Massimo for telling us that if we had one day, we should see the Pitti Palace over the Uffizi. Otherwise I would have missed the *Magdalene*."

Maeve shook her head. How could Lucy have a favorite when everything they looked at was the cream of the crop? Florence was a living, breathing museum city, and Maeve had fallen for its splendor.

"Let me articulate, Maeve. You know how I love my Charlestonians and they all went abroad, our ancestors, too. Well, my favorite museum house in town these days is the Aiken-Rhett House, and in the art gallery of the house, there are many copies of Renaissance art that they purchased while here in Italy. In the collection there are two nineteenth-century copies of the *Magdalene*. Isn't that fantastic? In fact, while they were abroad, Cousin Joseph Aiken was supervising the construction of the art gallery."

Maeve smiled at her sister. "See, even while in Italy you are still thinking of home. No, you will always live in Charleston." She laughed.

The hours sped by with so much to see and do. By six thirty, they were wandering back to the train station, and as the vendors were closing their stalls, they quickly purchased scarves, ties, pashminas, and each two purses. They boarded the train at 6:50 with ten minutes to spare and fell into their clean, comfortable seats sated and happy. Lucy quickly donned a rich teal pashmina and laughed.

"Do you even know, Maeve, how many scarves you bought? I looked out of the corner of my eye and thought, how will all that fit in her suitcase?"

"I have no idea, but the silk ones were down to two for ten euros, and the pashminas are really very nice cashmere, and they were two for twenty euros. The purse vendor threw in a wallet. That was lovely, wasn't it? Besides, they are so light, they will take up no space at all."

Lucy viewed her sister's loot as Maeve spread the myriad colored scarves between them, and she laughed, draping them on her shoulders, her head, and winding them around her neck. Her upper torso was a veritable Joseph's coat of color.

They knew they had pushed themselves hard on this trip and that Europeans, especially Italians, would think that they had rushed through their stay. They each had a sensibility and could process and appreciate things quickly. Besides, this was the first of what would hopefully be many trips seeing it all together. They would be back, as Italy had struck with them a chord.

Maeve walked her to the train station. Lucy was taking the eight thirty train to the airport. The sky was fresh and new, and she felt revived, still aching, but now in charge of her life. She hugged her sister on the platform and asked her about her flight. When was she leaving?

Maeve gave her a sheepish grin. "Actually, I'm not. I'm staying two more weeks. While you've been journaling each night, I've been hammering on my dissertation. Massimo suggested that I go to Orvieto, another beautiful town. He has family there, and I can rent a tiny apartment for two weeks for about three hundred and fifty dollars. It's just perfect. I just feel so alive here, and it's as if all my creative juices are just flowing. I'll e-mail you and let you know how it's going."

"Oh, Maeve, I think we must do something nice for Aunt Aurora, as she gave us such an exquisite gift. Good luck, honey! I love you!"

As the train pulled out of the station, the sisters waved frantically. Lucy had tears in her eyes, not of sadness, but of happiness. The trip had given her back her confidence. Her heart was not healed, but she would be fine.

She checked through customs at the Atlanta airport and sought out the gate for her final leg home. She was tired, but happy. Italy had been an amazing experience, and Prague as well. She thought how lucky she was to have so many people in her sphere who loved her and were generous of spirit. She bumped down the aisle with her rollerboard and carry-on. No heavy books this trip. There was no time to linger in bookshops this time. Instead she would patiently hunt her reference materials online. Mentally she was clicking off her list, a concise book on Rome, a guidebook of the Villa Borghese, one of the Colosseum, and then two from Florence addressing the Palazzo Pitti and the Galleria dell'Accademia. She stopped in front of her assigned seat, 26 F, and quickly placed her carry-on on the seat. As she was ready to place her rollerboard in the overhead bin, a hand touched her shoulder. She turned to see a tall, handsome man with dark auburn hair and hazel eyes more green than brown. He smiled at her, showing even white teeth and a dimple to the right side of his mouth.

"Let me give you a hand with that," he said, smiling at her.

She smiled back at him and let him hoist the baggage above, storing it in the bin before he stowed his own.

He sat down next to her, stretching out his hand. "I'm Gus Wolfe."

"Lucy Cameron, nice to meet you, and thank you so much for taking care of my luggage."

"Heading to Charleston then?"

"Yes, home after almost three weeks in Europe. You?"

"Same. I was in Paris for a little more than a week. A guy that owns the real estate company that I work for has a house there. It used to be owned by Diana Mitford, and it is awesome. Original chandeliers and everything; the furnishings are a little over the top, and I felt like I was living the life of the rich and famous."

"That's pretty amazing. I met her sister a few years ago, Diana Mitford's, that is. The Dowager Duchess of Devonshire, an extraordinary woman. She lives at Chatsworth in Derbyshire and does everything in an exceptional manner, including raising chickens. Those sisters were amazing."

"So Her Grace was gracious?"

"Yes, ever so much." Lucy laughed. "In fact, after I returned, I sent thank-you notes to all of the people we met at the program. I had taken a picture out of her dining room window and for once had perfectly captured my subject, a beautiful *jet d'eau* with bright geraniums in the foreground. Don't you know a month later I received a thank-you for my thank-you, and she said she did not have a photo from that angle, and she thanked me and signed it 'Debo.' I was very touched and honored."

He smiled at her and asked her if she was from Charleston. She said yes, born and bred. She told him about her journey, leaving out anything having to do with Sam. He laughed at her anecdotes, and they realized they had many acquaintances and a few friends in common. Before she knew it, the plane was descending, dropping in the air, and circling for the airport. He gave her his business card and asked her if he could call her. She said absolutely and that her number was in the book.

She walked out of the airport. It was twilight, and the warm November day was cooling off, but she could smell home, the smell of pluff mud and the paper mill. He asked her where she lived, and when she said downtown, he inquired if he could give her a ride. He lived in Canonborough, so her house was on the way. She thanked him politely, but told him she had already arranged for a friend to come get her and she was probably circling around right now. He said he'd wait to make sure her friend showed up. They chatted for fifteen minutes, and he offered her his services again. The Honda Civic sidled up to the curb, and Katie lowered the window.

"Hi, Lucy, I hope you haven't been waiting too long."

Lucy introduced Gus to Katie. He asked Katie to pop the trunk, and he placed Lucy's rollerboard inside. Lucy thanked him again, and he answered that he would be calling her soon.

After unpacking, she called Gabriella and thanked her for running the shop and said she would be in in the morning, why didn't she take a much-deserved week off, with pay, of course? She called Diana and inquired if she could pop by to pick up her big woof, as Diana and Weston had busted him out of the big house the day before. Yes, please come by, Diana said. She unzipped her bag and pulled out the silk scarf in a shade of cobalt blue for Diana and a paisley tie for Weston, items she had purchased in the market in Florence before she and Maeve had boarded the train.

She handed Diana and Weston their gifts and hugged Toulouse to her. He had enjoyed his day spent with Annabel, Diana and Weston's golden retriever. Lucy gave them an abbreviated version of her trip before acknowledging that she was whipped and had just hit the wall. Weston said the tie was perfect and told her not to worry about Toulouse, as he had had a big day in the park playing fetch.

Diana thanked her and was happy to see the sparkle back in her friend's eyes, even though she noticed that there were tired lines around her eyes and her mouth.

Chapter 16

"Mr. Wicham is blessed with such happy manners as may ensure His Making friends—whether he may be equally capable of retaining them, is less certain."

Pride and Prejudice, Jane Austen

It was almost Thanksgiving, and Ben and Sebastian were planning a holiday feast for thirty of their closest friends. The guests would arrive by three, and dinner would be served buffet-style in Ben's backyard. He was proud of all the progress he had made to the 1940s house he had purchased in Park Circle. This was the first of many entertainments that he would host. Those closest to him were begging for him to throw a game-night party where they would play Cranium, Pictionary, or Operation. Diana and Lucy were partial to a game named Moody that had to have been invented by girls because the straight men never seemed to be able to win. It was all about tone of voice and identifying moods. As Ben was looking over menu items, his cell phone rang.

"Hey Lucy, what's my favorite girl up to? Yup, I am. I am going over the menu now. Sure, I'd love you to bring a broccoli casserole, and sweetheart, can you come early and help us? Sebastian already agreed to help. It's going to be casual, but I just want everything to go well. Absolutely you should bring Gus. It will give us all a chance to meet him and see if he's good enough for you. Oh, he'll be coming from Columbia, I see. Well of course you should ride over with Sebastian. Then Gus can take you home."

Lucy hung up the phone. She loved the holidays, and it all started with Thanksgiving. She hadn't asked if Sam and his Jess would be there. She didn't want to know. No, Sam was probably headed to Salem, back home with his family, many cousins, and friends.

Sebastian and Lucy arrived at Ben's at eleven, thinking that they would have enough time to prepare everything. The house was in a state of turmoil, as Ben hadn't finished the cleaning or the vacuuming. His vintage front-load washer that he had found on Craigslist had backed up and overrun, leaving dirty water throughout the kitchen and down the hall. He had not noticed that the water had continued its flow as he was cleaning the bedrooms. He had tried to push the door to, and the grommets would not set. He finally turned off the water valve, and the small waterfall trickled to a halt. Now he was on his hands and knees, sopping up the lake that spread before him with his best towels ineffectually swishing water back and forth.

Sebastian looked at Ben. "This, my friend, is why I rent. Now why don't you tell me where my Shop-Vac is, and we'll clean this up."

Ben started cursing and noted that all of his plans were critically behind and there was no way they could ever get everything done in time, and exactly why did Sebastian have the Shop-Vac, and the best power tools, when he didn't own his own house? There was no way he could now make his mother's favorite casseroles, the Carolina Gold rice that he had purchased for ten dollars a pound, his grandmother's oyster dressing, or the recipe for collards that he loved so much from the Junior League's cookbook. Lucy said nothing about how collards needed to be started early. Instead she looked around for a telephone, realizing almost immediately that Ben no longer had a landline.

"Ben, baby, give me your cell phone."

She soon had enlisted Ella, Violet, and Rachel to whip up casseroles of all kinds, squash, green bean, and sweet potato. She dialed Katie, and when she got her voice mail, she crossed her fingers, asking her to make six packages of Uncle Ben's instant rice. She then dialed Drew and Sheff. Yes, they could bring the corn bread dressing. In fact, Drew had just purchased fresh Folly River oysters. No problem, and yes, there would be plenty.

"Okay, guys. We're set. I'll start on the front rooms."

She picked up newspapers and magazines and threw them into paper bags and stored them under the bed in the spare bedroom. She quickly looked at the DVDs and removed all the adult material and filled another bag. She vacuumed the gleaming oak floors and mopped them, marveling at Ben's color choices of burnt sienna and warm beige. His grandmother's Arts and Crafts furniture suited the room, the settee with a warm, worn leather seat facing the fireplace and the two chairs sitting companionably across from it. The bookcases were lovely, and their hardware was reminiscent on a small scale of what she had seen at the Isaac Bell House in Newport. The Stickley dining room table was dressed with an Art-Nouveau-style table runner, and he had placed a bouquet of autumn leaves and fresh flowers on it that complemented the space. Within an hour and a half, the rooms looked tidy and clean. The men had finally finished cleaning and were straightening up the kitchen. Ben mentioned something about the bath. Sebastian looked at Lucy when he heard Ben curse at the top of his lungs.

"The tub's backed up now. What am I going to do?" Ben hollered.

Lucy and Sebastian peered in the bathroom. Sebastian said, "Just flush the toilet and see if it's okay. Maybe it's not tied into the same line."

The toilet flushed without incident. The three were crammed into the small space, standing on the original basket weave black-and-white tile. Lucy marveled at the sleek lines of the new sink and toilet that Ben had bought at the year-end sale of the expensive store on East Bay Street." Why don't you try it again, just in case?"

Again the toilet flushed. Ben wanted to try it for good measure, and it worked. Sebastian turned on the sink. The water burped and gurgled and then ran freely.

"Well, as long as our friends can use the toilet and wash their hands, you're good." The friends eyed each other and began laughing uncontrollably.

Ben shook his head and said he needed to bail out the tub and he needed a cocktail. Sebastian and Lucy found themselves in the kitchen, and amidst nervous giggles, they started going over the menu. Sebastian noted that all they really needed to do was fry the two turkeys, place the hams in the oven to heat them up, and boil the shrimp. He had brought all the salad fixings, and it would take them no time at all. After all, it was an hour and a half until showtime.

Rachel came in at 2:00 p.m. carrying a squash casserole in hand; she told Lucy and Sebastian that she had spoken to Ben about sharing the tasks. Cooking for a large group was no easy feat, but he had refused wanting it to go just the way he wanted. Men, just typical. Sebastian asked her to not be so harsh.

Lucy was making the roux for the gravy, hoping that Katie had gotten the message and wouldn't be late. Ben was in the yard, checking the plates and napkins. He had spent last night polishing the silver, starching the tablecloths, and folding napkins. Now they were bundled together in fan folds with raffia attaching them together. The white tablecloths from his grandmother topped the makeshift serving tables of sawhorses and plywood. He had borrowed some outdoor furniture, and the tables were set with white linens and a low centerpiece of rosemary, popcorn berries, and coleus with their leaves of lime green and burgundy. It would be fine; he just knew it.

Rachel was making pitchers of Bloody Marys, adding fresh parsley and cilantro from her garden, and Sebastian and Lucy scoured the cupboards for alcohol to flavor their sauce. Sebastian held up a bottle of Drambuie for Lucy's inspection, and they laughed together as she added a smidgen. He said it tasted wonderful and added a few more drops. At last the concoction was perfect, and the three friends nodded to one another. The hams were cooking, the turkeys frying, and all was well.

By three o'clock guests were slowly trickling in. They nibbled hummus and pita chips, crab dip, and crackers and shrimp. Katie showed at three thirty an enormous bowl of rice in hand. Lucy thanked her profusely and said it was the best team effort ever. Thank God for the pies that Ben's widowed neighbors had baked, pecan, pumpkin, and Key lime. Lucy found herself whipping cream with a whisk as Sebastian placed ice cream in a glass bowl. They looked at each other, giggled, and she pirouetted toward him, whisk in hand, and he kissed her firmly on the mouth.

"It was all serendipity how it worked out, wasn't it?"

"Absolutely," she laughed.

By five thirty the group had dwindled to twenty, and they were throwing horseshoes even though the light was dim and the full moon rose like a large butterscotch Tootsie Pop in the sky. Diana and Weston had arrived, and Rachel, Diana, Lucy, and Katie were placing out the games. The air had turned cool, and Katie, always the Girl Scout, built a brilliant fire in the hearth.

Gus arrived a little after seven, as he had driven from Columbia, where his family lived. He said hello to the guests, seeking out Lucy. He found her in the kitchen talking quietly with Sebastian. They were washing dishes in the sink, and Gus couldn't help but notice the new stainless steel dishwasher and wondered why they weren't putting it to use.

Yes, he told Lucy, he had had a wonderful time with his family. His mother had made a nouvelle variation of Thanksgiving, and they had eaten at one. No, he hadn't rushed back, but was glad he came, as he knew several people there.

"You know how this city is," he said. "You could see people every day and then not see them for years." He offered to dry so that Sebastian could store the dried dishes.

Sebastian whispered as he passed her, "Those midlands people sure eat early."

Lucy smiled at him and shook her head. She was suddenly lost in her conversation with Gus. He was smart and witty, and he was always paying attention to her needs. He was engaging and complimented her, and she felt that he found her not attractive, but pretty.

The crowd had moved inside, and they heard the others selecting teammates for Cranium. Rachel walked into the kitchen and told them that they were playing with five teams of four and it just might get a little crazy. Lucy filled the sink with hot water and soap, soaking the rest of the pots and pans. The casserole dishes were lined up on the clean kitchen table, as was the platter that belonged to Drew and Sheff. Katie's rice bowl lay neatly beside it.

Sebastian entered the dining room and said, "My friends, rue it and weep, for the scullery crew is about to whip some ass."

Ben reminded Sebastian that he had an architect and an historian on his team, so he wasn't worried, not in the least. Lucy giggled, thinking that her team would be pretty amazing, Sebastian, a tenth-grade social studies teacher, knew everything from ancient history to current events. Gus could act out scenes in detail, and she could draw even with her eyes closed.

"Who's our fourth?" Lucy inquired? She hadn't seen him, but she felt him. He was leaning nonchalantly against the wall. His mouth was drawn in a hard line that she referred to as the stick mouth, and he was eyeing her, or maybe Gus, with the stink eye.

"Actually, Ben, I really can't stay that long, so perhaps, since Sebastian's team is so good, they don't need a fourth."

Ben was horrified. All the teams were diverse and had strengths. He couldn't imagine Sam's rudeness. "Sam, they need the fourth. Otherwise it's not fair, you know that."

Lucy looked at the two friends and said, "Sam, either you are in or out, your pleasure, but we will win regardless, and if you're not happy to join our little party of three, we will just assume that you have too much prejudice against us for some stupid reason."

Weston let out a sigh. "Can somebody tell me what's going on? This is a game. That's it. Let's play."

Ben added, "Sam, you knew we were going to play. Let's just get on with it."

Lucy didn't see his Jess. She was still mad at him and didn't care if he stayed or left.

Sam angled near the group of three and said, "Fine, I'm in."

Sebastian, ever cheerful, hugged his friend and said, "The holidays make us all a little crazy."

They were winning. Sebastian had spelled "rhododendron" backwards, Lucy had drawn "rat race" successfully with her eyes closed, Gus had expertly acted out Britney Spears, and Sam had answered "Seeker," the position that Harry Potter played in Quidditch. The group was laughing at their own foibles, and the house was filled with a sense of mirth.

By ten thirty the game was over, and the party broke up. Lucy saw Sam look at her crossly as Gus opened the car door for her. Getting in, she shook her head and thought that that boy from Salem still had too much power over her.

Gus said that he had a good time, but what was it with Sam O'Hara? It wasn't as if he'd been drinking. Why had he been so rude, and how did she, Lucy, know him? Lucy said that they were all friends, but that she and Sam were not that close, and yes, he did get on her nerves. Sometimes he was just plain rude and annoying. Gus mentioned that he had known Sam when Sam was in college, as Gus had been in the same fraternity, but he had graduated a handful of years before. He was a bit proud then, and in fact, Gus had tried to help him out with a business deal after Sam's grandmother had passed on, but Sam was disdainful of the idea—just like a Yankee—and then Gus found out that Sam had met with the investors and they'd backed him for a separate, very successful, small real estate venture and hadn't included Gus. That's just not how it worked. What a bastard.

Lucy felt a headache coming on. It was frustrating that she had feelings for Sam, and now Gus was just wearing her last nerve to a frazzle with his "poor me" story. Sam wouldn't have done that. If she knew anything at all of Samuel O'Hara, it was that he did not speak poorly of others.

She remembered one night when they had dined on Sullivan's Island and she told him of the one rude Ann Taylor sales associate who had been mean to Violet during the end-of-the-season sale. She had told Sam she knew who this woman, "Cherie," was, and can you believe it, she had been a pole dancer at lunch at that nasty strip club on King Street Extension, and all the boys called her "Cherry." She had laughed out loud, but then later, as they walked on the beach with the phosphorous gleaming the small waves white and the stars beckoning from the heavens, Sam chastised her nicely and said you never knew how people arrived at certain destinations in their lives and you never knew the journey they needed to take. He said this while holding their shoes in one hand and her hand in the other. Lucy was quiet that night, feeling just terrible for what she thought was a silly story. She had become quiet and hadn't said a word over the two bridges and then home. Now as she and Gus headed home, she thought about that night and how Sam had later apologized for being so straightforward. He had taken her into his arms tenderly and kissed her into oblivion and then had made her reach new heights of splendor.

No, she thought, *Something is wrong with Gus's story.*

She was quiet as Gus pulled into the driveway, and she got out of the car before it had pulled to a true stop. He shut off the car and armed it. He walked her to the stoop and took her keys from her hand and opened the door. She wondered what was with the key thing, first Sam and now Gus. She had never had men take the keys from her hand and open her front door for her before. She hurt. Her head was shattering off in a million pieces. Something was very wrong, wrong indeed. She told Gus she didn't feel well and he should go. Toulouse came running and started barking, causing the new neighbors' dogs to start a Stravinsky concert. She didn't want him here; she couldn't explain it. Before she knew what was happening, her new neighbors were in the house. She knew he was a doctor—tall, gifted, smart, and handsome with almost black hair and dark blue eyes, straight, strong nose, eyebrows like wings, and a sensual mouth. His wife was beautiful, an artist whom she had taken classes with at the Gibbes. She heard him say something like "drugs," and she shook her head in the negative before all went black.

She woke feeling woozy and sick. She didn't remember Bennett telling Aslyn that it would be quicker if he took Lucy in the car to the ER, what with the holiday and the amount of wrecks, domestic disputes, et cetera. He had given Gus a scathing glance and asked him to leave, giving his wife of five years Lucy's keys after locking the house. It was 11:30 p.m., and the hospital had been relatively quiet. Lucy remembered in a haze that two doctors, one male, one female, had discussed whether they should pump her stomach or give her charcoal. She remembered being sick and smelling a terrible smell, and her tongue had tasted awful. She was exhausted, and her heart raced, and she started to cry because she felt so miserable.

What seemed very soon after, she heard Bennett's quiet, deep voice. "Okay, girl, we're going home."

It was 6:00 a.m., and the ER had been steadily filling up. She was no longer in any type of danger and was allowed to go. She slept woozily in the car and brooked no resistance when Bennett told her she would be staying in their guest room. She nodded her head solemnly, grateful that, yet again, God and the universe had given her sanctuary. Aslyn looked worried, but it did not diminish her beauty. She was tall, with a heart-shaped face, strong cheekbones, and eyes that turned from green to gold. Her hair was a natural shade of auburn that swept past her shoulders. Lucy had met them soon after she returned from the continent, and she recalled that Aslyn looked like a younger Julianne Moore, but even more beautiful.

Aslyn's cool hand was pressed against Lucy's forehead. She held a bag of frozen peas to Lucy's neck. "How bad do you feel, Lucy?"

"My head hurts terribly, my throat is so sore, and my stomach hurts. I don't remember what happened. Toulous was going to bite Gus, then the two of you were there, and then nothing."

"We were sitting outside enjoying the evening when we heard Toulouse make the most unbelievable growl—we hear everything with your windows open. We ran over, and Bennett was furious when he saw your eyes all dilated, and then you almost passed out. He wasn't sure what was wrong with you, but decided that you needed to go the emergency room immediately. He drove you himself, not wanting to wait for an ambulance since we're so close to the hospital. You've been here with us the entire day, Toulouse too. We didn't want you to be alone. Bennett's checked your vitals, and he wants to know who was at the party. He's sleeping right now, as he was up with you all night. Someone gave you what was probably a date rape drug."

Lucy shook her head. "Who would do that? It was my pack last night, all my favorite people, no one new."

"What about that Gus guy? He's new, isn't he?"

"Yes, he is, but I don't think he would compromise his position in the community like that, and we've not been seeing each other that long. So that doesn't make sense."

Aslyn perked her ears. The twins, well, not really twins, Irish twins not quite a year apart, were stirring from their nap. She looked at Lucy and was ready to apologize that she needed to leave her and check on them.

Lucy took her hand and said, "You need to check on your pack. The little ones are waking. I need to rest for a while, and I want to thank you so much for caring for me."

Aslyn beamed her smile and squeezed Lucy's hand. "If it's okay with you, I'm going to feed my brood. They're always so hungry."

"Aslyn, after they eat, will you bring them in here, and maybe I could read to them?"

"Absolutely."

Lucy closed her eyes and worried her brow. None of her friends would ever do that, slip her a Mickey. That was crazy. She thought again about the strange feelings she had had for Gus at the end of the evening, that she didn't like him much. She needed to listen to her gut and not her heart, and even her heart wasn't that excited. No, something was wrong there. Her boy was beside her, licking the cool bag of peas and her face. Within an hour the children, Liam, three, and Marguerite, two, were on both sides with Toulouse, yawning at her feet. She read to them, stroked their beautiful faces, his a likeness of his father with dark hair and eyes a deep shade of green, and hers like her mother's with a cerulean gaze and an auburn cap of hair.

By eight o'clock that night, Lucy felt she had overstayed her welcome. Yes, she was fine. She would call them tomorrow. She thanked them for their kindness and went quietly next door with Toulouse by her side. She wanted to call Diana and tell her what happened, but in the end, she kept her own counsel. She would not bad-mouth Gus because she could not prove that he had done anything wrong.

Chapter 17

The Grand Essentials of happiness are: something to do, something to love and something to hope for...

Allan K. Chalmers

Thanksgiving had been early this year, so she still had two weeks before she prepared for Christmas. Her dad and Rut would be coming in the middle of December. Her father had a business meeting, something to do with a nonprofit leadership program, and they would celebrate Christmas early at her house, just the three of them.

Maeve had hammered out her dissertation while in Orvieto and was scheduled to defend it in the spring. Her professors were thrilled that she had finished her dissertation in not quite three years' time. One commented that it was not unusual for that to happen, though, with students who had been in the real world for a while. They knew what they wanted and set out to attain their goals. Maeve was happy about her topic and felt that it would open up new scholarship of her favorite author. She enthusiastically explained to Lucy that Italy had opened the floodgates and she was good now. Strong, yes. In fact, she believed all her past misgivings were based on anxiety, and Italy had cured her of that, and she hoped it was for good. She and Lucy needed to confront their past, and she felt that if she spent a week in Charleston, they could do just that.

Besides, that was when Grandmere would be celebrating her big day. She was getting older, and she wanted a large family gathering at the house on Legare Street. Maeve would be there. No, she was sure to come, as Grandmere had told her she would be eighty-seven soon and she wanted a celebration with all of her family, not just the ones who were a bit pretentious, but her dearest granddaughters. And wasn't it just wonderful that Aurora and Georg would be there, too, as he was conducting one of his pieces at the Kennedy Center in December?

Sam didn't like the idea of Lucy seeing Gus. In fact, he just didn't understand what she could possibly find attractive in him. He had always been a shifty, self-absorbed ass. He was a taker, and he would take from Lucy. Sam knew that too well from the past. He knew that he had treated Lucy poorly, and he felt bad about that, carrying on with her while he was trying to figure things out with Jess. At least he had tried to be kind when they had the talk.

He still felt guilty when he remembered that last night. He had held her in his arms, thinking that it would offer her comfort. He had never intended to kiss her, but when she looked at him and he saw the pain in her big dark green eyes, he found himself lost in her odd, old-fashioned beauty. She had always been too good to him, always so generous of her time, her cooking, her body. He could not forget her laugh or her creativity, whether she was working on a project or in the bedroom. He tried not to think about her body, how it fit so perfectly to his own, how she would stretch like a cat and watch him with her eyes half closed. He wondered if she had succumbed to Gus's personality. He had to admit Gus always charmed the women, whether college coeds or their mothers.

He would never forget, when he was in college, how Gus had ruined his own girlfriend's mother's reputation. Gus was twenty-six and had secured his real estate license. He had enough charm and business sense that he was becoming quite successful with his clients. He met the older woman through an acquaintance, and she was easily impressed by his confidence, good looks, and charm. She was forty-four, pretty, sad, depressed, and married to a philanderer who drank too much and served on City Council. Her daughter lived in Harleston Village and rarely saw her parents, as she blamed them for her own life's dysfunction. Gus had carried on with the woman for more than six months in her South Battery Colonial Revival house during the afternoon, after she had completed her daily volunteer commitments with the Junior League, the art museum, and the hospital.

She referred to him as her young friend and introduced him to contacts, friends, and neighbors who all connected him to others, increasing his financial largesse. That hadn't been enough for Gus. He'd eyed the framed photographs on the elegant sunporch of the house and memorized the images of Charlotte's only child, Emily. He met Emily, wooed her, and two-timed both of them at the same time. Emily was besotted with him. She had told Sam how she hoped that Gus was the one because she was smitten with him.

Around Christmas, Emily had stopped by the house and let herself in, meaning to retrieve a dress to wear to a fancy party to which Gus had invited her. She assumed her parents were out as they always were that time of day. She heard a noise in the guest room and saw that the door was not shut properly. Assuming the worst, that there was an intruder in the house, she had quietly peered around the corner of the door, and in the reflection of a mirror, she saw her mother in Gus's arms, with Gus taking his pleasure as he had with her. She was outraged and shocked to see them together. She quietly let herself out the back, where the door did not creak, and then raced to her car parked in front. Emily had called her father immediately, her anger so fierce, and she blurted out what she had seen, not mentioning Gus by name while hoping in her own deluded mind that Gus loved her. Emily's enemy was her mother, Charlotte, the Mrs. Lonelyhearts who had ruined her own life and others' by her deceitful and lascivious nature.

Emily had cried out the entire saga to Sam that same day, and Sam knew that Gus had seduced the mother. His heart went out to Emily, but he felt sorry for her mom, who had always been so very nice to him, hoping that he and her darling daughter, as she had put it, would have a lovely and successful life together, not realizing that they were just friends.

A tearful Emily had told Sam a month later that, when she confronted Gus about the seduction of her mother—Mrs. Robinson—and herself, Gus had implied that her mother was a finer person in all aspects, including the bedroom, and that he had simply been tempted by viewing her picture-perfect image in her own parents' house. Emily transferred that following semester to Wofford, where she lost many credits, as she had been in her senior year. It took her an additional year to finish, and then she'd left the state altogether to start a new life in Atlanta. Gus had never been exposed, as Charlotte would not tell her husband the name of her young lover. Her life was in public ruin; she'd fled to her parents' home in rural Kershaw County and was divorced within a year, in accordance with South Carolina law.

Emily's father remarried a woman seven years older than Emily nine months after the divorce. The marriage was held on Folly Beach with a justice of the peace and the reception held in the house and yard of a post-Hurricane Hugo beach house with outrageous turrets that could sleep eighteen. The younger Mrs. Robinson was a natural beauty with a scheming mind and little class or education. She kept father from daughter at any holiday or gathering. In the end, Emily had said it was for the best, as her father had a penchant for anger and now blamed Emily for all his misfortune. His new wife had brought no connections nor money to the table and was quickly running through the funds he had worked hard for and inherited as well. His life was now one where he would return to managing his insurance company to pay for her unneeded augmentations, excess jewelry, and twice-a-week visits to the spa for a massage, a seaweed wrap, or the like.

To Sam's knowledge both mother and daughter were still estranged due to Gus and his nature. Besides this sordid narrative from Emily—Sam heard from her several times a month—he later discovered that, during the divorce proceedings, Gus had used the older woman's credit card and charged ten thousand dollars' worth of merchandise, trips, electronics, and clothes, in order to seduce others, and the game had continued.

There was another tale amidst this saga, one that related to Sam and Gus. Gus had told Sam about a potential business deal the summer after Sam had finished college, but there seemed to be a great deal of smoke and mirrors. Eventually Sam handled things in his own way and on his own. He had learned a great deal from Gus, mostly what not to do.

Sam was finished with his thoughts. He ambled to his refrigerator and realized the last of the milk had gone sour, the cheese was moldy, and the rest was simply what single guys kept—cereal and condiments.

Lucy looked in the fridge and made a list. She talked out loud while Puccini's *Turandot* played softly in the background. "Hmm. Toulouse, we have a problem. We have condiments and very little else. You must thank your lucky stars, darling, as I never run your food out. So, Dad and Rut will arrive in two days, and I must go to the store, but first, a list. Okay, buddy, here's the deal: shrimp for an appetizer, broccoli casserole, Cornish game hens. We have raspberry vinaigrette for the marinade."

She looked at the expiration date and smiled, noting that it was still good. She would mix it with raspberry jam and spices and lavish it on the birds.

"We'll do new potatoes with rosemary rather than rice, cognac gravy, salad from the garden, and then we'll make oyster stuffing; oh yes, and carrots for you. Ahhh...dessert. I am not getting out my torch this year for crème brûlée. This year we will go to Saffron and see what treats they have to offer."

Toulouse leaned his strong frame into her, and she patted his shaggy head. She would buy fresh head-on shrimp from the shrimp lady on the corner. Eggs, bacon, and bread, muffin mix, she mumbled, would come from the PIG. They would be going out to dinner one evening, so she only had the two meals to plan.

She pulled into the parking lot of the Piggly Wiggly on Meeting Street with her list in hand. After locking the car, she looked up and admired the azure blue sky with the puffs of cumulus clouds. She watched as one cloud turned from the shape of what appeared to be a sheep to quickly change into the form of a large rabbit. She giggled to herself thinking that life and all its glory was just wonderful.

***

Sam felt her before he saw her. He felt her energy, and he knew it was Lucy. She had a way about her that exuded confidence, happiness, and absolute joy. He watched her from the produce aisle as she said hello to many of the staff. He remembered, *That's Lucy, always waving and smiling and saying something nice to everyone.* She was in her head, he noticed how she smiled when picking out portabello mushrooms and then disappeared and reappeared rapidly filling her basket along the way. He had forgotton how quickly she moved with grace and decisiveness. His own basket was empty save for the bananas that he had placed there before he felt her in the store. He had always admired how she never used a shopping cart but could pack a basket like no one's business. She was curious like that.

He asked her once why she didn't use a cart, and she'd said, *"Sam, doesn't that seem so old and fuddy-duddy? People with shopping carts always seem so bogged down. A shopping basket is freeing, and if you run into someone you don't want to speak with, you can just act like you came for simply a can of soup and be on your way."*

He remembered her laugh that day, and he had asked her if that truly was the case. She hemmed and hawed and said well, actually, she had dated this man who was totally unsuitable for her, another engineer—what was it with engineers? She used to run into him regularly, and he would follow her to the checkout. Thank goodness she only had a shopping basket. As it was, she had spent forty-five minutes listening to him talk to her about a project that he was working on, another development on John's Island of loops and cul de sacs, where an urban dweller would use half a tank of gas only to find oneself at the same cul de sac that you had left thirty minutes previously, with clear-cut lots and enough vinyl siding to kill the world.

She was now headed for the checkout, and Sam wanted to follow her. His intentions were to tell her about Gus. She thanked the clerk, thanked the bagger, and picked up her Whole Foods bags covered with illustrations of coffee and mugs. The bags must have weighed almost thirty pounds, yet she threw them over her shoulder effortlessly and jauntily walked out of the store.

He followed after her and was stopped at the door by the security guard. "Sir, do you plan to pay for those?"

Sam looked down and noticed the bananas in his basket. He placed the shopping basket down and said, "I'll be right back." As he exited, he saw the flash of the Karmann Ghia's brake lights. He picked up his pace, only to see her pull out and turn onto Spring Street. He jumped on his bike, knowing he'd catch up with her at the light. It always seemed that the light at Spring and King Streets remained red for eternity. It was now imperative that they should talk. The light turned green, and Lucy's car disappeared.

He went back to the store and picked up his bananas and finished his other purchases. Stupid, just plain stupid. After putting away his purchases, he ambled about his house and decided he needed to get on his bike and head to Hampton Park. He needed to cycle and get his frustration out and let the park soothe his edginess. He didn't know why it was so important to tell Lucy about Gus. It just was.

Lucy unpacked her groceries, storing them in the refrigerator and in the cabinets. It was four o'clock, and the December light was starting to fade. She had an hour's time to walk Toulouse before dark. Toulouse happily walked alongside Lucy to the park, with his bobbed tail wagging all the way. They admired the cassia and its yellow blossoms. The sasanquas were in full bloom, and the camellias were everywhere she looked. She ticked off the names in her head: Pink Perfection, Alba, and her favorite, Betty Sheffield Blush. They stopped in the east field near the gazebo, the only remnant left of the West Indian Exposition of 1902. She let Toulouse off of his lead and threw the tennis ball to him with her

Chuckit! Toulouse could run for hours. Lucy needed to tire him out since he had been filled with boundless energy earlier. As she threw the ball, she noted that they had the run of the park. There were just a handful of joggers and no one else. Toulouse was frantic for the ball, so she pitched the ball high in the air and was temporarily blinded by the waning light of the sun. She didn't see Toulouse and started calling his name. It was time to give up their game and head home. Toulouse was happily barking, and she noticed a familiar figure walking his bike and talking to her dog.

What on earth is he doing here? she thought.

Sam looked at Lucy, smiled, and said hello. Toulouse was licking his hand and nudging his head against Sam's leg. "I thought that was you. I saw the two of you while I was lapping the park."

"Hello, Sam, how are you?" Lucy said stiffly.

"I'm well. Listen, Lucy, I wondered if I could talk to you?"

Her hair was shorter, and her cheekbones looked razor sharp. The look suited her, and he noticed how her pink-tinged mouth was so full in her heart-shaped face.

"Don't you think we've said enough to one another? What could we possibly talk about now?"

"I want to talk to you about Gus. I know the two of you are seeing each other, but I need to tell you that I've known him for about ten years, and he is just bad news. Everything he does is tinged with malice, and I think you should know that he is just not honorable, and I really don't want to see him hurt you."

"Really?" she intoned critically, cocking her head to the side while pursing her mouth at him. "Well this is certainly rich. And tell me, Samuel O' Hara, just who exactly promoted you to become the CEO of my personal life? And exactly why, in your infinite wisdom, would you think you might advise me as to whom I should see?"

"Look, Lucy, I don't want to argue, all right? I just think it's important for you to know what's gone on in the past."

The sky was turning the dark, rich blue hue of a Crayola crayon, while clouds tinged with reds and golds were streaking through. It would be twilight soon and then full dark. She looked hard at him. Anger tinged her cheeks pink.

"Look, Sam, Toulouse and I need to head home, and I really don't want to continue this conversation."

She turned her back on him and stalked off. Sam stared at her retreating form, noticing that she looked good in her little jeans. He shook his head thinking he just didn't want her to be hurt. He knew he had hurt her, and she had been hurt before by the guy she called the not-boyfriend. He had to admit she was right; it wasn't any of his business who she dated. He would go home. The temperature had dropped, and it was almost dark. Jessica was working late at the hospital, so he would eat alone, again.

Lucy was furious. She stalked home, walked up the stairs to the stoop, and walked back down. Still fuming, she walked Toulouse to the Ashley River, hoping that the sight of the cool water and the full moon would temper her anger. The bastard, she thought, rat bastard, who did he think he was to tell her about Gus? She didn't care about him. Although he had called several times after "the incident," she refused to see Gus.

In fact, one evening not so long ago, she watched *Pride and Prejudice*, and when Lizzie said to Wickham, *"Go, go. I will not have you back,"* she, Lucy, ensconced in her den dressed in dark teal-colored flannel pajamas with black velvet-covered buttons and bows on the cuffs, intoned those same words in reference to Gus in between taking bites from her rocky road ice cream. Funny, in all of her life, she had never eaten anything while lounging on the sofa. Barwicks and Camerons just did not eat anywhere else but at the dining room table. She wanted to say those same words now, but she couldn't. She had wasted too much time in Praha and Roma on that man from Salem, Mass. She just could not possibly expend more energy upon him. For all she cared, he could hole up in his private man-cave and draw hieroglyphs. In fact, after the Gus Wolfe disaster, she was temporarily steering clear of men. Three for three. Cooked, fried, done.

Lucy's father and Rut had flown in a day early, on Wednesday night, and had taken her to dinner Thursday at Cypress, where they enjoyed exceptional food, wine, and service. On Friday they had dined at Rue de Jean, where Lucy ordered the mussels in cauliflower sauce, and her father ordered the steak with pommes frites and Rut the duck confit. They spoke of politics and the possibility of a woman or an African-American man being president. Her father was encouraged, as he thought that the nation was ready for a change. Rut was thoughtful and complimentary to her, and she noted that her father's relationship with him was one of respect and love.

She reveled in their company on early Saturday afternoon when she served up her special dinner at her house at two thirty in keeping with Charleston tradition. She had ironed her mother's damask tablecloth, and the napkins were folded to emulate the bird-of-paradise flower. She brought out the Cameron silver that her father had given her so many years ago and polished it until it shone brightly. Her father noted that, for December, her cottage garden was quite colorful, and her grass was almost perfect. He reminded her that he thought grass was far more difficult than other plant materials, and he was proud that she soldiered on and hadn't hardscaped it all.

They spoke about her trip to Rome, and Rut surprised her with all of his knowledge. He was a retired orthopedist who loved travel, good wine, and good food. He was also knowledgeable when it came to history and the arts, and like the few other surgeons she knew, he painted on the side. He reminded Lucy that he and her father, John, had met in Rome so many years ago, a few years after Lucy's mother's death. They had struck up a conversation while they were viewing the Colosseum, each traveling alone. John was trying to sort out his grief, and Rut, short for Rutherford, was simply enjoying a much-needed vacation away from his job, his life, and the demands of the HMOs. It was curious how they had so much in common, and then six months later, after a great deal of correspondence, John had visited Rut in San Francisco, where he lived and practiced medicine for Kaiser. John, with his studies at the Citadel and his training in the army, had closed that closet door, and it was Rut who had patiently taught him that this lifestyle was not an aberration, and when you were given the chance to love again, you should take it. It had taken John a little longer, but in the end, he knew where his path lay.

Lucy knew they had always been faithful, just like her dad had been faithful to her mother so long ago. Lucy asked the two of them if they had told Maeve about her father's feelings towards their mother before he came out of the closet. No, why would they? Maeve had been a part of their household before she went to college; surely she knew. No, she didn't, and Lucy told them about the conversation she and Maeve had had while staying at Lake Tahoe. The two men, both handsome in their midsixties, looked perplexed and sighed.

John said, "I made a mess of things. I suppose I thought she knew. Before I met Rut, there was no one for me but your mother, and when she died, I felt I would be lost forever until Rut and I began to know each other. I need to explain to Maeve that I loved your mother with all of my heart."

Rut said that he, too, had been wrong, by not explaining and he sincerely thanked Lucy for bringing this matter to their attention. They would tell Maeve when they went home.

John Cameron and his daughter Lucy walked Toulouse in the park while Rut stayed home and watched football. They passed the Citadel, and Lucy was frank as she told her father that his institution of higher learning was the absolute worst regarding historic preservation, as they had knocked down several historic structures because they weren't quite seventy-five years old and they could do so. The buildings had started failing due to the institution's lack of stewardship. He was indignant about that, as he had donated to the bell fund for Summerall Chapel, where he and Lucy's mother were married.

She told him that she loved him and that she was glad he had met Rut in Rome so many years before, as it was the city that had healed her, made her thirst for knowledge, and want yet more. Her father turned her in his arms and lifted her off the ground as he had done so many times in her childhood. He told her she was beautiful, called her his *bella* Lucinda, his life, his world. She cried and laughed at the same time and rushed to tell him about all her changes, all that she was giving up to live a happier life with tradition in tact but without the rules. She told him that this weekend had changed her too, that he and Rut made her want love and a relationship, because all of her life she had just basically goofed up, especially with the last ones.

She wanted something real, not like the relationship in one of her favorite movies *The Illusionist*, where Edward Norton's and Jessica Biel's characters get back together because their love is unbreakable, and the Philip Glass soundtrack makes you cry in such a heart-wrenching manner. No, that was the kind of love that happened in movies, very rarely in real life. What Lucy wanted was someone who had eighteen qualifications. She fished out a worn sheet of paper from her pocket and began to read her list aloud to her father. He listened as she articulated that what she wanted in a partner was a man who would share her interests and she his, everything from bike riding to the arts. She wanted someone who would be respectful and whom she could respect, someone who was financially responsible, and he must love dogs. He should want to spend time with her friends and she his, and he should be honest and true. As she read on, she finished with one sentence. "He must be physically, legally, and emotionally available."

Her father mentioned that she didn't mention money or looks.

"Dad, I've been trying to move forward with my life. I'm trying to figure it all out, and I wrote this list a while back, well, about a year and a half ago, and I've been dragging it about ever since. I don't care if he has money as long as he's responsible and pays his bills on time, and I don't care if he's handsome or not. Yes, both would be a bonus, but truly those are superficial attributes. I want someone who is basically a decent, good guy that I'll be able to have fun with, but will be responsible and will love me. I'm trying to let go of my rules, my angst, everything that holds me back. In the past I've been judgmental towards people, and to be honest, I've been a snob in a way. I'm just trying so hard, and as I've focused on the little things in life, I have felt happy beyond compare. It's as if I've had an epiphany that I need to live this life fully. I just can't surf anymore; I need to dive into the water and swim with the current, letting it carry me away to a new adventure, even if there's a riptide. Maybe, and please don't take this wrong, but maybe after Mom's death and your leaving, I bought too much into Grandmere's society?"

"Oh, darling, you have worked hard. Everything has been more relaxed this visit. You made everything so comfortable and nice, no long list of things to do or orchestrated events. Rut and I both noticed it. Even your Christmas tree was different, not as formal as it has always been, and look at you. In the past you would have dressed to the nines for dinner, and yet this time, you have been more casual, even wearing jeans and a sweater today. Rut noticed that you didn't wear your standard hat or cape when we went out to dinner. You seem much more calm, and you smile and laugh more than you ever have."

"Dad, I had help with the tree. I met the most wonderful family this summer that live in the neighborhood. They are tenants of Stella and Mack's. She, Maria, is a first-generation American. Her family is originally from Mexico, and her husband, Ernesto, is from Chile and just received his citizenship a few years ago. Suffice it to say, he's helped me with cutting down a dead water oak, and she always leaves food for me, just wonderful dishes. I had them and their two small children, Maximillian—well, we all call him Max—and Clara, who is just a darling, over to my house for dinner. I made them Low-Country dishes that were probably extremely bland compared to the spicy cuisine they provide me, and we all decorated the tree. There were no rules this year. I didn't say what I've always said—well, repeated what Grandmere always said, that too few lights would make people think you were cheap, and too many, then you might be considered nouveau riche. No, this year I threw all caution to the wind, and we all participated. One of the German erzgebirge angel's wings was broken, but that's what glue guns are for, and then little Clara dropped what I thought was my prized Käthe Wohlfahrt angel. It shattered into pieces, but I didn't mind, especially when I looked into her forlorn face after it happened. It's only stuff, right? And this learning of a new family's hardships, love, and passion to succeed in America is far more important than a glass bauble that I watched for seven ridiculous days on eBay."

He took her hand in his. "My dearest Lucy, you always have had a knack for making the most wonderful friends, and when others would have been angry about the broken ornaments, including yourself last year, it shows that you are showing progress. I do want to ask you, though, do you want to talk about your relationship with the contractor? I understand if you aren't ready to discuss it, but I'm here for you."

"Well, I'm still mad at that guy, Samuel O'Hara from the Northeast, but Charleston is so small, and we just run into each other. I have to tell you that sometimes I look at the toe of my foot, especially when I'm wearing boots, and I consider, wouldn't it feel good to connect the toe of my boot with his jaw? That would fix him or give him a good old bruise. I loved him. I was just crazy about him. I would see him, and I would think that I had never been as happy in my life in anyone else's company, but in the end, he had a former girlfriend, and she moved back, and *poof*, we were over. I must admit that's why I want to meet someone else, because somewhere out there, there is someone that will be good for me. Although I'm still hurting, I know I'll get over him. It's just a matter of time, and Dad, I'm not going to force anything like I have in the past. No square pegs in round holes."

John hugged Lucy to him. "There, there now. Anger is a healthy emotion, and you'll meet the right person, I assure you. You just need to get out there, have fun, be less serious, and you have to remember you will kiss a few frogs along the way. Not everyone is the one, so take it slowly, and date a lot."

They strolled home enjoying each other's company, and Lucy couldn't remember a more wonderful time with her father since her childhood.

They were back in San Francisco now, ensconced in their 1907 Victorian house, a painted lady furnished with a mixture of fine antiques, casual furniture, and enough books to fill a lifetime of reading. As they had promised, they spoke to Maeve together and had a three-hour discussion regarding John's marriage to their mother and the tragic accident that had changed all of their lives irrevocably. Maeve was still processing, trying to figure out how their father could not have known that he was gay, and was challenged by this generational difference. Maeve would be arriving in less than ten days to be a part of Grandmere's celebration. She would stay several days, mostly with Lucy, but a few on Legare Street. Lucy was excited to see her sister and could not wait to discuss so much that had been revealed.

Chapter 18

"Hope" is the thing with feathers –
That perches in the soul -
And sings the tune without the words -
And never stops – at all –

"Poem 254", Emily Dickinson

Business at the gallery was steady, and Lucy would meet again with Sadie. Her sister had passed, and she was ready to unload more works of art. Sadie said that her apartment was packed with second-tier items and that it looked as if it was that of a Russian émigré's, floor-to-ceiling with art and antiques. She had to unload it soon, as she was afraid she would fall over the jumble and then break a hip, and that just would not do. She had met a wonderful bridge player who happened to be a widower and was an adept dancer. You never knew what possibilities were there. It was best if Lucy came sooner rather than later and helped her sort through the lot, as she wanted to invite the gentleman for tea and to see her Christmas decorations. The extended family had taken all they wanted, and Sadie wondered how on earth did an old woman continue to end up living in chaos when, in truth, she was trying to simplify her life. Lucy had assuaged her and told her she had a friend she could suggest who would probably take the furniture. Sadie implored her to come alone first so that they could assess the goods together.

Lucy found herself on Tuesday in Sadie's comfortable apartment. The space was packed with furniture mostly in the Empire style, but High Victorian as well. Lucy looked at a huge, ostentatious bed.

"Sadie, are you going to keep that?"

"No, absolutely not, nor the dresser or that wardrobe. I would feel as if I were sleeping in a Renaissance chapel surrounded by gargoyles and buttresses. Why Cordelia loved this monstrous Victorian stuff was always a wonder to me. My taste is that of my mother's, Charleston furniture that I inherited, with its simple English lines. Darling Cordelia was never interested in that. She thought it was boring."

Lucy looked closely at the furniture before assessing the art, Charleston Renaissance pictures and an original portfolio by Alice Ravenel Huger Smith. Lucy called them all by their first names, feeling that they were her special dead friends. She came across several paintings all done by the same hand. She was not familiar with this particular artist and said so to Sadie.

"Oh, those works were done by Eola Willis. As I remember it, her story is so typical of the Gothic South. She was born to one of Beauregard's officers in the eighteen fifties. After the war, there were pitifully few men to marry, as so many had died, and she never married. Her family had a bit of money, though, and she traveled extensively abroad and then later studied under William Merritt Chase. She never married, but for over thirty years she gave a series of Lenten lectures. I think she saw herself as a scholar of art and antiquities. She lectured on ancient Italy, the Dock Street Theatre, old Charleston, and such. She was an odd bird, and I remember in my twenties, when she died, she seemed sad and old and slightly pathetic, living in a house on Tradd Street where she rented rooms. But then again, many people rented out rooms in the fifties, and the old seem horribly decrepit to the young. Thankfully, my family did not have to rent out rooms, but we rented the back houses. Mother always said that you should try to rent to those you knew, as they would be more gentle to their environs. Back to my sister's things, what are we to do with all of this?"

Lucy looked at Sadie, smiling at her. "I'm pretty sure that bedroom suite was made by Herter Brothers, and it should do well at auction, along with the sofa and settee, maybe in New York. When I was in Rhode Island for the summer school, we saw similar furniture in a few museum houses. Much of the other things will probably do well at the auction in Columbia or Asheville, while some of the smaller things, the footstools and such, can be sold locally. Why don't I call my friend and see if he can arrange it for you? He can probably store it in his warehouse until it's sorted out. I will take the art off of your hands, and especially the works of Miss Willis. Sadie, what I don't understand is, why didn't you hire an appraiser and have them handle it all?"

"Well, Cordelia's will was specific. The nieces, nephews, and my grandchildren were to go through it all after I did. They were to take what they wanted, and then Stella was to have her share too."

Lucy raised her eyebrows in amazement, wondering how Stella took care of so many of these aged ladies.

"Oh, yes, Stella kept Cordelia in perfect order. It made much more sense for me to look at the things in the light of day rather than have them stored in a dim warehouse. I don't really know what I was thinking. Maybe Cordelia had something she wanted me to see, but alas nothing."

Lucy said that perhaps they should look in the dresser and see if there was a hidden drawer. They did just that, finding a false front behind a small box built inside. They removed the front and found a locked feature.

"Hmm," Sadie said. "I wonder if any of the keys I have left still work." She fished around with the keys and found one that turned the lock; inside were packets of letters and several journals. A note lay on top.

Thank you, Sadie. It is yours alone. The story of my life. So many things you will be able to piece together if you want. It won't be a daunting task, but with the cost of your retirement and your excellent health, it just may help if you are interested. I did have a glorious many days on Earth, and you above all know how I cherished living life. Your beloved sister, Cordelia

"Oh dear. This was not at all what I expected, but then again, that was Cordelia..." Sadie noted with her voice trailing off. "Darling, let's have some tea. Now let me tell you about my gentleman. He has the most lovely manners. He's simply divine and from Richmond. He treats me with such courtesy. One of his sons lives here and another back in Virginia. I have met them both, and they are just very dear. In fact, I've asked him, my gentleman, Lucas Semmes, if he will accompany me to Lily's party, and he has agreed. Isn't that marvelous?" Sadie went on to tell her how they spent time together, playing cards, going to movies, and attending the symphony.

Lucy sipped her tea from the fragile Chamberlain's Worcester cup and agreed. "Quite wonderful, Sadie, I'm glad you've met him." She was happy for Sadie, but she couldn't help but wonder why she, Lucy, continued to be single in a world where everyone she knew was meeting someone perfect for them.

She queried Sadie more about her sister.

"Oh, Cordelia, it's hard to think of her gone, and now this." She held the documents in her hand. "She was a free spirit at a time when that was against the rules. She left Charleston and moved to California and had all sorts of affairs with powerful men and owned her own stylish boutique in Los Angeles. She came home after our mother died and moved into a beautiful house on Chapel Street at a time when many people were moving out of that neighborhood. She would throw lavish parties where the most eclectic guests were invited, including that man from England that became a woman, you know. She married at fifty in her drawing room and wore the most beautiful celadon-colored dress. Her husband, a widower, was ten years older than her, a retired Navy captain that had been stationed at the base. He adored her, and she him, and he always said that she made him exquisitely happy all of his life. Personally, I think it was because she never allowed him to become bored. She arranged what she called their play dates, and every day she had planned something amusing for the two of them. Funny, when he died last year, she said to me that she wouldn't be on this earth for long, as she needed to follow him quickly to the next life. Odd, isn't that?"

"I don't know, Sadie. Stella has said that about Mack, that when it's his time, hers will come soon after. Maybe that's what it's like if it's the love of your life. I wouldn't know."

"Lucy, don't look sad. He's there. You just haven't met him."

Lucy finished her tea, collected what works of art she could, and kissed Sadie's cheek. "I'll call you soon, and we'll have your apartment looking just right before your hot date next week."

Sadie laughed and waved to her from the door.

By Friday, Sadie's apartment was back to normal, and Lucy found herself at the historical society researching her new dead friend, Eola Willis, whose papers were part of the collection. Since she was not completely satisfied, she went online and searched for other paintings that had previously been sold and then placed a call to Huger Sinclair, knowing that he would shed light on her subject.

Diana called to remind her that she was having dinner at their house the next night. Lucy told her that, yes, of course, it was on her calendar and she had already found a bottle of champagne so they could toast the season.

"Oh, and Lucy, you don't need to dress up, but we do have another dinner guest that Weston would like you to meet."

Lucy arrived on time wearing jeans, a black sweater, and a leather jacket. Diana told her she looked perfect. Diana, always chic, was adding last-minute flourishes to the hors d'oeuvres tray, fresh rosemary and edible pansies and nasturtiums. Lucy asked her friend how her business was doing. It had been almost two weeks since they had spent time together. She also told her about Sadie and her gentleman caller.

They laughed together, and Diana said, "A girl has to work it, even if she's in the adult facility."

Lucy told her that, on her way home from seeing Sadie, she had counted six signs that said "Find Romance in Charleston," and a phone number was listed below. Wasn't that strange? So if a single person was driving alone at forty-five miles per hour, which was the legal limit, how in the world, if they indeed wanted to find romance in Charleston, how could they write down the number without causing an accident? Diana placed her palm to her forehead and began to giggle. That was a quandary, now wasn't it?

Amidst their pealing laughter, they heard a knock on the door. They were laughing so hard that tears streaked down Diana's cheeks and Lucy's face had gone completely red. Diana called to Weston to get the door, as the two friends' laughter was uncontrollable. Weston mumbled something about silliness as he opened the door.

His friend Michael entered carrying a bottle of wine. He was tall, broad-shouldered, and lean with dark eyes and dark, curly hair with a dimple on the right side of his mouth. He looked at Weston and said, "What's up with those two?"

Weston shook his head at his wife, who was softly laughing, and Lucy, who was still giggling. "Some girls never grow up, and these two can laugh at anything, and it's something about signs. Sometimes I just need some backup."

"I know what you mean. I have two sisters at home, and they are silly like that with their friends as well."

The introductions were made, and Lucy took an interest in the new architect in Weston's firm. He was witty, smart, and nice and a fan of Frank Gehry, which made Diana happy. The four enjoyed dinner of pork tenderloin, wild rice, and broccoli fresh from Diana's garden. They discussed new projects and the upcoming Carolopolis Awards that would be presented in January at the Preservation Society of Charleston's annual meeting. Weston suggested that perhaps the four of them could go to the meeting together. After all, it would be interesting to see what projects were awarded, it was always a good time, and even better, it was held at the Riviera Theatre with its Art Deco design. After dinner they played Pictionary, and Michael volunteered to drive Lucy home in his Porsche Boxster at almost one in the morning. Lucy thanked him for the ride, and he walked her to her stoop. She told him it was nice to meet him, and he said likewise. She waved good-bye and greeted Toulouse on the other side of the door.

"Toulouse, I have just met a man that I like—how nice for me—and he did not take my keys out of my hand to open my door. Hmmm. Maybe this is the respectful one. No matter, as the Five for Fighting song goes, there are plenty other fish in the sea. This time, no maniacal behavior, I will just meet people and take things as they come."

Toulouse cocked his head to the side, which made Lucy giggle.

"Okay, big boy, let's let you out, and then we will fall into the land of sleepyheads."

Lucy woke the next day. She was tired and stretched and yawned before leaping out of bed to grind the coffee beans, half hazelnut, half regular. She giggled to herself as she thought about the night before. Michael was fun, and he was relaxed yet smart, and most of all she liked that he wasn't as attentive as Sam had first been, or that creep Gus Wolfe.

She hadn't told Diana about her concerns regarding Gus. She would have to do that soon, before there was a mishap, but then again, maybe she was imagining it all. Maybe someone else had placed the Mickey in her drink thinking it was someone else's drink, but weren't those unpleasant and depressing thoughts? She shouldn't blame him truly, should she? She shook her head and decided that she would not think about it, not today.

She took her furry boy to the dog park, thinking about the list she needed to create. In three days' time, Maeve would arrive, and then her Grandmere's party two days after that, and then Christmas. It would all be a whirlwind. As she threw the ball to Toulouse, she saw the familiar red vintage Jaguar convertible that belonged to Brooks. It was a beautiful car, and it was a good thing it came with its own tool repair kit. He parked the car and entered the double gates, strode to Lucy, and hugged her.

"Listen, Lucy, girl mine, I want to introduce to someone that you absolutely must meet. He's some sort of astrophysicist, and he's fantastic, just the guy to get you over my friend, the Yankee that treated you so poorly."

She looked at Brooks, her best friend for so many years, smiled, and shook her head. "I loved that Yankee, you know, and I just hate that he's friends with all of my friends."

As she threw the nasty saliva-and-grass-encrusted ball to Toulouse, Brooks looked at her shaking his head. "That thing is just disgusting. How can he fetch for hours?"

"More like days, honey, he could just fetch for days."

Yes, Brooks was coming to Lillian's party, and he wanted to bring his new friend for Lucy to meet. Yes, she said he could bring his friend, but remember she and Maeve would be ladies-in-waiting to Lillian and her friends in their eighties and nineties, and she just did not know if she would be able to spend much time with them. But on second thought, all of their gang would be there, and they could meet him too. How did that sound? What was his name again?

"Dante. He says that after he thought about concentric circles as a young man, he started looking for stars."

"Hmm. Sounds like he has a sense of humor."

"Baby, Lucinda, you will love this guy. Everybody does."

"Brooks, exactly what does that mean?"

"I don't know. Even straight men are attracted to him."

"You?"

"No, I imagined him for you. I'm still in love with Desiree."

"You are not. Yes, she's smart and beautiful, but she's still the manipulative bitch she was at Ashley Hall more than twenty years ago. Let her go. She just divorced her third husband, is that right? Never worked at anything in her life but her beauty and feminine wiles. I imagine this guy will end up paying a pretty penny, too, just like the others. She's also had a ton of work. How many injections of Botox has she had? Clearly, we're almost forty, and that is an option, but why not embrace those fine lines that we've earned? No, Brooks, buddy, don't go there. She's hurt you too bad in the past. She's just a horrid creature who finds herself superior to others. Truly, when has she ever done something nice that hasn't been based on self-interest? When has she been good to you? Not to mention that mother, always making comments about my mom's death."

She threw the ball to Toulouse with more force than necessary, and it flew over the fence and rolled into the street. A shiny green Lincoln Continental from the 1980s, with expensive wheels, booming rap, immediately crushed it. *Sorry, my boy, about your luck. Game's over,* she thought.

Brooks eyed her. "Don't you think you're being a little harsh? When was the last time you spoke to her? She called me the other day, and we had a nice conversation, and I have to tell you, Lucy, she's changed."

"Just be careful, Brooks. Last time it took you years to get over her, and all you did was work, and I worried about you so. Maeve is going to want to see you, and she's here for only one week, so please check your calendar and let me know what night you want to come to dinner. Brooks, I'm sorry if I sounded critical about Desiree, but she has never deserved you. You are too kind, too generous, and too good."

"I'm not sure if I should say thank you, Lucy. Anyhow, I'll get back to you about dinner plans and will definitely see you at Lillian's bash."

Maeve's flight arrived on time, and Lucy was happy to see her dear sister. Since their trip in the fall, they had become closer than ever, writing e-mails, calling to check in with one another. Maeve was preparing for the defense of her dissertation, and she was searching for full-time employment at one of the universities. She hoped to teach at Berkeley, but it was a long shot, and she may have to teach at one of the small colleges until she had more experience. She told Lucy that it was important for her to publish, but she could not possibly think about that, as she felt her fingers were still cramped from all that writing and typing.

Surprisingly, Maeve was not tired even though she had taken the red-eye. What did Lucy think about shopping on King Street and then getting a cup of coffee? Lucy and Maeve parked in the garage at Marion Square and first headed south. They tried on ridiculously short dresses made of diaphanous materials at some of the high-end boutiques and were horrified at some of the prices. Maeve was dying to go to Saks, and while searching through the sale rack, she found a beautiful teal cocktail dress that had been marked down four times. It was a size ten.

"Look, Lucy, it doesn't look like a ten, does it? It's more of an eight. I'm going to try this on."

Lucy started pulling out other potential dresses for Maeve and found a light fuchsia dress with black lace trim. Another was a shimmering cobalt dress that a young Audrey Hepburn would have worn. She selected three more dresses and headed to the fitting room. She called softly out to her sister, and there Maeve stood outside of the dressing room. She looked stunning in the dress, and Lucy hadn't noticed that the skirt puffed slightly out with a tulle underskirt. Maeve's waist looked tiny, and the dress complemented her dark hair and eyes. Lucy showed her sister the other dresses, and as always, trusting Lucy's taste, Maeve tried each one on. They both kept looking back at the iridescent teal number, and it seemed to glitter at them, slyly whispering, *You know you want me, and I'm only $64.98*. Maeve tried on the dress for the third time.

"Lucy, I just love it, but I didn't bring any jewelry that will match it."

"Maeve, I have those beautiful turquoise earrings that you got me in Santa Fe and the necklace and bracelet that Dad gave me. They will match perfectly. Wasn't it nice of Grandmere to give us both a check for the dresses?"

"It was, She's so dear. And with our bargain dress prices, we can buy shoes! I think she wants her two granddaughters to shine. It's almost as if she wants to help us find suitors. I always have to remind her that Ray is mine and I his."

"Well, after my debacle, I'm ready to meet a houseful just to see what's out there. Even though it didn't work with Sam or that Gus or the not-boyfriend, I think it's time to test the waters. Just to see, nothing serious, just having fun, right?"

The sisters strolled northward and were enticed by shops named The Finicky Filly, Luna, and LulaKate. They walked into Bob Ellis, where Maeve showed off the dress to the competent salesperson. Lucy wandered the store and didn't see a pair she wanted to afford that would match her dress. Maeve called to her, and Lucy saw a most beautiful pair of shoes adorning her sister's feet. They matched the dress perfectly, being open-toed sandals on high platforms.

"Oh, but Maeve, can you walk in them?"

"Yes, I can, and they are comfortable due to the platform. Remember, my feet are a nine and a half, not an eight like yours. That's why I never trip and sprain an ankle. I'm well grounded."

Lucy laughed as her sister thanked the clerk and went to pay for the shoes.

They looked in the window at Copper Penny Shoes, and Lucy eyed a pair of open-toed Italian pewter-colored pumps. They were ravishing. Maeve arched an eyebrow. The sisters laughed as they dashed inside. Lucy flipped the Italian-made shoe over, and there was one size eight left. They were 50 percent off, but the hundred-dollar price tag was still too high for her to consider. They would match her shimmery gray dress perfectly that she had purchased at a consignment shop in West Ashley. The dress had never been worn, and Violet had told her that she absolutely must buy it as it flattered her figure better than anything she owned. She didn't know the designer, but once home, she Googled "Philosophy by Alberta Ferretti" and found that, for seventy-five dollars, she had purchased the dress at a fraction of the original price.

Maeve was egging her on, reminding her that she had saved so much on the dress. "Just try the shoes on. They're gorgeous."

Lucy did as told, and she wandered around the store thinking that, for pumps, they were very comfortable. The style was reminiscent of the fifties with thin heels and scalloped edges, and she didn't want to take them off. Maeve convinced her sister that she must have those shoes. As Lucy handed her debit card to the sales associate, she heard a familiar voice behind her.

"Mother, you must see these shoes. I have thought about them all day and night, and they have only one size eight left."

Lucy hoped that Desiree was talking about her new shoes and hoped that she could spite her. She signed the receipt, thanked the staff, and together Maeve and Lucy stopped and said coolly, "Mrs. Radcliffe, Desiree, nice to see you."

Walking out the door, they heard a very petulant Desiree complain and raise her voice to the nice girl who had helped Lucy. Yes, indeed, Lucy had won this round. She couldn't wait to see Desiree's face at the party once she saw Lucy's newest acquisition. The Radcliffes had always been acquaintances of the family, and Mrs. Radcliffe would bring her newly single Botoxed daughter in tow.

Chapter 19

I was present the other evening by invitation, at a splendid entertainment and dance...to a numerous assemblage of the first families...We retired to supper...which was very profuse and elegant, all served up in India China and cut glass...

Letter about Charleston, Charles Caleb Colton, 1799

Lucy and Maeve arrived at the Legare Street house two hours before the great event. The caterers had everything under control, and the floral designer, from Diana's shop, was placing arrangements of peonies, bells of Ireland, hydrangeas, and holiday greens around the rooms. A beautifully bedecked tree reposed in a corner of one of the double parlors. Lucy was supervising the goings-on, making sure that the chaos was controlled. She noticed that the elegant house was spotless and that everything was in its place. Bless Stella, she thought, for always keeping it all so straight and nice.

Maeve was helping Grandmere dress for her special occasion. Grandmere's elegant dress came from Berlin's, on the corner of Broad and King Streets. Over the years, she had been a loyal customer, and the staff knew her tastes exactly. Grandmere had mentioned that she was amazed, as always, at the high level of customer service that was awarded to her.

The dress was a long velvet gown colored a soft midnight blue that matched Lillian's eyes. She wore the sapphire necklace that had been Arthur's mother's and the sapphire-and-pearl earrings that Arthur had given her for their fifth wedding anniversary. Her knees ached and her hips creaked, but she had made it to this year, and she was grateful for all that she had been given. She told Maeve at six to go change, as she wanted to properly show off her granddaughters. She reclined on the Empire meridienne, still admiring its gilded winged-paw feet. She remembered the day that Arthur had brought it home saying that it was said to have belonged to Varina Howell, the wife of Jefferson Davis, the president of the Confederacy. He had placed it in this very room, near the window so she could laze and read her books. He had always been so kind and generous, and she missed him every day, as she did her one daughter, her darling Celeste, who had predeceased her. She wrinkled her brow and thought of her Cameron girls, losing their mother so young, and how they were both so strong. They were both getting older now, and she wondered if they, either one of them, would enjoy the delights of motherhood.

Lucy knocked on the door at 6:40. "Grandmere, it's showtime, and your guests will be arriving shortly."

"Lucy, I do believe I've been ruminating about my life, but now our audience awaits, and we should arrive as actors on the stage."

Lucy giggled and kissed her grandmother's cheek. "I love you, Grandmere, and you'll be the most beautiful belle in all of Charleston tonight. Let's hope Sadie's gentleman caller has strong nerves so he's not tempted by you!"

Lillian swatted at her granddaughter's hand. "I am not at all interested in Sadie's new love interest." She then rolled those beautifully made-up blue eyes.

Lillian noticed that Lucy had straightened her curls, and her blondish hair fell in a stylish cap. Lillian thought the dress was beautiful, made of a silk blend, and when the light caught, it shimmered silver light. The three-quarter-length sleeves were tightly fitted. While the lines were clean and straight at the bodice with a v-shaped neckline, the skirt flared out and came a few inches above the knee, showing off her long legs and narrow ankles. She wore her great-grandmother's jadeite necklace, a piece that Lillian never preferred, remembering it on her own mother, but Lucy had linked it to a short chain, and the large circular piece of jadeite set in its Art Nouveau silver setting looked fashionable and chic. Lillian then noticed the shoes.

"Darling, I had a pair like that once. No, they weren't metallic, but the shape was almost the same. I remember how I was so excited to wear them. My Arthur was taking me on a dinner date a few years after Gardiner was born. I hardly slept the night before, as I was so excited and I found the shoes so beautiful."

Lillian thought that Lucy had not looked so good in years. Her darling granddaughter seemed giddy and young, and she thought she was finally really happy inside.

They entered the double parlors. Lucy had placed several canes strategically around the room for Grandmere's access. Maeve had lifted her eyebrows and commented, *"Thoughtful and smart, otherwise our mature girl might be worn out by the time it's all over; I know I will be."*

Maeve's dark curls were pinned up, and she looked sassy in her teal dress. The four-inch silk pleated straps accentuated her strong shoulders and well-muscled arms. The borrowed turquoise jewelry matched perfectly and completed her outfit. Lillian commented that she had the prettiest granddaughters and they were so very smart, successful, and nice, kind and generous girls. That Maeve, though, she had a wicked sense of humor, honed like steel.

The first guest arrived just before seven. Maeve knew what Grandmere was thinking. The beautiful socialite had grown up outside of Orangeburg, where those types, Grandmere would infuse, always are prompt and don't quite understand the fifteen-minute rule; it must be their German heritage, always orderly and on time. Her husband was a businessman who had moved back to town following an early retirement as a CEO for a Fortune 500 company. His wife had died after a hard, complicated illness, and he married Susie nine months later. Mrs. Radcliffe called Susie a money-chaser, and Grandmere thought she should know all about that, what with Desiree's lifestyle, but no, Grandmere liked Susie. Besides, men often needed companionship. If they loved well once, chances were they wanted to test the waters and find that feeling again. It may be that he had loved his wife so truly and deeply that he needed that again and that he could not die on the vine; this actually was a compliment to his wife of so many years. Susie gave him bliss wrapped up in the package that was her smile, her joie de vivre, and her constant passion for life.

She was pretty in a petite, blonde-haired, blue-eyed way, and he was still young and wanted one more chance of love in this thing called life. When Frederick Sanders played golf, which was approximately three times a week, Susie would bring her Bichon, Charlie Dog, to the Legare Street residence and read to Lillian. They reread classics, *Wuthering Heights*, *Jane Eyre*, and everything by Austen, from *Sense and Sensibility* to *Mansfield Park*. They were currently reading *Bleak House* by Dickens, and Grandmere would lay on the chaise lounge with the sun dappling her pale, lined face. Susie would sit cross-legged on the high Tester family bed where so many Barwick children had been born and read to Lillian. In true Southern form, she would call her Miss Lillian, and Lillian, in her dotage, just wanted to be called Lily by her, for some unknown reason. Lily was her pet name, and no one new called her that, but Susie was different. Susie was dear, with giddy childlike enthusiasm, and she possessed a sense of innocence.

Susie reminded Lillian of a boy from her childhood, when she would go to cotillion on Wednesdays for dance lessons. She had been so uncomfortable. Her feet were large, and she always seemed to get the steps wrong. A young boy named Conscience, who hailed from a small town in Jasper County, had entered her life and helped her navigate the dance steps. He was the distant relation of Mrs. Johnston, who led their class. His parents were poor, as so many during those days of the Great Depression, and he had been sent to Charleston because he was too slight to work the farm, and the family could not afford to feed another mouth. He would say, *"I'm your conscience. I am, I am."* He would tease Lillian and talk to her about his family. They consisted of uneducated, hardworking sharecroppers, although he was a quick boy of thirteen who read voraciously. Mrs. Johnston would place the needle of the Victrola on the 78 records, and they would line up girls on one side of the room and boys on the other. He always managed to be her partner and dance with her. His feet were smaller than her own, and he would tease her and say, *"I'm dancing with boat-foot girl. She keeps me on the ground."* He danced well, and with his gentle teasing, he made her relax, and they would complete the steps with little incident. His gentle prodding and his kindness helped her build her confidence. She never forgot him, his passion for life, his innocence, or the kindness he showed to her. When she was sixteen, she heard that he had been in a terrible tractor accident. His life cut short before he was seventeen.

Susie was like him—exuberant, fun, and she could best Lily at backgammon and checkers. She held out her hand to Maeve and then Lucy. "I'm Susie Sanders. I know I'm early, but I wanted to check on my best friend before the big event."

Lillian hugged Susie to her, and Susie slipped a small package into her hand.

"It's nothing, and it's silly, but I made it for you. Miss Lillian, thank you for your grace and your friendship."

Lillian opened the small package to discover a beautifully crafted origami bird. "Susie, it's so very beautiful. Thank you."

Susie offered to help the sisters with anything they needed. They said all was in place, but they thanked her for her offer. By seven thirty the party was in full swing, and the sisters took turns checking on their grandmother. Aurora and Georg were holding down the fort introducing themselves to Lillian's friends, young and old. Gardiner and his wife, Rachel, were delightful, and even the cousins and their spouses, Russ and Stephanie, Blake and Molly, seemed relaxed tonight. The house glittered, chandeliers sparkled, and the mahogany furniture gleamed in the candlelight. Stella could not help herself and checked on the caterers in the kitchen. Lucy followed her in and smiled as Stella nodded in approval. It was her kitchen, after all.

By eight thirty Gardiner asked the grandchildren to round up the guests for the toast. Grandmere was positioned in her favorite wing-backed chair. The toast was beautiful as he noted Lillian's many accomplishments over time, being a past president of the Junior League, serving as a board member on various boards and institutions, and most importantly, being the best mother, wife, and grandmother that a family could have. There was a great noise as guests chimed, "Hear, hear!" and clinked glasses in honor of Grandmere. Lucy looked behind her and noticed a familiar pretty face with dark, long hair and blue eyes. What in the world was Sam's Jessica doing here, she thought. Standing next to her was James Weathers, Lillian's doctor of fifteen years. She watched as they exchanged glances and thought, *Oh, Samuel, your girl is cheating.*

"Maeve, we need to introduce ourselves to Dr. Weathers's date. As you know, Garndmere wants us to say hello to everyone."

Maeve looked at her sister. Something was going on, she just knew it. The girls wound their way through the crowd, saying hello to the many guests and thanking them for attending Grandmere's big event. They said hello to Mrs. Radcliffe and noticed that Desiree was cozying up to another woman's date. Lucy and Maeve said hello to Dr. Weathers and introduced themselves to his date. She was pretty and had a melodious voice. Her name was Jessica McManus, and she was so pleased to be in Mrs. Barwick's beautiful home. She answered Maeve's questions: Yes, she loved living in Charleston. She was originally from Kingstree, but she had attended the Medical University, where she now worked. Did Lucy and Maeve live in town? Maeve answered for the two of them. She replied that Lucy lived near the Citadel, but she lived outside of San Francisco and was visiting mainly for the party. They chatted of this and that, and the girls thanked the guests for coming and moved on.

Lucy waved to her friends who had gathered on the large Greek Revival piazza with its heavy leaded pendant lights.

They were all there, Diana looking gorgeous in a chocolate velvet dress and Weston in his kilt and formal jacket. Brooks had brought his acquaintance Dante, and true to his word, Dante was absolutely gorgeous. She noticed Maeve's beauty as she said her hellos, and watched Brooks retrieved a cocktail for her sister. Maeve and Rachel always found something to discuss, and they were laughing, probably talking about various guests or the inappropriate questions that old Mr. Rutledge asked every woman under the age of sixty-five.

Susie sought out Lucy at nine thirty. "Lucy, it was so nice to meet you. I just wanted to tell you that I adore your grandmother. We have so much fun together, and this party was so lovely. Please pass on to her my very best, as there is such a crush around her that I can't possibly slip through."

Lucy hugged her. "Thank you for coming, Susie. It's obvious that my Grandmere certainly enjoys your company, and I appreciate that you spend time with her."

"We enjoy the classics, and I love to read to her. I was never close to my own mother, and well, Miss Lillian makes me feel special. We have such a nice time together. Well, I must go. Frederick is coming home tonight, and I want to be there to greet him. He stays awfully busy for someone who is retired."

Lucy smiled at Susie as they said good-bye. Funny, Lucy thought, she rarely hugged people upon first acquaintance, but there was something about Susie that just drew one to her.

The guests began to leave around nine forty-five. Maeve said that Grandmere seemed tired yet happy. Lucy stood by the door to the second-floor hall with its sculpture niches, appreciating the Hiram Powers statue of Persephone as well as the Italian copies of other Masters picked up in the mid-nineteenth century by wealthy ancestors on the Grand Tour. Mrs. Radcliffe and Desiree were saying good-bye. Gardiner and Rachel thanked them for coming. Desiree walked by Lucy, and Lucy told them how nice it was for them to come and she knew that her grandmother greatly appreciated that they were part of her celebration. Desiree looked at Lucy's outfit and then noticed her shoes.

"Where did you get those beautiful shoes, Lucy?"

"Oh, I just picked them up a few days ago at Copper Penny. Actually, the day I saw the two of you."

"Well, it was nice to see you."

"Good night."

Lucy turned to the doorway, where she saw Maeve smile at her.

"Ah, Lucy," she whispered as she walked to her, "you are so very bad. You had to make sure she knew you had them."

Lucy looked at the floor and then at her sister, grinning mischievously. They looked out the window, and they saw Desiree talking strongly to her mother as they headed down the street to Mrs. Radcliffe's house on Tradd Street.

"Indeedy, dear sister, I think you got her." Maeve giggled. "She was always so jealous of you, your relationship with Brooks, and everything else."

"Do you think so? I just thought she liked to be cruel to me. I would never have thought she was jealous, and besides why would she be jealous of my friendship with Brooks? He was always smitten with her, you know?"

"Life is a curious, complicated thing, and I think Desiree just always wanted what you had, always. Remember, in school, you were given parts in the plays in which she always auditioned and then you had more badges when we were all Girl Scouts?"

"That's just silly, Maeve, craziness, I tell you. I just never liked her or trusted her."

The girls were changing into pajamas by eleven, cozily ensconced in Lucy's house. A fire burned bright in the fireplace, and Maeve sat in front of it with Toulouse cuddled in her arms.

Gazing into the fire, Maeve said, "Thank goodness tomorrow will just consist of brunch with the family. I'm a little done in after tonight, but it was fun, wasn't it? And why was it so important to meet Dr. Weathers's date? You were a little odd about that. And this Dante guy, he's just beautiful, isn't he? That kind of beauty would just wreck me. I would just worry who would throw themselves at him and who would tempt him. I'm so lucky to have Ray. Although we have the conservative quotient, he would never look at another woman, and there is great comfort in that."

"I agree with you about Dante. He's too beautiful, and there is something else there too, isn't there? A certain charm and sexuality. When I shook his hand, I had that weird feeling of this connection. I can't explain it, but it made me think of that scene in *Like Water for Chocolate* when the two characters are consumed with passion and they literally catch on fire. Weird, isn't it? Dr. Weathers's date just happened to be Samuel O'Hara's Jessica. I thought it was her, but I needed to know for sure."

"Oh my, that makes things complicated. She was clearly his date. Did you see how he had his hand on the small of her back?"

"I know. I quietly kept my eye on them. They are clearly a couple. I just saw Sam a few weeks ago, and I know she's still seeing him too."

"Gosh, what intrigue, and she seemed nice as well. Maybe she and Sam have an open relationship? So many people do that these days. I suppose it's very modern. I couldn't do that. It would be far too confusing."

"No, Maeve, Sam can't do that and won't do that. He's not made that way. He loves this girl to distraction. I just know he can't be clued in to her behavior."

"How can a cheater seem so nice?" Maeve queried.

"That is a question I cannot answer, Maeve. Poor Sam."

"How can you say that, dear sister? He treated you poorly. He does not deserve your sympathy. Sometimes I think you are so in love with wanting to be in love that you would forgive any of these guys just so you are in a relationship. Lucy, you let the not-boyfriend take advantage of you, and the same was with that Sam. Next time around you need to place Lucy and Lucy's priorities first, not other people's. You also need to calm that passionate nature of yours. It tends to get you into trouble."

Lucy looked at her sister and pursed her lips. "Maeve, don't let's say cruel things. I loved Sam, we had fun together before anything intimate happened, and I might remind you that I dated the not-boyfriend for over a year. I am getting better at this relationship thing. I chose to not see that Gus guy ever again after Thanksgiving, and in the future I will put myself first, or at least I'm going to try. Maeve, I'm giving up some of the old rules, like being judgmental and being snobby, but I'm also going to make sure that when someone is disrespecting me, I will let them know that. I'll make sure that I'm not always available. If anything, that's what I've always done wrong."

"Good. It's easier said than done, you know."

"I know. I just want to have fun, none of this getting-serious business, no questioning if the person is the love of my life or my soul mate. I want to do things like go to the Gibbes and see the new exhibit, maybe with that architect Michael. Diana is planning a bowling night for a group of us at the Rifle Club in early January. My new neighbors are so good, and I can always spend time with them and kidnap the children and take them to the park. I can keep busy. That's never been a problem."

"Lucy, have you finally told your friends about Thanksgiving night? You cannot act like it didn't happen, and it will happen to someone else. We both know that."

"No, but I will, and soon. Maeve, what did you think about that nice man from Richmond, the appraiser?"

"Sadie's gentleman caller's son, right? I thought he was nice enough. I didn't spend much time talking with him, though. Why do you mention him? You're not his type. You know that, don't you?"

"Absolutely, I'm thinking he's the perfect person for someone else. Anyway, he's handling an estate in Richmond, and he told me that there are pieces of art associated with Charleston. He invited me to visit in early January and see if I'm interested in anything. He actually offered to let me stay at his house located in The Fan. Richmond's not so far away, and I figured Huger may want to go with me. I thought his name was interesting. It's Raphael Semmes. I suppose he was named for his ancestor from the Civil War, who was the captain of the *CSS Alabama.* It's pronounced 'RayFeel' and 'Rafe' for short."

"How do you know this random stuff, Lucy?"

"I guess I just have a good memory. The cannons of the *CSS Alabama* are being conserved at the conservation lab at the old Navy base."

"With the *Hunley*, then?"

"Yes, that's right."

"That's sort of odd, isn't it, this six-degrees-of-separation thing."

"No, not really, that's how it always is here. More like three degrees."

"Just another reason for me to stay in California."

"Oh, Maeve, I always find it so comforting that everything fits together in such a tidy way."

Chapter 20

All truths are easy to understand once they are discovered; the point is to discover them.

Galileo Galilei

January 2008

Huger's party was another successful event, and Lucy's dinner partner was the astrophysicist who was a friend of Brooks's. Huger had been introduced to him over the holidays and felt that he would make an excellent guest. Lucy asked Dante about his name, and he responded that his mother had been a lit major, and she also loved everything Italian. His brother's name was Rudolfo because she loved Puccini's La *bohème*. Lucy laughed and asked if his father had any say in naming his children, and he replied that his father was so over the moon with his mother that he would have let her name them anything, maybe even Jell-O.

He said he would call her and perhaps they could go to lunch or dinner. She replied that that would be nice.

Lucy had asked Huger if he would be interested in making a road trip to Richmond with her in the middle of the month. January was always gloomy, and Rafe Semmes seemed very interesting and affable. Huger said he was sorry that he had missed Lillian's big day, but he had made a prior commitment to meet an old friend in Chicago. Lucy said that Grandmere understood, and she was sure that Huger had heard from her. Certainly, he intoned, she had graciously sent him a note thanking him for the majolica plate that he had sent her.

Lucy made the arrangements, and they would be driving up on the tenth and coming back on the thirteenth. Huger didn't trust the Karmann Ghia, and its seats were uncomfortable, so he offered the use of his Infiniti as long as Lucy did most of the driving. Lucy knew that Katie needed a break from her roommate and asked her if she would house-sit and take care of Toulouse. Katie agreed. Her roommate was awful, borrowed Katie's clothes, and ate her food. A stay at Lucy's would be wonderful, and she thanked her friend profusely. She was just so grateful that her lease would be up on the first of May.

Lucy and Huger made good timing and arrived at the Greek Revival house in The Fan at 6:00 p.m. The house was large, with large parlors and a sumptuous dining room. Rafe Semmes had exquisite taste, and his furnishings complemented the architecture. Lucy admired the Duncan Phyfe classical chairs with their klismos form and gilded paw feet. The sofa was exquisite, covered in heavy red silk fabric with gold fleurs-de-lis. The walls were painted a soft, buttery yellow and the trim an off shade of white. The ceiling medallions were robust and were finished with Greek keys. Lucy admired the bookcases with the many volumes on art and antiques. Huger was amazed that their paths had never crossed, as they had so many friends and colleagues in common. Rafe had also attended the prestigious English summer school, and over dinner the three discussed how the summer school had changed their lives in a wonderful way.

Rafe was an excellent host, pouring his guests fine wine and indulging them in a delicious dinner of beef tenderloin, au gratin potatoes, and fresh sautéed vegetables. The two men drank coffee with dessert of fresh berries with a sweet cream sauce. The bedrooms were tastefully and expensively furnished, and Lucy couldn't wait to sleep in the high carved bed with its opulent coverlet and hangings. She said good night at ten thirty and thanked Rafe again for his hospitality.

The next day, the trio visited Rafe's business warehouse, where the lot of furniture and art was temporarily being stored. Lucy looked about her amazed at the myriad abundance of furniture and art. Rafe drew her attention to several painting storage containers marked: Charleston provenance. Tables covered with conservation materials boasted small sculptures and sets of porcelain. He explained that he wanted to make sure that the family received the highest amount for their items, and oftentimes things that did not relate to the area did not sell well with locals. Rafe told them to look about, don't be shy, as they knew their subjects better than he did.

"Rafe, Huger, look. This is funny. Here's my new dead friend's work." There in front of her were four landscape paintings of Charleston's renowned plantations bearing the broad stroke of Eola Willis.

"Hmm. A few Huttys, a few Smiths, and Taylors. I'm interested in all of this. There's my friend Prentiss Taylor, too. Hmm, who would think? Huger, look, there are a few Abe Schwartzes. That's odd. You don't see them often, as so many people find his work naïve and associate it with outsider art. Rafe, I'll take those as well. I have an acquaintance that likes his style."

Huger and Lucy left early on the fourth day. They agreed to stay in touch. Huger commented that Rafe had been an excellent host, and Lucy noted that they seemed to have a great deal in common. They landed back in Charleston in record time, under seven hours. Lucy thought it was perfect that all the works of art fitted so nicely in the Infiniti's trunk, and Huger commented that he had no idea why he bought the small sculpture of a winged Pegasus. Truly, he already owned enough gewgaws.

She was settling in at home when she realized that she now must get her friends together and explain to them the situation with Gus Wolfe. It was time, and it had almost been six weeks since it had happened. She pulled out her laptop and typed their names in and sent the e-mail. It was short and simple. *Truth be told,* read the subject line. She typed the rest.

Dear friends—it's important for me to have you over. I need to tell you something, and I need your good counsel. Please say you can come on Thursday, in three days' time.

She sent the e-mail and signed off.

Katie called Violet that night. "Did you get that e-mail from Lucy? Sort of cryptic don't you think?"

"I don't know, Katie, but usually when she gets us together, it's important."

"Violet, don't you think she's been acting curious lately? I know she was really busy around the holidays, and she couldn't really talk to us at the party, but, there's something there. I just took care of her house, and she hasn't even called me yet, and I had a few photos made of Toulouse while she was gone and put together a little book so she could see what a good time we had together. Just odd."

"Don't fret. She probably had this on her mind and just came home. Didn't you say she was coming back only this evening?"

"You're probably right. I'll just put the date on the calendar, and I won't worry until I hear from Lucy," Katie said.

"That's exactly what I would do. Bye-bye."

Lucy had been busy in the gallery. She rearranged the walls with some of her new inventory and then placed the other works of art within their proper categories. She took digital photos and began e-mailing her client list. She finally called Katie. Her message went to voice mail, and she thanked her wholeheartedly for taking care of Toulouse and said she had a small gift for her that she hoped Katie would like. Hopefully she would see her on Thursday night.

Thursday came quickly. Lucy had put together a cheese platter of Brie, chèvre, and Morbier from Earth Fare, the small grocery store that sold the finest quality of goods in the South Windermere Shopping Center. Her children, as she called them, next door called it The Tomato Store, as its marketing materials showed a tomato above its name. She picked up pâté at the Harris Teeter. They always had a good selection this time of year, and she added grapes to her basket, and a couple of bottles of wine. The friends would arrive at seven o'clock, and she would have everything ready.

Ella was the first to arrive, followed by Rachel. Katie and Violet came together. They were waiting for Diana; she had some last-minute orders to fill and would be a little late. By seven thirty they were all together, sitting at the dining room table. Ella was the first to broach the subject. Lucy told her tale of Thanksgiving night, Gus in the car, feeling nauseous, Bennett and Aslyn coming to her rescue, Toulouse's reactions, the ER, everything.

"Someone at the party slipped me a Mickey, y'all, and I think it was Gus. I've known everyone else there for years, and he's the only one suspect that I have." She looked around the room and saw her friends' shocked faces.

"That's pretty huge, Lucy. I'm surprised you have waited this long to tell us," Diana said a bit crossly.

"I guess I just wanted it to go away. I wanted to think I had made it all up. Bennett asked me the other day, before I went to Richmond, if I had told all of you, and I said I hadn't. He told me it was not abnormal for some people to not want to discuss this type of topic, as sometimes the victims blamed themselves. I told Bennett that I would tell you right away, so here we are." She gave a weak smile.

Ella looked at her friends and sighed. "Bennett is right, you know, but if we want to find out who did this, then we need to know. We need to find out more about Gus. Really, all we know is that you went out with him a few times and that Rachel knows him through the Realtors Association, right?"

"I don't know him that well. I've met him at a few business meetings and cocktail parties, but nothing more," Rachel stated, crossing her arms and her long legs in front of her.

"He seemed nice enough, but almost too charming. I figured that was the salesman in him. But we don't really know him at all, do we?"

"No, we don't. In fact, Weston mentioned that it was hard to track him down on certain topics, and you know my husband—he can talk to anyone about anything," Diana added.

"The other thing is that, before Christmas, Sam found Toulouse and me in the park." At the many groans in the crowd, Lucy held up both hands. "Please let me finish. He suggested that I should not see Gus because he didn't want me to be hurt by his actions. I cut him off and didn't tell him anything, and I didn't listen to him either because I was still so mad at him, but y'all, this is what is interesting: Gus spoke poorly about Sam in the car on the ride home on Thanksgiving night, and I thought that everything Gus said just didn't ring true. The more I think about it, at the end of the night at Ben's, Gus was the only one near me. He stayed by my side, and I was flattered."

Violet looked at her friend. "Aren't we all still hating that guy from Salem?"

"Yes, Violet, but still, he offered me information, and I was too angry at him, and perhaps I wanted to hold on to my pride and just reject him and all he had to say outright. I just plain goof up all the time anymore."

"Hush, Lucy, stop with the blame. I'm so sick of the blame game. It just didn't work out with Sam and you. He's not evil. It just didn't work out. Life is so complicated, and everyone has so many stories. It's time to fess up. Who has kept up with Samuel O' Hara, anyone at this table?" Ella asked.

"I haven't, but Weston has. Sam had contacted him regarding a house before you broke up, Lucy, and I must admit, I was hopeful that the two of you would work it out by Christmas. So I let sleeping dogs lie, to say the least, and I know this is no excuse, but we have all been so busy."

"You're right, Diana. So somehow Weston needs to ask Sam about Gus. Then we'll have more information. Anyone else?" Ella intoned.

Violet said no, as did Rachel and Katie.

Lucy looked at Katie, who was uncomfortably quiet, and she wondered what was going on there. Who knew, and maybe she was making too much to-do about everything.

The strategy was set. Diana would tell Weston everything and rely on him to gently prod Sam the next time they were together. Meanwhile Rachel would research everything about Gus. As a former paralegal, she had the skills.

Katie went to Violet's house and ensconced herself on the over-large sofa. "Violet," she said with her strong Columbia dialect, "do you really think Gus was capable of doing that? I'm just putting my teacher's thinking cap on, and I think Lucy's been a little odd, loopy too, and she's been so crazy about making changes. In fact, there's that odd thing about the Hispanic family that she's embraced. She'll say, 'No, Katie, I can't go to that movie. I'm going over to see the little ones today, Max and Clara, and they are having me to dinner.' She doesn't know these people. They are nothing to her. In the past she would visit my class and talk about art in the Low Country during history month; now she's making recommendations that I contact a poet or a composer, she says, to mix it up. Then there was all that Samuel O'Hara business; she acts as if she's over him, but still something's going on there. I feel sometimes that I'm cut off from them. Ella, I know, is happy and enjoying her new marriage, but Lucy and Diana seem to have become poker players."

"Be nice to Lucy. She's trying to grow, and she's giving up the rules. She's embracing new friends and mixing up her circle. She didn't go into hiding after the breakup with Sam very long. Instead she picked herself up, dusted herself off, and got back in the game. All of that is good. She's right, you know, about you contacting other professionals in the community. You'll meet more people that way, and we all can benefit by meeting new acquaintances and friends. I'm proud of Lucy for putting herself out there. Yes, she was hurt, but she is now looking for someone to share her life, or at least spend time with. We should do that, too, not always being content with being alone or with our friends. I might even call that math teacher that I went out with last year. Diana is ready to take her business up a notch, so she really has no time for any of us, Lucy included."

"I thought you said the math teacher was odd and that you didn't feel that drawn to him. Plus he lived all the way out on Wadmalaw Island."

"He is odd and quirky, but funny, too, and very smart. I might just call Sebastian and find out if Rich is still interested in me. It won't hurt to try."

Katie shook her head. Here was Violet getting herself out there.

A busy January led to a busier February, and Lucy was gearing up for March and April, which would bring thousands of visitors to the city. She and Gabriella were hanging works of art, making sure that each piece was set to its best position. Lighting was critical so each work of art could be clearly viewed. She smiled to herself as she straightened a painting, thinking how fun Michael was and how she enjoyed his company. They had gone out several times to the Gibbes, to lunch and dinner, and they always had a good time together. He was coming off a bad relationship and was not ready for anything serious, and she said that suited her just fine. He was her wingman, he was the perfect date, and when she was given tickets at the eleventh hour to a concert, he stepped up and gladly was her escort.

Dante was her second-in-line, and he, too, was a wonderful and charming date. She felt comfortable with him and realized he was far more interested in men than women. One evening at the symphony, she caught him admiring the same handsome man that her eyes had found earlier. She nudged him, and they laughed, and she told him it was a good thing that she was only slightly attracted to him, as otherwise things might become very complicated. He simply smiled his broad smile, showing off beautiful teeth, and told her likewise. He felt their personalities complemented each other, and that was a good thing.

Diana and Weston were happy for her to just have fun, and Weston was grateful to have the support of another man when the girls, as he called them, became too giddy. She hadn't seen Samuel O'Hara since December, and that was just fine with her. It would be Valentine's Day next week, and she needed to purchase seeds for her yard. Nasturtiums always made her happy, and Grandmere always told her to plant them around that holiday. She would go to the hardware store at lunch and purchase the bulk seeds. She rubbed her hands together with glee, already seeing their colorful heads appearing in her flower beds.

Chapter 21

Men when their affairs require
Must a while themselves retire,
Sometimes hunt, and sometimes hawk,
And not ever sit and talk.
If these and such like you can bear,
Then like, and love, and never fear.

"Never Love Unless You Can", Thomas Campion

Sam had almost finished the Greek Revival house. He had been searching online all morning for vintage hardware for the doors to complete the project. He already had a few prospective buyers, and he was glad that at least work was going his way. Jessica had come clean with him during the early part of January. She had been seeing a doctor while seeing him. In fact, the entire time she had dated Sam in the past, she had always had a crush on the man, but because he had been one of her instructors in school, neither one of them had acted upon their feelings. When she had returned to Charleston in November, she found herself often in his company at work. One thing led to another, and the next thing Jessica knew, she was seeing him more and more.

She had to be honest with Sam: Yes, she loved him, but it wasn't like it had been in the past, and James and she had so much in common, and she saw herself with James for the rest of her life. She was sorry, it was a mess, and she blamed herself for not being honest, but it all happened so fast, and she wasn't quite sure what was real or not. Her feelings for James had always been there. She didn't want to hurt Sam, and when they spoke in the fall that night, she had told him that they wouldn't be exclusive, even though he thought they were.

He asked her if she had slept with both of them during the winter months, and she had looked sheepish. Her eyes turned dark with sadness, and she said that she had never thought that she was a cheater because of their agreement. She had slept with James in December, and only twice, and that's why she couldn't sleep with Sam that month or in the first week of January.

Yes, she had lied and said she was too tired to be intimate with him. She had been so conflicted. It had hurt her, too, trying to not hurt him, as they had had so much past history. She was trying to move on with her life, and she couldn't see being with him in the future. The experience made her sick, and she found herself dry-heaving or crying all of the time. She tried to make him talk and discuss the situation, but he couldn't because he felt like slapping her, which he would not do.

He should have seen it coming, all of it, and if he was truthful with himself, he had loved her for so many years, but since she had been back, she had been different. She had changed. She was always so serious, and whenever they had had dinner together, she seemed annoyed. There was a working tic in her jaw. She was silent most times, and he could tell she was distracted. If anything, it seemed as if she was going through the motions, and who wanted to be with someone like that? He had asked her why she was telling him this now, and she told him about the party she had attended at the grand residence on Legare Street around the holidays and that she had met Lucy and had seen some of his friends as well. She knew that eventually the news that she had been James's date would get back to him, and she wanted him to hear it from her rather than from someone else.

Sam scratched his head and kicked the closest thing next to him with his steel-toe boot. *Damn it, it's been a month; I've got to get over her*. He was still angry and hurt, and he was disappointed in her and mad at himself. He had been duped by Jessica. If he thought about it, he had to admit that they didn't have much in common and that she didn't laugh with him or share his desire to build his neighborhood. She lived in a quaint kitchen house behind a large single house across from Colonial Lake in Harleston Village, a neighborhood she considered safe. She called him an urban pioneer. He didn't like that term much, as it suggested that his area of town was rugged and untamed. She didn't understand the concept of building a community; she just wanted to enjoy the amenities of the upper class.

He would plan a trip sometime soon, once this house sold. A couple of months in different countries would give him the time to sort things out. The tenants in his freedman's cottage were moving out March first, and it was time to live by himself. He was too old to have a roommate. It was time to make changes in his life. Maybe he would even consider moving back to Salem. He wasn't quite sure. His roommate was moving out next week to live with his girlfriend in Avondale, west of the Ashley River. He would list the America Street house on Craigslist, and it would rent within a few weeks. It would cover his mortgage and make enough to pay for the repairs and upkeep. An old clapboard house required maintenance escrow, just like old people on medication; it bled a person's checking account dry. He had spent too much time thinking about it all. It was time to take action on what he could control, and if truth was told, he was over the entire situation. He made a list of things he needed to get from the hardware store on East Bay Street. They carried copies of the hinges and knobs that he needed, and he would comparison shop. Maybe he wouldn't be so frugal, and he'd just buy what was needed and be done with it.

❧

Lucy cycled down Anson Street, cut across Hasell Street, and caught the light before she cut through the Harris Teeter parking lot and then headed to the hardware store. The day was clear with a brilliant blue sky, and the temperature was in the sixties. Just another reason to love this city, she thought. She locked her bike and headed to the back of the store, where the garden items were stored. She sighed as she looked at the pretty planters and the colorful French bistro garden furniture. Ignoring the beautiful objects, she went to the counter and asked the clerk for the bulk seeds. After purchasing several packages, she was happy that she would have enough seeds for her front beds as well as for those in the back and for her planters. She chose different varieties of nasturtiums, including Princess of India, Jewel of Africa, and the colorful Whirlybird variety.

She helped herself to the free popcorn, indulging in the small pleasure, and wandered down the aisles, as she was always intrigued with the store's inventory. She was admiring the beautiful reproduction Victorian hardware in front of her, thinking how lovely it was that someone locally was manufacturing it, when she heard his familiar voice. She looked up and cocked her head to the left, and there was Sam looking tired, dirty, and disheveled. She wondered if he had plumbing problems, as it looked as if he hadn't seen a shower in days. That was odd. Except for the time at Huger's, he had always maintained such a neat and clean appearance.

❧

Sam's gaze caught hers. He noticed that she looked like a schoolgirl in her knee-length plaid skirt and turtleneck with black tights and boots. Her eyes became big in her head when she looked at him, and he noticed that she was quietly munching popcorn. She was still thin, but not quite as thin as she had been in December. Holding the popcorn in her left hand, she held up her right hand in a partial wave. The next thing he knew, she had dropped the popcorn on the floor. He couldn't help himself—he just started to laugh, comic relief, and of course it came from that pretty, goofy Lucy. She asked the clerk for a broom and dustpan and apologized for making a mess.

"Don't worry, it happens all the time," the clerk told her.

By the time it was all sorted out, he realized that maybe he didn't need to shop for hardware after all. He followed Lucy out the door and looked at her as she donned Jackie O sunglasses and unlocked her bike.

"How have you been, Lucy? It's been a few months since I've seen you."

"I'm well, Sam, busy, and it's all good." *He knows. The word is out. But I didn't say anything. I kept my good counsel. Only Maeve and I know.*

"Lucy, will you oblige me for a few minutes? I'd like to talk."

What could he possibly want to talk about? she thought. "All right, but I only have about fifteen minutes. Gabriella and I are revamping the shop for the spring."

"Let's just walk to Waterfront Park."

They quietly walked together, commenting about the weather and making small talk. She didn't feel awkward with him. She felt calm, a feeling she had never had with him before. She could feel his sadness, and she felt sorry for him for loving someone who had, in the end, betrayed him. She realized that she was over him, and it felt good to finally feel that he didn't have the power over her heart. That last three weeks with him, or mostly without him, had been so hard. If she was truthful, each day she had felt like there was an incendiary device in her chest or strapped around her neck.

They sat on a bench and watched the water in Charleston Harbor change from green to blue. She was careful to keep her distance from him, as she was still a bit afraid that her body would betray her. She mentioned that the beds were planted with maybe ten thousand Johnny-jump-ups. He asked her what those were, and she pointed to the myriad faces of pink, purple, and yellow violas and said, "Those ones."

His voice cracked, and he said, "You should know that Jess and I are over, but you probably know that already."

"Why would I know that, Sam?"

"She told me she met you at a party over the holidays and she was with someone you knew."

"I did meet her at my grandmother's birthday party. She was with my grandmother's doctor, but Sam, people can attend a party with someone without dating them. I have a couple of guys that serve as my escorts quite often that I call my wingmen. Certainly, it is not my place to pass judgment."

"If you had known that they were there together, would you have told me as a friend, sort of filling me in, so to speak?" he questioned.

She turned her body toward him and said, "I'm sorry, Sam. I'm sorry if you hurt and that she hurt you, but it is, and was, not my place to tell. I don't gossip. Maybe I have in the past, but no longer, and if I had called you with that news, what would you have thought? You would have thought, there's Lucy, still mad, and now she is making things up, crazy wombat." She looked at him, smiled, and then giggled.

He started to laugh slightly at first and then harder. "You are absolutely right. I probably would have thought something like that. Although crazy—what was that, wombat? I don't think that word is in my vocabulary."

"So, was it okay? I don't know how to articulate it, but was the breakup okay or really awful?"

"Awful, just awful, Lucy. It was mostly because I never thought she would be dishonest and cheat, but then again, she didn't think she was cheating at all."

He told her then the story, leaving out what she didn't need to know.

She thought of all the things she could say to comfort him, and nothing came out right, so she placed her hand on her mouth, stifling any ineffectual words that would have streamed out.

Instead she looked at him and said, "It's craziness, I tell you. Craziness." They both laughed. "Do you feel a little bit better?" she inquired, tilting her head first to the right and then the left.

"I do. You always made me smile and laugh, even at my own expense."

"I need to go back to work. Why don't you walk me there?"

They walked their bikes to the gallery, and Lucy told him about all of her purchases, her trip to Richmond, and how excited she was for the upcoming art walk. She asked if he was finished with the house, and he said that he was very close and wanted to plan another trip. She asked him if he would be gone as long as last time, and he said no, just a few months. He was thinking of going Down Under—Australia, New

Zealand, maybe Fiji—and she said that maybe he needed to find comfort in the arms of a dark-skinned, sloe-eyed Melvillian beauty from the South Pacific who could offer him educational outreach, if he knew what she meant, and travel was all about having fun, wasn't it, and maybe that's what was needed to take the edge off.

He shook his head, laughing, and asked her if her imagination ever switched into hibernate or did it ever turn off at all?

She looked at his handsome, scruffy face and said, "Never," and shook her strawberry blonde locks. She was not a computer, and if she did turn off her imagination, she would be terribly dull, and no one wants to be around a bore.

They were in front of her shop, and he thanked her for listening and said he hoped he would see her soon. She stopped him when he went to hug her, and she smiled and said he couldn't touch her. They were beyond that, and she could talk to him once in a while, but he could not touch her ever again. She had to draw the line with him. She smiled at him, thanked him for holding the door, wished him good luck, and walked the bike in.

"Was that who I think it was, Lucy?"

"Yes, Gabriella, it was. Samuel Francis O'Hara. I bumped into him while buying seeds, and he had to fill me in on his breakup."

"Geez, that was selfish on his part. Doesn't he realize how he hurt you? And then, what, did he want your sympathy?"

"I think he needed to talk, and I was there, and I don't know...We took a walk, and he talked, and when he tried to hug me, I told him no, thereby establishing the rules of engagement, which I never laid down the last time with him. This way he will understand that he and I have boundaries and I'm not a doormat. See, with my heart and men, I haven't always done that. I need to give up the insignificant rules and abide by the few important ones, this week anyway."

February turned to March, and Lucy was busy at the gallery. She and Gabriella had sent out e-mail blasts to their regular customers and had the gallery on MySpace, LinkedIn, and Facebook. It seemed to be working, as they were receiving many hits daily from around the country. They were generating a small boom with their prints and drawings, and Lucy had agreed to add some contemporary artists' work. These were edgier works, not what she jokingly referred to as Charleston modern-day pretty art, conservative art for the tasteful palate. She didn't sell the contemporary pretty images of Charleston. Others could do that. She was branching out to the younger crowd that was just beginning to collect, mostly those people in their late twenties to midthirties. These younger artists tended to be a bit of work. Not that she didn't like them; she did. They just seemed to talk her to death. Her familiar dead friends brought her so much comfort, and besides, reading the letters they had composed or journals that they kept allowed her to concentrate on their words and what they contemplated as their body of work.

The young, vibrant artists seemed a bit brash, and she admitted to Gabriella that maybe she was losing her edge. Gabriella laughed at her and told her that she was never losing her edge—she was embarking on a new adventure, and Lucy always loved an adventure. Lucy's favorites included a photographer who scanned her sepia-toned images on vellum. She then drew on the paper with various shades of ink. Lines of poetry and lyrics were added in layers, making the pieces intelligent, heart-wrenching, and beautiful. The second was a forthright-thinking woman who painted before she ever embarked on her career as writer . Lucy had appreciated her early paintings, but the new ones had a tight madness about them. When looking at them, Lucy felt her soul would leave her body and return again, hurt, cleansed, and restored. The third artist worked in mixed media: metal, paint, and textiles. She was a pixie, yet her works were larger than she was and awe-inspiring, if not a wee bit dark. Lucy sighed. Very dark, indeed. She then wondered why she hadn't found a male artist. In her community, were the only ones cranking out the good stuff women? Maybe. She sighed again. The male artists she knew were cranking out the "tourist art." Maybe they were having too much fun with girls. This was Charleston, after all, where there are five girls to every guy, and that did not include the gay men who hadn't come out yet.

Embracing new artists was as hard as dating. "It wears people out," she said to Gabriella. "You know, there are so many things about dating that are maddening, and this is like that, but different, and the personalities...I don't know what to say, but boy howdy."

Gabriella laughed at her. "I know it was my idea, Lucy, but you dove in. You said we should branch out. You are acting a little old-fashioned, like Mr. Sinclair—I mean Huger—used to, and when Huger and I went to lunch the other day, he even said he was using the Internet. How's that?" Gabriella's dark, curly locks wagged about her perfect face.

"Of course you went to lunch with Huger. He's been taking everyone to lunch, and yet he's been turning me down for a while. I agree I'm being petulant, but our three moxie girls have me twisting and turning in all different directions. So, dear Gabi, is there something else you think we should do, or is there anything on your mind?" Lucy queried.

Gabriella sighed. "I have a lot to tell you, Lucy, and a lot to ask. To be honest, I've enjoyed the mayhem of the last two months, as it's distracted me from what I've wanted to talk to you about. First, let me quote you—it's all good. I think we should have a happening, like the Beat movement, but different. One night we should just clear all of our old dear friends out and have a night of our new edgy friends. We can invite the crowd that's in now, our clients and our friends, and we should not do it on art walk night. Maybe music, maybe find a poet, what do you think?"

"Oh, Gabi, it's a great idea. The next art walk is in early May. Let's see, maybe during Spoleto in early June, do you think? That will give the moxie girls time to get more work done. The food is a small issue, as I can make the crudités and cheese platters, and we can augment it with platters from caterers. We can post the invitation on the Web and link it to everything. You need to figure the invite piece of art, and include Diana, of course. You know she has such a fine eye. I'm thinking that we should tell Enid about this and see if she's available to perform. She has a way of mixing things up depending on the audience. What about that poet, Carlos, that smart friend of yours that volunteers for the Conservation League? Perhaps we should ask him to read a piece or two. I like his poetry on green living. Most importantly, the 'girls' use recycled goods in their art, so more 'green thinking.'"

"Yes, Diana has the best eye, and we'll ask her to do recycled arrangements, like she's done before. Remember the ones she did with the vines and dried flowers that she painted? She'll like that, I think. It will be my pleasure to do the invitation. This will be so fun. On another topic, and this is serious, I want to thank you for all that you have taught me, but I want my own space, and I want my own gallery. My grandmother has given me some money. Following my grandfather's death, she discovered that he had made tremendous investments, and she wants to underwrite me. I've been meeting with Huger to discuss how I would talk to you about this because I know how squirrely people in our industry get, but Huger said, 'Tell her directly what you want to do,' and then he winked at me. He never does that. And then he said, 'My girl will help you.'"

Lucy hugged Gabi to her. "Oh, honey," she said affectionately, "it is hard work and a dream, and you know all of that. You know how I scrimped. There was even a time that I worked three months straight with no time off. Most importantly, I want you to be a success, to say that I was one of your mentors. This is sad news for me, as I adore you, but good news for you. So, I am all ears. Tell me all about your plans."

Lucy met Dante for coffee and dessert at a quaint and upscale coffee shop on East Bay Street. The walls were finished in ochre-colored Venetian plaster, and the brightly painted bistro furniture reposed comfortably amidst cushy sofas and chairs. They ordered a slice of a delicious chocolate concoction and shared it. They usually met two Sunday evenings a month to catch up and laugh. She still met Sebastian and Benjamin on the other two after supper at Grandmere's. If anything, Lucy was a creature of habit. She told him Gabriella's news and how they were planning an event at the gallery. It would also be Gabriella's send-off. He asked her how she felt about the changes and asked if Gabriella's gallery would be competing with her own. She said no, that Gabriella's inventory was dramatically different, and then she laughed and filled him in about one of the artists whose work could be considered pornographic. He noted that that was what art was supposed to be about, pushing limits, and didn't Klimt and Schiele do that a hundred years ago? She laughed again and smiled at him as he fed her the cake off his fork. She liked that about him, the way he was familiar with her almost like a lover although they were only friends. He made her feel confident and beautiful, and she would lose herself in those beautiful chocolate eyes. He asked about Michael and questioned if he was being a gentleman, and was he calling and picking up the tab like he should? He reminded her not to fall too fast. She cocked her head to the right and to the left and laughed. They had kissed, and she did like kissing Michael, but she was taking things slow. She liked Michael, too, because she could enjoy his company without feeling like she would fall into a chasm. Truly, she did not know how she had become almost obsessed with Sam, as if he were the only one for her, the one you know that you wanted forever. But she was so much better; she had run into Sam in February, and she hadn't had that light-headed feeling that she always did with him. Dante picked up the check as he always did. He refused to let her pay, and when she tried once to slip her credit card to a server, he became annoyed and said he liked taking girls out and especially her.

They ambled out of the coffee shop, turning left on Queen Street. The houses built so close together sharing common walls graced the streetscape with their presence. She quoted Fanny Kemble, saying that when the English actress had visited the town in the 1830s, she said that the streets reminded one that they were in an old English town, or a city in France or Italy, and that it was pleasing to the eye, something like that anyway.

He told her that Fanny Kemble was indeed right. Did she see how the different houses and their colonial architecture complemented each other? He pointed out Venus in the night sky, taking her hand in his, and it seemed as though they were reaching for the star together. She placed her head on his shoulder as they passed window boxes filled with pansies, sweet alyssum, and cyclamen. She closed her eyes briefly and thought that she was very lucky indeed to have this beautiful man as her friend.

Dante walked her to her car on Broad Street. He opened her door for her, and in the shadowed night, he kissed her softly on the mouth. She smiled at him and thanked him for making her happy and for the coffee and dessert. He told her he was working on research, but he would call her midweek. Once home, she gathered Toulouse to her and hugged him tightly. He was almost five, and he had calmed down significantly and no longer nipped strangers on the rear. It was time to start taking him to work.

Chapter 22

"Loss of virtue in a female is irretreviable; that one false step involves her in endless ruin; that her reputation is no less brittle than it is beautiful; and that she cannot be too much guarded in her behaviour towards the undeserving of the other sex."

Pride and Prejudice, Jane Austen

The phone was ringing off the hook in the gallery, and although Lucy was helping her guest, she felt that something important was going on at the other end of the receiver. She finally packaged the small William Aiken Walker painting of nineteenth-century slave life, complete with a slave cabin and a cotton field. Gazing into the painting, a person could feel the heat of the hot Southern sun and note that there was not a breeze to come by. She had had the painting for more than three years and would not sell it outside of Charleston. It was too precious. A cheerful and handsome Jim Weathers stood before her and wrote his check. He told her that Jessica would be thrilled with the gift. After all, the wedding would be in just two months' time in June.

Lucy inquired as to their wedding plans, and he told her that they would be married at the Cathedral of St. Luke and St. Paul, where they worshipped, and they had booked Lowndes Grove, the early-nineteenth-century country estate in Lucy's neighborhood, for the reception. Lucy said she imagined that it would be lovely. Lowndes Grove certainly did shine with its glowing restoration. It was one of a handful of houses that retained its oculus. What's that exactly, he queried, and she told him about the circular window at the center of the ceiling that was a classical detail, like the Pantheon in Rome, but different. Of course, he said. He told her that Jessica was very organized and there were to be about 250 guests who were invited, including Lillian, and he wondered if Lucy would squire her. She said it would be her pleasure and congratulated him again. He noted that there would be several single men in attendance and perhaps she would meet someone that would catch her fancy. She giggled and thought it was funny how he would use such an old-fashioned phrase, but that was what endeared him to his patients.

She asked about their plans for the honeymoon, and he told her that they would be spending two weeks in Italy. He had a friend who owned a small house in Tuscany, in Montepulciano, and they would stay there and use it as a base to travel to Rome and Florence. Italy is glorious, she enthused. She smiled at him, gregariously talking about her trip in the fall and all that she and Maeve had seen.

"You must go to the catacombs, and you can't miss the Villa Borghese in Rome. Bernini's sculptures are exquisite, especially his *David* and *Apollo and Daphne*."

Of course, while in Florence, they absolutely had to visit the Pitti Palace and see its vast rooms of paintings and sculptures. He said he would call her before the wedding to borrow the guidebooks that she offered him, and he thanked her for her generosity.

After he left, Lucy checked her caller ID. *Odd, four calls from Katie.* She dialed Katie back, knowing that she would be in class. The phone rang twice, and Katie's voice was on the line.

"I have to talk to you, Lucy."

Lucy heard the noise in the background, fractious children, and Katie asked her to hold on. She heard Katie's strident teacher voice.

"Not one more word out of any of you, do you understand? Terrell, put that down. Jasper, enough. Angie, be quiet. I am taking two minutes away from you, and I will have no misbehaving. Do you understand?"

"Hey, Lucy, listen, can I come by tonight? I really need to talk to you."

"Sure, honey, is everything okay?"

Katie sniffled. "Not so much."

"I'll be home a little after six o'clock."

"I'll be there."

Hmmm, Lucy thought, *what is this all about?* Katie never answered her cell phone at school.

Katie was sitting on Lucy's stoop as she pulled the Karmann Ghia into the drive. She looked drawn and pale, her pretty face blotchy and tired with circles under her eyes. Toulouse bounded out of the car, ran up to Katie, and licked her face. Lucy hugged her friend to her and told her to come inside. Katie said that Toulouse looked cute sitting in the passenger seat, and Lucy told her that she had been taking him to work and that her patrons loved him. Lucy hunted in the refrigerator and took out grapes, cheese, and crackers and offered Katie a glass of wine. It certainly appeared that she needed a fortifying spirit, but Katie declined, picking up a cracker and barely nibbling on it. Her blonde hair fell and she placed her face in her hands.

Lucy looked at her friend and said to just let it out. “It can’t be that bad, can it really? And besides, whenever a door closes, God opens a window. Remember that from *The Sound of Music*? It’s true you know, Katie.”

Katie looked at her friend and gave her a brief and poignant smile. “I’m pregnant, Lucy, and I’m pretty sure that Gus Wolfe is the father.”

Lucy said nothing. She smiled at her friend and placed a hand on her blonde head, tucking the thick, long strands behind her ears. “Why don’t you tell me all about it?”

“Remember the weekend that you went to Richmond? I ran into Gus that Friday night, and he said, ‘Why don’t we get together sometime soon? I was so excited that I was playing house at your house that I invited him for dinner the next night. He came over, and he brought flowers, wine, and the ingredients for dinner. It was fun to cook together. That was something that Marshall and I always enjoyed before, you know, the breakup and divorce. We enjoyed each other’s company, I thought. Afterwards, we sat in front of the fireplace and just talked, and then I don’t remember anything else. The next day I woke up and felt sick, and my body was sore. I still had my period, so that wasn’t so surprising, as I always have those awful pains. So I just assumed I drank too much. I haven’t had my period since, and I just couldn’t possibly be pregnant, could I? So I took a pregnancy test earlier this week, and it was positive. I was so rattled that night that you had us all over, and I couldn’t talk to anyone.”

Lucy looked at her friend and said, “There, there, Katie, we’ll figure this out.”

“But Lucy, you’ve been so distant lately, and I’ve had no one to share any of my misgivings. Violet spends half of her time in the country with that math teacher, Rich, with the ever-changing facial hair.”

“I’m so sorry. Had I told all of you earlier this would not have happened. I am to blame for all of this. I don’t even know what to say except that perhaps we are looking for that elusive thing called love and then we all goof up. I really got it all wrong being embarrassed and insecure with what happened at Thanksgiving. I don’t know if you can ever forgive me.”

“I can forgive you, but I don’t know if I can forgive myself.” Katie responded.

“Honey, truly, you invited a man for dinner. What did *you* do wrong? Nothing. It was dinner. It was a date. It was supposed to be fun.

You didn't plan the drug or the date rape. *He* did. He needs to be turned in and we both know that."

"I can't do that, you know. I just can't go through that. A few days after, I faced the truth and, I was embarrassed. You know I never have more than two glasses of wine, and the next morning there were three bottles on the countertop. I just figured, I don't know, that I just lost control. I haven't done that since college. So I called him and apologized and said I thought we had a good time, and he seemed distracted. We went out a couple of times after that, but it was odd, and I felt that he was distant. He looked at me one day, down his nose, so to speak, and said, 'You're not very bright, are you? Do you teach elementary school?' And I said no, middle school, and he said, 'No wonder Charleston County schools are in such a deplorable state,' and I said that I had been named teacher of the year two years ago, and he laughed in a mean-spirited way."

"Oh, Katie, I am so sorry for all of this. I brought him into our sphere, and he is the worst kind of Mr. Wickham ever."

"Why does everything with you always go back to *Pride and Prejudice*? Don't you read anything else but Austen?"

"Please don't get mad at me although I deserve your anger. Austen was an amazing voyeur on life and its goings-on, from calamities to desperate love, passion and real love. We can really learn from her, even if it's two hundred years later. Truly she saves me. Right now I feel so terrible. If I had just told you, you would never have invited him."

"Thank you. Lucy, why didn't you tell us, really, *why*?" Katie dashed away the tears.

"Don't know. I guess I wished it had never happened. I denied it all and then Bennett told me that my actions were not unusual. I just fucked up, okay?"

"Okay."

"Katie, I've been a flipping mess for a while with the Sam thing. I didn't use my judgment with Gus. I've just been so confused. Samuel made me feel so good and in the end so bad. I really thought that maybe we could get back together, and I think I wanted to ignore how it all ended. Sometimes I wonder if I just want to have someone in my life. Someone that I can share things with and someone I can love and maybe have a baby or two. It's going to have to happen quickly, though, as I'm not getting younger, and I'll turn forty in some months' time. Gus just seemed nice and I thought, oh who knows what I thought. He is such bad news. I will tell you, though, both Michael and Dante have become blessings in my life. Well, Dante more than Michael, if I'm honest. I've learned that I can go out without feeling the panic that I need to seriously be with someone. So then maybe it is okay to just fly solo, and if the right person comes, so be it, and if children are part of the master plan, then that will figure out as well."

"Right, that's all good for you, but my life just sucks."

"I'm sorry and I'm sorry I just sounded completely self-absorbed."

"We all do that. Let's talk about something lighter. Take me to a place where I won't think about what I need to do, you know? I'm tired of thinking about this huge decision that will alter my life forever."

"Okay, I think Rich's facial hair is quirky and fun. You never know with him. Sometimes there's a goatee; others just a soul patch and then a full-blown beard. It's like us and different hairdos—ponytails, chignons, straightening, curls, you know the like."

Lucy tried to cajole her friend into a giggle, but it wasn't working. There was too much sadness in Katie right now and too much worry.

"Lucy, it's not working. I don't think anyone could make me feel better right now, I'm at sixes and sevens with how I should proceed with the new life growing inside me. Remember our last superintendent who became pregnant without being married? She was almost run out of town on a rail."

"I know. I remember it well. Okay. So you won't show for a while. We have two months to figure this out. Do you want me to call an emergency night? We all have been, yet again, so busy that we have not been together for a while."

"Yes, please, but not until next week or the week after, when I'm not barfing up a storm. Well, I may still be. Who knows?"

"It's going to be all right, trust me. You are surrounded by your friends. Katie, this is for your knowledge only. Remember when we first met six years ago and you thought I was sad all the time? When I was seeing who I thought was the love of my life, I became pregnant. William and I discussed it forever, to the point that I cried constantly. I don't know if that's what ended the relationship or if circumstances simply fell into place. I was terrified and felt so all alone, and I was thirty-two. He had proposed marriage and then backed out, and I couldn't think how I could responsibly raise a child on my own. I then miscarried in the fourth month, and I felt that I had brought it on, even though my doctor told me that the fetus had just not become viable. When people refer to pro-choice, they refer to the mother, the host, making a decision. Whatever that decision is, it is not an easy one. For me, the choice was made for me."

"Oh, Lucy, when we first became friends, we both joked that we had not been with a man in years. I thought you were just heartbroken. I had no idea about the other. I'm so sorry."

Lucy took her friend in her arms and hugged her to her. She mussed the gorgeous blonde hair, smiled into her blue eyes, and said, "Sweet sister, we will get through this, and that dog will be laid to waste. We will ruin him, believe me."

"No, we can't do that. He's from Columbia, and my dad plays golf with his dad at the country club, and I can't, well, won't tell my mother. She plays bridge with his mother, and they are both past presidents of the Junior League. It won't do. When we were growing up, I thought he was the most gorgeous guy ever, and he exuded such confidence. I had a crush on him, and to tell the truth, he never noticed me."

"So, you are about the same age, then?"

"He's a few years older, thirty-seven to my thirty-four. You know I married straight out of college, and that wasn't the right thing to do either, and by the time I was twenty-seven, it was over. I'm just not so good at this game."

"I don't think many of us are that good at this game. I think there is a great deal of chance to it all. Okay. Look, I will do anything for you. You just let me know, and I will help you navigate, be your compass, or something like that."

"I should go home now. I'm tired, and it's getting late."

"I'm here for you. You know that. I want to tell you that I love you, and I'll be supportive of your choice."

After Katie left, Lucy thought, *What a mess.* She had brought that cur into their sphere. Katie was right. This was her decision to make, and Katie did not want to stir the pot in Columbia. Katie's parents were always keeping up appearances. That is just what they did, no matter that their daughter was in the midst of making one of life's most dramatic decisions. Lucy knew what Katie would do. She would have her baby, nourish it, and raise it well. Her parents would not appreciate the situation even though it was the new millennium. Lucy knew what she *had* to do. She would contact the police department tomorrow and file a report. The hospital had her paperwork and she would go from there.

It was a Thursday afternoon a little more than a week since she had met with Katie. Lucy was scheduled to speak for fifty minutes to an alumni group about Charleston in general, focusing the last twenty minutes on the Charleston Renaissance. It was difficult at best to wrap up the history of Charleston in a fifty-minute lecture, much less both topics, but she had worked and reworked her slides and written notes on index cards so she would not go over, not a smidgen. She drove to the hotel on Calhoun Street and parked in guest parking. She was annoyed to heave her laptop with her. Most high-end groups provided her with one, and she could then pedal her bike to the various locations, as all of her knowledge, as she regarded it, was kept conveniently on her jump drive. But then again it was raining, pouring, in fact, so she would have taken her car anyway.

This group, she harrumphed, were moneyed enough to pay, just cheap. Even Katie's school had everything set up for her, but then they had their own media center. Poor Katie, she thought, what was she going to do? If all went well, no one at the school would notice her pregnancy. She smiled slightly, remembering one of Katie's students and her comment about Lucy's lecture on the Charleston Renaissance. The bright eighth grader said when she saw the slides, she felt that her sightseeing senses ran wild, like a dragon cheetah in a dust storm. She needed to adjust her attitude. These guests would enjoy it, they always did, and the gigs paid and kept her amongst the group of historians and scholars who were asked so often to give presentations. She needed to be gracious and simply be quiet. She opened her umbrella and hoped that it would shield her from the larger drops.

She strolled into the hotel, damp from the inclement weather. She found the Lord Ashley Room and introduced herself to Robin, the IT wiz who would hook up her laptop to the projector. Robin was a pretty twenty-something dressed casually in jeans and a white T-shirt. She managed to take care of the equipment and showed Lucy how to use the remote. Lucy thanked her, and soon they began talking about the images and the artists. Lucy told her about her upcoming show and invited her to attend. Robin gave Lucy her business card, and Lucy said she would send her an Evite. Lucy checked in with registration, only to be told that they would start a little late as some of the guests' planes were just arriving. Lucy didn't mind. What was fifteen minutes? Fifteen minutes turned into thirty that turned into fifty.

Finally the group was settled. They went through a round-robin, introducing themselves and giving a bit of autobiographical data. One gentleman, a retired chemistry professor, went on forever. He was older, probably suffered from dementia. Lucy thought it was nice how patient the other guests were with his rambling until she realized that he had rambled on for about ten minutes. If this continued, she would be here until morning. The other introductions were less lengthy, but all in all they were now behind schedule by one hour and twenty minutes, but who was counting?

Lucy was giving them the basic history and was into her program by twenty-five minutes when she caught the eye of the person supervising the event. She held up her hand, indicating five minutes. How in the world could she wrap it up in five minutes? She looked at the dementia don, as she called him, and he was fast asleep in his chair, snoring softly with drool dripping down his chin. She did a breakneck journey through the Charleston Renaissance and finished within seven minutes.

They thanked her for her time, and as several people held up their hands to ask questions, the director said, "We have no more time, and I'm sure you'll hear more about our topic on the bus tour tomorrow."

Lucy felt a wee bit puzzled, but realized that they were by now far behind their itinerary. She quickly packed up her gear and left.

Two ladies in their seventies followed her and said that she had been recommended to them and they were sorely disappointed at how she raced through the last half. Lucy smiled at them both and said that she was scheduled to start at four, but didn't start until after five because of the weather. If they hadn't had the thunderstorm, the other guests would not have been late. She heard them both sigh and say, "Ah..." and one had the graciousness to say, "Please forgive me." Lucy gave them both her business card and invited them to visit her shop during their stay.

Lucy pulled the Karmann Ghia out onto Calhoun Street. She could not see around the illegally parked Tahoe's hood. As she inched out, she heard brakes hit hard and saw the truck that had almost hit her. Her heart was in her mouth, and she realized that Sam was behind the wheel. He motioned her forward. She waved to him and completed the turn to the right. She looked in the rearview mirror and made a little wave. He pointed to a few empty parking spaces on their right, indicating that she should pull into one of them. She pulled in, and he pulled in behind her. As she stepped out of the car, she thought, what was it with them and SUVs and Calhoun Street?

Sam looked at her and asked if she was okay. She said she was a little rattled, as they had come so close to being in an accident. He had to know that she couldn't see beyond the SUV. He smiled at her and asked her if she had plans for dinner. She said no, that she was planning on picking up shrimp and boiling it at home for supper. He asked her if he could pick her up at eight. She acquiesced.

He was prompt. In the past she would have worn a pretty dress with little heels, but this evening she donned her Lucky brand jeans and a black top, adding black gladiator sandals and the chic black leather backpack she had purchased in Florence. He held open the door to his dark blue Z4 and asked her if Italian food suited her mood. They drove to Warren Street and sat outside on the patio of Pane e Vino, perusing the menu. She loved that the restaurant stated on the menu that cheese would not accompany seafood dishes. She never added cheese to her own seafood pasta at home, as she thought it masked the flavor of the fish or crustaceans. She ordered the shrimp pasta, and he ordered the pasta Bolognese. He asked her if she wanted to share a bottle of wine, and she said no, thank you, but she would like a glass of the Pinot Grigio. He ordered the same.

He asked her what she had been up to that day, and she embarked upon her lecture and how the guests were late, but that all in all it went well. He told her that he had met an acquaintance of hers who spoke about hearing her in the winter. Did she give lectures often? He didn't recall knowing that. She giggled and said there was a lot he didn't know about her and then mused aloud, wondering which lecture the person referenced. The acquaintance was a local Realtor who belonged to the Citadel senior group. That was her Women in Charleston lecture, she said. "Mavericks, Mothers, and Mavens" it was called, and yes, she knew the man, but not well, and if he was who she thought he was, he had questioned her about why the presentation concluded in the 1930s and not the present day. When you have only fifty minutes, you must pick and chose, she told Sam.

Sam told her that Allston Murray had come by the Hanover Street house and thought that he might have a prospective buyer. Sam gave him a tour of the grande dame, pointing out all of his work and showing him the photo album of before-and-after pictures.

"I'm sure you impressed him, Sam, what with all your hard work and talent."

"Thank you, I hope so. It seems his client likes to have some autonomy and is fascinated by life on the Eastside. He's a young writer who has a serious following, and he's intrigued with the house and the neighborhood."

"Well, that's all good in the hood. You can then let that expensive wooden bride of yours go and zip off on your next great adventure."

"Something like that."

The server cleared their plates and offered dessert. Sam looked at Lucy and asked her if she wanted to look at the menu. She smiled at him and said she was so full, as the pasta had been that good, and she didn't think she could eat another bite. Lucy reached for her purse in order to locate her credit card. Sam shook his dark head and said it was his treat.

He pulled up in front of her house and asked her if he could spend five minutes inside with her. Lucy didn't know why she acquiesced again; she just did. He didn't take the keys out of her hands like he had in the past. She sat on a chair and he on the Empire sofa with the winged paw feet. He apologized for his past behavior, and he told her that he had never forgotten her and he wanted to see her again. He would understand if she couldn't, but he really wanted to give it a chance, as he respected her, liked her, and enjoyed her company.

Lucy wasn't quite sure what to say, so she said nothing and let him continue. He was completely over Jess, and did Lucy know that Jess was getting married? As Lucy nodded her head, he went on saying, of course she did, as Jess and her fiancé had been at her grandmother's party. He hoped the two of them could go out to dinner, cook together, ride bikes, walk Toulouse, and watch movies. He wanted to teach her how to sail. How she had never learned to sail while living in the port city was anyone's guess, he said. She would take to a boat like a duck to water, and she would certainly enjoy seeing the architecture from the harbor. She was a fascinating conversationalist, and he liked hearing her stories. She made the world come alive with her bright eyes and her energy. Lucy continued to sit silently, in awe of his musings. He had always enjoyed her company and hoped that she would consider seeing him again. He had missed her and her laughter. He felt that they could make it a go.

Lucy wrinkled her brow and looked at Sam and thought, *Just as I am getting over him entirely, he waltzes back into my life*. She was bemused and shocked and could feel her heart race. Part of her wanted to say, *No, Sam this will not do, You broke my heart once. You'll break it again*. Yet another part said, *You, Lucy, have changed. Maybe it won't work, but what if it will? He made you happier than anyone ever has, and just when you look into those pewter eyes, you are lost forever. No,* her heart spoke, *banish the negative words from your mind and your tongue. Let the hopeful Lucy, the Lucy who has tried to be one with all and accepting, try it once more.*

He was looking at her, staring at her mouth. She smiled at him and said, "Samuel Francis O'Hara, you are one piece of work, and I mean that in the kindest of ways. Let me digest this all, please?"

"Sure, I'll go. If I don't hear from you by early next week, I'll call you, okay?"

"Yes, I'll call you, Sam. I just need some time to process all your words. You do understand that, though?"

"Look, Lucy..."

He was standing in front of her, and he took her hands in his, and she felt their connection. Her eyes were misty, and there was a great deal of emotion there. She pursed and unpursed her mouth and finally smiled a half smile at him. "Sam, just give me a little time."

He smiled at her, and she grinned back at him. After he left, Lucy washed her face and prepared for bed. She rustled in the drawer and pulled out a simple black silk nightie and tried to go to sleep. She slept, only to dream about Sam, and woke up at 3:00 a.m. Finally, after tossing and turning, she fell into a fitful sleep at 5:00 a.m.

Lucy was tired. Although she had consumed almost a pot of coffee, she could not shake the brain fog. She still could not believe yesterday's chain of events: the derailed lecture, running into Sam, dinner with him, and then his dramatic monologue. What on earth was she to do? She wanted to tell him no, she was no longer interested as she was afraid of getting hurt. She knew she wanted to see him, and she probably would let him take her out, but she couldn't let her friends know in the event that he wouldn't do right. That was the conundrum. If she didn't tell her friends, then what? Then she would be lost without her support group. She shook her curls and placed her head in her hands, sighing deeply. What had Ella said to her in January? Sometimes you have to let life take its course. Don't try so hard. Just let it be.

So now she must let it be, and if she was going to embark on this maelstrom, she would have to have a compass and a sextant to guide her. Who was she fooling? This was Sam, and she was like a small craft in the water enduring a hurricane with another behind it. She would need running lights, a laptop, and a GPS tracking device to find a safe port of call.

Chapter 23

Every man is surrounded by a neighbourhood of voluntary spies....

Northanger Abbey, Jane Austen,

The bell on the door gave a soft jingle, bringing Lucy out of her reverie. Susie came in, blue eyes shining, dressed in a simple and expensive gray-and-white seersucker dress.

"Hello, Lucy. I haven't spoken to you in a while and thought I might pop by and see how all is going, and I wanted you to check your calendar so that we can plan a field trip."

Lucy smiled at Susie, thinking that her Grandmere had excellent friends, both young and old. Lucy offered Susie a glass of iced tea. Susie told Lucy that the renovation of her small Victorian cottage in Springfield was completed and that she wanted Lucy to see it. No, she didn't know what she was going to do with it, but she had inherited it from her grandmother's estate, and could Lucy believe when her grandmother passed three years ago, she had just celebrated her ninetieth birthday? She wanted to see a nice tenant in the cottage, a couple maybe, who would appreciate its charming interior and sweet garden. Lucy said of course, a drive inland would be nice this time of year, and she would love to see the cottage in all of its glory. They agreed to visit the following Sunday, as Frederick would be out of town and Lucy's gallery would be closed.

After work Lucy walked Toulouse to Diana and Weston's house for dinner. The three of them had not spent time together in a few weeks, and Lucy looked forward to their time to talk together. It didn't hurt that Diana was making a beautiful salad and that Weston was grilling steaks. Toulouse was rummaging in Annabel's toy box, selecting and depositing toys right and left on the hardwood floors. Lucy apologized to Diana, who said not to worry. If Annabel allowed it, why would she mind?

Lucy wanted to tell Diana about last's night's turn of events, but she couldn't bring herself to do it. It was still too much like a dream, and she wondered if she had imagined it all. No, she wasn't even sure if she would call him back. Maybe for once in her life she needed to not be a blabbermouth about every minute detail of her life. Maybe she should keep this to herself until the five-month mark, if there would be a five-month mark. She wouldn't sleep with him, though. Not for a while, if at all.

"Lucy," Diana scolded. "You haven't listened to a thing that I have said. Why are you so preoccupied?"

"Er, I don't know. Just thinking, I guess. I don't know about what, though." She smiled at her friend and giggled. "Tell me about the greenhouse, Diana; it must be going splendidly."

"It is."

While they set the table in the yard, Diana told Lucy of her big find. She and a master gardener had been highly successful at cultivating a spring crop. Although she loved to garden and knew her plants so well, this retired teacher, Ida, could run circles around her, and she loved being in the greenhouse. Diana was saving bundles on the flowers she used to order, and now there was such an amazing inventory that she and Ida could plan for a week-by-week selection and let her clients know about it through e-mail blasts. She had almost doubled her profits in the month of March from last year.

The greenhouse was amazing. Who would ever have thought that when she listed "Greenhouse wanted" on Craigslist that she would have such a response? She finally settled on a greenhouse that was from the 1950s that a farmer in Orangeburg County was offering, and even better, when Lucy was high-tailing it to Richmond in January, she had met the man whose brother just happened to be a truck driver, and he said that they could assemble it on site. It was solid, beautiful, and every time Diana stepped into the space, she was overcome by the scents and the sheer oxygenation of it all. Ida was the kicker. She loved being there, and she kept the place spotless. Diana had been a little nervous at first about the investment, but it was all paying off nicely, and who would have ever known? And thank God for Rachel's involvement. She had found the right spot that included a well.

They were offering flowers for half price if you came by yourself to the shop and picked up a bouquet or five dollars off if you brought your own vase. She still added her signature curly willow, and what had drawn her to the site was that there were five mature willow trees on the edge of the property that she could harvest. It was as if the universe was manifesting all of her dreams in this rural lot in the heart of old North Charleston, just ten minutes away from her shop. Yes, she still had to buy willow branches from a vendor so she wouldn't overharvest the trees, but that was no problem. It was paying for itself and garnering her a more than modest profit. Lucy smiled at her dear friend and said she was so very happy for her. Weston called to his girls and said the steaks were ready and to come to the grill. They sat down to eat their feast as the sun began to fade. Diana lit the candles on the outdoor candelabra that hung in the tree above them, and Lucy felt, as always, surfeit with her very dear friends.

Weston looked at Diana and asked, "Did you tell her?"

"No, darling, it's yours to tell, not mine," she said.

"Lucy, are you still seeing Michael?"

"Michael is wonderful, but it's not there, you know. The chemistry and all. I enjoyed his company in January and February, and it was pleasant to have someone around while my heart was mending. I do have to tell you I always liked zipping about in his Porsche Boxster, and he was a nice and safe date, although he is not as entertaining as most of my friends. And then there is the work thing. I'm so passionate about what I do, and his work seems like it's just a job to him. Weston, I've seen his designs, and they are fine, but his renderings seem to lack the detail that yours have. I know that you are extremely talented as well as passionate about your work, and he seems a bit boring, like the engineers that I dated. I know this all sounds very superficial, and I'm sure I just insulted you, Weston, without meaning to do so. After a while it seemed as if the relationship took too much effort. We've decided that, although he respects me and likes me, I am also lackluster and boring."

"Certainly, he didn't say that, Lucy?" Diana queried.

"Honestly, he has more tact then that," Weston chimed.

"No, no, those were my words to him entirely. He is a good man."

Diana looked at Weston, held his gaze, and said, "Honey we need to tell her."

Weston looked at Lucy. "So, this means you won't be hurt if he asks someone out? Someone you know and don't like?"

"Oh, Weston and Diana, I wish him well, but I can't see myself with him down the road. The feelings just aren't there. He and I didn't last but eight weeks. If the feelings aren't there the first six months to a year, there isn't any reason to hang on to the relationship. That should be the time when there are very few faults to be had and when you want to talk to each other, to be with each other, and if that passion is not there, then it is not. In the end you waste each other's time, and later you will criticize each other, and that's not healthy. There is no reason to stay in the relationship if the passion isn't there. I also think, just if you like someone, there may be the potential for it to turn into love, but relationships are hard enough, and without the chemistry, if it is not there, that won't change over time. How can you justify being with someone you like as a friend and yet *not* love as a friend and a lover? Look at the two of you. After ten years, you are still crazy about each other, and I think your honeymoon lasted three years. With Michael, it wasn't there from the beginning."

They looked at each other and nodded.

"Then you won't mind if he asks Desiree out for a date?" Weston asked.

"Oh no! Poor Michael and poor Brooks. Brooks has always been mad about her, and they've been seeing each other since December. Please tell me what's going on with this situation."

Weston told her that Michael had met Desiree at a party a few weeks ago, and he found her extremely attractive and that she had flirted with him outrageously. She had given him her number and asked him to call her. They were going out on Saturday night.

"Someone has to warn him," Lucy said. "Someone has to tell him that she's a man-eater, a social vampire, and that she's hurt everyone she's married or dated."

Then again, it was not hers to tell. She looked at them both seriously and said, "I don't think Brooks will endure this so well. Someone must let him know. It can't be me, you know. Desiree and I have a past of unfortunate experiences, and Brooks will think I'm mean-spirited. Someone else must warn him."

Diana eyed Weston and lifted one winged eyebrow. Lucy could tell there was more to this story.

"Lucy, I'm to meet with Brooks and Sam tomorrow night for supper at Moe's; perhaps I'll ask Brooks to meet me earlier. You are absolutely right; you are not the one to tell either of them. I will have to do so."

"She always pops up, you know, like a bad seed ruining the garden or infecting the ornamentals," Lucy stated.

Diana was in full agreement. "Why can't she stick with her wealthy South of Broad out-of-towners? Why does Desiree have to bring her drama into our humble lives uptown, where everyone is pretty grateful to just live life and enjoy what they earn?"

Lucy and Diana loaded the dishwasher while Weston selected music for their listening pleasure. Lucy yawned, and once the dishwasher was loaded, she hugged her dearest friends and thanked Annabel for letting

Toulouse play with her toys, which she placed back in the open bin. She left, calling, "Good night" and "I love you," and her friends returned the rejoinder.

She walked Toulouse home thinking, *Yet again, another mess*. She realized it had been a little over a week since she had spoken to Katie, and it was time to make the call. It was nine forty-five, and it was a school night, so she would make the call in the morning.

Chapter 24

Trouble is the common denominator of living. It is the great equalizer.

Soren Kierkegaard

Lucy left a message for Katie and drove to work. She thanked her lucky stars that the gallery had come with one off-street parking space. The tenant of the six-hundred-square-foot apartment upstairs was able to get a parking decal from the city, and she parked on the street. Tenants always complained about parking, but that was how life was as an urban dweller. When she had purchased the property, she had allowed the tenants to park in the space, but now that Toulouse accompanied her on a daily basis, it made sense to take over her territory. Her shop was not far from the market, and she always enjoyed a steady stream of traffic. Customers loved Toulouse, and there were several carriage drivers who gave tours of the city and would come in just to pat his shaggy head. They always wanted to give him dog bones or some other processed dog treat, but Lucy wouldn't let them and gave them a half of a carrot instead to give to her most beloved woof.

Her mind was trying to process it all. First Katie's news, then dinner with Sam and his monologue, then Desiree's deceit of Brooks. She shook her head. The last ten days had been filled with revelations. Hopefully she would be busy today so she wouldn't have time to think. Because the Festival of Houses and Gardens was going on, Lucy saw a steady movement of traffic. A couple with tattooed sleeves on their arms parked their loud Harley-Davidson in front of her shop. They walked inside and looked about, making constant commentary about her inventory. She asked them where they were from and if they were visiting because of the tours. Yes, they replied they were spending several days and had come specifically to see the private residences. They were from Richmond.

"Ah," she said, "I was there in January visiting a new acquaintance." They asked who she visited, and she said, "Rafe Semmes, he lives in the Fan."

"Are you Lucy, then?" the man inquired.

"Yes. Yes, I am. Lucy Cameron at your service."

"I'm Jack Bonney, and this is my wife, Lita."

They shook hands, and Lucy said, "Very nice to meet you."

The woman said, "Actually, my name is Carmelita, Lita for short."

Lucy said she noticed a beautiful dialect there, and Carmelita said she was originally from Chile. They were entranced with everything Southern, especially the art. They knew Rafe from VCU, where he taught the occasional decorative arts class and where they both taught. He was a Political Science professor, and she taught latin studies. Rafe had told them to visit her shop, as they were sure to find something magical. She showed him the works she displayed, and they instantly needed an Eola Willis painting and one from Abe Schwartz.

"Funny" she said, "this same Abe Schwartz painting came to me in January from Rafe."

Jack said, "Yes, I know they were in my mentor's house." He had known Mr. Schwartz back in the 1970s, when Mr. Schwartz owned a gas station somewhere around here.

Lucy laughed and said, "Well of course you should have it, then."

She marveled at the woman's tattoos near her collarbones. They were two beautifully colored phoenixes, and when she raised her arms, the colored wings of the birds flared up, seeming as if they were in flight. Lucy told her the designs were beautiful, and the two guests laughed together. Lita told her that when she had left her abusive husband several years ago, she had the phoenixes emblazoned on her arms and chest as an epiphany. Jack said that when he asked his future wife out, he was concerned that his own arms that he kept covered during the day might put her off. When he picked her up for their third date to a concert by The Killers, he saw the art and immediately took off his long-sleeved shirt and proudly displayed his art in a short-sleeved T-shirt.

Lucy laughed and said, "And were the two of you done in from there?"

"Pretty much," he said, "or at least I was. It took her a couple of years of convincing and a great deal of conniving on my behalf."

Lita laughed at him and said, "I wanted to make sure you were after my mind and not my body."

Lucy looked at Lita and thought, *Who wouldn't be entranced with that?* She was gorgeous and confident. They agreed that Lucy would send them the paintings, and she charged their credit card. An hour later the phone rang, and Lucy answered it on the fourth ring.

"Cameron Fine Art," she said.

She hadn't spoken to her mentor in six weeks, and here he was inviting her for dinner the next night. She agreed and asked to bring Toulouse. Yes, absolutely. He was having friends of his from Richmond in town. He wanted her to meet them.

Hanging up, Lucy said, "Odd, just odd. I bet it's my Harley couple."

The dinner was lovely. Lucy had brought a nice bottle of wine, and sure enough, Jack and Lita were Huger's guests. She also learned that, while she had been muddling through all of her chaos, Rafe and Huger seemed to have managed to become a couple and that Huger Sinclair had been to Richmond several times. *Nice,very nice, indeed,* she thought.

She arrived home with a very tired dog at ten thirty. There were six new messages. She yawned loudly and knew she would return them in the morning.

It was Sunday, and Lucy had the day off. She was exhausted. She had been out three times that week, her brain was on overload, and she had garnered more information, good and bad, than she could bear. The phone rang, and she realized it was Katie.

"How are you, honey?" she said.

"Better, Lucy. I'm going to have the baby. If I can figure out my finances, I'll be okay. I just think I need to leave Chucktown for a while when school ends this year. I love this city, but I'm emotional, and I need quiet, comfort, and solace; do you understand that?"

"Yes, certainly, you need all those things. What can I do?"

"Nothing yet, and not the girls' night. I have to come to a place of peace and understanding."

"I understand. Let me know what you need, and I'll be there."

"I'm okay. Just keep in touch, all right?" Her voice wavered.

The phone rang again. It was Susie, reminding Lucy that she would pick her up at ten thirty for their field trip. Lucy had completely forgotten, but she couldn't be a flake and tell Susie that. Instead she quickly showered and dressed and was ready at the appointed time. They were in Springfield before they knew it, driving down shady streets lined with Victorian houses and cottages. Susie pulled the Mercedes Benz in the driveway and came to a halt. The cottage gleamed white in the late-morning sun, and it was surrounded by lush vegetation. The azaleas were in full bloom and Lucy thought, *This house is situated in a bower of earthly delights*, and told Susie just that.

Susie laughed and said, "Let's go inside."

The pine floors had been beautifully refinished and gleamed softly. The walls were painted a cream-colored hue, and Lucy was amazed at the amount of sunlight that poured in. It was a very cheerful and lovely space. Susie showed her the rest of the house, and Lucy said how charming it all was. The kitchen boasted new stainless steel appliances, and the black soapstone countertops and sink made the space modern in appearance. The sunroom off the kitchen was Lucy's favorite, with built-in glass-fronted bookcases lining one wall.

"Now you see why I want the perfect tenants. It's just too dear to let just anyone live here. My challenge, Lucy, is how to find the right ones. As I'm about an hour away, it would be hard to watch over it, and I don't know any local Realtors who could manage it. So, it's a conundrum."

"Yes, I can see that. It is lovely, though, with its two large bedrooms. Do the fireplaces work in both the living room and dining room? It would be ideal for a couple. The right couple, that is."

"Yes, the fireplaces both work, but I didn't install gas logs, as you always hear of tenants building regular fires on top of them, and they ruin them completely."

After a while they drove about town, and Lucy told Susie that Springfield was the quintessential Southern town when you thought about the South and how it was presented in books and movies. Susie agreed, but commented that it didn't have any industry, and the majority of the population worked outside the town limits, where they could find employment. Lucy mused aloud that this would be the safe haven that Katie needed. Susie wondered what Lucy meant. Lucy told Susie that a friend of hers needed to get out of town for a while. Actually, she wasn't sure for how long. Maybe they could meet each other and see if it would fit everyone's needs? Susie said that would be lovely. The sooner the better.

Susie dropped Lucy off at three thirty. Lucy walked Toulouse and then went back home thinking she needed a nap. She couldn't help but think that this could be the best solution for Katie. She could remove herself from the drama and be in a nice quiet spot where she could heal and plan for a new life. Still yawning, she quickly undressed and crawled in between the bed linens thinking that her life had been too busy the past two weeks and hoping that the coming week would be filled with far less drama and chaos.

She heard the phone ringing from a long way away. She stretched, yawned, and checked the alarm clock, noting it was early, only six fifteen. NPR was playing Celtic music, and it softly filled her house. She was tired. She checked her voice mail and realized she had missed three calls: one from Katie, one from the neighborhood association, and one from Sebastian. She had completely forgotten to meet Ben and Sebastian for dinner at Moe's. She called her friend and immediately apologized for not showing. He forgave her as long as she would look at her calendar and find an evening this week to go to dinner or for a walk. She thanked him, told him she was sorry again, and that she'd call him tomorrow.

She contemplated returning to the comfort of her bed and then thought if she went back to bed now, she would be up at three or four in the morning, and that would never do. She prowled around the kitchen, opening cabinets and the refrigerator, until finally deciding to open a can of tuna. She took the phone from its cradle and quickly dialed Katie's number. Katie answered on the third ring. After inquiring about her health, Lucy dove into her subject matter. She told Katie all about Susie's quaint and charming cottage in Springfield. She mentioned the yard, mature trees, and the sunroom. This might be the perfect match for all parties. She wasn't sure what Susie would charge for rent, but it couldn't be exorbitant. Mostly Susie wanted a decent tenant, and it might be the sanctuary that Katie needed. She gave Susie's number to Katie and suggested that she give her a call. They continued to chat, and Katie thanked Lucy again for being so wonderful and considerate.

A week later Susie and Katie met and traveled to Springfield. Katie was charmed by the cottage and the town and told Susie that this would be the blessed sanctuary. They came to an amicable decision on the rental agreement, and all the wheels were placed in motion. Katie would create a new life in a happy, quaint house in a charming small town. Susie identified with Katie, as she had been a teacher before being swept off her feet by her first husband, a little more than thirty years before. Charles had been twenty years older than she, but that is what suited her. She liked the security of being with an older man, someone who was mature and stable. They had had a wonderful life together, and when his life was cut short by a heart attack on the golf course, she was heartbroken, but then later she recovered, as there were so many memories to remind her that she and Charles had something that most people only dream of having.

Three years later she had met Frederick at an antique show in Charleston, and she had been taken aback. She had had that same feeling that she did when she met Charles, and look where she was now, happily living with the most kind, loving, and handsome of men in a nineteenth-century house on one of the finest and most picturesque streets in Charleston. She hoped that Katie would find someone who would give her all of those things as well.

She and Katie discussed everything, and Susie was happy to have Katie in the cottage, but what was Katie to do? Katie told her that she would only have money until August. She couldn't teach. Nobody would hire a single mother, as it would imply that she was not an appropriate role model, and she couldn't, and wouldn't, fabricate a husband; that would never do. But maybe she could tutor children after school. She thought that both her grandmother on her mother's side and her grandfather on her father's side would help her. Of course, she would pay them back. Maybe she would even start her own business. She sewed well. Perhaps she could even do alterations. She had never thought about that before. She played the piano well and had done so in church, and maybe there were children to whom she could give lessons. So, she told Susie, maybe she could cobble it all together and it would all work out to her satisfaction. She knew it would be more cost-effective if she were to work out of the house. Susie asked her about insurance, and Katie replied that she had gone online and her insurance would be good through the end of August, but then she had to try her hand at Cobra or something like it, and it would be expensive, but this baby thing was just that.

Susie pulled her gently to her and said, "Hush now. It will work out. Trust me."

"I'm sorry, Susie, but I am sorely frightened, and I feel that you and Lucy are my only friends in the world right now." Katie placed her head in her hands and dashed away tears of disappointment, hurt, and embarrassment.

Susie peered at Katie and remembered her own circumstances so many years ago, and her decision that had left her barren. Charles had never minded. He said he knew that he was selfish, but he just wanted to be hers alone and did not want to share her with anyone else; besides, children were overrated. Katie's situation would work out. She just knew it.

"Katie, dear, we are not your only friends, and you know that. You have lovely friends, and they will all step in and help you. I have watched your group from afar, and I remind Miss Lillian how lucky you all are to have each other. Not just the women, but also those very nice young men. I think now what you must do is plan the relocation. When exactly does your lease end?"

"May first, and I cannot wait, as my roommate has been dreadful, borrowing my clothes, my perfume, and eating my food. It will be a dream to live somewhere else. The only problem is where to live between that time and the end of the school term, which ends towards the middle of June, and where to store my furniture. There's not that much, but still,"

Susie laughed. "That is an easy problem to solve. You can move your belongings at anytime to the cottage, and you can stay in my carriage house until the third week in May, and it's completely furnished. Frederick and I had previously agreed to allow performers for Spoleto to stay from the beginning of the third week of May until the end of the festival. That means you will need to only find someplace else for the time that the festival ends, and then you can move back in until your transition to the midlands. Ask Lucy. She has an extra bedroom."

Katie smiled her brilliant smile and thanked Susie, but she couldn't possibly afford to pay the rent that Susie and Frederick would expect. Susie said that was not a problem. Katie would be her guest, and she knew that Frederick would feel the same way. The only thing that Susie would request was that Katie would take supper with them at least once a week.

Katie could not believe her good luck. Almost all of her problems solved by a petite, beautiful fifty-something woman whom she had met just once.

The For Sale sign had been up for five weeks, and the property was being shown on a daily basis. Sam was pleased with the comments, and although the house was being listed for its appraised value, he did not have a serious buyer. Allston Murray had called him that day to inform him that one of the Realtors in the office would be showing the property that day. Would Sam make sure that the photo album of before and-after-shots was available? Sam told him that that was fine; he would leave the photo album on the kitchen counter. The phone rang again, and he thought that it might be Lucy. She had said she needed time, but the Lucy he knew always called back within a few days, well, usually within a day, and here it had been a full week. He couldn't worry about that, though. He was going to look at another property. This one was situated on Aiken Street. It had been doused in a house fire, and the property taxes hadn't been paid in years. The price was low, but he wasn't sure if it would be a total bust and not worth his time or his effort.

Sam met the owner's son, a confident, smart man in his forties who worked at a local bank. He told Sam that he had no idea that his father hadn't paid the property taxes, and he was trying to figure it out. The family needed to unload the house because there were too many rentals to manage, and all of them had seen better days. This house was the worst, as there had been a grease fire in the kitchen, and that fire had also spread to the upstairs bathroom before being contained. His father had moved to a suburban neighborhood in West Ashley years ago, and the property manager had not kept the family up with the state of affairs. He had just recently gone to the Charleston County Web site to assess the properties his father owned and was surprised that his father had acquired over ten properties that he used as rentals in the city, and mostly on the Eastside. Several of the properties were behind in taxes, and now here he was having to do all of the damage control.

They looked around the small single house, and besides the obvious fire damage, the house was in relatively good shape. The kitchen had been part of an addition of an enclosed back porch. The construction had been shoddy to begin with and could easily be rebuilt. Sam pulled out his digital camera and notepad and started snapping away while making detailed notes. He asked Zeke how much he was willing to take for the property, and after twenty minutes of discussion and banter, they had come to an agreement, as Sam would pay cash for the property. Zeke's father would receive fifteen thousand less than the asking price, but then again, it was better for everyone if the house was someone else's problem. Sam was sure that, after all the paperwork was done, they could close within a few weeks. Zeke punched Sam's number into his cell phone and said he was looking forward to working with him. He had to run now for a meeting at church, where he had agreed to serve on the buildings committee.

Sam dialed Brooks, and immediately his friend was on the other end of the line. He explained the current situation, and Brooks checked his calendar and said the closing could be set up in two weeks' time.

"What's Zeke's last name? Is it Richardson?"

"It is. Do you know him?" Sam queried.

"I do. He's a great guy, really tapped into the community. He does a lot for the Boys and Girls Club, and I've worked with him on Habitat houses. He should know your Mrs. Annie, as I believe he worships at Emmanuel AME."

"Well, that's all good to know. I'll talk to Mrs. Annie too. She knows everything about everyone."

Sam whistled as he settled behind the wheel of his truck. His day was just about perfect. Now if she would just call, it would be even better.

Chapter 25

O! How this spring of love resembleth
The Uncertain glory of an April day.

The Two Gentlemen of Verona, William Shakespeare

Lucy knew that she had to call Sam, but every time she took the phone off the cradle, she became fidgety and nervous. *It's just a phone call, that's all.* She could do this. The bell jingled on the door, and she turned her attention to her customer. There in front of her was a delivery person, young, probably a college student, carrying the most beautiful floral arrangement. He asked her if she were Lucy Cameron, and she nodded and took the flowers. Placing them on the counter, she just knew that they had come from Sam. The arrangement was filled with peonies, bells of Ireland, and a profusion of stock of every different hue—white, pinks, and deep purples. Artemisia and rosemary added texture all the while large white snapdragons towered above them. It was finished with a few curly willow branches. How thoughtful, she thought, not only to send them, but to order them through Diana's shop, thereby letting her friend know that he was seeing her or at least making amends.

The bell rang again, and before Lucy knew it, she was caught in the day, helping customers, answering the phone, and returning e-mails. Finally at six o'clock, she turned the Closed sign to face the street. She sighed and smiled, looking at the flowers, thinking that she should make the call now.

She was absently patting Toulouse's shaggy head when Sam answered on the first ring. She thanked him for the flowers and told them how beautiful they were, and yes, she would meet him for supper this week. Thursday would be wonderful. Yes, she looked forward to hearing from him in two days' time.

Sam ended the call and thought that he had lied by omission, something he tried not to do. He hadn't sent her flowers, but who had? He would call a florist in town tomorrow, in the morning, and immediately have a bouquet sent. He called his accountant, Jillian, and asked her about florists, and she told him that there were only three that she recommended. One was Diana. Obviously he couldn't send them from her shop, he thought. Lucy had agreed to dinner, but they were not an item. That was out of the question.

Jillian sighed. "Sam, you have got to get it right with her, and buying gifts and sending flowers is just the beginning. If you weren't such a good friend and client, I would let you have it for not treating her with more respect. Buddy, you need to fork over at least fifty dollars to make it showy. No, Sam, showy does not mean over the top. C'mon now, you're not asking her to marry you; you are simply sending her flowers. You do know that I would never have put up with this crap from Curt."

"I know, I know, you always made him toe the line. It's just that sending flowers, in my mind, says we're more than friends and all, and we're still negotiating dinner, you know?"

"Hmmph, last week you told us both that you wanted to see her seriously. What is wrong with you today?"

"Nothing, Jillian, it's just...I don't know."

"Well, if you can't articulate it, maybe you should just let her go, again. You don't deserve her if you are all wishy-washy."

"I'm not all wishy-washy, and I've never been that in my life. I take risks; you know that."

She could tell he was getting annoyed, but Jillian was a straight shooter, and as a woman she felt sorry for Lucy. She had only met her once at an art opening. Her neighbor Gabriella had introduced them, and Lucy had been polite, funny, and nice.

"All I'm saying, Sam, you've danced this dance before. You always sent flowers to Jess. What's your problem with sending flowers to Lucy?"

"That was different. I suppose I just need to do it."

"I'd call them first thing in the morning, and I'd offer to pay an extra delivery so they get there before noon. Otherwise, she will know that you ordered them because she received flowers from someone else."

"Okay, maybe you're right, Jillian."

"Sam? Maybe right? How about right again, or right as usual. One more thing. Don't break her heart all over again. If you're being selfish, you need to recognize that emotion. Just promise me that if you are not feeling the love, you'll be honest with yourself, and if you let her go, you'll treat her decently."

"Yeah, okay, I need to go." He knew he sounded frustrated.

Sam drove by the America Street house and saw that Mrs. Annie's lights were illuminated. He called and asked if he could stop by and run a few questions by her. She agreed, and he quickly crossed the street and knocked on her door. He was always amazed at how tidy her house was. Everything cleaned and dusted, there was never a thing out of place. He asked her about Zeke Richardson, and she verified that he had always been trustworthy and decent. It was just a shame that Zeke's father couldn't, or wouldn't, keep up his properties and all of them were in a state of disrepair. She was happy that Sam could take on the Aiken Street house. It would be an excellent situation for both parties, and it would mean that another eyesore would be rehabilitated. It sure did drive her crazy when people abandoned buildings. It placed everyone else's home at risk, as well what with ne're-do-wells breaking in and starting fires. She asked him how he planned to get the work done with his upcoming trip. Sam told her that Sheff and he could probably get the kitchen and bath done by the end of June and finish most of the project sometime mid-July. That would postpone the trip until the first of August, but the other repairs were minimal: some plaster repair, rewiring, painting the interior and the roof. All could be done simultaneously, and Sheff had a friend who worked construction and could live there rent-free while completing the interior painting once the kitchen and bath were up to snuff. Unlike the Hanover Street house, it was small, around twelve hundred square feet, so it was all manageable, and the placed would be inhabited.

Sam inquired about the tenants in his house across the street. She told him that they weren't loud and seemed courteous and said hello. How did he like living in his cottage on Nassau Street? He said he liked its compactness, although he really did need to upgrade the bathroom. He had learned so much since that project, as it had been one of his earliest. For some unknown reason, Sam told Mrs. Annie about Lucy and the flower situation and asked her if she thought he was doing the right thing.

Mrs. Annie looked at him hard and said, "Sam, you shouldn't ever lie, but you did, so you have two choices: admit the lie or cover for yourself. If you choose the latter, you better make darn sure that you don't do it again—lie, that is. Once a lie starts, then there are always plenty more, and you are no liar."

Sam agreed and told her he wasn't proud of his actions and he was concerned about it all, as it hadn't ended so well before. She asked if he was talking about the pretty blonde girl who used to visit with him, and he said yes, she was the one. Mrs. Annie smiled a rueful smile. Why were nice men never nice to nice women, she wondered aloud, Lucy had always waved to her and said hello and would always acknowledge her if she saw her around town. Wasn't that considerate? Most young people don't go out of their way to say a brief hello to older people they have only met a few times. Sam had been chastised twice. If he were to get it right, as Jillian said, he would have to behave in a more gentlemanlike manner. He thanked Mrs. Annie, kissed her unlined cheek, and drove home to his freedman's cottage.

The next morning Sam called the florist second on Jillian's list. He just couldn't call Diana's shop. Plus, if Lucy asked...Well, nope, he would try the other two. The first florist said they were busy and could not guarantee a delivery before noon. He said he'd get back to them. The next florist's line was busy, and his message went to voice mail. He didn't know why he was so impatient; he just was. Maybe Lucy wouldn't notice if the flowers were late. No, she would notice. She always did notice that kind of thing. He was taking a chance, but that's what he felt he needed to do. The phone rang, with the florist's name popping up on the screen. Yes, they could make the delivery by ten thirty. No, there would not be an additional fee. And yes, they would call him and let him know that the flowers had been delivered.

After hanging up the phone, he thought, *This behavior is ridiculous. I just became OCD over that girl.* He shrugged his shoulders, thought about the color of her eyes, and muttered, "Oh well, oh well."

Lucy was looking forward to Thursday night. She wondered where they would go, hoping somewhere that they could sit outside and enjoy the spring weather. She was lost in her thoughts, smiling and feeling distracted, when she heard the bell. A delivery person brought her an amazing arrangement of hothouse lilies and asparagus fern. The flowers were beautiful and totally different than Sam's arrangement on the counter. They were a little showy, but then again, she couldn't think when she had seen such an abundance of tropical colors. These flowers were definitely not from Diana's shop. She thanked the delivery man and opened the card, wondering who had sent them. The card was simple and elegant and on heavy card stock. She read three words: *Lucy, Enjoy! Sam.*

What was this all about, she thought, and then she realized that she had not read the card of the other arrangement. She had simply assumed they were from *him*. She fished out the card from yesterday's arrangement and opened it. This card read: *Lucy, darling, it's been too long...Dinner, champagne, or dessert? Your pleasure. Love, Dante.*

How could she have been so stupid? She wanted to kick herself. Sam was not as sensitive as Dante. Of course Dante had sent the flowers, and she had called the wrong person to say thank you. Why had she made the assumption? Had Sam ordered the flowers yesterday? Or had he covered today after he didn't say anything when she mentioned the flowers yesterday evening? Who knew? She sighed. She didn't want to go to supper with him now. She just didn't.

Sam called her midday and asked her when he could pick her up. She said she had to work late; why didn't she meet him somewhere nearby at seven? Sam wasn't a fan of the restaurants in the Market area. He preferred unpretentious and casual dining on Upper King Street to the formal settings. He said how about Rue de Jean? She replied that that would suit her just fine, as it was on her way home.

At six thirty she was wrapping up the last updates to the gallery's Facebook page, and she tweeted information regarding the special exhibit in June. She looked at the clock and decided it was time to meet him.

Sam was at the bar when Lucy entered. He could tell something was amiss, and he regretted not saying anything when she had thanked him for the flowers. He tried to tell himself it was nothing; just let it go. She walked up to him looking fresh in a white embroidered dress that fell above her knee. She had on bright pink shoes, and a pink sweater was thrown around her shoulders. Her bangs had grown out, and she had cut her hair and straightened it. He missed the mop of curls.

"Hi, Lucy. You look pretty in those bright colors," he said with exuberance. He leaned in to hug her, and she stopped him short. "Would you like a drink from the bar?"

"Hi, Sam, can we just find our table? I've had a big couple of weeks, and I'm not sure I should stay out very late."

"Right." He settled his tab and found the hostess, who seated them outside on the terrace.

Lucy thought he looked handsome in his white-button down and jeans, but didn't say anything. She was angry at herself for yesterday, as she had spent the entire day acting like a besotted teenager over a stupid bouquet of flowers that she had thought he had sent. She was also irritated at him. Would he fess up? He really ought to, because if he didn't, well, then who was he really?

He asked her if she would like a glass of wine, and she said that there were several nice glasses of Pinot Gris. She ordered one that was not the most expensive, but a close runner-up. Sam eyed her, thinking that Lucy never ordered the least expensive glass of wine, but a glass for twelve dollars was not in keeping with her choices in the past. He thought it was best to say nothing and decided he would order the same. Their conversation was stilted at first, and then Lucy asked him to tell her about the possible sale of the Hanover Street house. He told her that it was generating a good deal of traffic and that he hoped it would sell by June first. He told her about the purchase of the Aiken Street house. Wouldn't that interfere with his journey, she asked. Not really, he told her, explaining the scope of work that the house required and his plans for its rehabilitation. She was impressed with how he had figured it out in such a short period of time, but then again, it was a much smaller project. He told her that he hoped to be on his way by August first. He would need to get his vaccinations and purchase his tickets soon in order to line everything up for his trip Down Under.

She chose the mussels in cauliflower sauce and he the burger with pommes frites. He asked her about the shop. She had so much news, she said.

"I met the most fun and engaging couple from Richmond, and they know Huger. Actually, they are friends with Huger's new partner. Oh, it's a long story, but I introduced Rafe to Huger in early January, and while I've been so busy with our season, I had just lost track of time. Anyway, they made a purchase, and then flocks of visitors had purchased prints and other works. Plus, Gabriella and I are planning this exhibit for June during the second week of Spoleto."

He smiled at her, as her infectious giggle pleased him.

Then she said, "Thank you again for the flowers. They were really lovely. I toyed with the idea of taking them home, but I spend most of my time at the shop, so they are best kept there."

Sam had just placed a French fry in his mouth, and he realized he had to tell the truth. They eyed one another, and he realized she was giving him what she called the stink eye and the stick mouth. Then she lifted her mouth in a slight grin.

He took a sip of wine and cleared his throat. "Lucy, I apologize."

"For what exactly, Sam?"

"You know, the flowers."

"No, Sam. I'm not sure what you mean. Can you explain?"

"Yesterday, when we spoke, it was, ah, just good to talk to you, and I was multitasking, and then I realized that I took credit for someone else's gift by omission."

"Why would you do that, Sam?"

"Why did you think the flowers were from me?" he said defensively.

"Don't know, nor would I after your dramatic monologue last week. I thought you were being kind," she said crossly.

"Sorry."

"For what, Sam?"

"For not saying what I should have. Our conversation was so hurried, and then you were gone. It all happened so fast. That's why I sent the flowers today. To make up for my actions." He cocked his head at her in what she called his proud Mr. Darcy demeanor.

"Sam." Lucy's eyes narrowed. She placed her fork down and crossed her arms across her chest. "Would you have admitted it, if I hadn't broached the topic?"

"Yes, sooner than later, believe me."

"It just seems like I forced your hand to send me the bouquet because I assumed you sent the first one. Would you have sent me flowers otherwise?"

"Yes, I would have done so," he said, thinking, *Eventually.*

Lucy harrumphed. "No, I don't think so. You never sent me flowers before. In fact, besides treating me to lunch or dinner, you have never given me anything in the past."

Sam was squirming a little inside. She was right, but why did women always need to be cosseted. Lucy's house was packed with objects, her garden was always in bloom, and she never wore the same jewelry twice. What was he expected to give her? Gift-giving denoted that there was far more going on than friendship, and there was a sensitive balance to giving when starting out or rekindling a relationship. God knows if you give them too much at the beginning, then they believe you are crazy about them, and they don't want that either, according to his sister Elizabeth. He had helped her paint, though, and didn't that count for something?

Sam eyed Lucy with frustration. "I'm sorry. Can we just leave it at that?"

"Okay. Can you please not do that again?"

"Yes. I won't do it again. Were the flowers I sent nice, though?"

"Yes, there were all types of lilies, ferns, and coffee beans, very dramatic."

"And you liked them, then? Not too large and ostentatious?"

"No, they weren't that, and yes, I did like them, very much. Thank you."

The two finished, and Lucy stifled a yawn behind her hand as Sam walked her to her car. He held the door for her and leaned in to kiss her on the mouth. She turned her face, and his kiss landed on her cheek.

She was still pissed. He could feel her energy. She was on high simmer. He asked if they could do lunch or dinner next week.

She smiled and said, "Yes, thank you," and then, "good night."

He walked home thinking he had made a mess of things. Why in the world had he contacted Jillian and then asked Mrs. Annie? He should have contacted one of his male friends, who would have told him not to worry, just explain that he had not sent the flowers when he took her for dinner. But who had sent them? He hoped it wasn't that asshole Gus; although Weston had told Sam that Lucy had not seen him for some time. Jillian and Mrs. Annie had seen it from her side, not his. Jeez. There's a reason TMI is Too Much Information. What had he been thinking? This relationship thing with Lucy was confusing at best. He needed a little alone time. Time to unwind, watch a movie, make his sketches and notes for the new project. Onward and upward, that was his mantra.

Lucy unlocked the door, greeted Toulouse, and took him around the block. Although she was still irritated and annoyed at Sam, her big, brindled furry boy always made her happy. He wagged his tail and would look back at her, showing a white underbite. She laughed with him and soon turned the corner to the house. Once inside, she changed into a silver silk nightie, yawned, and crawled between the sheets. She felt sniffles coming along and hoped it was allergies. She was too busy to begin to come down with a cold, and that would not do, not at all. She popped back out of the bed and washed vitamins and an aspirin down with milk and reread the directions for Zicam. She knew she would feel better in the morning.

April turned to May, and Lucy and Sam saw each other three times a week. She still felt that amazing feeling of intense chemistry for him, but she was starting to see him warts and all. The rose-tinted lens had finally lifted, and she was very grateful. One evening Lucy and Sebastian strolled through the park with Toulouse, and she spoke about him.

"We all adore your Yankee from Salem, Luce. Just don't let him hurt you again. You were so sad after the last time."

"I know. I just want to give it another chance when he's not encumbered by the beautiful soon-to-be married Jessica. She looks a little like a dark-haired version of Jennifer Aniston, sexy body, beautiful face, and everyone says she's kind and brilliant. That's some competition with someone like me, you know. I'll give you I'm attractive, and my body is okay, but she's like a siren, and I can see how Sam would have thrown himself overboard for her like in *The Odyssey*. And Sebastian, please don't tell anyone. You're the only one I've told."

"Jeez, the drama, and stop that condescending shit. You *are* beautiful. Girl, let it be. I think Sam was making peace before she came back to Charleston, and he always seemed totally into you. Now just let it be, one day at a time. Lucy, your friends will find out. You shouldn't play all innocent."

What was it with this "let it be" thing? First Ella, now Sebastian. She wasn't going to mess with it, though. If they told her to let it be, then let...it...be. How could anything be that difficult? But there it is.

Chapter 26

Begin at the beginning,...and go on till you come to the end:...

Alice's Adventures in Wonderland, Lewis Carroll

Katie had asked Lucy to call a girls' night at her house so she could share the news with her friends, the good and the bad. They were all there, and although Katie was nervous about what they would think of her and her actions in January, she was surprised to see how sympathetic they were. Besides Lucy and Susie, she had only confided in Violet, who had kept quiet, knowing that the situation was difficult for Katie.

Each one of them chimed in that something must be done about Gus Wolfe. Lucy then mentioned that she had filed a report with the police in March and that the nice officer had assured her that he would look into it.

Rachel said that life was full of unexpected situations and that a person just had to embrace her own decision and then let it take its course. Ella patted Katie's shoulder and said that she would be there for her friend in any way possible. Diana said that she thought this opportunity, although it may not seem so much so right now, gave them all the chance to practice their mothering skills. Violet smiled at her friend with a knowing glance that seemed to say, *I told you they would not pass judgment.* Katie told them that Brooks, Lucy, and Ernesto had helped her move her belongings into the cottage in Springfield the last weekend in April and that she was safely ensconced in the carriage house on Legare Street just a block from Lillian's house.

Lucy asked Diana if Weston had ever found out about Gus's and Sam's past. Diana said that Sam had told Weston little, but implied that Gus's behavior had never been chivalrous. Katie said that this baby was hers alone, and she didn't want Gus's taint to be upon it. The girls broke up, with each hugging Katie to them and telling her it would all work out in the end.

ꕥ

He was falling into the routine of seeing Lucy, and he enjoyed her company, her laughter, her smile, and her energy. Just this past Tuesday evening, she had suggested a field trip to the beach. She had packed a picnic basket with cheese, crackers, sandwiches, and bottled water, and they had laughed as Toulouse wallowed in the green water off of Sullivan's Island. As they walked back to the car, passing the fortifications of Fort Moultrie, she told him about the Seminole Wars, Osceola's capture and incarceration behind those very walls. He wondered how she stored all of that information in her head and told her so. She laughed and told him that history was one of her passions and that she just knew that he would be the same way if they were in Salem. He helped her dry off Toulouse before her furry woof jumped into the back of the Karmann Ghia. When she dropped Sam at his house, he asked her if she wanted to come in to look around his house, as she had never seen the interior of the freedman's cottage.

She marveled at how his furniture fit perfectly in the small space and complimented him on the faithful restoration of the faux painted paneling in the living room. The kitchen was simple, and she said she liked his choice of using large wooden shelving rather than cabinets. He told her that he had found them when he was looking for bookcases, and it just made sense. She nodded her head, running her fingers on the mahogany shelves filled with white dishes and glassware. Food items and canned goods were neatly stacked on other shelves. Toulouse wandered happily about, wending his way between them. She had touched his shoulder and told him that it was charming, quaint, and perfect. He had felt proud of himself, and it was important for him to feel that she approved of his hard work.

ꕥ

He had taken her in his arms and began kissing her, and before she knew what was going on, he was backing her into his bedroom, where he lifted her onto the bed. She had thrown herself into their kissing, kissing him back as deeply as he kissed her. He undressed her quickly and continued to kiss her, reveling in her soft skin and warm body. She was like a present in his hands as he looked at her lingerie, wanting to unwrap the white lace bra and the matching underwear. She had looked up at him, her eyes darkened with passion, and she had stopped him.

"No, Sam," she said quietly. "We can't do this yet."

He gazed at her face and told her, "I want you, Lucy, and it's been far too long. I've missed your body, your mouth, and all of this."

She wiggled from underneath him, hugged him to her, and whispered in his ear, "I need time, Sam. Please give me that, and don't rush me."

He helped her find her shorts and top, watching her closely.

"You look like a lion waiting to pounce on its prey." She laughed.

He laughed, holding her close to him, thinking that in the past when he would look at her, he wanted to kiss her, but recently when he gazed at her, he just wanted to hold her close to him and take her. He wanted to see those cat's eyes close halfway as she felt the ecstasy that they had shared in the past.

Lucy kissed his cheek. "I need to go home. So when do I see you again?"

"I'll call you tomorrow, Lucy."

The next day he smiled to himself, thinking, *Enough. I need to swing a hammer and get things done.* Sheff was meeting him at the Aiken Street house, and they would have their hands full since the demolition was done. They had a full crew this week, and they would begin framing the kitchen today and then probably finish framing the second floor of the addition by the end of the week. His phone rang, and Allston Murray's number popped onto the screen. After saying brief hellos, Allston said that an agent in his office would be showing the Hanover Street property again, this time to a potential couple. Sam said the photos were still on the kitchen counter and asked Allston what the clients did for a living. He said that the wife was a professor at the College of Charleston and her husband a school teacher. Sam liked the idea of teachers in the house.

Gus Wolfe showed the couple the Hanover Street house with a bit of irritation. Damn Sam O'Hara, why does he always make out so well? Here he was having to make small talk with an annoying woman who asked too many questions and a man who just smiled broadly and didn't speak at all. She thanked Gus and told him that they would let him know by the end of the week.

Gus had been pissed off for a while. He hadn't had as many sales as he was used to, and he hoped these two would just make up their minds. He also knew that something else was afoot. That jerk of a cop kept coming by his house. And then he had run into several of the members of Lucy's group at restaurants for lunch or dinner, around town, or at parties, and all of them gave him a wide berth. He wondered if it had to do with that stupid schoolteacher friend of Lucy's. He hadn't seen her since late winter, when she had become so clingy. She was pretty in an insipid blonde-haired, blue-eyed way. Lucy, on the other hand, was a catch. She had her own business and owned property. He should have just seen how that went without adding anything to her drink on Thanksgiving.

Zeke called Sam the following week to ask him if the Hanover Street house was under contract. Sam said that a couple had put in a contract at the end of the day last Friday. Why the interest?

"Sam, I know how hard you work on your properties, and the other day I was at lunch with Brooks when we saw one of my less than respected work colleagues having lunch with Gus Wolfe. Gus mentioned that he needed some help to work the loan so the sale would go through. It wasn't as if we were eavesdropping; they were just loud enough for us both to hear. This guy is always shady, but never gets caught. It gives our business a bad reputation. It would be a shame if the property ended up going into foreclosure if they can't make the payments."

"That's strange, though, Zeke. She's a professor, and he's a teacher. I'm only asking two hundred and fifty thousand for it, so they should be able to afford that. It's infuriating that Gus Wolfe is involved. We've known each other since college, and there has always been bad blood between the two of us."

"I don't know. Maybe they have too much debt, school loans and all that. I just wanted to give you the heads-up."

"Thanks, Zeke."

Sam was furious. Gus Wolfe always reared his ugly head, and he was the agent involved in Sam's house. He recalled Lucy calling it his wooden bride, and he thought of all the hours he had spent on it: repairing the piazzas, the bargeboards, all of it. It had been a labor of love and had tested his limitations. It had required him to sub out and supervise many workers, something he was loath to do. In the end he would not clear but maybe fifty or sixty thousand, tops, but he was building his neighborhood one house at a time. He had money in the bank, no credit card debt, the America Street property was rented, and the freedman's cottage was paid off, so he had very few expenses.

Sam met Lucy for coffee Saturday morning, and they strolled the farmer's market at Marion Square. She told him she had a hankering for a crepe, and he indulged her. While sitting on the edge of a fountain, she asked him if he had had nibbles on the house. Before he thought better of it, the entire story was out. His frustration, the call from Zeke, and then he topped it off with Gus's unscrupulous behavior in the past.

"Gosh, Sam, I'm so sorry to hear that. Gus Wolfe sure is a charmer on the surface, though, isn't he? He charmed me until, well, until I knew him better. He does know how to work it, all smiles and charming dialogue. He got Katie in trouble, you know, and now she's going to move to Springfield and have a baby. He's horrible, the perpetual wolf at the door." Lucy looked up at him and smiled ruefully.

"Lucy, I had no idea. I haven't seen Katie since Thanksgiving, and Sebastian and Ben haven't said a word."

"They wouldn't, Sam, but she will begin to show soon. She's packed on some pounds, so maybe that will disguise the baby until the end of the school year. It's been hard for her, but she is firm in her decision, and she will be a marvelous mother. I'm just sorry Gus is the father."

Sam chewed the inside of his right jaw and thought that if he had told her as he had wanted in December, would things have been different? Would she have believed him then?

"Lucy, someone did turn him in, right?"

"Yes. Someone did turn him in."

"Good."

They shopped quietly, both lost in their thoughts as they purchased fresh vegetables. Lucy let out a little squawk and pointed to the plant with thick leaves and blue flowers in front of her. Sam turned his head and looked at her with a frown forming between his brows.

"Well look here, Samuel O'Hara, borage for Toulouse at the farmer's market. I won't have to go to John's Island after all." She giggled.

Sam laughed, saying to Lucy, "You are always made happy by the simple things. You never require anything large and ostentatious."

"You're right, Sam, but sometimes I do like large and ostentatious things, like your hothouse lilies." She wiggled her eyebrows and smiled at him.

Just like that, with a laugh and a smile, she had chastised him. Why did women always hang on to a person's deeds or misdeeds? It was a quandary, that's for sure, he thought.

They cycled to Sam's cottage and talked for a while of this and that. Lucy stretched and stood up and said she would be late for her afternoon shift at the gallery. Next week was their big bash and all that. She told him that his haint blue shutters were wonderful in the summertime, and she liked the color he had chosen for his house. He mentioned that the color was from the Historic Charleston color chart, and the creamy yellow reminded him of Barbados. She leaned into him, kissed him squarely on the mouth, and said good-bye. He held her hair in his hand and went to kiss her back. Instead she buried her head in his neck, hugged him quickly, and was gone.

He had to admit, this Lucy was different. Still quirky, still fun, but with a quiet confidence, and he liked it.

Katie had called Brooks to thank him again for his courtesy on helping her make the move to the midlands. He told her he was glad to help and that he had always been fond of her. She quickly hung up and thought, *Brooks, our Brooks, has been fond of me?* What exactly did that mean? Truly, really, what in the world could that possibly mean? Maybe she was emotional, reading too much into it. She couldn't wait for Lucy to come home so she could ask her if there was insight there. Maybe it was her hormones. Lucy said she was raging, crying one moment and laughing the next. In a few weeks' time, she would move to the country, by herself, and be all alone. She went into Lucy's spare bedroom that had been previously dubbed the closet, patted for Toulouse to join her, and hugging him close, promptly cried herself to sleep. It was three thirty in the afternoon.

Lucy turned the sign in the window from Open to Closed and locked up. It was comforting having Katie with her, but the mood swings made her a little crazy. Then again, who wouldn't be crazy with all of the plans that needed to be made? This was huge and mind-boggling. Katie was good, always having dinner ready, although Lucy's size-four dresses were becoming a little snug. She was happy that she could occasionally cycle to work to minimize the damage. Funny, she thought. A favorite dress that she had held on to for ten years that fit her, albeit loosely, was a size eight. So was she a size four after all? She doubted it. Screw Wallis Simpson after all. Who cares to be too rich and too thin?

She entered the house. No Toulouse, no Katie, no hors d'oeuvres like hummus and pita chips or brie and crackers, just silence. Lucy took off her shoes and tiptoed through the house thinking, *Something is up. I just know it.* She quietly peeked into the closet, the room with its rich azure walls and High Victorian bed, and saw Katie's tear-stained face with a quiet Toulouse tucked under her arm. His chocolate eyes gazed at her, and he smiled, wagged his tail, and immediately nuzzled Katie.

Gosh, now we have to get in the big guns, she thought. She had to mix it up for dinner, two people who Katie adored: beautiful Dante and fabulous baby friend from my childhood, Brooks.

"Hi. I need you right now. I have a pregnant, hormonal woman who has taken my dog hostage in my spare bedroom. Can you come to dinner? Yes? Can you help me cook, because Brooks needs to come and help with damage control. Thank you. Dante? I love you. You will bring shrimp? I just need some special assistance right now. Thank you."

"Brooks, what are you doing? Of course, Spoleto and the after-party, how nice."

"Is something wrong? These tickets were a king's ransom," he said.

"Brooks, Katie is sad, holding on to Toulouse like no tomorrow. I don't even know how he can breathe. I'll pay you for the tix. No? Desiree and Michael will be there? How do you know that? What? They're an item? I'm so sorry. Yes, please. If you come, I will do anything, clean your house, mow your yard, you name it. Thank you. You can always make the after-party."

Dante would bring the shrimp, she would run to the store and buy salad fixings, vegetables, and pasta, and all would be well.

***

Katie woke at seven. Her throat was dry, and she felt sorry for herself. She wondered what was going on in the kitchen; there was such a racket. She smoothed her hair and wandered down the hall and saw the three of them: Dante peeling shrimp at the sink, Brooks angled in the doorway, and Lucy boiling water by the stove. She smiled slightly and said hello and apologized for not remembering that they were coming to dinner. Lucy said not to worry; it had been an impromptu decision. She thought that they needed to mix it up and enjoy male companionship.

Brooks asked what he could do, and Lucy asked him and Katie to set the table. Katie pointed in the direction of the sideboard and told Brooks to pull out the blue place mats and the matching blue cotton napkins. He looked at her curiously and said that Lucy never used place mats at the dining room table.

"She does now," Katie said raising her eyebrows. "Our Lucy is becoming more relaxed. Besides, she's been so busy with planning the event and Gabriella's send-off. I think it's going to be something."

The four enjoyed dinner, laughing and telling stories. Brooks told them about the poetry reading he had attended at the Dock Street Theatre. He said it had been hilarious. The author was a heavy woman in her late fifties with long gray hair piled in a tight topknot. She wore a tight black dress adorned with sequins, and her poems all had erotic themes.

"The funniest line I can remember was this. 'As my hands traverse my body, I remember your tongue, its taste, its texture lapping me as a river, washing me in its glory until I enjoy that blissful *petite mort*.'" Brooks laughed outrageously.

"I don't think that's so bad," Katie said. "She was remembering a lover, and her work couldn't be that bad, or she wouldn't have been asked to perform."

Lucy was laughing noting that Brooks was probably horrified at being in the audience, of which he knew probably one half, wondering what they thought he was thinking, and she said so.

"Lucy, that's absurd. Why would I care what other people think of what I'm thinking? It was just teetotal funny that this woman read these poems like she was going to have the big *O* right then and there.

Dante laughed also and said, "Did anybody go the poetry slam a few years back where this guy rapped an entire poem about his penis, which he called the love machine? I know exactly what you are talking about, Brooks."

Lucy was laughing again and said, "You should have been with me that day, Dante. I had Grandmere in tow, and she was outraged. She thought the rapper was disgusting. Plus he had all that crazy red hair sticking out in spikes."

"That was the one. Spoleto is wonderful. You never know what you'll see."

Katie only went to one or two of the performances. She usually chose something tame, like seeing a quartet. One year there had been an impressive quartet that played only Balkan music. She would be lucky if she could fit in a performance this year with her situation.

Brooks noticed that Katie had become quiet, and he asked her if she was tired.

"No, not tired, just a little overwhelmed with everything."

"Katie," he said. "We're all here for you. Don't feel you have to do everything on your own. I told you I'll go with you to get you settled in. In fact, maybe we should all go and make a weekend of it? What do you think?"

Dante and Lucy said they would have to check their calendars. Lucy was interviewing assistants and would have to be there several weekends to help open and close the gallery. She had several promising applicants, one named Gertrude who went by Trudie, a charming interior designer who also painted. Her work was quite promising, and Lucy hoped she would be perfect.

The men left by ten thirty, and Lucy and Katie said their good nights. Brooks would still be able to make the after-party if he chose to do so.

"Thank you, Lucy, for asking them over. I had been so sad earlier, and Brooks and Dante are so very special."

"Well, they like you, and Brooks was certainly attentive."

"He was, wasn't he? I've always liked him, but he just...I don't know. I always seemed to not be in his league. He's a downtowner and all, and I don't know..." she mumbled.

"Katie, he's not like that. He's very successful, I'll give you that, and he could live south of Broad Street, but he's more of an uptown guy. We like how our neighborhoods are all mixed up. We like the casualness of Moe's being our favorite neighborhood bar, and we like that our neighbors actually live here. Downtown has changed since I grew up there. C'mon now, Katie. I never knew you were interested in Brooks. He'd make a perfect husband and father."

"I guess I never thought of that."

"Well, just return his calls, and see where it goes. You never know. One thing for sure is that he is one of the most honorable, reliable, and decent men I know."

"I guess I need to let it be. Violet told me that the other day. She seems to spend a lot of time with Rich these days."

"Indeedy, it seems that we must just let it be. Maybe that's our mantra." She hugged her friend and said good night.

Katie called from her room, "Is it okay if Toulouse sleeps with me?"
Lucy stifled her yawns. Katie needed Toulouse. "Katydid, Toulouse is yours for the night."

As she closed her eyes, she wondered if it had just been this morning when she had kissed that handsome man from Salem. She thought of his pewter eyes as she drifted into sleep.

Lucy had convinced Katie to go with her to a concert at St. Matthew's Lutheran Church at five, but before they went, she needed to weed her beds. The phone began to ring. She stopped pulling what seemed to be mountains of Florida betony, took off her garden gloves, and turned the receiver on.

"Hi, Brooks. I hope you were able to make it to the party, and where was it?"

"I did, and it was in the garden of this amazing house on Lamboll Street. A High Victorian that I had never seen, all paneled wood and stained glass windows. I saw Michael and Desiree, and I suppose, yeesh, that I'm calling to say you are right. How in the world did I think I was in love with such a self-absorbed individual? She came over and chatted with Diana, Weston, and me, and then your Michael wandered over. He hangs on her every word, and then they have this stupid thing that they do. He raises his hand and waves and says hi, and then she says hi back with a wave."

"He's not my Michael, Brooks, nor was he ever. I'm glad that Diana and Weston were there."

"You'll find this curious. After they moved off, Diana said that, although Desiree was pretty and charming, she lacked substance. She then said that she felt I should be with someone that I could grow with in time."

"Well, that was nice and true. We all need someone that will challenge us. What are you doing this evening? Do you want to join Katie and me at a concert at St. Matthew's? It's at five, and it's free."

"Sure, and I'll drive. The Jag's on the fritz, so I'll pick you up in the Toyota since it has AC."

Lucy giggled thinking that Katie's Honda's AC was on the blink, and the Karmann Ghia had never had it. True to his word, Brooks squired them, Katie in a pretty yellow sundress and Lucy in a pale pink skirt with appliquéd black poodles and a black T-shirt. Lucy looked about her, admiring the German Gothic Lutheran church with its vivid stained glass windows. The church was exceedingly cool after the heat from outside, and she wished she had brought a sweater. She heard a familiar voice behind her and turned to see Sam in khakis and a white shirt. He asked if he could join them. Brooks stood, shook his friend's hand, and said by all means. After a little rearranging, Sam sat next to Lucy and said he didn't know that she liked Bach.

"Yes, he's one of my favorite composers, and when I looked through the Piccolo Spoleto program, I knew I didn't want to miss it, you?"

"Yup, one of the very best. I'm glad I saw you."

After the concert, Sam asked them if they were up for a bite to eat. Katie said that she needed to prep for the morning, and Brooks said he had stayed out too late the night before. Lucy didn't want to bail out on Sam, and in fact, she could feel that intense feeling that she had when she was around him.

He looked her in the eye and said, "Lucy, then it's you and me. Why don't we walk down the street to Chai's and get a bite?"

"Do y'all mind?" she asked Brooks and Katie.

They said not at all, and before she knew it, Sam had his right hand on the small of her back and was walking, pushing her gently north on King Street.

"I like your skirt, Lucy, too bad you couldn't find one with Bouviers on it, though," he gently teased.

They talked of this and that, and he asked her what other performances she planned to attend that week. As they sat outside drinking in the heat and beauty of the city, she noted that she was taking Grandmere to a noon concert at Memminger Auditorium in the middle of the week, and then the party at the gallery was on Saturday from seven to ten. Was he planning to attend?

"Yes, I'll be there. Can I help you with anything?"

"Thank you, no, Sam. I think I have it totally under control. I'm pretty excited about the artists' work. We'll be installing it this week and putting my familiar friends up for a couple of weeks. I just hope their art sells."

"Why the concern? The works are not overpriced, are they?"

"No, it's not that. It's just it's a little, well, some of the works are large, and others very dark and edgy, and I'm just not sure what the market is for it. I'm testing new waters right now, and it's not that I'm uncomfortable, but I'm just not totally at ease with it. The food will be fine. Carlos will read some poetry at eight, and then Enid is scheduled for nine o'clock, as she has a concert at Mt. Zion AME church at seven."

"That's the church on Glebe Street, in the middle of the campus of the college?"

"Right, that's the one."

They walked to Sam's house, and he drove her home. He said he'd check in on her around mid-week, and maybe if she had time, they could take in a concert, or poetry reading, or this or that.

Chapter 27

My momma always said life was like a box of chocolates...
You never know what you're gonna get.

Forrest Gump, Forrest Gump,

She picked up Grandmere at eleven thirty for the concert and dropped her in front of the auditorium. She found parking easily on Coming Street and thanked her lucky stars. The concert was beautiful with pieces written by Chopin and Liszt. After the concert, Grandmere ambled slowly with her cane and asked where Lucy had parked. Lucy told her that she was less than a block away. Grandmere wanted to stroll to move her ancient body and get it going, she said. She asked Lucy about her upcoming event.

"Dear, do you think you'll have a good crowd considering there are still so many concerts and plays this Saturday?"

"I hope so, Grandmere, and the crowd we're cultivating would probably attend the Piccolo finale and not many of the classical programs; this event will be catered, and the artists think that their friends will all come. I'm hoping that buyers will attend." She smiled brightly.

Before they knew it, Lucy had pulled in front of the Legare Street mansion, and she wondered how long Grandmere could amble about its three floors. She helped her into the house, kissed her on the cheek, and told her she loved her. Grandmere thanked her for taking her to the concert and wished her great success for her party.

"Lucinda, one more thing."

"Yes ma'am?"

"We did enjoy so much having Katie in our midst; Susie and I both miss her company. She's a very dear girl and rather smart. I'm just so sorry she has to go through this situation by herself."

"I know, but we will all be there for her, whatever she needs, and there are a bunch of us to help. I just hope the move to Springfield will be okay and that she won't be too lonely. I know she especially enjoyed playing your piano when she visited you."

Sam was having a week. His mother had called to say they were coming on Thursday and staying until Sunday. Didn't Sam remember? He and Elizabeth had given them the Spoleto package for their anniversary. They were staying at the Mills House Hotel and had tickets for the opera, the play, chamber music, a jazz concert, and a spirituals concert. She really wanted to see the marionettes, and his father thought that might be fun as well. She was so excited, and she hoped that they could see their son at least one evening, if not two. Sam adored his parents, but he had hoped to see Lucy, but between their schedules and his parents' visit, he wasn't sure how it would all work out to everyone's satisfaction.

Sam called Lucy on Wednesday and asked her how her preparations were going.

"Sam, I'm ahead of schedule. Everything's up and priced, so now it's quiet—well, somewhat—until Saturday."

"Lucy, a friend of mine who is a local composer is having a concert on Friday at five. Would you like to go? I can meet you there if that is convenient."

"Yes, thank you, Sam. What kind of music is it? Classical? That suits me just fine. I'll ask Gabriella to close. Where's the concert? Okay, at the City Gallery. I haven't been in there yet. I'll wait for you outside. Thank you."

Lucy was excited. Her e-mail had been humming all week, and she hoped that she could accommodate everyone who said they were coming. Thank goodness for the small courtyard off the street and the parking space. Gabi said they should plan on placing a few chairs in both spaces and place a temporary screen of bamboo to make it more intimate. It would be a crush. She was looking forward to the concert, and she hoped the rumbling in the distance wasn't a storm on the way. Storms in May were always torrential, with much of the city flooding within thirty minutes if the tide was high.

Lucy donned her raincoat and took her umbrella with her. It had been constantly raining for about an hour, and she had ridden her bike this morning when the sky was blue and not a cloud scuttled through it. Here she was hoping that her umbrella would not turn itself inside out. She arrived at the City Gallery in ten minutes and was grateful that only her black ballerina flats with their ribbons were soaked through. She waited under the awning until five minutes to five. She then handed the ten-dollar bill to the volunteer and sat down in a seat, wondering where Sam could be. The music began a few minutes later, and Lucy was enchanted with the sounds of the violin, viola, and cello. The pianist moved like one with the instrument, and Lucy sat transfixed. Before she knew it, the players had stopped, and the piece was finished. It had been magical, and she knew this friend of Sam's must be the new Aaron Copland, the piece was so moving. At intermission she purchased a bottle of water and looked for her most favorite friend. Humph. Still no Sam.

He heard on the radio that the Crosstown was flooded. He shouldn't have spent so much time at the salvage yard. He had thought his timing would be perfect. It must be high tide, and the only possible way he could get around the flooding was to wend his way back and forth and traverse the high streets of Charleston. He took King Street to Grove Street, then turned south on Rutledge Avenue. At Moultrie Street, the cars were at a standstill. He inched the truck closer to the intersection and made the turn and turned again onto President Street. He splashed the truck through low puddles until he reached Congress Street. He turned east onto Congress Street. After indicating to the driver of the car to his left that he wanted to go straight, the car at the corner of Rutledge Avenue and Congress Street backed up slightly, causing a cacophony of horn-blaring from the car behind it. He had a few inches on either side of the vehicle between the car to the right and the car to the left. He sailed slowly through the intersection to realize that he was clear. He could see the Crosstown. It was impassable with cars stalled and water clearly above their wheel wells.

He was now on his way to King Street, then to his house. At the corner he looked to his left, and just as he imagined, the intersection of Huger and King Streets was under enough water to cover the hoods of two cars, a Volvo and a Subaru. Both would have damage totaling around two thousand dollars each. He felt sorry for the owners and was glad that he knew this town. He would miss the first part of the performance, but there was nothing he could do. It was now five. He ran up the shallow stairs of the cottage and quickly changed his clothes. After finding parking, it was a quarter past five, and he could gain no admittance until 6:00 p.m. All he could do was walk to the Blind Tiger and order a beer.

Lucy was sipping her water, hoping that Sam hadn't flooded out one of his vehicles or, even worse, that he had been in an accident. As intermission was coming to a close, she found her seat and realized that someone was sitting in the vacant seat next to her. *Oh well,* she thought, *that's how it goes with open admission.* She smiled and said hello to the handsome man and his pretty wife, both in their early sixties, she figured. They said hello back. The room filled up quickly, the performers began and she was again lost in the music.

He saw her and realized that she was sitting next to his parents. Didn't they have something else scheduled at the exact same time? Had they met? Shit, this was a mess. He wasn't ready for her to meet his parents, was he? Yes, she was amazing, but he hadn't told them that he was seeing her. There was a reason why he had kept that private. Just last night at dinner, his mother was hinting that he should just find a decent, good girl and settle down. Wasn't Sam always saying that there were lots of girls in Charleston? His mother was hoping that he was not afraid of commitment. He wasn't; look how long he had been there for Jess. He wasn't even sure if he would come back here after the trip. He hadn't made up his mind about the future. He might just sell it all and move back to Salem, start over there.

At the end of the concert, and after a great deal of applause, the crowd called for an encore, and the musicians obliged them. Lucy turned to her neighbors and asked if they enjoyed the performance. The woman was petite and said, "Very much," with a New England dialect. Her husband agreed. Lucy asked if they were visiting for Spoleto from the Northeast. She told them that she hoped they would enjoy their stay and the festival, then said good-bye and headed for the door.

Sam saw his parents turn to get their coats, and he literally pounced on her as she exited.

"Hi, Lucy, I'm sorry I missed most of it. Would you like to get a bite to eat at the Blind Tiger?"

"That would be nice, Sam. Did you get stuck in the rain?"

He placed his hand on the small of her back, walking her quickly down the street.

"I did. You know how hard it is to navigate the water."

"I do. Sam, slow down. I just splashed in a huge puddle and soaked my shoes, again. Are you all right?" Lucy looked hard at him.

"I'm fine. I just had too much caffeine today." He then noticed that muddy water had splashed her pretty light blue trench coat.

Red Bull, she thought. *I hate the stuff. It makes you all jumpy.* But everyone she knew seemed to drink it. She never could understand how it got mixed up with vodka. It's just a wonder that it didn't stop the person's heart right then and there.

Sam called his father on Saturday morning. He had some downtime. He had dropped Lucy at home by eight thirty the night before, and she was eager to get a good night's sleep before her big "happening." He had gone to bed early, only to make a list of what he could do on the Aiken Street property the next day. Refreshed, he pulled on clean jeans and a T-shirt from Moe's Crosstown Tavern. He thought their logo of "Having a good time on the bad side of town" was hilarious and somewhat true.

"Hi, Dad, how are you and Mom faring? Right, right, it's like a nor'easter, but different. Wow, really, you went to Edward's concert and then to the opera? I bet you were exhausted after all of that. I mean, that really is a lot of culture to take in. *Così fan tutte* by Mozart, right? So you enjoyed it? Good. What's the plan for today?"

"We're going to take in jazz this evening at seven, and your mother is downstairs right now trying to locate tickets for the marionettes. This was the best gift that you and Elizabeth could have given us. We were wondering if you would like to go to dinner with us around five. We thought you could meet us at the hotel earlier, and then we could walk to dinner before we take in the concert."

"That sounds great, Dad. I'll see you at four o'clock. Give Mom my love."

He thought of calling Lucy, but knew that she was busy, so instead he headed to the Aiken Street property. He had found solid wood cabinets for the kitchen at the salvage yard, and they rested on the floor. He had gone back yesterday to see if they had any more when the rain began. He figured what he had was enough and that he would look for appliances next.

The washer and dryer would be installed in the bathroom upstairs, and that made more sense anyway. They were progressing nicely on the house, and he might just be done with it all by the end of July. He was mentally tooling and retooling his trip, and he thought it would be good to take a break, see a new country or three, and just recharge. On Monday he would need to call Allston Murray and talk to him about Gus and the house. He just couldn't bear to think that it could be sold to someone who couldn't afford to maintain it.

He met his parents at four. His mother had been successful at securing tickets for the show, and they had enjoyed seeing it in the intimacy of the Dock Street Theatre. On the walk back to the hotel, they had stopped by an art gallery with some intriguing works in the window. Wasn't it funny, they met the nice girl who they had sat next to them at yesterday afternoon's concert. She was very nice. Sam's mom prattled on that this was exactly the kind of girl that Sam should meet, charming, polite, and smart. His father mentioned that he had purchased a painting from the gallery. It was dark, but hopeful too. His father described the piece as mixed media and that it was a watercolor of a slave cabin under a large oak tree with a brilliant blue sky in the background. In the corner of the work were sentences from a narrative of a man who had been enslaved. The excerpt from the narrative came from the Works Progress Adminstration's oral history project of the 1930s and was from the Low Country. It was quite poignant, and his father had to have it, his mother added. The young woman at the gallery would send it to them, as it was too large to take on the plane.

"Thomas, her name is Lucy, isn't that right?"

Sam knew he had to tell them that he knew Lucy. If she sent the package to them, she would have taken down their names.

The gallery was packed, and red "sold" dots were flying on the walls next to many works of art. Lucy was happy to see that there was almost an equal distribution between the three moxie girls. She felt him before she saw him. It was always like that, some kind of primeval thing going on between them like primates, peacocks, or swans. He smiled at her, and she smiled back. She thought he looked handsome in his khaki pants and his dark blue polo shirt. He told her congratulations, and she said thank you as she touched her hand briefly to his chest. At nine Enid started performing jazz songs in the courtyard, and soon the crowd was singing along with her to the tune of "When the Saints go Marching In."

"Lucy, I know you're probably going to be pretty beat tomorrow, but my parents are in town, and I wondered if you would like to meet them. They fly out in the afternoon, and I wondered if you might go with us to brunch?"

"That would be very nice, Samuel. I wondered if the O'Haras from Salem were any relation to you."

"Yes, well, my sister and I gave them a Spoleto package for their anniversary, and I completely forgot about it until they called on Thursday. Anyway, Friday got away from me and then the monsoon and all that..." He trailed off.

"Hmm. Right. So would you be introducing us had they not made the purchase of the painting?" she inquired with a smile on her face.

"Yes, absolutely. It was just figuring out their schedule and yours. I didn't want to bother you today, what with your event."

She didn't say what she was thinking, which was, *Why didn't you mention it over appetizers last night?*

"Okay. Listen, I have to start cleaning up and all. Just call me in the morning." Why did she even bother with him, she thought. If his hand had to be forced, first by her own and then by his parents, was it really worth it?

Sam walked home. She had dismissed him just like that. Maybe she was just tired and overwhelmed. He liked her teal striped dress; it looked like something from the sixties, very retro. Did she realize that when a guy introduces a girl to his parents, that it's a really big deal? It was saying without the words that this person is important to me. Besides you never knew what would fly out of parents' mouths that might make you feel uncomfortable, like the time when you were three and you shit in your pants. He would call them all in the morning and coordinate the brunch, and he would pick up the tab.

Lucy woke up early and stretched. She could smell the coffee brewing and thought maybe a roommate wasn't such a bad thing after all. She hadn't heard the phone ring, but he had said he would call, and she would just not worry. She walked into the kitchen still dressed in her pink-and-white striped slip.

Katie was at the kitchen table sipping coffee and patting Toulouse on the head. Lucy asked her what she had done the previous evening, and a slow smile crossed her face.

"Brooks picked me up, and we watched a movie at his house. It was fun and cute. *Must Love Dogs*. Brooks had Cokes and popcorn, Skittles and chocolate bars. It was as if we were at the movies."

"That's nice. I like that movie. The main character loves *Doctor Zhivago* and goes on and on about it. So would you like to go with me for a stroll in the park? I think our boy could use the exercise. It's early, so it shouldn't be too hot yet."

Katie agreed, and the two donned shorts and T-shirts and ambled down the street. Lucy told her all about the event the night before. It had been far more successful than she could ever have imagined. More than one half of the inventory had sold, and she was thrilled for her artists. There was a champagne toast to send off Gabriella, and Carlos's poetry and Enid's singing were a tremendous hit. Katie mentioned that the roses in Hampton Park were exquisite and the beds more beautiful than she remembered.

"Lucy, what are your plans for today? I think I'm going to see if there are any free concerts and ask Brooks if he would like to go."

"That's a marvelous idea. I am going to brunch with a friend..." she said, her voice trailing off.

"Oh, and who is that? Our ever-favorite, Dante?"

"Er, actually, it's...well, it's Sam. His parents are in town, and I met them at the shop. They bought one of the pieces of art, and then one thing led to another. I don't know. It's complicated." Lucy turned her face to Katie, looking her squarely in the eye, thinking, *Don't judge me, girl.*

"Wow. That's big now, isn't it? You haven't seen him for months, and he's ready for you to meet the parents? That's a huge step for a guy, you know, the parents and all. Have you been seeing him for a while, then?"

"Oh, Katie, a couple of months—dinner here and there, a picnic, lunch, things like that."

"And who knows then, Lucy?"

"Just you and Sebastian. I wanted to give it several months to see, well, I guess just to see if it would stick. Last time, it ended after four months, and I was devastated. This time I wanted to see if we could get past five months, and then I would tell my friends; but you're staying with me now, and he'll call today, and we share the phone. Wish me luck?"

"So Diana doesn't know, which means Weston doesn't know, and Sebastian does know, but Ben doesn't know. Ella doesn't know, which means Ryan doesn't know. Does Brooks know or Violet? Rachel?"

Lucy shook her head. "No, Katie, you and Sebastian are the only ones, and I hope you will respect my privacy and not let on. I need to keep this to myself right now, please understand."

"I do understand, Lucy. I wasn't ready to tell any of y'all about my situation, but once I did, I felt so much better."

"Right, still, I don't want Violet saying about the first breakup shame on him, and on the second, shame on me."

"I agree, but she's changed since she's met Rich, and all for the better. I think she would understand. As you say, this is yours to tell, not mine. I won't gossip, I promise."

Chapter 28

When love is not madness, it is not love.

Pedro Calderon de la Barca

Sam had called her at ten asking if eleven thirty would work. She said yes, and he told her he would pick her up a little after eleven. She wasn't sure what to wear. She had met Sam's parents twice now. She would address them as Mr. and Mrs. O'Hara, as she couldn't remember either one of their first names. She shouldn't wear something too casual, but not anything too fancy, which would show that she was trying too hard. She sorted through her closet that held her summer clothes and couldn't find anything appropriate. The white dress, well, too white, and what if she spilled something? The poodle skirt, too girlish. No suits, that would make her look like she was uptight. The heap of clothes was growing on the bed. Then she found it. Yes. It was the Alberta Ferretti dress she had purchased at the consignment shop on Upper King Street.

"Thank you, girls at Butterfly!" she said aloud.

The dress was a blend of linen and silk and had a soft grayish-green shimmer. It wrapped beautifully at her waist, and the skirt was full without being too full, as it fell an inch above her knees. It was an adaptation of a dress that could have gone on a safari—well, sort of, she thought—with epaulets and large pockets. Dressy, but understated. She added a bracelet from her great-grandmother, its delicate silver links linking seven cameos of varied hues of basalt and taupe. Simple silver hoops were added to her ears, and a necklace that she had made when she was thirteen. It consisted of two Victorian fop watches from some Barwick or Carpentier ancestors and fell right below her collarbone. She was slipping open-toe Ferragamo sandals onto her feet, another consignment find, as she heard the doorbell ring. She was excited, true, but she didn't have that feeling as she had had a million years ago when Sam had squired her to the wedding and she had been a maniac. Sam said hello to Katie and looked a wee bit uncomfortable in his standard uniform of khakis and a polo shirt.

"You look stunning, Lucy," he said as he opened the door to the BMW.

"Thanks, Sam, you look handsome. I like the color of your shirt," she said with a smile.

He noticed that she had not straightened her hair, and the mop of curls softened her face.

Brunch was a delicious concoction of shrimp and grits with a tasso sauce, eggs, bacon, sausage, and the works. Sam graciously had introduced Lucy to his parents, Thomas and Catherine, and she said how nice it was to meet them again.

"So Lucy, how long have you owned your own gallery, and what made you choose the type of art that you sell? I was quite intrigued with your inventory," Sam's father enthused.

Lucy beamed. "I was actually an assistant to a family friend. My degree is in art history, and it just made sense to work for Huger. He taught me a great many things, and then when he decided to retire, he offered me first refusal to buy the business. I was able to buy the building as well soon after. The works that you saw yesterday are not typical of what I usually carry. Usually I sell works of art relating to the Charleston Renaissance, but my assistant Gabriella encouraged me to branch out. So there it is," she said with a giggle.

"Do you rent the upstairs as well? Thomas was very pleased with his purchase, Lucy. Now I'm not sure where we will place it, but I'm sure you already have thought about it, haven't you, darling?" his wife beamed.

Lucy noted that the upstairs apartment had always stayed rented, and for once in her life, she didn't say that it paid for a little more than half her mortgage. Lucy liked the way that Sam's parents were so easy with each other and affectionate. During the brunch, his father touched his wife quite often on the hand or shoulder. Catherine asked Sam how he had met Lucy.

Sam was thoughtful, thinking if he should mention their first meeting, Toulouse nipping him in the rear, and her rudeness about the apartment above her house, and quickly changed his mind.

"We met through mutual friends, through Ben and Sebastian, when I came back from Asia."

Lucy remembered that evening fondly as she recalled his storytelling, something she had found so attractive about him. They discussed Sam's projects and Sam's parents' work at the university. In fact, because Catherine loved everything about France, they were returning for three weeks this summer, visiting Normandy, Honfleur, Caen, and of course, Paris. Did Lucy travel often? Lucy told them about her trip to Prague and Italy in the fall and said she just wanted to visit Italy again and again.

Sam liked the way that his parents were responding to Lucy, and he was happy that she asked them polite questions without sounding nosy. She laughed a lot, and his parents laughed with her.

"Sam, wasn't that right? That day we went cycling, you told me about your uncle, remember?"

Sam had been lost in his own thoughts, thinking that she looked fresh and beguiling, so he hadn't paid attention to her questions. He smiled at her and said, "I'm not sure, Lucy. I've mentioned him to you on several occasions."

"Yes, you have, but your mother now says that he's in excellent health since he had his operation." Oh God, he thought. Why would they begin to talk about ailments when they were eating?

"I just think that is wonderful, Catherine. I know that Sam was so worried about him last year this time."

"Yes, he's doing quite well, and Sam, I don't know if he has called you, but he has met someone, and I think he's quite serious about her."

Here we go, he thought. *Now my mother will tell her all about Uncle Sam's love life. No one wants to hear the gory details of why someone has been a permanent bachelor*—please.

His father looked at him and said, "He wants you to meet her when you fly up before you leave for Australia. We'll be back from France by then, so it should be a great time for us all."

Lucy smiled at Sam and thought, *Well, maybe there's hope for you and me, honey, and then again, well, I'll cross my fingers.*

Catherine asked Lucy if she had any pets, and Lucy told her of her Bouvier, Toulouse. Catherine and Thomas had always had Airedales, and she mentioned that Bouviers had an easier nature. She had had one growing up as a child. Their current dog, Murphy, was always jumping the fence and swimming in the water.

"Lucy, you can't imagine how many times we've had angry parents call us from the shore saying that Murphy had upset their small children, as if they felt that Murphy was some sort of large beast."

Lucy placed her hand over her mouth, stifling a giggle, and said she knew exactly how that was, as children in her neighborhood were always asking if Toulouse was a brown bear or a black bear.

Thomas winked at his son, looked at him, raised his eyebrows, and smiled a smile of genuine approval. They continued their conversation over dessert and Sam couldn't help but notice that his parents seemed to like her.

Lucy said her good-byes to the O'Haras and said that when they were in town next, she would give them a tour of her city. They invited her to visit them the next time she took a jaunt to the Northeast. Sam hugged his parents and said that he would see them in not quite two months, and they said their good-byes.

Today had gone well, he thought as he drove her to her house. He opened the passenger door for Lucy. He walked her to the door and said he probably needed to take a look at the Aiken Street property to make notes about it before he and Sheff started work on it tomorrow. She asked if he wanted any company, and he said yes, that would be great. She said she'd meet him there in forty-five minutes if that was all right? She needed to change her clothes and pop on her bike.

Sam was at the house when Lucy arrived. He heard her brakes squeal and thought that her bike needed a tune-up.

"Hi, Lucy," he called.

"Hi back. This is amazing. You showed me the pictures, but I had no idea how far you have already come. The addition is completely framed, and the Sheetrock is up. I'm really impressed!"

He swung her into his arms and kissed her firm on the mouth. She was in the air and kissing him wildly and thought, not for the first time, how much she cared for him, how handsome he was, and how much she needed the touch of him, his strong arms and strong back. He placed her down slowly, and she stood on her tiptoes, kissing him again.

"Shh, girl, now stop. We'll both be getting into trouble, and you said to take this slow, right?"

"What's the harm in kissing, Sam? It's just a kiss."

"It's never a kiss with the two of us, and you know that. It never has been just that."

Run one for the home team, she thought. He showed her the rest of the house, and she was excited, knowing that this project would be an easy one for him. After stifling a yawn, she said she should be leaving to tend to her flower beds. He asked her if she wanted to come to the cottage and watch a movie. She thought of it and thought that her beds were overgrown and needed tending. She just couldn't spend the whole day with him, could she?

"Yes, Sam, that would be very nice."

"Then let's place your bike in the truck." At her questioning glance, he smiled.

"I needed to bring some things from my place, and I don't have a basket like you do, nor would everything have fit."

She nodded and smiled as he effortlessly lifted her bike into the bed of the truck. They went home to his house, and he walked her bike inside, knowing that if he locked it to the balusters, the baluster would be sawed through within moments, and he would have an unnecessary repair to take care of, and she would never reclaim her bike.

"Lucy, why don't you have your bike registered with the city?" he asked.

"Why would I pay fifteen dollars to do that? Whoever steals it will just strip it off."

"I dunno, when my bike was stolen, they found it because it was registered."

"Then Sam, you must be one lucky guy, because I've never heard that to be true."

They watched *Indiana Jones*, and then Sam said they should watch something else. He placed the DVD in the slot, and it was *Must Love Dogs*. Lucy commented that Katie and Brooks had watched it just the night before. She didn't know what it was; she was just feeling sleepy. All that good food at brunch or the good company?

Sam felt her nestle closer and then held her head as she slowly slid into his lap in full slumber. He wondered what she was wearing underneath, and he felt the sheer urge to peek. He could barely see her panties, as her shorts had slipped down a bit, and he saw that they were some filmy number in a size small. He would remember that. He would not check the size of her bra because that would take too many machinations, and if he were caught, she would think he was a skank or a perv. He'd figure that out later. He wasn't ready to buy her lingerie yet.

The movie ended, and Sam's legs were cramping. He carefully and quietly carried Lucy to the bedroom. He couldn't think of anything better than to nap with her. Lucy woke a half hour later. She had dreamed that Sam was holding her in his arms, and there he was, quietly lying next to her with one arm thrown around her shoulder and the other tucked about her waist.

"Brooks? It's Katie. I know I sound nervous; it's just that Lucy never came back from brunch, and we're supposed to go to our concert, and I don't know what to do about Toulouse. It's too hot outside for me to take him for a walk. What? She went with that Sam guy. Just let Toulouse in the backyard? Really? I guess that's okay. We did walk him this morning. Okay. I won't worry. It's just...I don't know. I worry about her. I suppose you're right. I just wish she'd carry her cell phone. Why she even bothers to have one makes no sense to me. All right, I'll see you in a little while."

June slipped by quickly. Lucy was trying to rearrange the gallery so she could exhibit her dead favorites and her new favorites. She had established a rule with the moxie girls. They couldn't spend their time brewing and stewing in her gallery. They were darling, but of a generation where the term "What the fuck?" was common, and that just would not do with Lucy's loyal clientele. She had squired Lillian to the wedding of Jim Weathers and Jessica, and it had been a beautiful affair.

Gabriella had purchased a commercial building uptown on Huger Street. It had been built in 1917 as a grocery store on the first floor and as a residential unit above. It was perfect for what she intended. The downstairs unit would serve as a studio and as a gallery for special events, and she would live above it. Lucy was thrilled to see it. Yes, she agreed with Gabriella the downstairs unit was a little rough, but it had great bones. More than three-quarters of its pressed tin ceiling was intact, the concrete floor could be stained later, and the bead board on the walls was in great shape; its paint just needed to be scraped and reapplied. The windows provided wonderful light, and Lucy thought that Sam could advise Gabriella as to whom she should use. The work would be cosmetic and not structural. No, he wouldn't do the work. His hands were busy with the Aiken Street project. Gabriella mused that some people thought they were seeing one another again. Several of their mutual friends had noticed the two of them together at dinner in restaurants and at the farmer's market. Lucy didn't know what to say, so she smiled slightly and said nothing.

As they entered the second-floor unit, Lucy said, "Gabi, I think you live in a tree house with all those live oaks around the property, the fantastic French doors, and those windows. It's so cool you won't have to turn on the AC until the Fourth of July."

"Good thing too, Lucy, as I don't have AC."

"Well, you can always add two window units until you figure it out. They're not that expensive anymore, and I have a spare, just in case, for the rental above me and the one above the gallery. By the time winter comes, you will have figured it out. This space is perfect, and the only thing left to do is the kitchen. The space is small enough that you could be quite creative and spend little money on it. I adore the old sink. I wouldn't change it a bit, and I wouldn't sand the floors. Just oil them, and they will be beautiful. Has the space rented, then, down below?"

"It has. You were right in suggesting that I use it as a working gallery. I have three artists, and the rent is a little less than half my mortgage. As you said, they are responsible for the utilities, trash, et cetera. The bathroom downstairs works, and you are very right; the work is mostly cosmetic. They'll move in by August first, and somehow all this construction will be done by then."

"Gabi, just call Sam. He'll advise you to the construction needs. He'll write down all your questions in that notebook of his, and he'll get back to you within a week. Your tenants aren't living here, and you are providing them space for a very reasonable amount. I would take my time and hire the workers that you are comfortable with. You don't need it to be pristine, just encapsulate the lead paint and then tell them about your work program. I'm sure that they will be fine with it."

The girls hugged, and Lucy told Gabi how proud she was of her. She wished her good luck and told her to call at anytime. Starting a business was scary and anxious-making.

Sam called Lucy and told her that he would look at Gabriella's place tomorrow. He was hungry. Could he pick her up, and they could go to Basil? He was hankering for Thai food.

She said of course. Would seven thirty do?

At dinner Sam asked her if she planned to go to Brooks's Carolina Day party, and she said of course. He told her it never made sense to him that there wasn't a big celebration for the Fourth of July. Why didn't they do something this year at her house, invite about fifteen or twenty of their friends and have a cookout? Nothing special, hamburgers, hot dogs, some sides, wouldn't that be a good time? She said that would be wonderful, perhaps they could make the list by the weekend, and they could split up whom to call or e-mail.

He dropped her off and walked her inside. He shut the door, patted Toulouse on the head, and twirled her about, kissing her madly. He gently placed her on her feet and said, "I'll call you soon, and this year, you're my date for Brooks's party."

She didn't know what to think. This Sam seemed far more interested in the two of them. It was nice. Very nice, indeed.

Lucy walked to Diana and Weston's house two days later. They were sitting on the porch enjoying the shade and an occasional breeze.

"Hi, I'm glad I found you both here. I wanted to invite you to a cookout on the Fourth of July," she said and smiled slightly, as she knew she had to tell them about Sam.

"Lucy, it will be hot as blue blazes, but that will be fun, won't it Weston?"

"Do you need me to supervise the grilling, Lucy?" Weston asked, his blue eyes twinkling.

"Well, er, actually, no." She squirmed.

"Lucy, what's going on? Is there a new man in your life that you haven't told us about?" Diana giggled.

"Well, he's not new, and I'm not so sure how to begin to tell you, but Sam and I ran into each other back in April, and there it is. I didn't want to tell anyone about it until we had hit the five-month mark, as I well, I just wasn't sure how it would all sort out. He wants the party, and he plans to grill. We've never had a cookout together, and to tell the truth, I'm a little bit anxious."

"Lucy, you're a great cook. Why should you be anxious when a cookout consists of the easiest food ever?" Diana laughed.

"True, very true." She couldn't say the casualness of it all put her off just a tiny bit, could she?

"Would you like me to make a salad, then?" Diana asked.

All Lucy could say was, "Yes, please, and the one with pine nuts, mesclun, and balsamic vinaigrette?"

"Absolutely. How many are coming?"

"You two, plus eighteen of our mutual friends. Maybe more." Lucy grinned.

"Oh my," said Diana, and then she looked at Weston and laughed.

"Girls, it will work. We've all had that many plus more at our houses. Lucy, just relax."

"You're right," she said. "Well, I'm off to meet Sam so we can go over the list! I'm actually excited. Thank you for always being the best to me."

"Bye," they said in unison, and Lucy unlocked and locked the gate behind her of the white, wooden picket fence so Annabel wouldn't think of going for a walk on her own.

Diana gave Weston a look, raising her beautifully arched eyebrows. "Did you know?"

"No, but I suspected. She had to be the one to say." He smiled.

Diana touched her husband's hand, and he pulled her to him, gently kissing her surprised mouth.

Lucy drove to Sam's house with Toulouse serving as a co-driver. They sat on his narrow piazza of the freedman's cottage, going through their list of invitees. She noticed his courtesy that he had placed a bowl of water for the shaved Toulouse, looking charmingly like a baboon with too much facial hair.

Sam said, "Go first. Your list will have all of our mutual friends."

"Okay. This is what I have. Diana and Weston, they're confirmed. The others I haven't asked yet: Ernesto, Maria, and the children; Sadie and her gentleman caller, Mr. Semmes; Stella and Mack; Drew and Sheff, Sebastian, Benjamin, Gabi and her date of choice, or alone, Paul and Phoebe and their kids, Aslyn and Bennett and their children, Katie, she'd have to make the drive from Springfield, but she can stay with me, Brooks, of course, Ella and Ryan, Violet and Rich, and Dante." She checked off the last name and beamed at him. "You?"

"Many of the same, but I want to invite my friends Jillian and Curt, Mrs. Annie, and Zeke and his family, and what about your grandmother?"

"Grandmere goes to Russ and Steph's usually for the Fourth."

"Why can't you ask her? I'd like to meet her."

Lucy felt the pressure. *You've met mine; I need to meet yours.* "Okay, I'll ask her, but truly this will be a jumble of people in a tight place, and she operates with a cane, and sometimes that is not easy. Well, let me tally. That's twenty-nine, plus children, and Diana will make her delicious salad. I'm sure others will offer too."

He agreed. They split the list evenly and said they would make the calls. He hugged her to him and said he'd call her the next day.

The phone rang. Allston Murray's name popped up on Sam's screen. Sam jumped right in.

"Thanks for calling me back, Allston. I'm concerned about the buyers for the house. Suffice it to say, I've heard that they may not be able to afford it, and I would be disappointed if the wrong person was in that property. I know it's business. Can you just check it out? No, I'm not saying that you are unscrupulous, but one of your agents might be."

Sam clicked off the phone and hoped for the best. The cookout would be in two weeks, and he needed to make the calls.

Lucy charged through her list at work. The gallery was quiet, and it gave her the opportunity to multitask. Ernesto and Maria couldn't come; they were invited to a party on John's Island. Sadie and her Mr. Semmes were a go. He still drove and would squire her. Could she bring dessert? Stella and Mack said of course they would come. Stella would make mac and cheese, and then she offered to pick up Grandmere. Lucy left messages with the rest and then tidied up the shop.

Sam called Ben and Sebastian, who both agreed to attend and offered to bring beer and coleslaw. Sam made notes as the calls were returned. Paul, Phoebe, and their children were a go. What could they bring? Potato salad? Perfect. Jillian and Curt would be at a party on Sullivan's Island; could they drop by later? Zeke said he would have to check with his wife, but he thought they could make it for a while. Brooks said that he and Katie couldn't make it. There was some sort of celebration in Springfield that Katie wanted to go to, so he would be out of town. Mrs. Annie said she was happy to attend, and could she bring her niece and her wild rice salad?

Dante called Lucy back. He had been invited to a boat party at Rockville. Aslyn and Bennett said they were happy to come. Would Lucy like her to bring her seven bean salad? Ella and Ryan were off to the Grand Canyon for their summer vacation, so they were sorry to miss it. Rachel was a shoo-in and would bring an appetizer. Violet had called her back, saying that Rich's mother was in town and they had already made plans.

Drew called Sam back and said he and Sheff would bring boiled shrimp and his special cocktail sauce. Gabi said she had met a nice guy through one of her friends, and he had invited her to a party on Folly Beach.

Sam called Lucy and asked if he could stop by after work. Lucy said they should look around the small backyard and figure it out. She then reminded Sam that she needed to get her bike back from his house. When he arrived, he told her that he thought they could do the yard work that weekend, and then it would be perfect; just cut back some plants and mow the lawn. There would be twenty, including them, and then the children. He thought they could set up another table outside, and they would be set. He had an extra table at the America Street house that he could bring a few days before. Lucy agreed and thought the food was best kept inside; what did he think? He said that would be perfect.

He thought they could use paper plates. At first Lucy was shocked, and her response was "absolutely not," and then she thought, *Relax, this is a cookout, and why should I wash twenty or more plates?* Besides, maybe in the past she had been a little uptight. It was all taking shape in her head, and she was beginning to feel not only calm, but anticipatory. It would be fun and easy with everyone bringing their signature dishes.

Sam met Lucy at her house the day of Brooks's Carolina Day party. It was a Sunday afternoon in the low nineties, and they walked through Hampton Park to Brooks's house. Sam remembered the silly hat she had worn that time that he had seen her a year ago. Today, Lucy wore a pretty skirt with a T-shirt and flat sandals. He thought she seemed so much more calm than last year. Her energy was there, but also a sereneness that left him feeling content to be in her company.

Brooks welcomed them, told them the beverages were outside in coolers and that he was glad they could come. Sam asked Lucy if she wanted a glass of wine, and she declined, saying that she was so hot it would probably go to her head, but water would be nice. Sam fished a Bud Light out of the cooler and found a bottle of water for Lucy. As he approached, he noticed that Lucy was squatting and talking to a neighbor's child who held something clutched in her palm. Lucy was telling Erica that ladybugs were a delightful presence in a garden and that the little girl should set it free. Besides, wouldn't it be nice to see their polkie-dotted friend fly? The girl was having none of it. She was probably four, and Lucy, wiggling her eyebrows, giggling, and cajoling, made the child pull her closed hand to her chest. Sam handed her the water and asked her to introduce them to her friend.

She said, "Erica, this is my friend Sam. Sam, Erica. Erica, Sam."

Erica beamed at him, and he smiled into her freckled face.

"So what did you find? A lizard?"

She shook her red curls. "No."

"A bee?"

She shook them again. "No."

"Hmmm. I know, you found a rare fox-tail squirrel, but it must be a tiny baby, as it wouldn't fit in your hand."

Erica giggled, the pure sound of the innocent, and opened her palm to show Sam her treasure. The ladybug lay in her hand for a moment, and then it moved its delicate wings and flew to a grouping of zinnias.

Sam looked at Erica's face and said, "I bet if we watch closely, we can see her."

The little girl nodded. Lucy laughed at him, touching his arm, and mouthed "thank you."

They spent the early evening chatting with old friends and new, and by eight o'clock, Sam said, "Let's go home."

As they crossed through the park, Sam took Lucy's hand in his own. It just felt right to do so.

Chapter 29

"The food itself is often the entertainment at social gatherings such as the barbecue, the oyster roast and the fish fry. Everyone pitches in and joins the cooking, then sits down at the communal table when all the food is prepared."

Hoppin' John's Lowcountry Cooking, John Martin Taylor

It was the first of July when Sam's phone rang. He stepped outside of the Aiken Street property and answered it. Allston Murray asked Sam if he could come down to the office. It was imperative that he talk to him sooner than later.

"Allston, why can't you meet me here at the house? That would be more convenient."

"I would prefer the privacy of my office, Sam. I have a few questions for you, and it is of absolute consequence that no one overhear our conversation."

"All the better that you come here," Sam said.

"Sam, I know that you are busy, but I would really appreciate it if you could come here. Besides, I have some paperwork that might interest you," Allston Murray said stridently.

Sam ended the conversation. He would be there at 4:45 p.m.

Sam walked to Allston Murray's office, which was located on Broad Street. What had Lucy said to him once? Oh yeah, in the colonial period, it had been the widest street in America. Funny how he could hear her in his head sometimes. He hadn't had time to shower or change his clothes, and he arrived in jeans and a T-shirt. When he announced himself to the receptionist, she curled her fifty-something lip at his appearance. Whatever, he thought.

Allston Murray invited him into his office and asked him to take a seat. The office was nicely appointed with the hand of a designer: sofa and chairs that coordinated, Allston's large mahogany desk sat squarely in the room, and expensive wooden Venetian blinds adorned at the windows. The art was interesting. A portrait of a long dead Murray above the desk, something that was probably a Halsey and a McCallum, two artists who Lucy enjoyed, and then on another wall, a large painting that he thought he had seen at Lucy's gallery.

"Great office. Is that a Halsey and a McCallum? Now this looks familiar, dark, but interesting."

"You're right, of course. I knew both William Halsey and his wife, Corrie McCallum. They were both very talented. That one is new, and my wife expressly told me I could not bring it home. It came from Lucy Cameron's shop. I believe it's quite good and somewhat disconcerting." Allston stated.

"So, you went to her show in June?" Sam asked.

"I did. That girl reminds me a lot of her mother, very creative, yet different. I knew her mother from a distance, she was a few years younger, but everyone wanted to be in her sphere. I feel her daughter is like that."

Sam nodded, thinking this town was all about whom you knew and who knew you.

He sat down across Allston Murray, the large desk looming between them. Allston began talking about his concerns of the Hanover Street house. He was happy that Sam had brought to his attention his questions regarding one of his agent's behavior. He had been looking into Sam's complaint and had spoken to the agent directly. He also was inquiring about the potential buyers' ability to afford the house, and a friend at the bank was looking into every possibility of fudged reports of credit. He wanted Sam to know that he was taking this sale very seriously. At this time, they were scheduled to close in just about three weeks.

Allston Murray inquired if he could offer Sam a drink, and Sam said, "Just water."

"You won't mind if I have a bourbon, do you, as I have a few questions I'd like to ask you."

Sam could see the clock on the phone. It was now five thirty. He was to be at Lucy's house at six to finish up the last preparations of a party that he had insisted upon. He had a feeling he would be late. Allston Murray asked him about his associations with Gus Wolfe. Sam quietly told him about their interactions in college and then beyond, choosing what he would and wouldn't say. Allston asked him if he knew anything about his current personal status, and Sam replied that he could not say, but that he had been told that Gus had recently acted in a dishonorable fashion, but then again, who knew both sides of the story?

"I was playing golf with a friend of mine, and he told me about this sweet girl that was living in his kitchen house. It's a long story, but supposedly, she is pregnant, and Gus is the father and won't take responsibility."

"I don't think that Katie wants anything to do with him. He was toxic to her, and she's moving on. She's a very quiet, but resilient woman."

"I'm just sorry for her. There's nothing I can do for her, though, poor thing," Allston Murray stated.

Sam was annoyed. "Actually, there is something you could do. I know when I contract out work and there have been issues with child support or other things, I've leaned on those people. Now maybe you don't want to, or maybe you can't, but there is a way to do the right thing with her. Jeez, Allston, we're talking about a schoolteacher who has left her position, is going off running into the midlands to figure it out, and she faces the expense of a baby. That's huge. Gus Wolfe should have to pay for half of the expense, or at least some of it. He's not a child, but a man who should be held accountable for his actions. This is not the first time he has done wrong, and you know it. I know that you are a decent and good man, but those attributes cannot be said about Gus Wolfe."

"Maybe you're right, Sam. I'll get back to you about the buyers. I hope you won't consider pulling the listing?"

"No, I'm not going to do that. I just want what's best for the house."

He pulled his cell phone out from his pocket and turned it on only to realize the battery was dead.

It was six thirty. Sam hadn't called. That was odd, Lucy thought. He was usually so punctual. She couldn't worry about it, though. It was only time, after all. The new assistant, Trudie, was working out splendidly and would work on the third of July so Lucy could take the day off. Lucy thanked her lucky stars that everything in her life was coming about so nicely. She checked her list. She would need to vacuum the house and straighten the kitchen. How did it get cluttered so quickly, she thought as she placed newspapers and shredded bills and credit card applications into a bag. After tidying, she looked at the phone, noting that it was six forty-five.

Sam pulled in front of her house a little before seven. He was frustrated. She would probably be mad at him for not calling, or at least annoyed, but there was nothing he could do.

"Hi, Lucy!" he called through the screen door.

"Hi, yourself. Just getting off from work, then?" she said, smiling at him as she let him though the door.

"Look it, I'm sorry I'm late. I had to meet with my Realtor, and it took longer than I thought, and my phone died."

"Oh, and did you take the time to give it a proper burial?" she teased.

"Sorry."

"It's all right. I was just going over the menu and have decided that you will have to pick up condiments, sodas, and beer. I'll get the wine, hamburgers, hot dogs and the rest," she said.

"Why can't we shop together? I wanted to shop together."

Was he whining? Sam had never whined before. She didn't know if she liked that.

"Sure, we can shop together. Sam, I need to get my bike from you. It's been at your house for almost a month. Can you bring it next time, please?"

"Sure, sure, it's been taking up too much space at the house anyway," he said, tugging a lock of her hair.

He opened his notebook, and they prepared the list together.

Sam was installing windows to the addition, whistling while he worked. He had purchased them at Historic Charleston Foundation's warehouse, and they perfectly matched the other two-over-two paned windows. The process with this house had been so easy, with much of the approval being done at city staff level and limited tweaking by the Board of Architectural Review. In fact, he had never had a project that went through the first time that the application was heard.

The party was a success. Yes, it been hot as hell, but it had been fun, and he had really enjoyed hosting a party with Lucy. She always made things seem effortless, and her house and yard had looked perfect. He was glad he had brought the horseshoes and the bocce ball set. He was relieved that their mutual friends now knew that they were seeing each other. It was a lot easier that way, and why not? Lucy was great. Who wouldn't want to be with her?

He had made her happy with the bike. He recalled how she had thanked him for bringing it. As she was placing it in the corner of the small yard, she noticed the new tires, and then she tried the brakes. She had turned to him and smiled, and then she giggled as she saw the registration on the frame. She ran to him and threw her arms about his neck, thanking him for his thoughtfulness and generosity.

Mrs. Annie had called him today to thank him for the invitation. She told him that she liked Lucy and that she was "quality." She had also enjoyed meeting his friends. She had no idea that he had so many nice friends, and all were so thoughtful, offering her this and that;

wasn't that dear? He had been a little nervous when he met Lucy's grandmother. She was a wonderful woman, so spry, and she looked so youthful. Sure, she needed a cane, but how many people heading toward ninety didn't? The day had been perfect and the night even better. He smiled broadly, thinking about Lucy's laughter as she curled up next to him in bed, showing him the beautiful and silly pictures in her pop-up book after all the guests had left.

Lucy was straightening the frames of the art in her gallery, thinking about the day before. It had been an amazing time. She and Sam had a few odd moments while putting it all together, but nothing that hadn't sorted out within moments. She liked his Mrs. Annie, and Zeke and Sandra too. They were so nice and genuine. Ben and Sebastian had helped him at the grill, and everyone had brought the most delicious food. Ben had warned her about Sebastian's spiked watermelon, and she had stayed clear of it. It was nice that Stella and Mack had picked up a beautifully coiffed Grandmere, and she thought she would call in a little while to tell them thank you. Sadie's gentleman caller was quite the flirt, and it was touching how he was constantly touching Sadie's hand—and once Lucy caught him touching her lined cheek. Lucy shook her head. *Our girl might be getting some in that swanky party palace that doesn't seem like a retirement home,* she thought.

She had been surprised when, after all the plates were cleared, Grandmere had made a pronouncement that this was the best Fourth of July party she had ever attended. Unbeknownst to Lucy, Grandmere had had Mack place champagne in the coolers. As friends were delving into desserts from Saffron and Cupcake, Lucy heard the first cork of the Taittinger let go, and before she knew it, everyone was sipping bubbly out of plastic cups while nibbling desserts on paper plates. It had been one of the most spontaneous and happy moments of her life. Sam had charmed Grandmere. He had been a delight, asking her if he could fix a plate of food for her and then making sure that she was surfeit. He had chosen to sit next to her grandmother while eating, and Lucy had been left to her own devices. That was of little consequence, as she sat next to Mrs. Annie and her niece, balancing Zeke and Sandra's son, David, on her knee with a plate of food in her hand.

She was happy to meet Jillian and Curt, friends of Sam's. She had met Jillian once, but on reacquaintance, she liked this no -nonsense woman who seemed to be able to talk about everything under the sun. Diana and Weston said that the party had been splendid and they would see her soon. As Rachel said her good-byes, she had winked at Lucy and said that she liked Sam, and it seemed that they were very companionable together. Sebastian and Ben were the last to go. Ben had kissed her cheek and smiled his beautiful smile at her, making her giggle. Sebastian had kissed her on the mouth and whispered, *"Have fun, my girl."*

She thought that Sam couldn't have been better, so hospitable, and funny too, and when had he found the time to drop off her bike and get it serviced? New tires and brakes, and he had registered it for her. She initially wanted to ask him the cost so that she could reimburse him for the expense, and then she thought that her thoughts were impolite and she should just thank him instead, and she did so. He had smiled at her, crinkling those beautiful pewter eyes, and the next thing she knew was that her arms were about him and he lifted off her feet and swung her around; before she knew it, she had kicked her heels up, and one of her sassy black sandals sailed past their ears, which made her laugh even harder. It seemed so hilarious to her that her shoe could have given either one of them or both a concussion.

She turned on her computer and waited for it to boot up. Placing her left hand to her mouth, she blushed, thinking that what had happened between them later was a magical moment. She realized that there was something so physical between them, and although it scared her just a little, she liked it very much.

July flew by so fast, and before she knew it, Lucy realized that Sam was preparing for his big trip. They were walking Toulouse in the late evening on Folly Beach, enjoying the Morris Island Lighthouse with its rust-and-white-colored stripes in their sight.

"So, tell me, Sam, what is your itinerary like for this trip?" she asked.

"The idea is to go home for about two weeks and then fly to Australia, see the sights, bum around for about three weeks, then head to Fiji for two weeks, then off to New Zealand for about three weeks. So I'll be gone for two and a half months. The goal is to see new things, learn about different people, and to grow. Even though there has been lots going on lately, I'm not sure if this is where I'm going to land, Lucy. I'll give you that Charleston is a beautiful city, and I've enjoyed living here, but I've been here for twelve years, and I've missed the Northeast and all it has to offer. Everything is so close by, you know; from Boston alone there are so many towns just a car drive away, and a short one at that. So we'll see. There is my uncle's business to consider as well. I know he wants me to take it over, and I feel a family obligation to do that."

"Of course," she said, trying not to feel frustrated. "Well"—she beamed at him—"you will figure it out. You always do." She looked down, noticing that the wet sand covered her feet, then looked out to the gray-green water.

"Lucy, why are you so quiet?" he asked tugging her hand and holding it firmly in his.

The breeze picked up and cooled her hot skin, and she thought, *I can't tell him my thoughts or what I feel for him.* She smiled at him crookedly and said, "Just thinking what the color of the water will be like over there. I'm sure it will be hot in Fiji, but what about Australia and New Zealand?"

"Mostly in the fifties and sixties. It will be like late winter and early spring here. To tell the truth, I'm looking forward to the cooler weather. Sometimes in the summer here, I feel like I'm not as focused, as it's too hot. So, yes, I'm excited. I've been planning it pretty well and plan to take my bike with me." He smiled at her.

Lucy drove him home and dropped him off in front of the cottage looking bright and pristine in the twilight. He kissed her on the mouth and thanked her for asking him to go to the beach, and then he patted Toulouse's furry head.

She didn't know why she felt like crying; she just did. She took off her sandals and placed her sandy feet in the white tub and then held the shower sprayer to them. As the sand washed down the drain, she thought that he had planned this trip before they ever began seeing each other again. She had two choices. She could become sad and get grumpy or she could make these next two weeks special. It would be easy to fall into the first category, doing the poor, pitiful me thing. What was it that she had heard from Tony Robbins, the thought guru? Oh yes. The four *R*'s. Resistance leads to resentment, which leads to rejection, which leads to repression. None of those words were good alone, much less linked together.

He was going on his big trip whether she liked it or not. If she was honest, she didn't dislike the idea of him going on this journey. What she disliked was that he may not come home to Charleston—and to her. So, what she had to do was enjoy this time with him and make every moment a special one. They didn't have to have fancy dinners or anything like that. What had Sadie told her about her sister Cordelia? Oh yes. Play dates. That's how her husband never became bored. It was what it was. She would just remind him that she was fun-loving and playful and that there was no one who was like her. As she tossed and turned in her bed, she told herself to embrace the contrast. She could only control herself, and if Sam moved back home to Salem, then she had to let it be.

Sam called Lucy the following day. He told her he was tidying up his projects nicely and that he wondered if they could get a bite to eat later that evening. She said that sounded nice; where did he want to go? He thought Santi's was a good choice. They had such authentic Latin food. She wondered how she could mix it up, add some fun touch. In the end, he picked her up, and they enjoyed a pleasant evening talking and laughing, she eating the shrimp-and-avocado salad and he enjoying tacos.

By Wednesday, she called Diana. She hadn't come up with a solitary plan for them. Maybe she wasn't a very able planner.

"Lucy, calm yourself. Pop by the house tonight, and let's see if Weston and I can give you some good suggestions."

Lucy wandered down to Diana and Weston's house with note cards and a pen shoved into her shorts pocket. She leaned into the breeze and thought, *It's so hot,* and said so to both of them as she climbed the steps of the front porch.

"So, Lucy, what's the challenge?" Weston asked.

"As you both know, Sam is leaving in a little less than two weeks to go on his big adventure. He's not even sure if he plans to return to Charleston, and I, well...I guess I wanted to give him a proper send-off, you know? I don't want it to seem over the top, just remind his subconscious that I'm fun and all that." She ended breathlessly.

Weston shook his head, and Diana laughed. "You are fun," she said. "In fact, everyone loves that about you, Lucy. That's why you have such good friends. You always have that great energy about you, and you are caring, honest, and kind. Your guy from Salem should know all those things, plus the fact that you look fantastic."

"So, how can we help?" Weston asked.

"Well, Weston, if Diana was to surprise you with a few things, what would they be? Fun things, like play dates."

"That's pretty easy. Let me see. I always like to go to a RiverDogs game. There is nothing better than catching the cool breeze off the Ashley River at the Joe," he said, referring to the Joseph P. Riley, Jr.

ballpark. "Kayaking, that's something I like to do, and I want to visit the Russell House. I haven't been there in years, and I've heard that the restoration is incredible. Sam would like that, especially since they've repainted all of the decorative finishes. Food is always good, and none of the stuff you two want to eat, and then again, a good action flick. How many times have I been forced to watch movies over again, like *Stranger than Fiction*, *Pride and Prejudice*, and that one where the divorcée goes to Italy and buys a villa?"

"I thought you liked *Under the Tuscan Sun*, honey?" Diana asked.

"Sure, once or twice, but every six months?"

Lucy had never thought that he would find the movie boring. She loved that movie; in fact, it was one of her favorites. "Okay, Weston, what do you suggest?" She had the note cards at the ready, her pen held sharp as a dagger.

"*Glory* is a classic. Plus, Lt. Robert Gould Shaw was from Boston. *Kingdom of Heaven* is another good one, and any of the *Ocean's* movies. For the silliness factor, I'd suggest *Anchorman* or *Wedding Crashers*."

"Okay, let's see then. I can suggest we go kayaking and see the Russell House, a game at the Joe, and then movies in between with unhealthy takeout?"

"Yup, I think that would do it. Any ideas, Diana?"

"She looked at him and said, "You like the *Harry Potter* movies, too, and Lucy owns all of those, so it wouldn't look like she's trying so hard. Lucy, this has to seem effortless on your part. Otherwise, well..." Her words drifted off.

"What she wants to say, Lucy, is don't make it look like you've planned it at all."

"Right, okay. I think I've got it. No anxious behavior, assert myself by driving the car, so to speak, and then let him lead the dance. I take a step back, and then I duck and punch? Wow, this is madness. No wonder I was single for so long; this is *work*!"

"It is work, Lucy, but this time around you've been getting it right. Besides, what in life that's worth it isn't work? Just continue to do it," Weston said.

She hugged each one of them to her, shaking her head while laughing, and thanked them. She told them she loved them and shut the gate behind her. She chose not to walk directly home and instead found her way to the banks of the Ashley River. The sun was going down, and the sunset was extraordinary as it tinged the sky and the water with golds, oranges, and reds. She waved to her neighbors, Karen and Dan. He was washing down their kayaks with a hose, and she asked them if they had enjoyed paddling. They said they had, and if she ever wanted to borrow one of theirs and throw in, she could use their dock. She said thank you, and she might take them up on that one of these hot evenings.

She could hear the phone ring before she entered her house. It was Sam, asking her what she had been up to. She said she had gone for a walk and told him about her neighbors and their offer of the kayak. He had his own, he said, and maybe they should do that sometime this week, just get on the water and cool off.

"That sounds great, Sam. Why don't I call them tonight? What afternoon is better for you? Right, Sheff and Drew gave you their tickets to the game at the Joe for Friday? That was nice. Sure, I'd love to go. Then maybe we could kayak on Sunday afternoon. Okay, I'll ask and call you back. Saturday? Oh. I haven't gotten to Saturday yet. Yes, certainly I'd like to see you then, too, maybe a bike ride? That would be perfect." She hung up the phone and whistled. The universe had set everything into action, and the first act of this play was looking promising.

Chapter 30

Man is the hunter; woman is his game

The Princess, Alfred, Lord Tennyson

They were passing The Battery, and Lucy felt the perspiration run down the back of her neck. Somehow they were stuck behind a tour bus, which made them slow down and brake harder than intended. As the bus continued its way down East Battery, Sam suggested that they take a left on South Battery and turn down Meeting Street. She suggested that they take a break and sit in the garden of the Nathaniel Russell House. There it was. They were enjoying the shade under the arbor at the back of the garden, and Sam commented that it was beautiful, a virtual paradise.

"Sam, have you been in the Russell House lately? Maybe we should go inside. All the guests that come in the gallery always rave about it. I haven't been in it in years. Maybe we should go in and just cool off in the AC?"

"Lucy, look at us. We're in shorts and T-shirts, and I don't know about you, but I'm sure I smell pretty ripe."

She noticed two overweight guests walking through the garden. Their clothes were sopping wet with sweat, and their shorts were crawling up their robust thighs; she and Sam looked like movie stars in comparison, and she told him.

"Lucy, I don't have my wallet. I'm sorry."

"Sam, I have mine—let's just do it. C'mon."

"Okay. Now if a docent wrinkles her nose at us, you better not get your panties in a twist." He grinned.

"Humph," she replied. He didn't know her little surprise. She had something up her sleeve, she hoped. As he was looking at the books in the kitchen house that served as a gift shop, she purchased the tickets. The sales associate tried to sell her the double ticket to include the Aiken-Rhett House, and she said no, thank you, they were local and had visited that antebellum beauty just a while back. Their tour guide was a lovely, slender woman in her sixties, perfectly coiffed and wearing a Chanel suit and Prada shoes. She spoke with a clear Yankee dialect.

Sam found himself asking her if she was from Massachusetts. She said that, before retirement, she had lived all her life in Marblehead, and now she and her husband split their time between the two. In fact, they were heading north next week, a little later than they usually did. He told her he was originally from Salem and had lived in this port city for more than ten years.

Good, Lucy thought, no strident and conceited guide, but a lovely woman who did not look down her nose at their sweaty bodies. But then again, all the guests were drenched. It was, after all, July in Charleston.

Joan was entertaining and knowledgeable, listing that Russell was a merchant who hailed from Rhode Island. She spoke about the family and their fortune and pointed out the beautifully crafted Charleston-made furniture. She was direct about Russell's involvement in the slave trade and then succinctly spoke of the meticulous restoration that Historic Charleston Foundation had accomplished. As they entered the stairhall, Lucy looked for the trompe l'oeil, hoping that the guide would mention it. She crossed her fingers. Sam's eyes were huge as he marveled at the free-flying staircase. Funny, she thought, noticing the four men who craned their necks to see the construction of the stair through a Plexiglas opening. One of the other visitors asked the guide about the painted cornice.

"Now, that cornice is a restoration of the original that was discovered through stringent paint analysis. We don't know who the architect was or if there was one. What we do know is that an Irish man named Samuel O'Hara created the original painted cornice, as he had taken an ad out in the paper suggesting that prospective clients view his painted decoration at the house of Nathaniel Russell. That also allows us to understand that this painted decoration could be viewed from the entry through those rosette doors, as that was a public space and this a private one."

Lucy was overjoyed. Yes! Sam could now share this story with his family, most importantly his beloved uncle. He looked gobsmacked, and she smiled slightly, remembering Weston's and Diana's words. The thirty-minute tour came quickly to a close, and Lucy couldn't help but notice that Sam was beaming. He thanked the guide and asked Lucy if she had any cash. He wanted to place it in the donation box. Lucy never kept cash in her wallet, but she had ten dollars and gave it to him freely. He placed the money in the box, and the two of them exited, thanking their guide again.

"So where do you live?" she asked the two of them.

Lucy responded that she lived near the Citadel in Wagener Terrace, and Sam said that he lived on the Eastside.

"Oh," Joan had said. "Don't mind me. I suppose I thought you were married."

Sam was baffled. What did *that* mean exactly? He was so excited, though, that he paid little attention as they walked to their bikes that had been locked up to a No Parking sign on the street.

"Lucy, that's my ancestor that she mentioned. Did you know that?"

Lucy feigned ignorance. "Sam, wasn't that amazing? After the research you've done, you've found his work? It was absolute serendipity. I was simply hot, and it seemed important, if not necessary, to cool off. It's a beautiful house, isn't it, and the art and furniture are exquisite. Aren't you glad that we went inside?"

He hugged her to him, holding her in her ragtag jean shorts and white T-shirt. There was something, if he would admit to himself, about Lucy. Maybe she didn't know about the house and the painted decoration, but she had created a moment of magic that he had never expected. Even when she was quiet, which she had been of late, she was the most wonderful and considerate woman he knew.

He was leaving tomorrow. He would come to her house for breakfast and then drive the BMW to Massachusetts. He would stay with friends in Washington, DC, for two days, and then *poof*, he was gone for three months. She would miss his company and try to stay busy. She had started to strength train in April, hoping to turn last year's tankini body into this year's bikini body, and she hoped that the discipline of the weights, the love of her friends and family, and her job would sustain her and make the time sail by.

Chapter 31

All human actions have one or more of these seven causes: chance, nature, compulsions, habit, reason, passion and desire.

Aristotle

He was in Logan Airport. So much had happened in the last two weeks, it had been a whirlwind. The last couple of weeks in Charleston had gone by so fast, and his time with Lucy seemed so short. The buyers of the Hanover Street house had not worked out, but the science fiction writer who had been previously interested and then looked at Savannah as a retreat had shown interest again. Who knew? Lucy had called it his wooden bride, and the house was that; he treasured it immensely and wanted the right buyer for it.

It seemed that their relationship had shifted in those last two weeks. Lucy was always easy to be around, but there was a change in her. She was more steady and calm. He thought about how they had spent one evening watching *Harry Potter and the Sorcerer's Stone* while eating pizza out of the box in her den, and then she had surprised him with a pillow fight. He could hear her laughter in his head, and he smiled. She had been so damn good to him. He called her, and his voice went to voice mail.

"Lucy, I'm flying *out*! Thank you for everything. I'll stay in touch. E-mail me, okay?" His flight number was called, and as he stepped in line, he said, "Lucy, thank you again."

She came in from her bike ride, only to see that she had missed his call. She thought of him constantly, and it had only been two weeks that he had left. This would never do, she thought, hitting the number one button on her phone in order to listen to his message again.

She remembered the day they had toured the Russell House. Just a few days before that, she had picked up the Gateway Magazine and had read an article about the seven local museum houses. There the sentence was before her.

"This neoclassical mansion has always been known for its free-flying staircase, but the masterful painted decoration shows the sophistication and wealth of Charleston's inhabitants. The architect and contractor are unknown; however, the decorative painter, Samuel O'Hara, left his legacy by taking an ad in the newspaper at the time."

Those last two weeks had been amazing. She had wanted them to be special, and it was as if every time she turned around, things were handed to her just like that, falling into her lap, making it look like she wasn't trying to make things so special. She thought of her good luck and was grateful for all of the days and evenings they had spent together. So, now the rest of summer was in front of her, and she had to stay busy.

August flew by, and Lucy saw a steady traffic at work. Her moxie girls had created a sensation in June, and now their work seemed to fly off the walls. She marveled that certain designers were purchasing the works for offices and commercial spaces.

One evening she came home to find Brooks sitting on her stoop. She hugged her friend to her and asked him how he had been.

"I never see you, Brooks. You always seem to be popping up to Springfield. I've missed you."

"I've missed you too, Lucy. Can we take a walk?"

"Sure. Let me change clothes." She changed into shorts and a cotton camisole. It was hot—well, when wasn't it hot in August?—and the sun shone overbright. She added sunglasses and a ball cap.

"Are we taking Toulouse?" Brooks asked.

"No, it's too hot. I walked him this morning, and I'll take him before dark is upon us," she said.

They walked through Hampton Park, quietly talking about his work, her gallery, and their friends. She asked him how Katie was doing. She had talked to her last week, and she sounded happy.

"That's what I wanted to talk to you about, ask you for your good counsel, so to speak."

"Go on then," Lucy said, punching his arm.

"I've spent a lot of time with Katie this summer, and we seem to have the same values. She's a great girl, and she's very organized. I'm very comfortable in her company too. I'm thinking about asking her to marry me." He smiled at her.

"Do you love her, though, Brooks? You haven't said anything about that, and are you two attracted to one another? Do you have fun together?"

They sat on a bench, and Brooks took Lucy's hands in his own. "Yes, I do love her, and the intimacy that we share is different and better than I have ever had. I can see myself growing old with her. I've never thought about needing or wanting children, but with Katie, I do. I think we will enjoy that." He smiled.

Lucy placed her hand over her mouth in a thoughtful gesture. "How does Katie feel abut you, then?"

"She told me over the weekend that she feels that I have been her constant star through her pregnancy and that she loved me. We have similar interests, and we do have fun together, playing cards and board games. I know this seems to have happened so quickly, and I don't quite understand why I never paid attention to her in the past, but her nature suits me, and I believe mine suits her. I think it was also that I was no longer blinded by Desiree. Katie is so different from her," he said.

"Well, then, Brooks, I think you will need to buy a ring!"

"Right, and that's where I need some help. She just doesn't seem like the kind of girl that would like a diamond ring. I was thinking about a sapphire in a platinum setting, or at least that's what I've been advised by the jeweler. What do you think, Lucy?"

"I think you are probably right. I've never been keen on a diamond, not that I have to worry about that," she giggled. "Why don't I close the shop at lunch tomorrow, and we can take a look at what you're considering?"

"That would be perfect."

Wow, Lucy thought later as she turned down the sheets and crawled into bed. She knew they were spending time together, but who ever thought that Brooks and Katie would be an item and who ever would have thought that her baby friend would consider marriage? It was wonderful, and she was happy for them. Everything seemed to be sorting out for Katie; she just hoped that Katie loved him.

The ring was beautiful, and Lucy told him so. Brooks was going to Springfield on Friday, and he would let her know how it went.

Lucy was mowing the yard on Saturday evening, thinking it could not be hotter and she couldn't wait until the fall. Violet had called her earlier to remind her that she would be turning forty in exactly two weeks' time and that she should have a party. What did Lucy want?

Lucy didn't really care about a party. Why didn't they just get their friends together and go to Moe's or Santi's for dinner? That would be nice, wouldn't it? Violet agreed.

Lucy finished edging the yard and was looking forward to a much-deserved shower. *I wonder what Sam is up to,* she thought. It had been four days since she had received an e-mail from him, and he would soon be heading for Fiji. Could it have already been almost three weeks since he landed in what he referred to as "Oz"? His e-mail had been chatty; he had just visited the Art Gallery of New South Wales, as the day had been a rainy one. He wrote on to say that she would have loved the Pissarro exhibit, as it had been wonderfully done. His last few days would be spent visiting Sydney's environs, primarily the Blue Mountains, where he was joining a group to trek that natural wonder, then off to Fiji. She wouldn't hear from him for a little while, as on his trek he would be away from communication. He was feeling good about his plans for the future, and he missed her. She had replied that she hoped he would have fun. Maybe he planned to bring back a boomerang, too! She typed: *Be safe* and then thought better of it; she wouldn't want him to think she was a worrywart. She hit the backspace button until the six letters were erased. Instead she added: *Miss you too, Lucy.*

An ecstatic Katie called to say that Brooks had just proposed with the most beautiful sapphire ring. Lucy could hardly understand her as Katie and Brooks were talking at once. She told them congratulations and asked them if they had settled on a date. Katie started laughing and said they would elope. They were planning that now, maybe even Las Vegas. Lucy started laughing, thinking that she would never have thought that Katie and Brooks, individually or together, would ever venture to Las Vegas. Then again, the most surprising things happened, didn't they?

Allston Murray had e-mailed Sam. He wrote thanking him again for bringing up his concerns about Gus Wolfe. Gus was no longer an agent at Murray and Associates Realtors, and had Sam not made him aware of the situation, he probably would not have chosen to make the decision that was necessary. The writer was very much interested in the Hanover Street house and had met with a local landscape architect. He was considering putting in what he called a pleasure garden with a lap pool. Sam thought that was hilarious. Who ever thought that someone would make that kind of investment on the Eastside? He couldn't wait to tell Lucy and Mrs. Annie. He e-mailed Allston Murray Brooks's contact information and told him that Brooks could set up the closing when he came back from his trip to Las Vegas. Yes, he was enjoying his trip; he had just come back from snorkeling in the beautiful waters off of Fiji.

Sam was sipping a cold beer and talking to some Australians at the bar. They were exchanging stories of their various travels. A man named Charlie was telling Sam that he and his wife had spent a couple of months in America and that they had visited Charleston and Savannah. They had visited in September, and he had no idea that it was still so hot that time of year. He had enjoyed the different places, especially Fort Sumter and Drayton Hall. Charlie asked him how he liked Australia, and Sam told him that three weeks was just too short a time to see what he needed to see. He had started his trip in Queensland and had taken a week-long trip in the hinterlands behind Cairns. He had cycled, sea kayaked, and gone white-water rafting. The package included hot air balloon rides and snorkeling off the Great Barrier Reef. He had snorkeled and dove off of Lady Elliot Island. There he explored coral reefs and shipwrecks in the clear blue water. He had seen so much, including volcanic crater lakes and rain forests. He had taken a sailing excursion off of the Whitsunday Islands. Later he had camped on Hook Island. From there he had spent an evening enjoying the amazing view from Hill Inlet on Tongue Point. In Sydney, he had spent three days taking in the sights and two days in the Blue Mountains. While there he had spent time walking the Jamison Valley, where he saw the Three Sisters Rocks. He had learned about the Dharug people, their art, and their culture when he visited the Aboriginal Cultural Center.

Charlie asked Sam how he was able to take so much time off of work to travel, as most Americans he had met only had a few weeks of vacation a year. Sam said that he worked for himself rehabilitating houses. Charlie asked him if his wife or girlfriend approved of such a long excursion, and Sam said he had planned this trip before he started seeing Lucy, again. She was very supportive, he said. In fact, she was not like many girls he knew at all. Charlie ordered another beer and said that he and his wife of fifteen years took vacations together and that each one took a week during the year on their own to get away from it all and that it had made their marriage stronger. Sam was amazed that Charlie was openly discussing his married life with a stranger, but then again, that's what happened on these trips. It was like that on the first leg of his flight to L.A.

The passenger next to him was a woman originally from Iowa who had family in Boston. She was only in her fifties, but looked far older. She had worked as a truck driver and went on to tell him about a twenty-year affair she had had with her neighbor. He had no idea why she felt the need to tell him her tale of woe. What had she said about the man? That's right. She liked him plenty—his wife, not so much.

He wondered what it would be like to be married and have trips like Charlie was talking about. He wasn't sure if he did get married if he would want his wife to take a week off of their life. There would have to be a great deal of trust on both sides to do that. Later that night Sam thought about Lucy, thinking that she never questioned his "adventure," as she called it. In fact, those last several days were so comfortable and enjoyable. He could see spending a great deal of time with her.

Lucy called Mrs. Annie back. "Hi, Mrs. Annie, you said that you had some drawings that you wanted me to see? Sure, I can come by anytime this week and take a look at them, if that's convenient. Do you mind if I bring Toulouse with me? That would be wonderful. Okay. I'll see you on Thursday."

"Hi, Susie? It's Lucy. I know, I know. Who would have ever thought, but it's wonderful, isn't it? No, Brooks's family is not the issue. They are wonderful. Katie's parents are, well, not a challenge, but a problem. Right. He will get them in line. That's our Brooks. But I'm sorry about the cottage, and now you have to find new tenants and all. Really, I had no idea."

"Lucy, it's that Sadie. She has all those contacts at Bishop Gadsden. She and Lucas joined us for drinks, and Lily was the one to tell them about Katie and Brooks's good fortune. Within a week my phone was ringing off the hook, and before I knew it, the cottage was rented to a couple from Columbia wanting to raise their young children in a small town. He's some type of consultant and flies in and out, and she is a designer, of handbags and shoes, who works at home. So, it has all worked out to everyone's satisfaction."

"Wow, Sadie certainly has surprised us, now hasn't she? Last year she seemed so old to me, and this year she has just blossomed. She's always getting out there, and I believe her social calendar leaves mine in the dust," Lucy noted.

"I think she's in love with Lucas, honey. It's amazing what love can do to a person, transform them and all that. Plus the yoga helps to keep one limber. Lily's been going with me to my yoga class, and she swears that she hasn't felt so good in years. She doesn't use her cane so much, but I might add I'm glad leg warmers have come back in style, as she is never without them."

"Susie, my Grandmere, in leg warmers, as in *Flashdance*? No way, you are teasing me, aren't you? Of course you were. Of course she wears yoga gear. You had me going there for a second." She giggled. "Well, will I see you this weekend? I'm going to pop by Grandmere's on Sunday for a little while."

"Yes, I'll be home. Why don't you call me when you get there?" Susie said.

Lucy hung up the phone thinking that this would be a busy week. She would head over to Mrs. Annie's on Thursday evening after she closed the gallery, and then she would join her friends for a birthday celebration on Saturday evening. She still had a hard time thinking she would turn forty, but then again, forty was the new thirty. *Oh, what nonsense,* she thought.

Mrs. Annie met Lucy at the front door and led her and Toulouse into the living room of her tidy and straight single house. Lucy marveled at Mrs. Annie's crystal vases and said they were beautiful. She looked about her, noticing what she thought were several Edwin Harleston paintings on the walls amidst photographs of family members. The wallpaper was probably hung after Hurricane Hugo; it had that late eighties look. Mrs. Annie asked Lucy if she wanted anything to drink, as she had just poured herself a sweet tea. Lucy thanked her and said that that would be nice.

"Lucy, I wanted you to look at a few things that I have. I'm not really sure what to do with them, and I think they need to be somewhere else than this house," Mrs. Annie said.

In front of Lucy were two large sketch pads from the 1920s. She leafed carefully through them, noticing sketches made for portraits and landscapes of the Low Country. Clearly, they must be Harleston's work, and she said so. Mrs. Annie said they were. Her late husband's father had been a friend of the artist and subsequently had been given the works at Harleston's death. Mrs. Annie felt that they were too important to have in her own house, and she did not want to sell them, but maybe Lucy knew someone at the Gibbes Museum of Art who might be interested? Lucy said she thought she could make the phone call if Mrs. Annie was so inclined. Mrs. Annie said yes, and perhaps she would get a tax deduction? Lucy told her that she would go with her if that would make her feel more comfortable and that she had done this before with Sadie.

"Lucy, have you heard from Sam, lately?" Mrs. Annie inquired

"I heard from him today, in fact. He's been snorkeling around Fiji and taking in the sights. He seems to be having a wonderful time, and I won't be surprised if he extends his stay. The Hanover Street house is under contract, so I think he's a bit relieved about that." She smiled.

"Yes, that must be a relief, especially after all that work he put into it. Do you think that he'll come back to Charleston, then?" Mrs. Annie asked.

"I don't know. I think he misses his family and the Northeast. He can easily do what he does here up there; plus there is the question of his uncle's business and all. I guess we'll see."

"Well, I certainly will miss that young man. He is just such a thoughtful neighbor and kind too. In fact, I received a postcard from him today from Australia. He seemed to thoroughly enjoy himself."

Yes, he is enjoying it, Lucy thought, feeling a little jealous that she had not received a postcard from Sam, but then again, he had been conscientious in sending her e-mails. Lucy took her leave from Mrs. Annie, telling her that she would call her soon.

Chapter 32

Twenty years from now you will be more disappointed by the things that you didn't do than by the ones you did do. So throw off the bowlines. Sail away from the safe harbor. Catch the trade winds in your sails.
Explore. Dream. Discover.

Mark Twain

She drove to Grandmere's thinking how fun her birthday dinner had been. Ben and Sebastian had commandeered two long picnic tables at Santi's, and sixteen of her friends had joined her in a boisterous celebration. At one point Weston had sat next to her, asking her why hadn't she been born in March, when the temperature would have been cooler. Diana had playfully swatted her husband, telling him not be rude. She was happy to be with her friends, and they all sipped margaritas and mojitos, toasting her big day.

Earlier that day she had walked Toulouse on Sullivan's Island, where they enjoyed looking at the city's skyline from the beach. Toulouse had bounded through the front door, and Lucy bent over to retrieve the mail on the floor. There, amidst advertising and the neighborhood newsletter, was the postcard. It was very large, with an image of Sydney's opera house. On the back Sam had scrawled: *Lucy, greetings from Sydney! This is an amazing place, wish you were here. Hope you like the L&O card. Yours, Sam.* She had no idea what L&O meant, but she liked the card very much. She had immediately placed it on the fridge, securing it with two magnets.

Lucy entered the house and called to Grandmere.

"Out here, darling," she called from the piazza.

Grandmere had the table on the piazza set with a white linen cloth and her Limoges porcelain. Lucy couldn't help but notice that there was food enough for a small army and the table set for five. Before she knew it, Grandmere, Susie, Stella, and Mack were singing "Happy Birthday" to her. Lucy almost started crying. It was so dear of them all to be here, and she told them so. Stella and Mack gave her the latest cookbook by the Lee Brothers, and Susie gave her a lovely mahogany box inlaid with mother-of-pearl. The card inside was touching, Susie's beautiful cursive told Lucy to remind herself that she needed a magical creation box to store her mental treasures until they came to fruition. Inside was a generic frequent flier card from a credit card company, and Susie had scrawled: *Lucy Cameron, one free ticket to Italy*, which made her smile. Grandmere surprised her with a short necklace and a matching bracelet made of jadeite and pearls. Lucy said they were exquisite and wondered where she had found them. Grandmere smiled at Susie, and Susie smiled back.

"Darling, your great-grandfather did enjoy his travels, and many years ago he went to New Zealand and purchased a necklace for my mother. The tradition, as I was told by my mother, is that greenstone, or the nephrite, that you see is bought as a gift and not for one's self. It was a longer strand, and Susie suggested that I take it to the jeweler and see if they could shorten it to make it more fashionable, and there were enough pearls and stones left over to make the two-stranded bracelet. They even matched the Art Nouveau clasp. Wasn't that clever? I do hope you like it," she said with eyebrows raised.

"Oh, Grandmere, they are beautiful," Lucy said.

Grandmere clasped the necklace to Lucy's neck, and Susie fixed the bracelet at her wrist. As Lucy walked into the parlor and peered at herself in the large pier mirror, she thought that Grandmere seemed less fragile, and she noticed that the cane was nowhere in sight. The jewelry was just perfect and suited the cream-colored linen dress that she was wearing. She didn't know if her birthday could be any better.

Sam was enjoying his respite on Fiji. He and Charlie had become fast friends, and he liked that Charlie just showed up one morning and had told Sam, *"Now no more drinking at bars at night and sissy snorkeling in the day."* His friend had a small sailing vessel, and they would set sail. Could Sam help with the rigging, or was he just talk? Sam laughed and said that he knew how to sail, and yes, he had spent too much time on leisure activities. They would meet at five tomorrow morning and begin another adventure.

This trip was so much better than his trip to Asia, and he didn't think anything could top that. He liked these Australians he had met, their easy sense of humor, and he enjoyed the island people; but then again, he was reminded of his mother's e-mail yesterday. This was simply a different time in his life, and he had changed from the last big trip. That was what was so wonderful, Catherine had said; travel changed your life. She told him not to worry about Uncle Sam. He was doing better than they all expected, especially with the company of Beatrice, who continued to charm them all.

Lucy had e-mailed him and told him that she was heading to San Francisco to see her dad, Rut, and Maeve. They had sent her a ticket; wasn't that generous? It seemed as if her birthday was stretching out now for two weeks, and then Mrs. Annie had called again. They were to meet with the lead curator at the Gibbes next week. She had told him that Enid—remember her, the songbird at Huger's that New Year's Day?—had shown up on her stoop and had serenaded her to a jazzy version of "Happy Birthday." Could a girl's fortieth have been any better? And it wasn't over yet, as her friends David and Celia wanted to take her to the new dive bar on Upper King Street for another celebration when she returned from San Fran. She added that she missed him and signed off: *Lucy*. Not *Yours, Lucy*; not *Love, Lucy*; just *Lucy*.

He e-mailed her back saying that they were taking to the high sea, ha ha! Thanks for helping Mrs. Annie, and he hoped she would have a great time with her family. He would write her again this time from New Zealand sometime late next week. *Yours, Sam*. That should help her along, shouldn't it?

⁂

Lucy and Trudie had agreed to take on two young male artists' work. They were both talented. Geoff's work was whimsical, with crazy animals leaping in the air amidst powder puff clouds and strange houses in the background. The other, Darryl, whom they had nicknamed Seurat, dabbled in a large type of pointillism and painted portraits, landscapes, and seascapes. One of the moxie girls had jumped ship and gone to Gabi's studio, as there had been one artist who had not quite worked out, but Lucy didn't mind, as that space was better suited for her large pieces. All in all her life was very grand. Who would have thought about all the changes that had happened in such a short period of time?

She had received an oversized card from Sam, and she had to give it to him, he was having a wonderful time. This one was of Fiji, showing a magical landscape and a cerulean-colored sea. It read: *Lucy, Swimming and snorkeling in blue waters and then went sailing, where I climbed like a rat in the rigging. Sounds like you had an L&O time for your birthday. See you soon! Yours, Sam.*

She had no idea what L&O meant. Was this some kind of Down Under thing, or was it something that had been exchanged between them that she didn't remember?

He had no idea what all had occurred since his last missive. She had gone to visit her father, Rut, and Maeve. Ray had been out of town over the weekend, and a joyous Maeve told her she was pregnant. No, she and Ray were not getting married. They needed to talk some more about that. Well, of course, she told Lucy, he had proposed for several months now, and yes, she was only two months along, and she was moving into his large condo in Pacific Heights with its most amazing view. He had already cleared space for her books, and he had decided to get rid of some of his clunky furniture to make space for her Arts and Crafts sofa, chaise, and desk. The apartment was situated in a painted lady, a late Victorian, and he had a full floor with a large living room, dining room, and two bedrooms as well as what must have been a sewing room that would be perfect for the nursery. The kitchen had a vintage gas stove that worked, and off from its French doors was a charming terrace. No, she wasn't worried that he would freak out when the baby came; their relationship was very strong indeed. She couldn't be happier, she told Lucy as they walked down the sheer slope from their father's house to the gourmet store down the street.

The men were overjoyed. They would be grandfathers, and it was about time too. The three of them had delighted themselves by eating fresh oysters at the Ferry Building, while Maeve chose a savory crepe stuffed with vegetables and cheese. They had wandered the market and purchased fresh fish, vegetables, and pasta for the evening meal. Rutherford had made them laugh afterward, as he had played silly ditties on the Kawai piano, its ebony wood gleaming. He had a beautiful voice, and when he played show tunes, they all chimed in, mostly off-key. Lucy was disappointed to leave them on Monday morning. There had been such a sense of family, and the occasion had been joyous. Besides paying for her flight, her father had given her an octagonal silver locket inlaid with an amethyst stone. He told her that he had given it to her mother, and it now belonged to her. Maeve had purchased her a rare first edition of Isak Dinesen's *Out of Africa*, and Rut had found silver earrings with amethyst drops. Again, Lucy was so thankful of the largesse that her family had given to her.

She couldn't believe that it was already Friday. There was so much to say to Sam in an e-mail. Mrs. Annie had been quite successful in turning over the sketch pads and getting her tax deduction. She had invited Lucy to her house after work and had presented her with a small pastel landscape painted by Edwin Harleston. Lucy had demurred, saying she could not possibly accept such a valuable gift, and Mrs. Annie had told her that forty only comes around once. They had laughed together, and Lucy thanked her profusely. Lucy was working Saturday for Trudie, as Trudie had a friend who was performing in an old-fashioned musicale that evening at a private residence on Thomas Street in Radcliffeborough. Trudie was needed to schlep the wine and make some of the light hors d'oeuvres. Nothing fancy, perhaps open-faced sandwiches and stuffed cherry tomatoes.

Lucy said she was more than willing to help if needed, and Trudie said, "No, thank you, just come, and bring Gabi. I do so like her."

It was quiet on Saturday, and Lucy started her e-mail to Sam, regaling him with the stories about San Francisco and her sister's pregnancy. She told him that Raymond was even becoming a more liberal Republican; was that an oxymoron? She asked him if he had finally heard from Brooks, and had the sale progressed on the house on Hanover Street? Brooks and Katie seemed to have enjoyed their honeymoon and were happily ensconced in Brooks's house across the park. Wasn't that all something? Had he heard the latest about Gus Wolfe? She imagined he had. Rumor had it, and she really didn't like to be a gossip, but on this topic she had to say that she was glad he was let go and people were saying that even his best clients were shunning him, as a number of men had been implying that his business transactions were far from ethical. That's what Huger had heard, anyway, in the back bar of the yacht club. She was a little tired from all this birthday business and it had all been wonderful fun, but now it was time to get back to work. The art walk was scheduled for the first week of October, which was in exactly two weeks' time, and she and Trudie had plenty to do to arrange the new and the old works together. She had asked Gabi's friend Carlos the poet to write a line or two about the couplings of the works, and he was diligently working on this for her. It would be fine, if not a little bit anxious-making, and she was excited, hoping her new artists' work would sell.

Lucy pulled the Karmann Ghia into Gabi's parking space. As she got out, Gabi hollered from the second-story window that she was coming down. Lucy thanked Gabi again for taking care of Toulouse while she was in San Francisco and Gabi said that Toulouse was such a joy and even slept with her every night.

"I love that dog so much, Lucy. It is making me tempted to get my own. Maybe I should go online to the Bouvier rescue site. What do you think?"

"I think that's a great idea. You just have to remember that they are quirky dogs. They back up, you know, when they meet people, like a truck—*beep, beep, beep*—and then sometimes they nip. Toulouse used to nip people in the rear, remember? He even got Sam, the first time we met." Both girls laughed.

"They are also so very sensitive, so you can't raise your voice too loudly, or their feelings are easily hurt. Besides that, I would have no other breed." Lucy smiled.

"So Lucy, I'm sure that was a great first impression between you and Sam."

"Actually, it went downhill from there. He was looking at the apartment to store his electronics while he traveled to Asia, but I didn't know that. All I saw was that he wore these heavy work boots, and I couldn't stop thinking about the *thunk-thunking* of those boots above me, so I wasn't over-polite. Besides, he looked a little rough, you know, five o'clock shadow at one in the afternoon. Now it all makes sense, as he's a contractor, but then at the time, he just seemed to me as a handsome, scruffy man who would probably make a lot of noise. Funny thing, first impressions are, aren't they?"

Gabi started laughing. "Yes, they are. The guy I met on the Fourth of July seemed so confident and self-aware, and then I found out that he lives with his parents and can't hold down a job. Well, I wonder who we'll meet at our soiree this evening?"

They pulled up near St. Mark's Episcopal Church, with its Greek Revival edifice overlooking Thomas Street. Gabi mentioned that she had been in the church once and had been awestruck by the beautiful stained glass windows. Lucy agreed and said it was a handsome church, and its history was very important to the African-American community.

They crossed the street and rapped on the ornate dolphin-shaped knocker of the wooden Regency-style house. A woman in her late fifties welcomed them and introduced herself as Daisy. They followed her into the house, through the center hall, soon to be greeted by Trudie. Before they knew it, they were surrounded by twenty people of all ages. The concert would be relaxed as traditional musicales were, with food being laid out on the dining room table and drinks served from the sideboard.

Trudie explained how things went. The musicales were always held in private homes of Serena's students.

Serena had been trained at Juilliard and was proficient at piano and violin, and as Trudie said it, she had the voice of an angel. She had toured for a few years with several prominent musicians and had performed at the Metropolitan in New York, the Lyric Opera in Chicago, and at various festivals around the country, but those bright lights were not for her. She preferred to teach at the College of Charleston and take on older students who had decided to come back to music after retiring, having raised children, or those who had strayed away from their instruments as adults. Tonight's program was one focusing on the Romantics. Each student chose his or her pieces and would sit at the Chickering grand piano that Daisy and her husband, Byron, both students of Serena's, owned. The setting was exquisite, resplendent with a late Victorian rosewood sofa and settees and late Duncan Phyfe chairs with rosettes carved in the top rail. Various dining and side hall chairs were placed about the room for guests, yet many mingled and stood.

The pieces were beautiful: Chopin, Liszt, and Brahms followed by a lively waltz by Strauss. After each piece, the small audience clapped enthusiastically and then nibbled at the food table laden with delicious tidbits that each had prepared. The entire affair was so genteel, which Lucy told Darcie, Serena's partner, a funny and charming woman in her late thirties. The final piece was by Grieg and was a performance on violin and piano. Serena's long fingers were poised at the piano, and then a tall, handsome man strode by, apologizing for being late. Lucy had not heard him, but felt him at first. It was Dante. He was dressed in a tuxedo, his chocolate eyes twinkling, and Lucy thought him to be one of the most cherished men in her sphere. He played the violin with such beauty and intensity that at one point Lucy was forced to close her eyes and pay attention to the music, pushing everything else out of her mind. As the music ended, the crowd clapped loudly and asked for one more piece on the violin. Dante obliged them with an Hungarian rhapsody that left everyone breathless. After the performance, he placed the violin in its case and hugged Lucy to him and said it must have been weeks since he had seen her at her birthday celebration. He invited Lucy, Gabi, Trudie, Serena, and Darcie to his apartment behind the main house. His apartment was beautifully furnished, of course, Lucy thought. They all discussed the performance, and Dante and Serena had joked that how he had been able to perform was anyone's guess, as he was an unfaithful student at best.

They all sat on his terrace, sipping champagne, when Dante pulled her to him and said, "You have a little frown just there." He touched her forehead in between her brows. "Is anything amiss?"

"No, not really, I've been having a few unsettling dreams the past few nights, that's all."

"Tell, me then."

"It's always the same. I'm on a bridge, and traffic is zipping by, and I'm in a car and not in a car at all, and the bridge is shaking, and I feel that I will lose my balance, and then the bridge changes to a footbridge, and there is water beneath me, and I'm falling, but Sam is there, and he tells me to just jump, and I'm awfully scared, and I can't jump, and he says, 'Take control. Jump,' and I finally do right before the bridge gives way. Some days, before I wake, I dream he's pulling me from the water, and other days I have this perilous feeling that I will be plunging into an abyss." She sadly smiled at him.

"Where is he now, Lucy?"

"New Zealand. I think he arrived there yesterday, but I can't be sure."

"I wonder if that man of yours is bungee jumping then. I've not been to New Zealand, but I hear there are unlimited opportunities there to take in the sport. It may be more, you know. It might be that you are finally learning to trust him, taking the leap of faith, and it's a bit worrisome."

"Maybe you are right, Dante. If anything, you always make me feel so much better."

"Good, let's banish maudlin thoughts and have another glass of champagne."

Their group broke up at nine thirty, and Lucy took Gabi home. They talked endlessly in the car about how fun it was that they had attended and how fortuitous it was that they had been invited. Lucy screeched hard on the brakes as she was turning onto Huger Street from King Street. There in the headlights was a small terrier-like dog with huge eyes. She pulled the car over and asked Gabi to get out. Between the two of them, they cajoled and coerced the reddish-blonde dog to get in the back of the car.

"Lucy, what are we going to do with him or her?"

"I don't know, Gabi, but I couldn't just let it run in the street."

"I know. Come on, let's take this fuzzy mini-beast upstairs."

Lucy took off the belt that she was wearing and fixed it around the worn red collar. They took their burden upstairs and checked her out. She wasn't covered with fleas, but she had a stink about her. Maybe she had been sprayed by a skunk? In that case, ketchup was in order? No ketchup? No, but Gabi had tomato sauce; that should do, shouldn't it? The girls hauled her into the tub, soaking themselves as their purloined canine shook with fright. Gabi scrubbed her with the tomato sauce, leaving it on for five minutes. She then rinsed the dog, and both women stuck their noses to her fur. She smelled better, that's for sure, they agreed. Gabi then rubbed her best shampoo into the pup's fur, rinsed her again, then added conditioner before they both dried her off. Lucy noticed that there were no tags on the collar and wondered where the dog had come from. Gabi mentioned that she was probably another stray dog, but it was odd that she had a collar. The dog would remain at Gabi's for the night, and then they would decide what to do with her the following day.

Gabi called Lucy the next day to say that digital photos had been taken. She had left messages with animal control and the SPCA. She would have to wait to hear back from them tomorrow, but maybe she and Lucy could place signs up around the neighborhood? She had made twenty-five and would contact the newspaper tomorrow and run a Lost Dog ad. Meanwhile, could Lucy spare some of Toulouse's food? Lucy agreed to help her friend and bring the food over.

Gabi had fallen in love with the dog overnight. Lucy noticed that she followed Gabi everywhere, and Gabi said she had called some friends, and all said not to take her to the SPCA. One of her friends had done that, and then when no owners came to pick her up, she had to pay them fifty dollars to bust the dog out of the Big House the day before he was scheduled to be euthanized because he had heartworms. Gabi had decided that she would take a few fliers to them and see how it went. Lucy passed no judgment on her friend. If the owners didn't respond to all the fliers in the neighborhood and the ad in the paper, then it was meant to be that Gabi and this dog should be together.

"You've named her?" Lucy queried.

"I have. What do you think of Josephine, Josie for short?" Gabi said as she scratched the dog's forehead.

"Just don't get too attached, Gabi, as her owners may just call you. I just don't want you to get hurt."

"Don't worry, they won't call. I just know it."

Lucy pedaled home, hoping that it would all work out. She called Dante to tell him how much she enjoyed the concert last night, and he said thank you and hoped she had had a good night's sleep without the bridge dreams. She had dreamed of music, she told him, and she had been in a field surrounded by wildflowers, and then she was on a horse thundering on the shore, but it was a beach she'd never seen. Perhaps it had been the champagne?

He laughed at her and wondered to himself where Sam was and what he was doing.

Lucy told him about Sam's cards, both oversized, and wondered if he knew what the term "L&O" was. She couldn't think what it meant, but then again, maybe it was an Internet term like "laugh out loud"? It had taken her a while to figure that one out.

"Lucy," Dante inquired, "is this in reference, do you think, to the flowers he sent you?"

"I don't know what you mean, Dante. The flowers were showy, but L&O?"

"I remember you saying to me that he asked if they were large and ostentatious, and you said to him no, they were showy. Remember that?"

"No, not really. Would Sam remember that? He processes about fifty percent of what I say and forgets one-third of what he says to me."

"Lucy, I can't fathom what he does and does not process. I'm just saying, if he is sending oversized cards and writes *L&O*, maybe it's his code for you. Don't you two have code words?"

"Code words, Dante? What are code words, for heaven's sake?"

"Those terms that couples share. You know, like when I was with Stasia, it was 'Oh, what a romp,' and that meant that one of us was letting the other know that we wanted sex. With Mark, it was 'Et tu?' Clearly that meant everything. He'd look at me like *Isn't this situation ridiculous*, but he wouldn't say it. Instead he would say, 'Et tu?' and we knew we understood each other."

"Dante, how can Sam and I have code words when we've never established them? I'm just not sure if I'm following you at all."

"Just try it, sweetheart. When you e-mail him next, throw in an 'L&O.' If it means 'large and ostentatious,' be playful. You are too serious with him sometimes."

"Serious? Me serious? I thought I was fun-loving. That's what all of you all say," she added with a harrumph.

"You take Sam too seriously, Lucy. He's a guy. He belches, he farts, and you have him on this pedestal as if he's one of your sculptures or a piece of porcelain. He's a man. He's going to disappoint you. You are going to misunderstand each other. That is part of life. Start acting with him as you act with all of your other friends. Lucy, don't get uptight with him."

"Dante, I wasn't uptight with him before he left, and I really worked on being relaxed. Sometimes, I think this entire relationship thing is too much work, even with him being thousands of miles away."

"You miss him, Lucy. Just remember to be your happy self, and it will all work out."

She hung up the phone and thought that that conversation had been odd, curious, in fact. What was Dante telling her in his man-speak, a language that she couldn't navigate at all. It might have been Russian for all the good it did her.

Chapter 33

Where thou art – that – is home –

"Poem 795", Emily Dickinson

Sam had been in Auckland's environs for a week and was heading to the South Island. His clothes were washed, his gear was packed, and he would pop into an Internet café, check his messages, and fire some back. Brooks had e-mailed that the closing of the Hanover Street house was complete, the mortgage paid, and Sam had plenty of money in the bank. He reminded his friend that he needed to reinvest that money soon, or the IRS would take a sizable chunk. Sam thought, *I know, I know.* Brooks asked him how Fiji had been, as he had not heard anything about it except that he had been snorkeling. He and Katie were settling in nicely, and who would have ever thought that they would actually have enjoyed Sin City for a honeymoon? It was so different from what they were used to being around that it had been a great time. She had even made him suffer through a Bette Midler concert, which turned out to be entertaining, but he wouldn't tell her that. Brooks went on about Gus Wolfe's downfall and ended the e-mail saying that Sam should be proud of himself for telling Allston Murray what a slimeball he was. Otherwise, he would still be playing the same nefarious game.

Sam read the next e-mail from his parents. Catherine and Thomas were both enjoying the semester; each had bright students, and they never tired of their subject matter. Beatrice had hired two brilliant painters, and his uncle was doing so much better concentrating on supervising their work. It was so much easier for him, and he looked younger than he had in years. She didn't know what would happen there, but she was hopeful. His father added that he hoped that Sam was having a good time and that he expected him to learn about the Maori people and their culture while he was traveling the natural treasures of New Zealand. *Check, Dad,* he thought as he still winced from the Maori-inspired tattoo that he had had done a few days ago on his right shoulder. Elizabeth had been home for the weekend from her job in Newport, and she chimed in as well.

He wrote his parents that he had learned about the Maori culture by visiting the Auckland Museum, where he saw an extremely large war canoe. He had also stayed to watch a performance of song and dance while there. He had visited the National Maritime Museum and had seen Maori canoes and immigrant ships and had toured the harbor in an old steamboat. He had visited the aquarium, and he was amazed as he traveled on a conveyor belt at the many fish, sharks, and stingrays as they swam around him. He had taken the bus to Mount Eden, where he had backpacked for two days. The views were incredible, and you could see all of Auckland from that vantage point. He had looked down into that volcanic crater before heading back. He had also taken in a day of sailing. He had met the nicest people and several who had crewed for the America's Cup.

The next e-mail was from Mrs. Annie, short and sweet, hoping that he was enjoying himself and that she missed her favorite neighbor. He skipped over a few others, as he saw Lucy's name further up in his inbox. That girl seemed to always be in motion, attending concerts, planting flowers, and now kayaking, which had become her latest passion. He remembered the first time he saw her. She was planting in her backyard, and he smiled remembering the smudge of dirt on her nose. She regaled him about the rescue of Josephine, Gabi's new dog, and told him she wanted to learn to play the violin, but she was afraid that all that scratching and sawing on the strings might give Toulouse a breakdown. She hoped he was enjoying his journey, and she knew he was having an excellent time. *Live in an L&O way,* she said and then signed the e-mail *Yours, Lucy*. He laughed out loud, and several people looked at him. She had figured it out, finally.

Sam was headed to the Queenstown region, where he would hike the Routeburn Track for a few days. He enjoyed the isolation, but missed the company of others. He pitched his tent the first night at Lake Mackenzie and met three men from America. They had planned the trip a year out and were good companions. They wandered through rain forests and subalpine tracks. On their way to Milford Sound, they took in the dramatic views at Key Summit with the Eglington and Greenstone River valleys below them.

He spent two days in Wellington, not long enough to see the sights, but just enough to whet his appetite. He walked by Victorian buildings located on steep hills and visited museums, including Old St. Paul's, with its striking stained glass windows and exhibits of the city's early history, and then found himself at the doors of the National Tattoo Museum, where he viewed striking works of art.

He knew he needed to pick up trinkets for Elizabeth and Mrs. Annie and books for his parents. He had made his purchases and was wandering down Bowen Street when he saw a pair of earrings in the window. They were beautiful, and they were exactly something that Lucy would wear. The door shut behind him, and a beautiful woman smiled at him. He asked her about the earrings in the window, and she brought them out, placing them on a green velvet cloth on the counter. They were from the 1920s and were drops of pearls and greenstone linked together with a sliver of silver. She noted that greenstone was a popular native gem and that it was historically intended to be given as a gift. He didn't ask her the price, just handed her the credit card.

"Your wife will treasure these, as they are delicate, yet modern in appearance. Would you like me to wrap them for you?" she inquired.

"Yes, please," was all that Sam could say.

She placed the earrings in a green velvet box that had the jeweler's name embossed inside the lid. She then wrapped the box in a filmy piece of paper and tied a bow on top. As Sam left the shop, he found himself whistling. He was ready to head for home. This had been an amazing adventure, but he was ready to be on his native soil.

It was Tuesday, and Lucy was grateful to the weather gods for the beautiful days with brilliant blue skies and temperatures in the sixties. She had found a used blue beach cruiser at a pawn shop the week before, resplendent with a white basket. She and Trudie called it the shop bike, and they had painted it with crazy flowers and butterflies. Lucy had gone to the dollar store, where she purchased plastic flowers and butterflies and they had hot-glued the objects to the basket. They took turns riding it to the post office to drop off mail or to the Harris Teeter to pick up lunch. They were becoming fast friends, and Lucy was proud that Trudie's works had been selling. She had recently been commissioned to paint a mural at one of the local hotels, and it made them both giddy with excitement.

She wasn't sure where Sam was, but his last e-mail said that that he would be winging his way home, wherever that was, she thought. His tone was chatty, and he had said that he had had enough adventure for a lifetime, or at least for a couple of years. He still couldn't believe he had bungee jumped over a ravine, gone parasailing, cycling, trekking, snorkeling, scuba diving, and sailing. He had left his bike in Wellington at a home for orphaned boys. He had pretty much mangled it with all the miles, but some kid would enjoy what was left of his battered Trek. He would simply need to buy one in the States. He was safe, she thought, on his way, somewhere. She squinched her eyebrows together and shook herself, reminding herself again that, even if he didn't come home to Charleston, she had had a wonderful time getting to know him, and he had changed her life for the better. All those crazy e-mails and the large postcards. She had begun to cut and paste them, and by now they made up eighteen pages front and back. She would treasure those memories always.

Sam stayed for three days in Salem recovering from his trip and enjoying his mother's cooking. He had told his parents his many stories, and one evening his uncle Sam and Beatrice had stayed for dinner. Beatrice and his uncle had known each other for years, but she had lived on the West Coast and he in Salem. When her daughter and son-in-law moved cross-country, she decided to contact Sam O'Hara and ask him if there was enough work to sustain her. He said there was plenty in his company, and he would enjoy having her join him, as he had always respected her talent. She had sold her house and her business and moved just like that. They had been working together since March, and now it was October, and they seemed to be doing just fine. Sam couldn't help but notice how his uncle laughed with her and how at dinner they touched each other. She teased him mercilessly, and she seemed to get on beautifully in the kitchen with Catherine. Odd, thought Sam, his mother never really allowed anyone to help in the kitchen except Elizabeth.

Lucy arrived home with Toulouse in tow. The children were playing in the front lawn, and a much-harangued Asyln sat watching them, sitting on the stoop.

"Aslyn, honey, do you need a break?" Lucy called.

"Yes, please. They've been at it all day and no sign of a nap. Now it's six, and it's too early to put them in bed."

"I walked Toulouse earlier, so it's a matter of putting down his food. I can come over in, say, fifteen minutes and read to them. Would that be helpful?"

"Thank you." It was all that Aslyn could muster.

Lucy entered the house, picked up her mail, which included bills and a notice of an upcoming estate sale. She placed the items on the table, fed Toulouse, changed clothes, and shut the door behind her.

The cool breeze waved by her face, and she heard the wind chimes in the background as she read them *Olivia Saves the Circus* and *Olivia Joins a Band*. She was in the middle of the third book, one about numbers, when she realized that they had fallen asleep in her lap. She carefully carried Marguerite in her arms to the kitchen.

"They're asleep, but I could only carry one of them," Lucy said.

Aslyn retrieved a drooling Liam, and the two women carried them to their cribs. Asyln left the night-light on, thanked Lucy, and asked her if she wanted a glass of wine.

They walked into the living room, and Lucy started giggling as she pointed to the *Teatro Olivia* paper theater. Paper figures, costumes, and sets were tossed about the large mahogany trunk that served as a coffee table.

"It's not funny, you know," Aslyn said. She had tiny lines around her eyes, and blue shadows formed under her eyes. "I tried everything today. We went to the park, I took them to Charles Towne Landing and let them run for three hours, I let them color with chalk, and finally I brought out the theater. I know they are too young for it, but I was at my wit's end. I even played the music for *Turandot* and *Swan Lake*, hoping that that would work, but to no avail. I changed the script of *Romeo and Juliet* so no one died, and out of nowhere Liam says, 'She dead. That girl dead.' And there was Olivia with her paper Juliet clothes on, and I thought, *Mommy is just about dead too.*" Aslyn smiled slightly.

Lucy hugged her to her and said, "I bet Mommy is beat." She placed her forehead to Aslyn's, and the two started laughing quietly at first and then louder.

"Sh," Lucy said.

"Sh back," Aslyn replied.

"I better go. Does Bennett have call, then, tonight?"

"Yes. It seems he's always on call or at meetings. My life is just so chaotic right now."

"Aslyn, I can never repay you and Bennett for that night so many months ago. Why don't you schedule a date night once a week, and I'll take care of your pack of two. You need to have a date night once a week or every ten days. Besides, my future with you-know-who is uncertain, and I need the distraction."

Aslyn thanked her, and Lucy crossed the yard to her door. There was a card of some type in the mail slot. The picture was of some type of tropical plant that was unfamiliar to Lucy. On the back of the oversized card from the botanical gardens in Wellington, Sam had written the following: *Hi, Lucy. Hope this finds you living in an L&O way. The expedition is nearly over, and I am sad to see it go. What sights I have seen. Love, Sam.*

The phone began ringing, and her nosy down-the-street neighbor was on the other end of the line.

"Damn postman. Ever since Harold retired, our mail has been all screwed up. I told Bobby that he needed to just walk the card down to you, but oh no, not my husband of sixty years. He has to rev up the Lincoln and drive the car. Well, honey, you did get the card, didn't you?"

"The postcard, you mean?"

Lucy heard Mrs. Musselman light up the cigarette on the other end, Pall Malls or Basics. Yuck, Lucy thought. The woman was in her eighties. She needed to quit, but who was Lucy to judge?

"Yes, the card, and it said 'love, Sam.' Very romantic, if you ask me. That's from that young man that you used to see, right? And sending you a card from around the world? That's something."

"Yes, that would be the one," Lucy said breathlessly and peevishly. She wanted to look at the signature again.

"Well, I'm just glad he didn't dump you. Bobby had wondered where his car has been. I told him that you weren't being dumped again. I could feel it in these old knees."

Honestly, how can she feel what was going on with her and Sam in her knees? Please! Lucy thought. Instead she said, "Mrs. Musselman, thank you for being so kind to ensure that I received the card, and please tell Mr. Musselman that I appreciate his courtesy."

"Really, Lucy, what else do we two old New York farts have to do but spy on our neighbors? It keeps our old lives interesting."

She got off the phone thinking how could an eighty-something-year-old man still allow himself to be called Bobby, but then again, he had brought her the card, so she should have no complaints.

Sam thanked his friends for their generosity for letting him stay the night in their house in Falls Church, Virginia. He would leave in the early morning before they awoke, as he needed to get home in record time. He mumbled about a closing, and they thought he had closed on his house a while back. He said this was another one, but he wasn't consistent, and April and Scott were stumped. She had said so as she plumped their pillows before they went to bed.

Sam left at 5:00 a.m., feeling a bit like a thief in the night. He just wanted to be home, in his house, with his stuff. He wanted to sleep in his own bed. Shit, he had been gone for a little more than three months, and he missed knowing what was happening on the street. Besides, he needed to sort his pictures before he became confused about where he had been and what he had done. His notepads had been at the bottom of his pack, and even though he had been so conscientious of keeping them dry, some of them had gotten wet and were indecipherable. He could always review his blog, and that should help him sort it out.

He was on I-95, and it was smooth sailing. He knew he would hit bad traffic outside of Richmond, so he planned to take back roads. North Carolina seemed endless. He turned up his radio and heard a sad Mary Chapin Carpenter tune complaining about peaches and appliances on the front lawn. He slowed down, knowing that North Carolina state troopers always pulled you for speeding. He sailed into South Carolina thinking, *I'm home soon*. He was antsy. He knew that Brooks's friend had moved out of the house a few days ago, and he hoped it was straight, and he wished it was clean.

Lucy was on a high. She didn't know what to think, and she was happy that Trudie was off today, as she would probably divulge too much. She hummed about the shop. Although she had few customers, she tried to keep busy. She kept thinking about the card and wanted to call Mrs. Musselman and thank her again, but then again, no, because she would have to listen to that one's mouth, which was harsh at most and strident at least. She loved her business, didn't she? Truthfully, not when it wasn't busy, and as good as Trudie was, she missed Gabriella's energy.

Sam arrived on Nassau Street at four thirty. He had been caught in a stall of cars before he had hit Florence. What a mess. He was tired, sweaty, and he stank to high heaven. He walked into his house, switched off the alarm, called the company to reprogram a new code, and looked about him. The cottage was clean, cleaner than he even kept it, and there were cookies on a glass plate covered with plastic film and a note: *Sam, Welcome home, world traveler! Much love! Katie and Brooks.*

He showered, put on fresh boxers, set his alarm, and retreated to his bed. Home.

Lucy called Asyln and asked if she should come and read. Aslyn was good, all was well, and did Lucy have plans for dinner? No, she didn't have plans, but she hoped to saw on the violin. Dante had helped her find one, and she should practice tonight.

"Okay, look, why don't I have Bennett run it over to you? It's just tilapia in a red sauce, couscous, and some greens."

Lucy said thank you. She picked up the instrument and started playing "Three Blind Mice." As she scratched along the way, Toulouse ran for cover. She became disheartened, and after Bennett carried over dinner, she picked and nibbled and changed into a simple cotton nightgown that fell to her knees. She promised Toulouse that she would become better and that the noise wouldn't be an impediment to their daily life. He looked at her in bewilderment and sank his head under the pillows in the back bedroom. The phone rang. She was annoyed. Now what?

Sam was refreshed, clean and lean. He had honed his body on his trip, and he was thin and muscular. He hoped she would like what he brought her. He fiddled with the box in his hand and slid it into the right pocket of his pants.

"Lucy, I'm home," Sam's rich voice intoned.

"Good, home then in Salem?"

"No, I left Salem a couple of days ago."

"Oh, home then on Nassau Street?"

"No, Lucy."

She peered out the front door and didn't see his truck or the BMW. She became nervous. What if he were around the corner? Oh gosh. She spied herself in the mirror. Her mess of hair was barretted, angling at all degrees, and she looked rotten, tired, and old. She rifled through her lingerie drawer and found the black Grecian chemise that could be worn over tights, maybe. She took out the barrettes, brushed her hair, pinched her cheeks, and dusted her lips with a berry gloss.

"Well, where are you, honey, living your L&O ways in my hood?"

She checked the front door. No Sam.

"Wrong door, baby."

She carefully walked to the side door. *No mania, please, no craziness,* she thought. She noticed his boots first.

"Lucy."

"Sam."

"Girl, you cannot walk outside wearing that!"

"What?"

"Lucy."

She shook her head slightly wondering what would happen next.

Sam swept her off her feet, and she laughed as she had never before. He kissed her deeply and looked at her face with so much want. He stepped through the frame carrying her backwards. She looked at him; holding his face closely in her hands. He was more gorgeous than she remembered, but most importantly he was home to her.

Sam smiled at her and kissed her mouth once more. She was beautiful, more so than he remembered, but most importantly it wasn't just her physical beauty that had captured him but rather her entire essence. It seemed that they had been away from one another forever and yet together for a thousand years.

"I'm home."

"You're home."

About the Author

Valerie Perry is curious about life. She lives in Charleston, SC with her amazing Airedale Terrier, Lady Winifred of the Lake. (Winnie)

Made in the USA
Charleston, SC
03 June 2015